BOW BEFORE THE ELF QUEEN
THE ELF QUEEN SERIES BOOK 1

J.M. KEARL

Bow Before the Elf Queen

MATE

By J.M. Kearl
Copyright J.M. Kearl 2022
All rights reserved

The characters and events portrayed in this book are fictitious. Any similarity to real persons, living or dead, is coincidental and not intended by the author.

No part of this book may be reproduced, or stored in a retrieval system, or transmitted in any form or by any means, electronic, mechanical, photocopying, recording, or otherwise, without express written permission of the publisher.

Cover design by: Janie Hannan Kearl

Dedicated to David Farland. If it wasn't for him this book wouldn't have been written.

CONTENTS

Name Pronunciation Guide	vii
Prologue	1
Chapter 1	11
Chapter 2	27
Chapter 3	42
Chapter 4	51
Chapter 5	63
Chapter 6	81
Chapter 7	88
Chapter 8	98
Chapter 9	107
Chapter 10	117
Chapter 11	124
Chapter 12	136
Chapter 13	153
Chapter 14	167
Chapter 15	186
Chapter 16	200
Chapter 17	208
Chapter 18	219
Chapter 19	239
Chapter 20	246
Chapter 21	260
Chapter 22	270
Chapter 23	286
Chapter 24	300
Chapter 25	319
Chapter 26	333

Chapter 27	346
Chapter 28	356
Chapter 29	373
Chapter 30	388
Chapter 31	401
Chapter 32	417
Chapter 33	429
Chapter 34	446
Chapter 35	464
Chapter 36	481
Chapter 37	493
Chapter 38	499
Chapter 39	510
Chapter 40	518
Chapter 41	536
Chapter 42	546
Chapter 43	556
Chapter 44	566
Acknowledgments	585
About the Author	587
Also by J.M. Kearl	589

Name Pronunciation Guide

Layala—Lay-all-uh
  Seraphina—Sera-feen-uh
  Tenebris—Ten-eh-briss
  Evalyn—Ev-uh-lynn
  Athayel—Ath-ā-el
  Aldrich—All-drich
  Fennan—Fen-en
  Atarah—Uh-tar-uh
  Zaurahel—Zar-uh-hel
  Mathekis—Math-eh-kiss
  Palenor—Pal-eh-nor
  Calladira—Cal-uh-deer-uh
  Svenarum—Sven-are-um
  Vessache—Vess-ach

Adalon
Dragon Territory
Redcresc woods
Briar hollow
Svenarum
Sacred stones
Vessach
Desert of Anahar
Lake Emmie

dwarf
land
fang peak
Brightheart
forest
castle
dredwich
calladira
newarden
palenor
Lake Lamora
Ranaheim mountains
doonafell
Rhegar's
tomb
the void

PROLOGUE

In a small cottage filled with warmth and light, nestled at the edge of the Valley of the Sun, a scream whisked butterflies from their blooms. The gentle cry of the newborn baby filled the bedroom, a sound she had waited to hear for nine months. Seraphina released her grip on the green fuzzy branch of the calming tree at her bedside. Its mystical properties reduced the pain during the contractions and pushing but hadn't taken it away entirely. It even curled around her wrist as if it knew she needed the assistance.

A sigh of relief passed through Seraphina's lips upon seeing the tiny baby held by the midwife at her feet. Finally, the child was here and well. The melancholy "what-ifs" raced through her mind as she pushed; many she knew had birthed children who never took a breath. It became more frequent in the last four centuries after most of the elves lost their magic.

"A girl." Her husband Elkin's voice trembled with emotion. "She's so small."

The warm summer air drifted in from the open window, carrying with it the scent of jasmine and citrus. Sun shone inside, filling the ivory-painted room with brilliant light. Outside a pink weeping lilac tree swayed in the breeze. What a beautiful day the child was born on. A good omen.

Leaning back into the feather pillows behind her, Seraphina smiled at the dark tuft of hair on her baby's crown, black, like her father. The baby curled her legs toward her belly. She was perfect, from her delicately pointed ears to her rosy, pink toes. Though the pain of birthing still lingered, overwhelming joy took hold. Tears pricked her eyes and her cheeks ached from smiling.

The midwife inspected the child before her, still covered in birth matter and blood. Seraphina looked at the midwife expectantly, waiting for her daughter to be placed in her arms. She wanted to see her girl's face, hold her, hear her heartbeat.

But the midwife's eyes were fixed on the infant's shoulder with furrowed brows.

"What is it? Why do you not give me my child?"

"She bears a strange mark."

Elkin, who still gripped Seraphina's hand, met her eyes briefly then looked to the woman, "What do you speak of? A birthmark?"

Tugging her hand away, Seraphina stretched her arms out, growing impatient. "Give her to me."

With the umbilical cord still attached, the midwife passed the wide-eyed baby to her mother. There was indeed a mark. Unlike any Seraphina had ever seen. A black birthmark against the child's pink skin the size of a small coin, shaped as thorny vines wrapped around the stem of a lily. Could it be or did her eyes play tricks?

Elkin exchanged another look with her. Foreboding as the mark may be, she pulled the baby against her chest and savored the first moments of her daughter's life.

THE CHILD's name and testing day came seven sunrises later. Each new elf infant was brought before the king to be presented and tested for magical ability. So few remained now, but there was always hope a new mage would be born.

A pit grew in Seraphina's stomach, heavy and twisting. The midwife spread rumors about the baby's mark so hundreds gathered in the massive hall of kings. Dressed in light colors of pastels and fine jewelry, the high elves expected this to be a wondrous day. Their beautiful, serene faces beheld smiles, hair of varied shades in intricate braids and styles.

Seraphina wore a gown of the lightest blue with gold embroidered trim and a golden necklace with a willow tree centerpiece, passed down from her mother and her mother before. Her soft, golden-brown hair was pulled up into a high bun to accentuate her pointed ears and cheekbones. But her breath caught as she stood frozen in the entryway. Why did she feel ill when everything about this day was beautiful and bright?

Elkin placed a hand on her back and with gentle pressure urged her forward. It was so quiet their light elven footsteps echoed. Eyes followed Seraphina and Elkin as they passed through the gap between the sea of elves under the looming white stone archways leading to the king at the end. Sunlight cascaded in from the colossal windows, ethereal as it reflected off the diamonds glittering in the king's golden crown. He was elegant in his fine green robes. But there was a harshness around his eyes. Rumors swirled about the once benevolent High King dabbling in the dark arts, seeking to grow more powerful, to have magic of his own.

At the end of the aisle this blond king waited, his eyes fixed on the sleeping bundle in Seraphina's arms. The white throne he sat on had a back so high the king could stand and it would take three of him to reach the peak.

With a gray staff in hand matching his robe, the light mage Vesstan stood to the king's right. His pale, straight hair was half tied up in ceremonial braids woven between a crown of silver branches. With a warm smile, he descended the five steps and met the mother and father at the altar. "Many have gathered here today for the testing and naming of this child. What shall she be known by from this day forth?"

Elkin cleared his throat. "She is to be known as Layala Lightbringer."

Seraphina held her child closer, patting the baby's back gently. She didn't want to part with her for the testing but she would have to. All mothers did.

The mage dipped his head, his wrists clinked from the silver bracelets as he touched the gray stone altar before him. "Please place the infant Layala Lightbringer here."

Seraphina's eyes met the king's, his chin raised slightly.

Impatiently.

She set the swaddled baby down gently, leaving a hand against her chest, careful to make sure she wouldn't fall.

The mage bobbed his head. "This will be quick, and do not fret; the child will not be harmed. I will say a few words and we'll wait for a sign. If nothing happens the child does not have magic."

Seraphina knew this. She'd seen it hundreds of times herself. No child she witnessed possessed magic. No sign ever came. Mage Vesstan, one of the last elves born with magic to exist in Adalon, touched the crown of Layala's head with his fingers. With but a few chanted words an onyx swirl of cloud amassed around the tip of the staff. It soon traveled like a serpent, winding and moving around the four of them until it circled only Layala. Flower buds appeared above the dark mist around her; the lily's blossomed into such a deep purple they nearly looked black.

Seraphina's chest ached. The birthmark and now this dark display of magic... What did this mean? What would happen now? What did they do with magical children? Her eyes set on Layala's petite plump face, so sweet and lovely. Seraphina's heart swelled with love but a part of her worried; how could there be darkness in something so delicate and beautiful?

Mage Vesstan jerked his hand away as if he'd been struck and turned to the king, mouth gaping

The High King rose, with greed in his eyes. "She has magic." He waved a hand to a female elf with her hands on a small boy's shoulders. His dark-brown hair curled around his angelic face, and his big green eyes searched the crowd nervously. This was the king's wife and child. Seraphina recognized them as they drew closer.

"See that it is done," the king boomed.

Panic rose in Seraphina, looking from the king to the mage. "See that what is done?"

"As the first to be born with power in over four centuries, this child will marry my son when she is of age. They are to be betrothed, bound by magic for now." The hardness in his eyes showed no sign of negotiation. "She will be a great weapon for our people in the future."

A weapon? She was but a baby, barely even a week old and he was calling her a weapon? Seraphina should be happy her daughter would be a princess, but her stomach dropped. It was all too much too soon. How could they claim Layala like this without her consent?

Before she could even protest, Mage Vesstan chanted. Seraphina looked to the crowd. The happy faces didn't understand the panic clawing at her chest, threatening to buckle her knees. She gripped her husband's hand. "Do something," she hissed.

"What can be done?" he whispered and pressed a hand on her shoulder. "We will be killed if we reject this claim. We can devise a plan later."

It was only moments, moments and a tendril of white light passed from the king's son, a boy of only three, to her baby girl, binding them together. A rune appeared on the infant's left wrist: the rune for *mate*.

The king nodded to a guard and then his dark eyes turned to Mage Vesstan. "Take the infant to the royal nursery. We must see to it that she is raised properly, trained, and kept safe."

The panic turned to anger. Seraphina snatched the baby into her arms and held her against her before Mage Vesstan could move. "You must not take my child from me. Allow me to raise her. I'll see to it she is trained," she said, bowing herself before the throne, begging.

"She will stay," the king announced. "And be raised by me and Queen Orlandia. Her safety is my greatest concern. Here in the castle, we can ensure that."

Seraphina turned in a circle searching for help but not a single elf stepped forward. "Let me stay with her, please."

"No, that will not do. Being raised by someone who knows nothing about magic will only weaken her."

Elkin's hand rested on the hilt of his sword, but he gave her a small shake of his head. Noncompliance would mean death. Guards moved in.

Rising, Seraphina ran.

Her eyes blurred with tears as she slammed into the crowd of elves. Gasps and murmurs echoed in the hall. They parted for her. No one moved to stop her and the baby, but they didn't stand in the way of the guards either.

She knew the servants' passages. She'd worked in the castle before, delivering goods.

The king shouted, heavy footsteps from those who followed her closed in. Ducking under a guard's arm, she made a dash for the closest corridor and slipped behind a tapestry that led into the servants' passage. Breaths coming faster, she sprinted until she rounded a corner and came face to face with a woman holding a wooden basket of fruit.

Seraphina's heart sang. It was her dear friend, Evalyn, one of the only humans to work in the city. She wasn't allowed inside during the testing but she'd found a way to be there nonetheless. "Take my baby," Seraphina demanded. "Take her to your home. Do not go anywhere near mine. I'll come for her."

Confusion glistened in Evalyn's eyes. "Why do you ask this of me?"

Footsteps and shouts in the distance made her heart slam hard against her ribs.

"Where did she go? Find her!" a male voice shouted nearby.

Seraphina pushed the baby toward Evalyn. "Please. Layala is magical. The king wants to use her. We can't let him."

Setting the fruit basket down, Evalyn nodded and gathered the infant into her arms. A moment passed between them; they stared at each other, a mutual understanding. Tears filled both their eyes. Seraphina knew she'd never see her precious child again, at least not in this life. "If I don't make it to your house by nightfall, take her far from here... Make sure she knows I loved her with my entire being."

Evalyn nodded, a tear glistening on her warm brown cheek.

Seraphina kissed her baby's soft head, inhaling her sweet scent one last time. She tore the generational necklace from her throat, giving it over to her daughter. "Tell Layala her father and I fought until the end for her. Tell her one day she will need to fight, too."

Chapter 1

— TWENTY-FOUR YEARS LATER —

~Love is a powerful force. It cannot be bought. It cannot be taken or stolen. Although sometimes it must be fought for, it must be given freely.~

The rain pelted the ground as if the tepid drops were the hooves of a thousand galloping horses. A crack of thunder boomed, and yet a shrill scream cut through it all. Layala's elf eyes saw well in the dark, but on this starless night, deep among the looming redwood trees, the darkness almost became a living thing. The low visibility only gave away outlines of the forest, leaving the origination of the scream a mystery. It echoed from everywhere, bouncing off trees that should absorb. Skin prickling, she returned to her task.

She pulled her hood up, covering her waist-length

black hair and crept low among the ferns and shrubbery, listening for a whimper or movement. Every seventh day she visited the statues made in honor of her parents with a bouquet of rich blue forget-me-nots. It was the least she could do when they'd sacrificed their lives for her. The most she would do was yet to come.

The fluffy white pup her aunt tasked her with watching snuck out upon her return as the storm brewed, and darted into the Redcrest Woods, the backyard of their cottage. The woods here smelled of mild spice with damp mossy undertones and a hint of sweetness, but tonight, a rotten egg odor drifted on the breeze.

Putting her hand on a crumbling fallen log, Layala catapulted over and dropped low when another shriek ripped through the air. She slowly pulled a dagger from her leather belt. It was a war cry, the sound of an animal or something on the hunt, searching for a meal. She didn't want to let the words cross her mind, but *pale ones* cursed by the long-dead Black Mage screeched like that. She'd first heard them when she was a child, like a dying wildcat. The noise made her cringe to this day. If there was one nearby, she must kill the creature or risk it getting to the others in town.

A tiny whimper caught her ear. She searched the underbrush and stopped on the shivering pup partially hidden under a fern frond. His white fur was muddied brown from dirt and grime. Letting out a quiet whistle, Layala scooted toward him, holding out her hand. "Come on, Dregous." He perked up and began retreating backward. *This dog is going to get me killed,* she thought. Before he could run off, she dove, rolled, and scooped him around the middle, shooting to her feet.

"Bad puppy," she whispered as she held the pup against her and started back for the house. "Why do you run away at the worst times? Do you like being wet and cold?"

"Mmmm," a deep voice purred from behind her. "I smell she-elf."

A cool sensation ran from the base of her neck down her spine. Goosebumps erupted along her arms. She gripped her dagger tighter and barely turned her head, catching a glimpse of the pale one merely feet away. It was the heavy rain that prevented her from hearing his footsteps. His unnatural white pallor and hair were a stark contrast to the night around them. Even in this dim lighting, the smear of blood around his mouth was visible, dribbling over his black lips and down his chin. The ashen circles around his eyes and that sickly white of his skin, must have been smooth as an eggshell before he turned, was now cracked, and wrinkled like a desert floor thirsting for water. It must be hungry.

"Don't come any closer," she commanded in her sharpest tone. "For if you do, you won't like what comes next."

"Sounds like a challenge." He charged letting out a horrid shriek.

Layala's boots drove into the soft ground as she took off, the pale one right on her heels. She risked a glance backward. A clawed hand was within inches. Using her forward momentum she flipped onto the log, and whirled around, sights locked on the damned creature. The dagger flew from her fingertips. When the blade drove straight into his forehead, a dying groan drew from the pale one's lungs. His legs gave way and he fell to the mossy ground in a pile of awkward limbs.

Still holding Dregous close, Layala covered her mouth and nose with her cloak and hopped down from the log to get a better look at him. This was the first pale one she'd seen in years. What drew it here to Briar Hollow from the Void? It couldn't have been her magic. She hadn't used it since she was young. Perhaps the curse was spreading? No one in Briar Hollow knew how pale ones were made once the Black Mage passed. Some suspected it was like a disease now, infecting elves and killing humans.

She wanted to take her dagger back but thought it best to leave it just in case. Getting too close could be dangerous. If it spread like a plague, she didn't want to catch it. Becoming that *thing*, a vile, man and elf eating beast set on serving a master that no longer lived. What they truly wanted was to make all elves like them, a twisted shell of the person they once were.

She wasted no time heading back home. Shoving

through the round cottage door, Layala closed it tightly behind her and dropped the iron latch. With a palm on the warm wood, she caught her reflection in the smooth metal. The light blue eyes staring back at her showed the fear still making her hand tremble. *That was close.* She shuddered at how near the pale one came without her knowing. If he'd wanted to, he could have pounced on her back. Elves had naturally light steps, usually unheard by humans and barely audible by their own kind, and the pale ones were no different. She might have picked up on his presence before he got to her, but it wouldn't have been enough time.

Holding her palm out, she brushed her fingers across the leaves, vines and stalks of the many plants hanging from the cross beams above as she walked into the sitting room. Aunt Evalyn obsessed over collecting the rarest of foliage. Some would bring luck. Others would put someone to sleep for a week. The one with the bright blue berries and black leaves with sharp edges could cause near-instant death, and the burnt orange leaves of the Pottifer enhanced speed and energy for hours when ingested. Layala had eaten a couple of the leaves once and outran a horse at a full gallop.

The arched red brick fireplace roared as did the tea kettle over it. She dropped Dregous in his crate then grabbed a hook to remove the kettle and stop the ear-piercing whistle. Once it was out, she took off her wet cloak and hung it on the pewter hook by the door.

As she settled down in her rocking chair with a

blanket and a book, her mind drifted to flashes of a wildflower meadow. So quick it was almost as if it never happened. Then inaudible whispers of strange voices seemed to fly through the room. Echoing everywhere but nowhere.

She placed her hands on her temples, gritting her teeth. This had happened more lately. Flashes of strange places—places she didn't recall ever being, but it was the voices, never clear enough to understand anything. What was it? Why did it happen? Was she suffering from delusions as a side effect of her magic she refused to use? A heaviness settled on her shoulders recently, like someone always pushed down. It was a feeling that something bad was going to happen and she couldn't shake it.

Two boisterous singing men sounded close outside the cottage, saving her from the voices that abruptly cut off. Pounding on the door followed the singing. "Aye, Layala! Come have a drink with us!" Ren shouted.

"You know you want to!" Forrest sang.

An unwanted smile tugged at the corners of her mouth. Did they have to drag her out nearly every night? It had become so routine the people in town practically expected it. "You boys need someone else to entertain you for once," Layala hollered as she folded her arms.

"Only the fair Layala will do," Ren said, peeking his head in the window above the gray washed-stone sink. She should have pulled the curtains closed. Ren waved at her with a crooked grin.

Sighing, Layala lifted the latch and opened the door to the pair. "By the looks of things, you've already started drinking without me." Ren's dark blond hair was curly and usually unruly, but extra so this evening despite that the rain had stopped. Forrest's glassy brown eyes drunk her in as he leaned on his forearm against the doorway, more to prop himself up than to look savvy no doubt.

She wasn't wearing anything special; black trousers, knee-high boots, a sky-blue long sleeve top that buttoned at the wrists and showed a little cleavage, not much, but what seemed to be drawing Forrest's eyes tonight was the black corset around her waist. Most of the women in town wore dresses or skirts, and she would too if the fabric didn't inhibit her movements.

"We might've had a couple but the real fun starts when you join us," Forrest said, and raked his fingers through his dark brown hair. He'd let it grow just past his shoulders recently and it looked good on him. He smiled lazily, and a sharp pain hit her chest. He resembled his older brother so much. Even though it had been over two years since Novak passed, it was still hard to look at Forrest sometimes.

"I suppose I can come out for a little while." All she'd planned to do was read anyway, so she could get her mind off the pale one she killed.

"Yes!" They slapped palms. "Aunty Evalyn is on a roll tonight."

"Oh, is she?" Layala grabbed the dripping cloak and threw it back on. "How much has she won?"

"Enough that Baker Oswin owes her two weeks of fresh bread." Ren put an arm around her shoulder. "We'll be over to enjoy some of that, of course."

"Of course," Layala added with a smile. Her eyes drifted to the woods. Should she tell the boys? No, there was no need to scare them when the creature was already dead. But what if he wasn't the only one? She couldn't worry about that now. It's not as if she could go looking for more at this hour.

The boys sang a song about wine and pretty maidens up until they stopped at the entrance of the Smoky Dragon Inn and Pub. The wood sign hanging from the pole above was of a standing blue dragon with smoke rolling out of its nostrils. Another sign was nailed to the door and it read: *No Elves. No Dwarves. No Sprites.* Layala was the only exception to that rule.

The Smoky Dragon was where the town's folk gathered in Briar Hollow for entertainment. Layala and the boys walked inside to air hazy with pipe smoke, the stench of ale, and a hint of cinnamon potpourri. The potpourri was Aunt Evalyn's doing. She insisted that the dirty old man smell had to be masked with something good.

The pub was set up with several round tables full of men and a few women playing cards to the left, and to the right was the drinking section. Candles burned above on the oval metal chandeliers hanging off the wood rafters, giving the room a warm yellow-orange glow.

Loud chatter and clinking mugs rang in her ears. Sometimes with her elf hearing the noise overwhelmed her senses. She learned to tune much of it out over the years.

Briar Hallow's horse trainer shot to his feet, throwing his cards down. "How can you win so often?!" He shoved a stubby finger at the man across from him, one of the young guards. "It isn't possible."

"Old Boris is at it again. Always accusing people of cheating when he's lost everything," Ren drawled. "Maybe Layala will toss him out on his arse once more." Forrest and Ren snickered.

She hoped that wasn't the case. "I only did that because he grabbed my behind."

"The black eye was the best part. Lasted a solid fortnight, it did," Ren said. "The men at the training yard ridiculed him endlessly."

"I know. I was there," Layala said, smiling.

Aunt Evalyn waved them over to her table, her golden bracelets clinking. Her shawl, bright with red, blue, and yellow floral patterns, hung loosely around her shoulders. "Boys dragged you in here again, I see." She grinned and patted the rickety, wooden chair beside her. "Have a seat."

It wasn't long before Layala knocked back a couple mugs of ale and had a pipe in her mouth. She didn't enjoy smoking; in fact, she downright despised the stench, but it made the men bristle and she wanted that. After what happened to Forrest's brother Novak because of *her*, she'd never love a man again.

More ale. Smiles came easier. Her head felt a little lighter, her body warmer. Aunt Evalyn started telling stories about Layala's mother and father. She always did this when she had too much to drink. At least she hadn't brought up Novak tonight. There was only so much talk of death a person could handle.

Aunt Evalyn's stare was fixed on the foam in her metal mug. "I can't believe it's been almost twenty-five years since..." she trailed off. "I loved your mother like a sister. She was one of the only elves that ever treated me, a lowly human, with decency and respect." She snorted, shaking her head. "If only I could have done more. If I could have convinced her to come with me."

"She wouldn't have left my father to die alone. You raised me. Kept me hidden. You did what she asked."

"You know what the last thing she said to me was?"

Layala sighed and nodded. "One day I'd have to fight." Although it had been so long now, nearly twenty-five years since the High King of the elves killed her parents, it was hard to believe the day would ever come.

"Yes, and she was right." She slammed her hand on the uneven tabletop. It rocked and shifted, nearly spilling the contents of Layala's mug. "One day he will come for you, Layala. I've trained you. The folk of this town kept you hidden. Not a one has ever breathed a word outside these borders about you and who you are, but I fear this peace we have found won't be forever." Her Aunt's crooked finger got much too close to Layala's nose. Evalyn's black curls had gray at the temples now and her deep brown skin had earned some wrinkles around the eyes. "He will come. And you know what needs to be done. What you need to do."

Bringing her mug to her lips, Layala took a drink. Her eyes unfocused as she stared at nothing. She'd kill that bastard. That's what she would do, and his heir, too, cut that wretched bloodline from this realm. And finally put a stop to those who murdered innocents in her name as they hunted her for magic. She hadn't spent countless hours in fight training and mastering weapons with the guard chief for nothing.

A giant of a man, Briar Hollow's only blacksmith, practically fell into the chair across from Layala and Evalyn. His drink sloshed over the sides. "Boys said you wanted to test your knife skills, *elee*."

She was *elee*, slang for elf—an outsider. Even if the word was to protect her identity from a passerby who might hear her true name and suspect, the title painted her as different. All her life she wanted to fit in, but she couldn't change her pointed ears, or the way she moved a little too quickly. Even if she could pass as one of them for a brief exchange, humans still sensed something alien about her. Inherently knew she wasn't one of them somehow. Distrusted her.

Layala glared at Ren, who stood off to the side of the table, waggling his bushy eyebrows. Her eyes flicked to the burly man, and she drained the entirety of her mug. "I don't want to humiliate you, but if you're in the mood to be embarrassed, by all means, take that bet," she said and took off her cloak. A couple men whistled. Layala rolled her eyes. "Oh hush, I removed my cloak not my top." Human men were so easily aroused. She pushed up her sleeves to her elbows, more for show than anything.

"You can take that off too!" someone yelled. "We won't mind."

"Oye!" Forrest shouted and put his hands on Layala's shoulders. "She is a proper lady. Don't harass her."

"Thank you," Layala said. "So who is to be? You, John?" He should know better, but her looks deceived. She was tall, slender, with big blue eyes and elvish beauty, but they forgot how often she trained. To become the deadliest she-elf in all of Adalon was her sole obsession for years.

"Nah, me apprentice, James," the blacksmith John boomed, waving over the skinny teenager leaning stiffly against the wall in the corner.

With wide eyes, he approached. "Yes, sir?"

"Go stand against the wall there. Back flat. I gots a bet with Ren, says the elee can't stick an apple to the wall off yer head. He say she can."

Those big brown eyes of James slid to Layala. The

bump in his throat bobbed. "M-me? Let the elee throw a knife at me head?"

"Yes! Hurry boy," John pushed him toward the wall. "If she knicks ye, I'll give ye a bronze shepin for yer participation."

"And when I don't, you still give him a shepin for his participation." She pulled a knife from her belt and set it on the table. If the boy was taking the risk, he should get some reward. "You have an apple?"

"Eh," the blacksmith patted down his person. "Didn't think so far ahead. An apple anyone?"

A small crowd had gathered in a half circle around them. Mostly men with smoking pipes in their mouths and mugs in hand. One woman with too much color on her cheeks and half her bust hanging out of her corset, stood center. There was a chorus of mumbled "no's" while the patrons looked amongst each other.

"I do," called a smooth, deep voice from further back.

The group collectively turned and opened a space to reveal a hooded figure holding a bright red apple in his palm.

"Have an apple." A sliver of amber light snuck under the hood to reveal an unfamiliar scruffy chin and straight nose. A stranger, here in Briar Hollow. Layala gripped her knife's handle tightly and the speed of her heart shot up. The tall, broad man walked past her, and goosebumps erupted over her flesh. She shivered with an eerie sense of familiarity although she couldn't fathom why. He placed the perfect apple on the crown of the boy's head.

Layala stared at this intruder even as he sauntered toward her. Some deep instinct inside her told her to run but she stood firm. Mud covered the man's black boots to his ankles, however, his dark cloak hung an inch off the wooden floors was pristinely clean, crisp even, suggesting he hadn't walked far. The cloak didn't look damp; he'd been indoors and not in the storm, but who here housed him? No one spoke of a traveler. The inn's rooms sat empty this time of year. The townsfolk always warned Layala or Aunt Evalyn if any unknowns came through so she could stay hidden.

After clearing his throat, Ren asked, "Any other bets?" He raised his jingling pouch, carrying on as if it was usual for a stranger to visit the Smoky Dragon.

The man's cloak brushed her arm as he stepped around her and made for the bar top.

After a moment's pause and no one moved forward, Ren frowned. "No takers? You have such confidence in the elee who's at least three mugs of ale in?"

"Even ten mugs of ale in I'd be able to do it," Layala bragged. She'd find herself flat on the floor with that number but everyone laughed. The skinny teen trembled and slammed his eyes shut.

"Quit shakin' boy," the blacksmith bellowed. "Yer gunna get yerself stuck like a pig. Maybe ye should put the apple in yer mouth."

More laughter. Now half the pub patrons gathered

behind her. Her gaze drifted toward the man at the bar top. His back was to her. He peeked over his shoulder as if he knew she stared. She jerked her traitorous eyes away, embarrassed she'd been caught.

"What's the holdup, elee? Nervous?" Blacksmith John jeered.

"Not even a little." Layala closed one eye, willing her fuzzy mind to focus. Years of knife throwing granted her confidence. The motion of throwing a knife was so second nature she didn't have to think. The whoosh of the blade gliding end over end cut through the air, and with a thud, stuck the apple to the wall. James sagged to his knees, murmuring a prayer of thanks.

Half the crowd cheered, others groaned.

"Oh ye of little faith, do you not know I'm the best in the hollow?" Layala smiled at John and winked. "Now give the boy his coin."

John slammed his hand on the table. "Damn it all, Ren." He pointed a large, dirty finger at Ren. "You knew she could. Forrest told me she'd miss."

"It's part of the game, John!" Ren laughed. "Of course I knew, that's why I made the bet. You owe me a new knife. I'd like my name to be on the blade too."

"Do I get one since I clearly bet on myself?" Layala added.

Bystanders burst into laughter then went back to other amusements, clearing the way to the bar top where Layala expected to find the man but he was gone. She did a quick scan of the room, and didn't find him among the many bodies. The knots in her stomach loosened, and feeling like a weight lifted off her shoulders, she took her seat by Aunt Evalyn again. Her secret was safe for another day.

"Nice throw." The hooded stranger made himself comfortable in the chair across from her. His rich soothing voice sent a chill down Layala's spine. "Where did a pretty elf like you learn to do that?"

Chapter 2

Layala quickly slipped her arm under the table and rolled down her sleeve to cover her rune mark. The humans had no idea what her tattoo was, but she couldn't be too careful with an unknown man. She reached up and touched her hair, her ears were covered, as always. He must have surmised she was an elf some other way.

Layala reached across the table, clasping her fingers around the edge of his smoky gray hood and tugged gently. "I don't like when strangers come into my town and hide their faces."

"So it's *your* town, huh?" The stranger pulled the hood back.

Layala bit the inside of her cheek to keep herself from frowning or giving away that she didn't like what sat before her; the male was sinfully beautiful. His dark waving hair hung loosely past his shoulders, framing his masculine face. Her inspection traveled over his sharp jaw to his scruffy chin then perused to his high cheekbones and straight nose. She froze on his emerald green eyes but the color was lighter than that, like when the sun hit the jewel just right and it almost glowed. She'd never seen eyes that color before. "You know there's a sign on the door that says no elves. Can you not read or do you always blatantly ignore rules?" she asked.

He was too perfect to be anything but one of her kind, even if he kept his pointed ears hidden under that full hair of his. Now she knew how he'd figured out what she was so quickly. The distinction between human and elf was plainly obvious in the subtlest of ways. She'd never seen another elf up close until this moment.

He smirked. "I read quite well, actually." He paused. His voice was also slightly different, almost divine, and fascinating in the way the timbre seemed to roll down her spine. "Yet you're an elf, and I thought you said this was your town. Does it displease you that the inhabitants don't like what you are?"

Aunt Evalyn watched intently but stayed silent. Layala could almost feel the anxiety coming off her as Evalyn bounced her leg under the table. An elf in human lands was always a worry, no matter if they were looking for her or not. No one here would have offered to house him, which hopefully meant he was simply passing through.

"I'm the one who put up the sign," Layala said, tapping a finger on the table. "Keeps out the riff raff." Occasionally a lone elf or two would come through

Briar Hollow, and she'd remain out of sight, but it was as rare as a dragon egg. She couldn't risk an elf who might report to the king they'd encountered a lone elf female in the human lands. And since the pale ones emerged, humans had a natural aversion to elves, which was understandable since for all anyone knew the sickness could be caught simply by breathing the same air. It was fatal to humans.

"And it's my town because I live here." She winced a little, she was giving too much away. She half smiled to recover and lifted her gaze briefly to her knife still stuck in the wall. Too bad it wasn't in her hand. "What brings you to Briar Hollow, stranger? Business or pleasure?" She wanted to get rid of him but didn't want to come off as suspicious either. The reward for bringing her, Layala Lightbringer, to the king must be astounding. She'd heard there were bounty hunters, could he be one of them?

He leaned in a little closer, his eyes locked onto hers, a hunter who'd found his prey. "I was here on business but having seen you, a little of both, I think."

Was she supposed to be the pleasure? Or was she the business? Layala rolled her eyes, even as her heart beat faster. "You think you can come in here and win my affection so easily?" she said in hopes that was what he meant; business would be dangerous. She checked her surroundings. Was the male alone or did he bring friends? Another cloaked and hooded figure stood by the door. Definitely brought an accomplice.

Forrest and Ren had followed the blacksmith to

the bar top so she couldn't send them over to investigate the second intruder.

"Certainly not, fair maiden. I'd be willing to wager it would be quite the challenge to win said affections." He winked and leaned back in the chair. It creaked under the pressure. "I find myself... interested in you."

Layala swallowed hard. Aunt Evalyn broke her silence. "Be interested somewhere else, troll. We have no want of your kind here."

"A troll am I?" He looked down at his rather broad form and picked at a fleck of dirt or something as equally invisible on his cloak. Then his gaze rose. "*Maker above,* I thought I was an elf. How impertinent of me not to know I'd suddenly become green and misshapen and," he lifted his shoulder and smelled himself, "and wretchedly scented."

Layala pursed her lips to keep from smiling. "One can never be too careful with trolls."

"Don't I know it," he said and smiled, revealing his pretty white teeth. "But male elves are much worse, I hear."

"Terrible," Layala cooed. "And hideous."

"Oh, the ugliest things around, certainly." His casual laid back posture shifted when he sat up leaning in again as if he wanted to tell her a secret. "But elven females, the most exquisite beings to exist. Most especially the one sitting before me."

Aunt Evalyn snorted and jiggled the dried crimson berries tied around her neck with thin russet twine. "Don't make me use these, boy."

"Ah, slumber berries," the stranger mused. "Wouldn't I have to ingest those for your threat to be legitimate?"

"I could shove them up your a—"

"Enough, Aunt," Layala said. "There will be no need for that. My dagger at his balls should be sufficient." Under the table, Layala tapped the tip of the blade she'd swiped off Aunt Evalyn's hip against his inner thigh. His next move would help her determine whether or not he was there looking for Layala.

To his credit he didn't flinch, but a small smile lifted his beautiful face.

Layala tilted her head toward the door. "You know where the exit is. Take your friend with you."

"Since I've taken a liking to my *balls*, I'll see myself out." He said the word "balls" with particular emphasis as if he'd never heard the term before. Perhaps it was a human thing. Ren, Forrest and the men she trained with said it frequently enough. After he stood, he paused. "I'm curious, where is your mate?"

He saw her mate rune? And although there were many runes, he knew what the mark was? Her chest tightened a little. "I don't know what you're talking about."

His eyes dropped to her covered wrist. "I think you do."

Maker, he knew, or at least he suspected. "You are dreadfully mistaken. I have no man in my life nor do I want one in it. And if I were you, I'd let it go. No telling what might happen to you if you don't." Her eyes flicked to the group of men standing behind him. They'd been watching closely. All it would take is a signal from her and they'd toss him out.

When he left with whoever stood beside the door, she waited thirty seconds then jumped up. She tore her knife from the wall, and with a blade in each hand, shoved her shoulder into the swinging pub door. Her gut said his interest in her rune mark wasn't coincidental and neither was his presence here. What if he'd come searching for her to report to the High King? She couldn't let him. She stepped onto the road looking both ways. Rain streaked down her face. She looked at the shadows of the alleys, searched for horses in the distance but he was gone, and the rain washed away any trace of footprints.

She tossed and turned all night in her woolen blankets, worried about the elf, or more likely, *elves* she saw. There was a pair. She woke up minutes before sunrise to bathe in the nearby river, in hopes it would clear her mind. It was cold but fresh. Aunt Evalyn would heat rainwater in a huge metal tub for her baths but to Layala it was a waste of time. She dipped a toe into the slow river to test the temperature; a chill ran up her body. The shock of it would make her nice and alert. Red-breasted robins chirped in the willow tree that hung above the water as the sun rose over the mountains. The sprays of lavender along the water smelled lovely. This was her favorite part of the day. The serene sounds of nature and no one awake to bother her.

Maybe she was wrong about the elf. She might have interpreted everything he said to fit her own paranoia. He hadn't waited outside for her. No one came to the house. But the unease in her stomach wouldn't go away.

With a quick check of her surroundings, she stripped her clothes and waded into the water. Sinking completely under, she popped back up, shivering from the frigid cold. She quickly washed her hair with goat's milk soap, scented with mint and lavender, then added some oils to the ends to keep it smooth and shiny. A horse whinnied somewhere nearby. Her spine tingled. There were no homesteads close. No riders came this way.

Layala whipped around to see if anyone approached. The tall grass on the bank swayed in the slight breeze but no one person or horse appeared. Still, she listened to the rushing water, the light coos of songbirds, the quack of a duck, and crickets chirping at the shore. Everything serene until the caw of a crow or raven drew her attention up to the branch it perched on. Its small head cocked from side to side then it fluttered its wings before it lifted off and away.

The blackbirds were always a bad omen. She

couldn't help but feel someone watched her. Dripping wet, she crouched low in the grass, and quickly dried herself with a cotton cloth then slipped on her clothes, ever searching her surroundings. If it was a pale one, she couldn't be caught off guard. If it was a peeping tom, she'd cut out his eyes.

The mate rune on her wrist started to itch, like the sensation of a healing wound. It had been doing that a lot lately, and she didn't know what it meant. She looked down at the ebony mark, lines in the shape of cascading triangles with two diagonal strikes through both. Cursing the thing, she headed for the cottage.

As she drew closer, her stomach dropped. The round front door was ajar and hung off its hinges. Either Aunt Evalyn threw a temper tantrum, which wasn't entirely unheard of, or someone... she broke into a sprint, her light elven feet carried her the distance with remarkable speed. She drew her dagger and stooped below the kitchen window. Slowly, she rose up and peeked over the lip of the mantel, peering inside. Many of the plants that once hung from the rafters were broken and splattered on the floor. Dirt and leaves and flowers everywhere. Years of searching and money wasted. It smelled strongest of jasmine and sweet pea, Evalyn's favorites, their beautiful petals crushed into the floor. The furniture was overturned and Dregous's crate was but splinters. She charged inside, ready to cut down whoever did this. No, not whoever. She knew exactly the pair. It couldn't be a coincidence that she met an elf the night before and now this.

Inside, she found no one in the main room or kitchen. Her boots crunched over broken pottery as she moved farther in. "Evalyn?" she called, stepping over a shattered plate from a set her aunt had made. Her cheeks burned and her heart beat faster as she hurried to her aunt's bedroom. She poked her head in to find it empty. She dashed across the hall to her room—nothing. When she turned back to the sitting area, she stilled; how she missed it before was beyond her. On the dark wood paneled wall where the intruders tore down Layala's childhood painting of a unicorn, someone wrote in blood, *You can't hide forever.*

If they hurt Evalyn, if they—no, she couldn't think it. She couldn't let her mind wander to that dark place. The High King already took too much from her. The pounding of hooves and horse whinnies had her running for the window. A black carriage with gold fixtures pulled by six onyx steeds roared up right outside her front door. The heavy breaths of the horses said they'd been running. *Maker above, they found me. He is here to take me.* She knew this day would come, but now she wished she could hide. She took a step away from the window with her heart beating like a hummingbird's wings.

She held both a dagger with a ten-inch blade, and a knife half that size and waited in the center of the sitting room. Her senses hyperaware as light footsteps hit the ground and moved closer. She tensed as a large, cloaked male stepped up but stopped in the doorway. Was it him? The elf from the night before?

"Come with me," he said sharply. "His royal majesty the High King of Palenor awaits." Something about him triggered familiarity. She didn't know if it was the roughness of his voice or the way he moved, yet it wasn't the male who'd sat across from her.

A sheen of sweat dampened her skin. Her arm twitched, ready to throw her knife if need be. An old familiar sensation bit at her fingers, tingling like when the blood flow had been cut off and then rushed back into the limb. Her magic. Bad things happened when she used her magic. "Where are Evalyn and the pup?"

The dark towering figure stayed silent, his face shadowed by the deep hood. What was it with these elves and covering their faces? It wasn't as if it made them less suspicious. The carriage outside was far from inconspicuous, so if their intent was to go unnoticed, they failed on a grand scale.

She tossed her dagger into the air, watched it flip end over end and caught it again trying to mask her fear with bravado. All she knew of the wicked High King was his ruthlessness. She'd heard stories over the years of the countless bodies left in his wake, starting with her parents. He burned down entire villages in search of her, his weapon. His desperation grew more as time went on.

Aunt Evalyn and her fought over whether or not Layala should turn herself over to stop the killing. But it was always Aunt Evalyn's words that kept her in Briar Hollow, "Your mother and father gave their lives to keep you out of his hands, Layala. Don't let their sacrifice be in vain. If they should come, we'll be ready but not until that day."

She didn't understand what the king wanted with her. Yes, she had magic, but it wasn't as if he could force her to use it against her will. Aunt Evalyn said there were rumors that the High King had been waiting for a magical child like her to grant him power of his own. A rune spell of some kind to steal her magic, they'd guessed.

Her mind raced through images of all the scenarios that could have happened in this cottage. What if the blood on the wall was Evalyn's? "If you don't tell me where they are, there will be one less elf alive in this room."

The male shifted slightly and waved at someone outside. A moment later, another cloaked assailant stepped into view, a female by the size of her, but what she held in her grasp had Layala's throat dry up. A knifepoint was pressed against Aunt Evalyn's side.

"Is this answer enough?" the female questioned. Again, her voice was familiar somehow. Layala would swear on her parents' stone statues she heard it before, but she couldn't have. She'd never even seen another female elf before. She didn't know these people.

Aunt Evalyn gave an almost imperceptible bob of her head. She wasn't afraid. There was no fear in her eyes. If anything, there was determination and readiness. "And the dog? If you killed him, I swear—"

The male groaned. "In a crate by the chickens."

Gritting her teeth, Layala placed her weapons back in their sheaths and held up her hands. "Let her go and I'll come without any trouble."

"Take me with you," Aunt Evalyn said.

"No," Layala snapped. She cleared her throat and softened her tone. "No. I'll go alone." Evalyn was safe here. If Evalyn came, they could use her to manipulate Layala.

Evalyn's eyes glistened. "Layala," she pleaded.

The female holding her aunt, dropped the knife to her side and shoved Evalyn in the back. She tumbled forward into Layala's arms. After making sure her aunt had her balance, Layala smiled. "It is well. You've readied me for this day. Tell Ren and Forrest it's time I face this and to let me go, and that I appreciate their friendship."

She nodded once. "You'll come back, and you can tell them yourself."

"I love you," Layala said and tore her gaze away before she started crying. She made sure her shoulder slammed into the large male elf as she marched outside. Was he the one who stood by the door the night before? Maybe this was an entirely different group.

The six horses stamped their hooves and tossed their heads. The door to the carriage was open, and she hesitated. Was she going to walk right in with no trouble after she spent her whole life hiding? What choice did she have? Now wasn't the time to be a coward. She took a deep breath and headed for it.

"Not so fast," the female elf said and reached for Layala's hips.

Layala smacked her hand. "Don't."

"You're not getting in that carriage with those weapons."

The king was foolish enough to come all this way? He must know she would loathe him. Was he in that carriage mere feet from her? When they said the High King awaited, she assumed they meant at his castle in Palenor. Narrowing her eyes at the elf, Layala pursed her lips. It would be stupid to attack him so soon. She must weigh the situation, find weak points, devise a plan, but she didn't want to give up her protection.

Large hands clamped down on Layala's shoulders. "Hand over the blades."

Reluctantly, she pulled the two from her waist belt and placed them in the female's hands. She stooped down and grabbed one from each boot and surrendered them as well.

"The one in your back pocket too," the male said.

She clenched her teeth; she thought she'd get away with that one. It was a small throwing star, sharp and pointed with five tips. She reached back and pulled it out, giving it over. "That's all the weapons I have." Of course, that wasn't all. Her magic was as lethal as any weapon forged by men or elves.

A sharp sting burned her arm as a barb pricked her

flesh. "Katagas serum, in case you get any ideas," the male said. "We know you're a mage."

Her magic slowly waned, withering away until she couldn't feel even a whisper of its energy. "What did you do to me?" She clenched and unclenched her hands reaching for the sensation of magic.

"It suppresses magic temporarily. If you prove you aren't a threat, we won't dose you a second time."

Feeling naked without anything to protect herself with, her whole body trembled as her foot reached the step of the carriage. She grabbed the handle, steadying her uneven breath. To be so close to the elf who murdered her parents stirred a fiery rage and a healthy shot of fear, an inferno blazing in her chest.

Her mate rune itched again as she ducked her head and entered the carriage. She stared at the masked elf sitting on one side of the cushioned interior. She heard it was tradition for the King of the High Elves of Palenor to wear a mask for ceremonial purposes but why such a wretched thing? And did he consider this that type of meeting?

The door slammed behind her, and she nearly fell when the whip cracked, and the horses lurched forward. Stumbling into the seat opposite of the king, she righted herself and placed her palms on either side of her for balance as the carriage rocked side to side. Two five-inch silver horns rose out of the mask that completely covered his face save for his nose and mouth. Even the eye slits were so narrow she couldn't see beyond. The two silently watched each other for what seemed like a long time. Layala pictured herself diving across the carriage and wrapping her hands around his neck.

"Are you King Tenebris?" Layala finally got the nerve to say.

"I am Thane Athayel." His resonant voice felt like a fingernail gliding lightly down the skin of her back. It too was recognizable, as if it haunted her dreams. But his voice did something the others did not, brought goosebumps to her skin.

Layala licked her dry lips, as a connection between the itching rune mark and his closeness struck her. "The Prince of Palenor." She laughed humorlessly. "My mate."

Chapter 3

Layala squirmed in her seat. She sat directly across from the most notorious killer in Adalon. Said to be deadlier with his bare hands than most warriors were with a weapon. Feared above all, even more than his father. Only rivaled in infamy by the Black Mage himself. And she was supposed to marry him—and murder him.

"Prince? No." He tilted his head slightly, making the morning light coming through the window reflect off his silver face covering. "I am High King of Palenor now."

She blinked several times as a mixture of shock, anger and elation coursed through her. "Is he... dead?" Anger because if Tenebris was dead she wasn't the one to end him. Why hadn't word spread of this?

"I would still hold the title of prince otherwise, wouldn't I?"

Layala arched her eyebrow. "How?"

The new High King didn't respond. He tilted his

head toward the sheer black curtains covering the windows.

"How do I know if you're who you claim to be when you hide your face from me?" Layala shifted nervously, trying to judge if his skin might be turning paler than was normal or if his fingers had grown claws. He could be attempting to hide his becoming a pale one. What if he wasn't Thane at all? He wore leather riding gloves, but as far as she could tell from the small amount that was exposed, his skin still had a warm golden tone to it.

"Would you recognize me if I took off my mask? Do you know what Thane Athayel looks like?" He sounded amused as if he already knew she didn't.

Embarrassed by her own ignorance, she glanced out the window at the redwood trees going by, dug her fingers into the red velvet fabric beneath her, and shook her head.

Rather than revealing his face, he pulled off a glove, then slowly tugged at the fingers of the other. What was he doing? Layala pressed herself further back into the cushioned bench, every muscle tense.

"You don't need to fear me. I will not hurt you," he said and rolled up his left sleeve. She didn't believe him. His reputation for brutality preceded his arrival. Would they use torture to get her to invoke her magic? Aunt Evalyn said they might. For all her training, she was still only one person. Thane would have thousands of guards and soldiers at his command. He had three right here, all of whom had to be his best or he wouldn't have brought them. Maybe even more soldiers she hadn't seen.

"Proof," he went on, "I am who I say I am." He showed his wrist; the mate rune matching hers marred his skin in the same place.

It didn't settle her nervousness. Her stomach knotted. "And the mask?"

"Perhaps I simply like it."

He'd only like it if he wanted to be intimidating—threatening, both of which he accomplished. Layala pressed her lips together, wishing she could see through metal.

"I am meeting my future wife for the first time since childhood. It's ceremonial for the High King to wear a mask in such cases."

Her cheeks flushed hot with anger. Layala fisted her hands at her sides. *Stay calm,* she demanded of herself. If she was ever going to get out of this, she couldn't lose her temper, couldn't show her hand this early in the game. "Your wife." She tried to sound even, cool but a little disgust slipped into her tone.

"You don't sound enthused about that."

"Should I?"

"Many females would."

Layala stared incredulously.

"But I suppose you wouldn't. You don't know me."

"Or even what you look like."

He tapped his foot lightly. "Does that bother you?"

"If you couldn't see me, would it bother you?"

"You are rather beautiful. Your eyes are the most

stunning blue, and your hair as black and shiny as a raven's feathers. The contrast is alluring. But what if I wasn't beautiful? Maybe I am afraid you'll find me hideous."

"Even if you were the most beautiful male alive, I'd still find you hideous. I know about you and your father's desperation to have magic and what you have done. And I have no doubt you're exactly like him."

"If I were exactly like him, you might be regretting your choice of words right now."

Layala bit down on her bottom lip. She needed to settle down. If she was too nice he'd be suspicious but if she was too hostile he'd have more reason to see her as a threat to watch closely. Lowering her voice to sound docile, she said, "He would hurt me?"

"Yes." His voice was firm, resonant.

"But you won't?"

"I said I wouldn't." He leaned forward slightly. "I apologize. We're getting off to a bad start."

She stared at him. What start would he expect? Pleasantries and smiles when he forcibly took her from her home?

They sat in quiet, the sounds of the creaking carriage and beating hooves filling in for their lack of words. He abruptly slammed his fist against the door three times, making her jump, and the carriage slowed to a halt. The High King then shoved the door open. "It's a long ride to Palenor. We'll stop only when necessary, for your safety." He stood up and paused, facing the door. "And we will wed soon after we reach Castle Dredwich."

We shall see about that, High King.

When he stepped out, she leaned forward to watch him jump onto the back of a tall, ebony horse with a mane and tail even she was envious of. His deep green cloak flowed out behind him as his horse jetted forward.

They were on the move again before she could get a good look at who else might be out there. She was jolted all over the carriage on the rough road for hours. They would have gone over Brackendaw Bridge by now and through Sweet Bell village. She used to go there to sneak away with Novak when they didn't want anyone to know he was courting her. Sweet Bell was far enough away no one knew them but close enough they could get there easily. Human and elven relationships were frowned upon. Layala wished every day she'd listened to those who warned them.

The carriage jerked and creaked, the clop of horse hooves pounded. She touched the red velvet interior for hidden compartments, slid her hands beneath the seats for any weapons, *something* she could use to protect herself, but it was frustratingly ordinary. She peeked out the window on occasion but no one rode directly beside the carriage. All she saw were the meadows, trees, and grasslands. She didn't even know how many she rode with. Certainly, the High King of Palenor would have a large company.

When it was dark, a deep voice said, "Woah,

woah," and they began to slow. Layala peeled aside the curtain. The stars twinkled above, and the moon shone down on a nearby apple orchard.

"I have to take a piss," the same male voice said, and the carriage shifted as he hopped down.

Layala needed to do the same and if they were going to go at this pace, she wanted to grab some apples. Her stomach protested for food all day. They didn't stop to eat. Apparently the king didn't find eating necessary. She pushed the door open and it was immediately slammed shut.

"Stay inside," the female said.

Layala glared at the elf. Her hood covered half her face but a shiny red braid stuck out. "I've been in here all day. I have to squat behind a bush, if you know what I mean."

"Fine. Wait." A few moments later the door popped open and the red-haired elf shoved a black cloak into Layala's hands. "Put that on. We can't risk being seen here."

Being seen as elves? Or Thane Athayel being seen here? It *would* be suspicious to see a group of elves traveling in the human kingdom of Svenarum, or would attract attention at the very least. Layala slipped it over her shoulders and pulled the hood up. She jumped down, her boots hitting the hard rocky dirt road. The High King must have gotten off his horse. She didn't find him and his absurd mask anywhere. She was surprised to find only three horses aside from the team pulling the carriage. That meant there was only the king, two guards, and one driver. A swell of hope filled her chest; her chances of getting away increased.

But she was curious—why would someone with a status such as his take a risk like this? He didn't need to fetch her himself. And why so few guards? If any number of rogues or certain groups knew where he was, it could be a bloodbath... unless he wasn't afraid. Thane was ruthless and savage when it came to destroying his enemies, unmatched when it came to the sword.

Taking in a deep breath of fresh air that smelled of wildflowers, she searched for a place to go. To the right of the road were the apple orchards and to the left was a small wood with oak and ash trees with full green leaves. Grass as high as her hips grew at their base which would provide cover for her to relieve herself. There was also a boulder as big as a horse... She knew this place. Gaudrey's Hot Spring was close, and where the spring was, a poisonous plant grew. Deadly enough to bring down a horse in minutes, and an elf... even faster. Guided by moonlight, she started off toward the woods with the female elf steps behind her.

"Stay close," Red sounded guarded, fearful even.

Layala twisted around but kept walking. She'd been in these woods before and it was rare to encounter any dangerous creatures. "There's nothing out here to be afraid of. And I don't need an audience."

Red hurried to walk in step beside Layala. "When

you've seen what I've seen, there is always something to fear. To allow you to wander off alone would make me daft."

"I'm not going to run away." She'd done enough running. Movement near the boulder caught her eye. The three males looked to be peeing on it. Having been around a bunch of men, she guessed they were trying to write their names. The laughter coming from them would say as much. She couldn't help but look for Thane, but she didn't know which was him.

"And why would I believe that?" Red asked. "All signs would point to you trying to go into hiding again to avoid your duty."

"Duty?"

"Yes, you are the High King's mate. His promised wife. Your duty is to be with him."

"And what is his duty to me?" Layala spotted a wide trunked tree that would offer privacy.

"To protect you."

"From who?" *If not Thane himself,* she wanted to add but thought better of it. It was he and his supposedly dead father she needed protection from.

Red didn't offer an answer. Layala huffed and made her way around the tree. Following, Red folded her arms and watched Layala as she loosened the buttons on her trousers.

"Are you truly going to watch me? Tell you what, if you don't hear it hitting the ground in a few seconds you'll know this was all a ruse to get away."

With a sigh, Red turned around.

"Why aren't there more guards?" Layala asked.

"Thane didn't want anyone else aware of where you were but just know we will keep you safe."

For whatever reasons they were concerned with *her* safety specifically. But the Athayels were the ones who'd been hunting her for the last twenty-four years. They were the enemy. "How did you find me?"

"Not my business to tell."

A steel trap that one. When Layala was finished, she walked right by her guardian and started for the carriage. The others were already waiting.

One of the males crouched adjacent to a small pile of branches and stoked a budding fire in the middle of the roadway. Another leaned his back against the carriage door, one heel hooked on the bottom step. The other male worked at unsaddling one of the horses. The three wore identical cloaks covering their heads and shadowing their faces, all about the same height and stature, but Thane must be the one leaning against the carriage. The other two clearly worked *for* him.

Her skin crawled when he pushed off the carriage. The bottom of his cloak flowed out around him. "Come, Layala."

Chapter 4

Layala swallowed hard and glanced at Red. What she looked for she didn't know. Reassurance, perhaps, that Thane wouldn't try to do anything. She knew he wouldn't kill her, he needed her magic, and murdered, only the Maker knows, how many to find her, but she was his promised mate—he may try to take what he thought was his. Thane moved toward the apple orchards and didn't look back to see if she followed.

"Go." Red gave her a gentle push.

Heart pounding, she put one foot in front of the other until she caught up to him. He no longer wore the mask but she still couldn't see his face, shadowed by the hood. Why did he ask her to follow him? She fidgeted with the hem of the cloak, waiting for him to say something. They walked silently until they reached the blossoming trees with plump red apples.

"You think me a monster." It wasn't a question. He

reached up and plucked an apple, then turned it over slowly.

Layala didn't respond, but she too grabbed a piece of fruit. It was hard and cool to the touch. He brought her over here to pick apples and talk?

Thane grabbed another and turned his cloak into a sort of pouch, dropping them into the fabric cupped around his arm.

"What have your humans told you of me?"

She found it an odd question and lifted her shoulder. There was a lot to tell.

"Nothing? Now that can't be true."

She cleared her throat. "Like you said, that you're a monster."

"Don't spare the details. They must be absolutely riveting."

The arrogance in his tone grated on her nerves. "I know you and your soldiers have killed hundreds if not thousands. The woodland elves fear you, and if the human kings knew you were in their land, it would be considered an act of war because of your brutality." She paused to gauge his reaction. He didn't move or say a word. And even though she couldn't see his eyes, she imagined he stared at her from under the hood. "And they say you fought alone against a hundred pale ones and killed them all."

He smiled, showing straight white teeth even in the darkness. "A hundred, you say? That would be impressive."

Her brows furrowed. "It's not true?" She expected

even if the number was inflated, he wouldn't correct her.

"It was closer to twenty, but even that wasn't an easy gander through the woods. I strained my back a little."

Her brows furrowed. Was he being facetious? Layala plucked another apple. "I've heard that you mark your flesh with each elf downed by your hand so others know how deadly you are."

"Interesting." Was all he said.

She nibbled on her lower lip, debating on speaking the last few things she had in mind. Was it a mistake to give away all she'd heard? If she wanted him to trust her enough to let his guard down she had to give him something.

"Is there more?" he asked.

"Plenty." Gruesome details of how he and his father hung bodies from the very walls of Castle Dredwich, bathed in bathtubs of blood, and did ritual sacrifices to the old gods of young females in hopes of gaining magic power. Monster was the perfect word to describe Thane Athayel. But she didn't dare speak those details. "They also said you've had many lovers. And that they go mad when you leave them."

"They say a lot of things, it seems. Why do these lovers of mine go mad?" He was smiling again.

You tell me, she wanted to say but shrugged. There were plants that could make a person mad if ingested for long enough. Perhaps the females were heartbroken that he used them only to discard them when he was bored of their company. The how of it didn't matter much.

"I would tell you not to believe everything you've heard of me, but I doubt you'll take my word."

There had to be truth to the rumors. Maybe it was only one or two lovers who'd gone mad. It might be they hung bodies of their enemies in trees rather than off the castle but rumors usually stemmed from the truth. And he didn't deny a single thing.

Layala plucked another apple and stuffed it into the pocket of her cloak. It could be at least a week on the road, and she hadn't eaten all day.

When Thane's cloak looked heavy with fruit, he started back for the carriage and his companions. "That's enough for now."

She pulled two more and then followed a few paces behind him. There were two obvious sword outlines under his cloak on his back, and she'd spotted a shine of silver at his hip. At least three weapons.

The others gathered around the small fire, sitting on horse blankets. One of the males tended to a small, skinned animal on a spit but no one spoke as she and Thane approached. Red hurried to the back of the carriage and returned with a wicker basket. She set it at Thane's feet and the apples were dumped in. Layala kept hold of hers. She stood awkwardly for a moment, watching the four of them sit in silence, each of them looking in a different direction. What were they searching for? She peeked over her shoulder at the woods, and then to the long road ahead. No other travelers were in sight, and she didn't hear anything but crickets, an occasional owl hoot, the quiet crackling of the fire, and a gentle breeze.

The empty blanket resting between Thane and Red was for her no doubt, but she'd rather sit in silence in the carriage alone than with a pack of murderous thugs. Before she could even turn to leave, Thane said, "Stay. Sit with us."

It didn't sound like a request, but she didn't want to be ordered around like one of his soldiers or servants. Aunt Evalyn said males in power didn't like females who were easy game. They enjoyed the hunt as much as the catch, but what he didn't know was she would capture him in her snare before he even knew he was the prey. "I'll be in the carriage."

"I wasn't asking," he said firmly.

"Neither was I."

All three of Thane's soldiers turned toward him. Layala marched for the carriage before he reacted. She threw open the door, slid inside, and slammed it shut. Her heart thrummed against her ribs as she sank into the seat. She waited with bated breath for the door to crash open and for him to drag her out and demand she obey him. The carriage creaked, but he never came.

Hours went by. She listened for any noise but hadn't heard their mumbled conversation for a while. She pulled the curtain aside. Judging by the moon it was well past midnight. The four of them lay around the fire. She nibbled on her bottom lip. At least one of them would keep watch, wouldn't they? But perhaps the Maker was on her side this night.

She popped open the door and slipped down the steps careful not to make a sound. The carriage rocked slightly when she stepped off but none of the elves moved. If she was quick, they wouldn't notice her absence. She dashed through the grass, her steps as silent as the dead. Guided by starlight slipping through the trees, she hurried through the woods, past the big boulder. She caught sight of the thin trail she searched for and followed the dirt that cut between tall grass. Steam rose from the small pool ahead. Gaudrey's Hot Spring. White lilies grew at its banks and blush blooms of the magnolia tree blossomed overhead. The hot spring had an egg odor but the floral scent from the trees masked it well.

She removed her boots and stripped down bare, not wanting damp clothes for the rest of the night and into the next day. After hanging her clothes on a tree branch she gave one more quick glance around to make sure she wasn't followed, and dipped a toe in the spring. It was warmer than the night air but not burning. She waded in up to her hips and pushed her right foot around in the sludge, feeling for the drop-off. When she found the place with no immediate bottom, she took a deep breath and sunk under. She swam down at least seven feet, feeling for the weeds that grew in the dark, warm water. A fuzzy string caught around her wrist. There it was, the poisonous plant Gaudrey's root. The story was Gaudrey's wife, a thousand years before, poisoned him with this plant's root by accident. She'd mistaken it for a medicinal plant for healing. Layala jerked it free as her lungs began to protest and kicked off the bottom.

She broke through the surface, inhaled deeply and swiped a hand over her face. After she blinked several times her vision cleared, she gasped. One of the hooded males leaned against a tree trunk, arms crossed. At least she hoped it was one of them. She didn't want to have to fight off an attacker—naked, no less. Could it get any worse? She still couldn't feel her magic, and she didn't have a weapon to defend herself against anyone else.

"Just thought you'd go for a midnight swim in the middle of a dangerous forest?"

Her heart hammered at the sound of Thane's voice. Her sight drifted to her clothes hanging on the tree branch next to him. She was completely nude, and how in Maker's name was she supposed to hide the Gaudrey's root? Would he even know what it was? It would be so much easier to poison them all and get away than try to kill Thane or the others by different, bloodier, more risky means.

He lifted her bralette from the tree and dangled it from his finger. Her cheeks warmed even more than they already were. But instead of allowing the fear of what he might do to her take over, she smiled. "Did you come to catch a glimpse of your future wife? Perhaps you wish to fully see your prize after waiting so many years."

She gulped, waiting for his response. He set the bra down, grabbed her cloak and after two long strides, he squatted at the edge of the pool. His hood was back enough that she could see part of his face. How she wished she could push it away more.

"As delightful as you no doubt are, now isn't a good time." The snap of a branch drew both their attention to the shadows of the trees. When nothing came of it he said, "But I must say, you do have a nice, round backside."

Her face twisted in disgust. "You watched me undress."

"I followed you to make sure you weren't running away or getting yourself into trouble. You chose to disrobe on your own accord."

"I didn't know I had an audience."

"You should learn to listen then."

She cursed herself. She should have been able to hear him. "You're obviously—light footed. But a proper male would have alerted me to his presence, not watched from the shadows." She nibbled on her lower lip. Speaking so freely was taking a lot of risk, but she wasn't a helpless victim and never would be.

"I wasn't thinking about propriety. I was busy trying to figure out your motive for coming here, and got a lovely little show in the process." He shifted slightly, dropping one knee to the soft grass. "Feel free to explain yourself."

She clenched her teeth together. The audacity it took to even ask that after he called her undressing a "lovely little show" was astounding. Like she was his property. But she couldn't expect anything more of him. His soldiers forced her into his carriage with the threat of her aunt at knifepoint, after all. "I'm not your slave. You don't get to demand things from me."

"Is that so?" He sounded like he was about to laugh. "My, aren't we in a precarious situation, considering I'm demanding that you come home with me. Demanding that you be my wife. So wife, explain yourself."

Maker, she hated him. Her heart thundered and she drifted backward in the water a little further away. If she could, she'd slit his throat right then and there. "I'm not your wife either."

"Yet, but you will be soon. There's not much of a choice in the matter."

Little did he know she'd get her choice. Another branch snapped somewhere nearby. The playful tug of his mouth drooped. "You need to get out of the water. It isn't safe here."

Was there something here he saw that she didn't? Another pale one? A troll or group of bandit men? Layala still hadn't moved to get out of the water swirling around her neck, and she wouldn't unless... "Drop the cloak and turn around first." If he'd already seen her backside, he didn't need to see more.

His mouth curled at the corners but he set the cloak down, stood and wandered to the tree. With his back to her, he leaned his shoulder against it as he'd done before and waited. The water splashed loudly as she climbed out and snatched up the cloak. She stuffed the poisonous root in the pocket and covered her front. Tiptoeing to the tree, she grabbed her clothes, first stepping into the underwear then sliding her bralette on. She kept her eyes locked onto Thane, whose back was a mere two feet or so from her, but he didn't turn to peek once. At least her captor showed decorum when it came to her modesty even if he was a barbaric brute in other ways. Which made her wonder if he was being nice to gain her trust or if he might actually care for her.

On the walk back, he kept tilting his chin toward her, but hadn't scolded her or threatened her as she expected he would. The silence between them grew heavy, like a fog. She felt so uncertain and nervous now.

"Is there something you want to say?" she finally blurted out. It was almost as if she knew he wanted to ask her something.

"What were you doing in that pool?" His light footsteps barely made a sound over the grass. The stealth was a little unnerving given his size. A human man of his stature would surely be louder, but she had to remember these were elves, not men.

"Bathing, what else?"

He halted and grabbed her arm before she could take another step. "You're lying."

Her pulse ticked up. The sound of blood rushing in her ears drowned out the whoosh of the wind. But she kept her breath steady, forcing her voice to stay even when she said, "Don't you think if I was trying to get away that I would have kept going? If I wanted to escape, I'd hardly stop for a swim."

"That's what is bothering me." He still hadn't released his grip on her arm but it was gentle enough. "Look, I know this isn't ideal."

"You forcing me to join you under threat?" she said flatly. "Or an arranged marriage?" Which resulted in the death of her parents.

"Yes," he said slowly. "But you don't need to be afraid of me."

"It's not the thought of you hurting me that I fear." Also a lie, but what she feared most was that he'd use her as a weapon to kill innocent people in his war. Or that he lied about his father being dead and was being the dutiful son to bring her home so King Tenebris could somehow use her magic for his own dark purposes which would again end in many innocent lives taken. He wanted power... would he invade Calladira and take over the woodland elves' land? With her strength, would their armies take the human kingdoms? They could burn Briar Hollow and enslave those who didn't die in battle. The thought made her sick.

"I won't take you to bed against your will either."

Was he so foolish he really couldn't know why she'd been in hiding this long? Her parents didn't die simply because they didn't wish their daughter to marry a prince. Most would consider themselves fortunate and blessed by the Maker to be chosen as his bride and become the Queen of Palenor, if she wasn't the last mage and he wasn't a war-mongering male.

His mouth hardened. "You think I'm lying."

"I don't know what to think." She started to speak more but he spun her around, clamped his hand over her mouth and brought them down to a crouch. His hulking form was pressed against her back.

She was about to bite down on his hand until he whispered, "Shhh," in her ear. "We're being followed."

Followed?! By what?

Chapter 5

"Twenty paces to the left in the branches of the Ash tree. Do you see it?" His breath grazing against her ear sent an involuntary shiver down her back. He dropped his hand from her mouth and she lifted her gaze. There among the branches was the outline of a large winged creature.

"A bird?" she whispered flatly. By its size and the shape of its curved neck it was probably a vulture

"A messenger," he corrected. "Its eyes are red."

"A messenger for who?" How could anyone use a bird as a messenger? "Do you mean it's intelligent enough to follow us and report back to someone?"

"I don't know, and yes." A bow and arrow were suddenly in his hands. He slid around beside her, planting a knee firmly in the grass. The twinge of the bow echoed in the night, and a loud squawk grated against her ears when the arrow pierced the vulture's chest before it fell to the ground. "It's time to move."

Days passed with only short stops. She brushed her fingers over the Gaudrey's root in her pocket often to make sure it was still there. All she needed was an opening. The breakneck pace stunted any opportunity to slip the poison into the food or drink, until tonight. They made a stew and left it over the embers to eat in the morning. Now was the only chance she'd get to slip in the Gaudrey's root. After nearly twenty-five years this nightmare would finally be over. She wouldn't have to live with the constant anxiety of looking over her shoulder anymore. She prayed that whoever followed them was after the High King, and not her, considering no one stalked her before he showed up.

Slipping poison into their food seemed a little too easy for something she trained for all her life, and a little guilt nagged at her when she thought of Thane's guards having to die along with him. But she couldn't get away free if she left them alive. She assumed that King Tenebris was indeed dead and that Red told the truth when she said Thane didn't want anyone to know where she'd hid all these years.

The moon was high and the lack of any murmuring voices convinced her they'd gone to sleep. She slowly pushed open the door and quietly put her foot on the step. She froze; a dark heap laid at the base. Was someone sleeping right there? *Ugh, of course there is!*

Three of her captors laid beside a small fire not far off but one of them, one of the males by his size, was wrapped in a cloak laying on his side right below her. Maker, had he been sleeping there every night or did he suspect her tonight? No, there was no way they could know what she planned.

This might be her best chance. If she waited until they arrived at the castle it would make her escape far more complicated if not impossible. Keeping her breathing shallow, she grasped the carriage handle and hung off, stepping over him and quietly put her foot down right beside his chest. If she jumped, he'd no doubt hear her. Carefully, she let go of the carriage, and stood over him, one foot still on the step and the other almost touching him. He didn't move.

She swung her other leg over and took in a breath. Confident in her mission, she started for the pot of soup. A hand latched around her ankle, and she gasped, barely holding in a scream.

"I knew it wouldn't be long before you tried to sneak off again," Thane said from beneath his hood.

Her heart lurched into her throat and she tugged her leg, but his fingers gripped tighter. "I'm not trying to sneak anywhere—I just can't be in the carriage anymore. I need fresh air." The moonlight revealed there was nothing around for miles but open land, not a house or even a mountain range in sight. This was called the Flats for a reason. The few scattered trees and boulders offered nowhere to hide. Likely nothing to eat either.

"Sure you do. You know we're being followed, and we are in unpatrolled human lands. There are trolls, wraiths, more than likely bandits, and pale ones. You must stay inside." His voice was barely above a whisper. Then his hand flashed out and he caught her wrist. "Now be a good girl and—"

She wrenched her hand away. "You're not going to drag me anywhere."

"That's where you're mistaken. I will. I'll throw you over my shoulder if I must. And I might even enjoy it a little."

She scoffed, but she didn't doubt he would. "You're just used to everyone following your orders, High King, but I'm not one to take them."

His mouth twitched. She couldn't tell if he was irritated or amused.

One of the males by the fire stood up chuckling; the driver, she'd come to know him by his rich black skin. They called him Fennan. "Having trouble with your betrothed, Thane? She's a feisty one," Fennan folded his arms. "Good luck taming her."

The other male, distinguishable by his lighter skin and the golden hair that sometimes peaked out from under his cloak hood, she called Sunshine. He smiled the most and with his hair color it just fit. He shook his head, "My coin is on Layala."

Layala gaped at them. *Taming her? Bets?* Was this how they spoke of all females? "*She* doesn't like to be spoken about as if she can't hear," Layala said. "And I'm not a beast that needs to be *tamed*."

A pale one shrieked somewhere in the distance. She lifted her head, searching the night. It sounded far off, but pale ones were fast. Was this what hunted them? No wonder they'd been so quiet this entire time.

"Grab what you can!" Thane yelled to his crew. He turned to Layala. "We're almost to the border. Get back in the carriage."

She slowly shook her head.

"Please," he said as if it caused him pain to utter the word.

A massive lake gleamed on the horizon, Lake Lamora, which meant they were but miles from the elven kingdom of Palenor. The lake served as a barrier between elven and human land since it spanned hundreds of miles between the two.

"I'm not getting back in this time." She didn't trust that the carriage could be pulled fast enough to outrun pale ones on this uneven road. "I'd rather run if you won't give me a horse."

"It's too dangerous to have you out in the open. Do you have any idea what a mage like you is worth?" The driver, Fennan hopped onto his seat. "Don't make us do this the hard way."

The other two quickly mounted the horses that remained saddled, but Thane didn't move from his spot in front of Layala. Instead, he whistled and his gigantic horse lifted his head from grazing nearby and trotted over. He stepped into the stirrup and lowered his hand toward her. "If you want to ride, it will be with me."

She stared at his outstretched hand, clenching her jaw. She didn't want to share a horse with the High King but a chilling wail broke through their silence and Layala's blood went icy. Then another cry, and another. There were many. Their screams sounded far off before; they didn't now. Pale ones were far worse than her captors.

She reached for her weapons on her belt and then cursed, remembering they weren't there. Her magic tingled down her arms like the spindly legs of a spider, itching to escape. They hadn't dosed her with the serum in a day and her magic wanted to let loose on whatever wished her harm. To destroy. But even if she now had the ability, she couldn't allow it free. It was too risky.

"What do you want us to do, sire?" Red asked, pulling her sword.

He twisted in his saddle when another shiver-inducing shriek pierced the warm air, but it was closer this time. Much closer. The hairs on the back of Layala's neck lifted. They left her vulnerable when they took her blades.

"They've been tracking us for days," Sunshine said. His sorrel brown horse whinnied. "Their forces may be large by now."

Thane's horse shifted nervously, grunting and

pawing at the dirt. One of his hands rested on the reins. "We make a run for Palenor. Cut the horses loose from the carriage. It will slow us down."

"Tracking us?" Layala's heart thundered as she looked along the grassy landscape waiting for them to appear. Was the vulture Thane shot used by them? Were they intelligent enough for that? "How do you know that?"

"We've killed three over the last four nights while you slept," Red answered. "There is no doubt."

How had she not heard the pale ones, let alone the creatures being slaughtered? Why were they being followed? She hadn't used her magic to draw them.

She sucked in a gasp when on the edge of the amber meadowlands the road bordered, at least ten pale ones charged toward them. Weapons of various kinds in hand, howling and wailing. Damn, they were fast.

Thane didn't wait for her to voluntarily climb up. He grabbed her arm and lifted her like she weighed no more than a small child. As soon as she straddled the horse, her back pressed against Thane's solid chest. His arms circled around her to grab hold of the reins and he nudged the steed's sides. "Make for Palenor. Do not stop until you see the sentries!"

Fennan and Sunshine quickly unhitched the six horses. The herd bolted for Palenor, their home. The driver hopped on the mare behind Red, and the other mounted his own horse.

The High King's horse reared up, Layala latched

onto the saddle horn. The wind whipped through her loose midnight hair as they tore across the land. She turned back, the pale ones weren't gaining, but they weren't falling behind, either. One wrong move and the group would overtake them. Would the horses be able to keep up this pace? Pale ones were notorious for their endurance; they could run for days and not tire, not even get winded.

Heavy huffs of breath shot from the nose of Thane's horse. The hooves slammed yet glided across the uneven road. The huge white-trunked trees with deep blue and silver leaves shaped like stars loomed on the horizon. Only the Forest of Brightheart had trees like that, luminor, they were called. The elven sentries would be among them, high in the thick branches, guarding their lands. If Layala's small company could make it another mile they'd be safe.

A horse scream forced Layala to twist, clutching onto Thane for support as she peered around him. Sunshine's horse had hit the ground, and he was trapped under the weight of it.

Layala cupped her mouth. *He's as good as dead*. Part of her didn't want to say anything. So what if one of her abductors wouldn't make it? She planned to poison them all not even ten minutes ago but that didn't include suffering and being *eaten* by pale ones. He was only following the orders of his king.

"Your guard fell!" Layala shouted over the rushing of the wind and pounding of hooves.

Thane's strong arms tightened around her when

he pulled back on the reins and turned his horse in a wide circle. He snarled a curse as Sunshine struggled to wiggle free. The horse on top of him wasn't moving.

Layala was shoved in the back and fell from the horse, barely managing to land on her feet. She glared up at the king who pointed to the Brightheart Forest, his horse stamping and turning. "Get to the trees! Stay out of sight!"

Red and Fennan were already riding back to aid their friend. The pale ones seemed to be going faster now; they smelled their chance to pounce. But there was a single pale one on a snowy white horse, hanging back. As if he were directing them. Layala had never seen such a thing. Never seen them ride horses, never seen them with a leader.

She hesitated, debating on rushing in to fight or running to get help. The cries and shrieks of the pale ones kept her frozen in place, watching in horror as they drew closer. Their evil twisted faces elated at the prospect of the feast before them. Her stomach cramped. *Do something!* She screamed at herself.

Layala turned, breaking into a sprint, her light feet flying. She pumped her arms, breaths coming fast, wishing she had a mouthful of the speed-enhancing leaves. Her eyes watered from the air rushing past. When metal clinked against metal, she turned her head. Sunshine was up and all four of the elves fought the group of pale ones with swords at close range. Too close.

She couldn't figure out why it bothered her to

leave them. She wanted Thane dead. She could leave him to rot on this road, to have his bones picked by the vultures and Adalon would be better for it, but the others... she didn't want them to turn into pale ones. She could use her magic to save them, but she didn't want them to know what she was capable of.

A flash of white caught her attention, and she skidded to a halt, nearly falling back as a pale one darted into her path. He smiled, revealing his pointed teeth perfect for tearing through flesh. "Come with me."

Chest heaving, she took several steps backward, putting a hand over her mouth and nose. "Stay away." She reached for her belt again out of habit, her breath ragged with fear.

The monster stepped closer, swinging his rusted jagged-edged sword at his side. "Come, dark mage."

She recoiled at the name. How did he know of her magic? How did they know who she was? "Stay away from me or I'll cut you in half."

"Yes, show us your power," he said, his black eyes gleaming. "My master wishes to see it."

"I will kill you if you take one more step." She might not have a choice but to use her power unless— he advanced. With a spinning kick she knocked the sword from his hand. It flew into the air. She snatched it, and with bent knees, held the blade point at the pale one, ready to strike.

With wide eyes, he stumbled back. She charged

and swung, missing as he maneuvered to the side. Another swing caught the arm he used to block; ebony blood oozed from his pale flesh. When she was about to hack down again, an arrow struck through his chest, then another through his neck. Layala jumped back as the body crumbled forward.

A group of elven sentries in navy and silver garb emerged from the thick woods with long ivory bows in hand, arrows knocked back. She looked at the fight still going on between the others. "The High King Thane is under attack!" she shouted, knowing that would make them run. The fifteen or sixteen sentries moved in swift unison. Soon arrows flew and the remaining pale ones dropped to the dirt.

Layala stood frozen, watching to see if any of the king's guards died. Sunshine limped with an arm around Fennan's neck for support. Red held her forearm but otherwise she appeared fine. Thane unfortunately, by his easy movement, didn't seem to have a scratch on him. His hood had also fallen but his back was to her. His shoulder blade-length deep brown, almost black hair in the night's dim light was half tied back and disheveled. He pulled his hood up before he turned, and the group of them made their way to her.

When they reached her, Thane leaned over on the horse's back, scooped her up by her arm, and swung her behind him. "You and I are going ahead."

As the horse trotted forward, when Layala lost

some balance, she begrudgingly grabbed onto his waist. "Why?"

He didn't reply as they rode far ahead of the others. They passed groups of sentries standing in small wooden outposts high above. Some leaned over the edges of the railings to watch as they went by. No one saluted or acknowledged him as their king. Perhaps they didn't know. Layala pulled her own hood back up.

They were on a small winding path, but turned off it, traveling away from anyone, deep into the forest where only animals scurried about. Silver-tailed squirrels chittered, leaping from branch to branch. One dropped an acorn on her head. She rubbed the spot, scowling up at it. The farther they went the more nervous she became. What did he plan to do with her? Why was he taking her where no one might hear her scream? She eyed the outline of his swords beneath his cloak. There were two. Perhaps she could get her hands on one.

When they reached a small clearing in the woods with wildflowers of all colors and glowing nighttime butterflies lifting and lowering from bloom to bloom, the High King stopped and slid down. He wouldn't even look at her as the moon cascaded through the opening of the canopy of trees, shining on him as if a beam of celestial light. Layala grunted at the thought of anything about him being celestial.

He whirled around on her. "How do they know where you are?"

The anger in his tone surprised her. It was the first time he'd shown any aggression toward her. Layala's heart beat faster, her breaths a little shallower and dropped to the ground. "Who?"

"The pale ones," he barked. "They've been tracking us since Briar Hollow. Tracking *you*."

It couldn't be because of her. They only knew where she was if she used her magic and she hadn't, not once. She learned that lesson as a child. She'd been practicing and a pale one appeared the next day, Aunt Evalyn was almost bitten, but the guard master saved her. When it happened a second and third time, it couldn't be a coincidence. From then on, she tried to bury her power, to forget it was even there. She wanted to be rid of the magic that so many others sought after. "I don't know what you're talking about."

He snarled. "I nearly lost one of my friends back there and that's your answer? What were you doing in that pool? Magic of some kind?"

"I'm not leading them to us if that's what you're saying, and I couldn't use my magic that night even if I'd wanted to thanks to your soldier poisoning me." She thought of the pale one on the horse. Had he gotten away? She didn't see him when the skirmish ended. He might have gone to get more.

Thane stomped toward her, his face inches from hers. His sweet breath smelled of honey and mint. Without thinking she reached up to shove his hood off; she wanted to look into his eyes, to see the evil behind them, but he snatched her wrist. "We kept you alive. The least you can do is tell the truth."

"I got help. Maybe *you* should say thank you." Layala attempted to shove him back but he didn't move, as if he'd rooted into the ground like a tree. "How did *you* know where I was? Your spies?" Her mind drifted back to the charming elf she met at the Smoky Dragon. He must have told.

"I've known where you were for years," he snapped. "Now tell me. Are you doing it on purpose?"

Her heart seemed to falter and she choked on her own spit. He had known for years? *Years*?! How? And if he had, why wait until now to get her?

"It's not me. I don't want to be one of those *things*." She ground her teeth thinking how she had heard of them more than usual the last few months. Whispers of them in neighboring towns. "I don't know why they're following us. If they knew how to track me, I wouldn't have been able to live in Briar Hollow all my life. I saw one the day before you came, but I don't know why." Yet it seemed both of them knew deep down she was the reason the group of them had been there. The one she faced called her dark mage, and wanted to see her power. The cursed ones were far from the Void and a group of them wouldn't likely travel this far north without reason. "Maybe they're following *you*."

"Why would they be following me?"

"You're the High King of Palenor, their greatest

enemy. Maybe they saw an opportunity. Can you trust your people?"

He whipped around, his cloak floating out around him as if it danced on air, and walked a few paces away. When he turned back, he came at her with a determined march. "I trust them implicitly. Get on Phantom. If we leave now we'll get to the castle at sunrise."

"Aren't we safe from them here in Palenor?" She figured once they crossed into the elven forest it would be well guarded, and they wouldn't have to worry about being tracked or ambushed. He'd certainly dropped his pretense of silence since they'd crossed the border.

"Safe?" Thane stepped closer. "No, Layala. We may be safe from an army of pale ones, but there are few you can trust."

What did he mean by that? Were there others apart from him that wanted to use her power? They kept saying they needed to protect her... "I trust no one here."

"Good," he said. "Now get on the horse or I'll put you on it."

She clenched her jaw, wishing she could punch him. But she wasn't ready to test her skills against his just yet. They called him the Warrior Prince; she supposed now they'd call him Warrior King. And by his large stature, the way he picked her up with ease, and how he cut down the pale ones with such lethal precision, the rumors were true. "Such a charming king. I bet all the females fall at your feet with a demanding attitude like that."

"They do," he said. "And with pleasure."

Layala scrunched her nose. The last word she wanted to associate this king with was *"pleasure."* After reaching for the saddle, she realized the stirrup was out of her reach. She murmured a curse, struggling to get up on her own. *Why is this beast so tall?* She glanced back to Thane smiling at her struggle.

"Need help?"

Unwilling to accept his help for such a simple task, she took several steps back, ran and leapt. After grabbing hold of the saddle, she pulled herself up.

He chuckled. "Most elven females would just take a leg up."

"Well, suffice it to say, I'm not most elven females."

He rubbed a hand over his smooth chin, still smiling. Layala narrowed her eyes, wondering what he could be grinning at right then.

"Would my betrothed prefer I ride front or the back?"

She pursed her lips to keep from snarling a harsh comment at his innuendo. Her foot flinched as she thought seriously about kicking him in the face. From her position it would be easy. Of the many options she chose to scoot back slightly, giving him space to sit.

"You must like holding onto me." He pulled himself up and settled in.

She placed her hands firmly at her sides, gripping the back of the saddle, hoping it was enough to stay on. He chuckled and they were off, riding through the green grass and in between the ashen white trunks of the luminor trees, back the way they came. "I thought we were going to your castle."

"We will. After we rejoin with my friends."

Friends? She didn't think he had friends, only people he used for his own gain. He was quiet for a while, the sounds of the forest filling in for lack of words; somewhere a creek trickled, there was also the light flutter of hummingbird wings as a pair darted by.

He finally said, "You don't know me, and what you have heard was less than perfect, so I understand your bitterness, but I'm not my father."

"I'm not bitter." Her lie rolled off her tongue easily. She was well past bitter. Vengeful, a more appropriate word. "I simply think that if you want to have me, you'll have to earn it. When I was promised to you, I was never your father's to give. You haven't even asked me to be your wife, just *demanded* it."

He half turned his head. "I'm not the one who killed your parents. I was three years old when they died. I don't even remember the day it happened."

Anger simmered inside her chest at the mention of them. "I know." But none of that mattered. Just because he wasn't directly responsible for their deaths, didn't mean he was innocent.

"You'll see."

She dragged her fingers through her hair, pulling through the tangles. "See what?"

The horse's hooves patted quietly on the soft ground of the forest floor. "One day you'll be in love with me."

Chapter 6

Thane turned enough to see her. She cut a glare that was cold enough to freeze a troll. He smiled, getting the reaction he expected. But his chest tightened. There was so much she didn't know. It's not as if he had a choice in marrying her, either. He didn't choose to be bound to her as a boy. But he was stuck with the magical elf everyone wanted to get their hands on.

A long silence passed between them. It wasn't awkward or tense as he expected. He felt calm and the steady hoot of an owl added to the ambiance. "Why did you destroy my house?" she asked softly. "I didn't even put up a fight when you came."

"Destroy your house?" He hadn't ordered Aldrich and Piper to do that. He'd simply sent them in to get her, and they'd all had to stay so quiet on the road a conversation about it hadn't taken place. "What are you talking about?"

"You don't know what your *friends* did? Do you

have any idea how long it took my aunt and me to collect all those magical plants? And the blood on the wall to top it off," she huffed, and then snapped her mouth shut.

Blood on the wall? "We didn't do that to your home."

She blinked in surprise. "Then who did?"

He swallowed hard, his mind whirring at the possibilities. If the pale ones were tracking them and someone destroyed her house before they got there... someone else knew where she was. The list of elves his father, Tenebris, sent to look for her was long. Hunters from all over Palenor and even some of the woodland elves of Calladira wanted the reward he'd offered. Perhaps one of them had stumbled upon her by chance, recognized her mate rune, and Thane happened to get to her before they could. Maybe they sent the pale ones.

"I don't know, but it wasn't us. And for what it's worth, I am sorry that happened."

"That means whoever it was might still be there. My aunt is in danger. I have to go back."

"Your aunt will be fine. Whoever it was is after you and would have followed us. It might have even been the group of pale ones."

"Can pale ones write? They wrote on the wall in blood."

His mind drifted to his father. He'd disappeared into the Void a month before and hadn't been seen again. Thane assumed he'd been torn apart. Hoped it, even. No one survived the Void. A son should miss a father, but Tenebris hadn't treated Thane any better than he had one of his subjects, like he was only born for one purpose and it was to serve. He'd seen to it that Thane was trained in the art of war and logistics, that he was schooled in many areas, but only on rare occasions did he spend quality time with him like a father would a son. Tenebris wanted to use him to find Layala. Convinced that through their mate bond Thane should know where she was, he'd sometimes beat him. Beat him bloody and bruised. It wasn't until he was older that the thrashings stopped because Thane put an end to it. Train the boy you harm to fight and it will come back on you.

Tenebris always insisted his motivation was pure. He believed Layala could rid their world of the Void and put an end to the pale ones for good, possibly bringing back magic to the elves. But Thane knew his father's obsession was twisted and evil.

"Not all pale ones are mindless beasts."

"Why should I believe it wasn't you?" she asked.

"Why would I lie about it?" he fired back. "If I did it, I'd tell you and maybe even brag."

"Prick," she mumbled.

Lord, this female had a mouth on her. "What was that?" No one had ever called him a derogatory name before her, at least not to him directly. He was the High Prince and now High King. It simply wasn't done.

"Nothing, your highness."

He didn't know whether to laugh at her audacity

or to shove her off the horse and force her to walk. If he didn't feel it was his duty to look after her, he'd leave her in the middle of this wood and go home.

He lifted his eyes to the dark canopy of the star-shaped leaves, silently cursing his father for attaching him to her. Yet, even if he wasn't, he couldn't abandon her now. If the pale ones got ahold of her... "Are you always so uncouth or is that reserved for me?"

"It's a trait of my lovely personality. A gift, really."

"How blessed am I to have such a one-of-a-kind bride," he said and kicked Phantom into a steady canter. A smile tugged at the corners of his mouth. Maybe a part of him enjoyed her brashness as much as he hated it. She was certainly nothing like he expected her to be.

She grabbed onto the fabric of his cloak. "I'd prefer Layala over 'bride'. Thank you."

"You're betrothed to the most attractive and charming High King there has ever been. You should be swooning that I call you my bride." He smiled.

She snorted. "Lucky me."

When they reached Piper, Aldrich and Fennan, the healers still tended to Aldrich's injured leg. He sat on the flat of a stump, his face strained. The medic touched his tender flesh and he groaned through the stick between his teeth and stamped his good foot on the ground.

Most of the sentries had gone back to their positions in the trees, but for the pair of healers that knelt in front of him. His pant leg was rolled up to reveal deep purple bruising from his ankle to halfway up his shin. His gold blond hair was damp with sweat at his temples.

"Is it broken?" Thane asked, dismounting. Upon closer inspection, the shinbones were misaligned and showed as much through his skin. He winced knowing how much that would hurt. "You'll need to set it and wrap it with franzen leaf." The plant grew here in the forest and was known for its healing properties.

Piper stepped to Thane's side and folded her arms over her abdomen. "He needs to rest for a few days. You should take Fennan and get her to the castle. I'll stay."

Aldrich cried out when the healers snapped the bones in place. Thane bit down, regretting asking his friends to come with such a small number. He'd put their lives in danger trying to be discreet, but they didn't complain about it. They never did.

Remembering he'd left Layala on Phantom, he whipped around. His rapidly beating heart settled when he found her still seated on the gelding's back while he grazed nearby. She could have trotted off while they'd been distracted and yet she'd stayed. Perhaps he could trust her more than he thought. He rubbed his chin, contemplating if he should wait for Aldrich to heal enough to travel or not.

The cooler evening air brought the chirps of luminor crickets. Thousands of their minuscule bodies scattered on leaves and on blades of grass lit with a yellow glow. Almost as if the forest floor became the night sky. There wasn't even a need for torches. The insects produced enough light. He loved to come here and marvel at nature. It was only in this place he ever felt at peace. The luminor trees and insects brought him calm. It was their magical property. And after some of the things he did, he needed that calmness to live with himself. Some of the things Layala thought about him were true, probably far worse.

Aldrich threw the stick from his mouth, making some of the luminor crickets scatter. He spit and wiped his mouth with the back of his sleeve. "I'll be fine. Go on ahead."

Always well-mannered, that one. He didn't want to leave Piper or Aldrich here but Castle Dredwich was the safest place to keep Layala. It hadn't been breached in over two millennia. If pale ones invaded here, the forest could be taken, and she could be captured. It wasn't far. Even if the last couple of weeks on the road left him sore and exhausted, he could make it. He'd ride through the night to sleep in his own bed at this point.

Tapping Fennan's shoulder, he tilted his head for them to go. One of the sentries brought Fennan a horse. A gelding that had pulled the carriage, now saddled. Thane grabbed onto Phantom's reins. Layala stared down at him. "Don't I get my own horse?"

Thane thought better of it. He didn't want to have to chase after her should she try to make a run for it. "You'll stay with me."

"I know how to ride."

"It's not your skill I'm worried about."

"You're afraid I'll run," she said flatly. "What would be the point? You and your friends would hunt me down again. It's not as if I could go back home." The sentry elves nearby watched them, not a single one breathed a word but their eyes fixed on the two with rapt attention, as if this was the theater and he and Layala were the entertainment. He hadn't wanted anyone to know he was here or about her, but that was out now. There was no reason to even bother with the hood anymore, but he kept it on to annoy Layala. It bothered her not to see his face.

Thane pulled himself up and let out a long breath. "We don't have a choice, and if you knew anything about our mate bond, you'd recognize that."

Chapter 7

Those ethereal glow bugs lifted from the path before them, rising into the night like burning embers of a fire. Layala reached out several times to catch one in her palms but they always slipped through. They stopped at a stream for water where the horses drank deeply. Layala splashed her face and washed her hands and forearms. For having been in the carriage most of the time she was remarkably dirty. Her mind drifted to home. Aunt Evalyn was left with a huge mess to clean on her own—hopefully that was all. If Thane was right and it was the pale ones, likely the leader who wrote on the wall, Evalyn was safe. But still, she worried that they could have hurt her after Layala was gone. Maker, she missed Evalyn already. If only there was a way to get a message to her.

They were so close to Castle Dredwich now. Her stomach ached at the thought. If the rumors were true it was a place of dread. Even its name spoke of it.

Thane protected her thus far but would that change once they arrived? What would they do once they reached the castle to get her to use her power? She could only imagine the kind of pain they'd inflict. Her escape must be swift.

When they emerged from the forest and rode to the top of a green grassy knoll, they stopped at its peak. Below was a great valley of houses and shops and farms, all the things of a large city. There had to be thousands of elves down there.

At the far end of it all rose a stone castle of thundercloud gray, built into the hillside. A waterfall roared to one side of it. There were many peaks to the castle, but the tower dominating the center was the highest. A navy blue flag flew at its top. The three emblems on the flag were a white sword crossed over an arrow and a war hammer through the center of both. The sun lifted until its golden light illuminated the city below like a beacon. All the roofs of the buildings were gold, and when the sun hit them everything glowed.

"Welcome to the Valley of the Sun," Thane said.

Something wonderful in her stirred. She'd never seen anything so fascinating. She heard stories of the Valley, but the words hadn't prepared her for its beauty. A part of her wanted to live here among her own people where she wouldn't be different, yet now that she was, she didn't know what to think. Her mind was caught somewhere between awestruck and panic. There wasn't much time now. Soon she'd have to kill the High King and doing so would cause chaos and disarray. She'd prepared for this time, but to think about something and actually do it was severely different in this case. She'd never assassinated anyone.

They didn't ride through the cobblestone streets or past the soon-to-be bustling shops. She'd hoped they would so she could see the buildings and architecture up close. See the elves at work on a normal day, a place she wouldn't get to see again, at least not for a very long time.

Instead, Thane took them around the city, riding along the lip of the valley until they reached the castle's stone bridge that carried them over a wide river. The waterfall sprayed them lightly as they crossed, and the thundering of it drowned out any other noise. The gate was a massive thing of silver swirling metal and spikes. When they approached it lifted.

Beyond the bridge, a cobblestone path led through the short-trimmed green grass. They passed trees with pink blossoms and luminors with the star leaves, shrubs and fountains and bushes of roses. They passed under archways of twisting branches with ivy vines wrapped around them. There were no bodies hanging from the walls as rumors said. No telltale signs of evil atrocities.

"It's beautiful, isn't it?" the driver said, watching Layala. With his hood back she finally saw his eyes, like swirling pools of cinnamon that contrasted beautifully with his black skin. "I don't know if I ever told you my name, but it's Fennan."

She brushed a stray hair behind her ear, remembering the name being mentioned before but she'd kept silently calling him the driver. "It's wonderful, Fennan. I've never seen anything like it."

"He is one of the three, other than myself, you can trust here," Thane turned back slightly. "You know the other two as well. Piper and Aldrich."

She wouldn't trust him or his friends or anyone else for that matter. Fidgeting with the dry skin around her fingernails Layala asked, "What does that mean? Will someone try to hurt me here?"

"I honestly don't know what might happen. But I do know that there are many with an unhealthy obsession with trying to obtain you." He paused. "You are still the only known elf born with magic in recent times. The others are dead or their magic has faded. Mage Vesstan is spent, living out the rest of his days in Calladira with the woodland elves."

"He's the one who bound us?" She knew, but she wanted to see what he'd say about it.

"Yes," Thane said. "He used one of the Black Mage's spells."

Something in her recoiled. She hadn't known that. "Why would anyone use anything created by him?"

He shrugged. "Because the Black Mage was the

most powerful mage to ever exist. Because he had the spell. No one else creates them."

She'd known that too, but to use magic that the Black Mage created was foolish. She'd studied his life, of the ruin he made of the world. When he was finally killed by an elf named Rhegar, after three hundred years of his destruction, Rhegar went mad. As if the Black Mage's final act was to poison his killer. She didn't know how he created the Void or the pale ones but it was him.

Thane cleared his throat. "This is your home now. You can have almost anything you want as my future queen."

Almost anything except freedom. She didn't respond. In her heart she belonged at the cottage in Briar Hollow. This would never be her home. She wanted to train with the men in the arena, search for magical plants with Aunt Evalyn, bathe in the river, live her life in peace without wondering when the High King would come for her.

When they reached the bottom of the agonizingly long set of stairs to the entrance, they dismounted the horses. A trio of guards took the steeds, barely giving her a glance.

"You must be hungry," Fennan said. "I know I am. Ready to eat a feast!"

Layala shrugged. She was hungry after their meager rations on the road, but she didn't want to eat with them. "I'd like to freshen up and I'm rather tired."

Then she could work out her plan to escape. Poison wasn't an option anymore.

A PAIR of maids with simple white dresses and black aprons met Layala as soon as they stepped into the entry. The staircases seemed to be endless, as did the ceiling. The glossy, gray stone floors sparkled like a starry night. Faint footsteps of patrolling guards echoed in the vastness above. She'd never been inside anything so grand before. Although it was magnificent and its beauty unmatched, the sheer size, and its foreign nature made her long for her small comfortable cottage. Unseen danger could lurk around every corner here.

"Please show this young maiden to the Starlight suite and see that she gets something to eat," Thane said, and didn't wait to see that it was done before he walked off with Fennan at his side.

The two dipped their heads and motioned for her to follow. One had hair of fire, darker orange at the roots and fading to almost blonde at the ends. The other had her dark tresses pulled into a tight bun atop her head.

"Welcome to Castle Dredwich. I am Reina," said the dark-haired elf.

"My name is Pearl." They walked on either side of

her like a pair of guardians. "How do you know our High King?"

She didn't sound as if she was prying, simply making conversation with a stranger. But of course they'd wonder who the female guest of the king was. Not knowing if she should say her name or not, she pursed her lips. He said to trust no one except the three she'd been brought here with. But who could she say she was? "I'm an acquaintance."

The two exchanged a look. "My, how interesting," Pearl said. "You're the only maiden he's ever brought to the castle, apart from those who work for him. And none have ever stayed in the Starlight room."

"He doesn't have mistresses?"

Reina and Pearl exchanged smiles. "None that we've ever seen." Pearl leaned in closer. "But don't think none of these scandalous maids haven't tried to move up in status."

"What does that mean?"

Reina nudged Pearl. "The dear is speaking of things not proper."

"So you must be special," Pearl blurted out.

What of the lovers that were said to go mad... was that a lie? She was beginning to think that the rumors she heard were simply that. So what was true about him and what was false? His lethality against the pale ones was evident. That was no lie.

Perhaps the maids simply wouldn't speak of it. But if she was the only one that meant the two servants would likely know exactly who she was or at least someone important to him. There was no point in hiding it then. "I'm Layala Lightbringer."

They both gasped and then slammed their mouths shut. Layala thought they might explode if one of them didn't speak soon. They climbed a set of glossy stairs and entered the first room to the left. When the door closed, Pearl all but squealed. "I cannot believe you are her! The High King's mate! The one who will destroy the Void."

Blinking in surprise, Layala rubbed her forehead. Surely, she hadn't heard that correctly. "Destroy the Void?"

Pearl's lovely face fell into a frown and she dropped her hands to her sides. "You've come to save us, haven't you? The kings have been looking for you for such a long time. Stolen away on your testing day. What a tragedy." Reina brushed her hands down her apron.

What sort of horse dung had these people been fed over the years? Stolen? "King Tenebris murdered my parents, and a dear friend took me to get away from him."

They exchanged another glance. "Is that what you've been told, sweetheart? You poor dear," Reina cooed.

Pearl had a hand over her mouth, shaking her head as if she felt sorry for Layala. "Fed numerous lies no doubt. At least King Thane was able to rescue you now. You are safe here."

Painting Thane as her rescuer? She should have

seen that one coming. Forcing herself not to roll her eyes, she stepped forward and examined the room. Ornately carved windows lined the wall on either side of the ivory bed. Green vines with sprays of pastel flowers grew from the ceiling like a chandelier and draped over the sheer fabric of the canopy. The same vines wound around the windows and could be pulled to act as curtains. The whole room smelled like fresh greens.

She ran her hand over the top of a silky chest at the foot of the bed. Out of the corner of her eye she thought she saw something small in a red hat scurry across the floor with quiet footsteps, but when she turned that way there was nothing. *Interesting.* She continued looking around; the room was stunning, more elegant than any she'd ever seen let alone stayed in, but she couldn't forget why she was here or be distracted by luxury. So she asked, "What happened to King Tenebris?"

"He died three weeks ago," Pearl answered and bowed her head momentarily as if to honor him. "Killed by a pale one in battle. Such a brave, honorable High King. I only wish he could have been here to see you, our savior."

Her stomach coiled, and a shiver wracked her. She couldn't be their savior. She had little idea of what she was even capable of with her magic but she knew for certain that its dark properties couldn't save anyone, least of all the entirety of Palenor.

Layala set her sights on the oversized plush bed

again. The soft ivory covers and mound of pillows looked like heaven after being trapped in the uncomfortable carriage for so long. "I need sleep. It's been a long ride here. Please leave me be." She'd lose her temper if they didn't get out. She always had a harder time dealing with stupidity when she was tired and talk of Tenebris being brave and honorable was the epitome of it.

"I'll bring you up some hot tea and a little something to eat." Reina dipped her head and the two of them left her alone to think.

When Reina returned with a cart of food and tea as promised, Layala sat up. "You can leave it next to me. Thank you."

"I hope it's to your liking, Lightbringer." She said the name with awed reverence then dropped into a bow. After lingering for a moment, as if she wanted to say something, she turned and made for the door.

Picking up the tea, Layala sniffed; it smelled of citrus and something else she couldn't quite name, Valeri Root perhaps, to aid in sleeping. She set the cup down on the wooden tray. "Wait, where is the High King's chamber?"

"Oh," she said, raising her eyebrows. "It's the room on the other side of this wall." She pointed to the left where a massive, marbled stone fireplace dominated.

"Thank you," Layala said with a feline grin. It was better they thought she'd want to go there for intimate reasons than what she had in mind.

Chapter 8

With the moon piqued at its highest, Layala's back pressed against the cold stone, the sharp edges biting into her flesh as she lurked in the inky darkness. Somewhere in the distance a water drop hit every three seconds. *Plop... plop... plop.* The musty smell of mold from lack of fresh air and sunlight penetrated her senses. Hand sliding against the rough stone for guidance, she took painfully slow steps, careful to not make a sound. The knife in her hand from the dinner tray the maid brought up seemed to grow heavier as she neared the outlined orange light of a secret door ahead.

You can do this. Her breath moved slowly past her lips with an intense control she'd trained for, making no sound. *You can do this.*

Thane's room was easy to find. Aunt Evalyn had her memorize the layout of the castle, from a map she kept from when she worked there, including the servants' passages. She spent a few hours navigating them, putting what was on paper to what was in front of her to ensure a quick escape. She even found the queen mother's and princess's chambers, unguarded and with no safeguards. They hadn't prepared for an assassin in their midst.

Fingers brushing the crack where the light from inside the room penetrated the dark passageway, she pressed ever so gently making the servants' entrance grind lightly, stone against stone. Intensely still, she waited for movement, for an alarm, a sign that he heard but only the crackling of fire greeted her.

If they get you to the castle, you will likely only get one chance at them, Aunt Evalyn said during her training. *Take it. Take it for your parents. Take it for you.* This was the only way to be free.

Opening the door hidden behind a framed picture wide enough to fit her body, she peeked her head out. She expected more grandeur from the elf king, more pompous and ornate gaudy decor. Not that it lacked in beauty but the bare simplicity of the cream-colored dresser with only minor details, etches of ivy leaves on the front of the drawers, and the plain framed ivory mirror across the room surprised her. A painting of a rearing white dragon near a high waterfall. A single fireplace with a bulbous silver vase on the dark wooden mantel.

The dim firelight created long shadows and hidden corners, but there in the center was a massive four-poster bed with silken coverlets of navy blue. In the middle lay the shape of Thane beneath. Two large rugs from pelts of white wolves sat on the ashen stone floor at the foot of the bed and to the side where the master would set his bare feet down.

Layala listened to his breathing.

Steady.

Slow.

Rhythmic.

A sign of slumber. Carefully, she stepped across the floor, heart booming like the black clouds above a tempest sea. Hand slightly trembling, she stood over him, finally getting to see his face. He wore no shirt, revealing his muscular upper torso and chest. From what she saw there wasn't a single scar on him... so he didn't mark his flesh with the number of kills. What rumors in Briar Hollow were actually true?

Her gaze moved to the fullness of his lips, accentuated in this light, as was the perfect smoothness of his warm ivory skin and the shadows from his sharp cheekbones. *Maker*, he was beautiful. His long, wavy dark hair partially swept across his face.

Her eyes widened. It was *him*, the mysterious elf who'd sat before her at the Smoky Dragon back in Briar Hollow. The male with charm and an easy smile. She thought he reported her, but it was Thane all along. How had she not seen it before?

Kill him, Layala. This is your chance. Your chance at ending the bloodshed. Your chance at justice. Your chance at freedom. But she hesitated to put the knife to his neck. If so many things she heard weren't true—was this a mistake?

His eyes opened. Her stomach lurched. In her panic, she tucked the knife behind her back. *What do I do now?!* Barely able to breathe, she pressed her free hand against his chest, leaned down and her lips crashed into his. A rush of energy shot into her—a strange exhilarating sensation she never felt before. She grew more confident he was distracted when his mouth moved in perfect sync with hers. Her tongue swept over his teeth and his body stiffened in surprise.

Pressing the sharp edge of the knife against his throat, she froze. Maker, why couldn't she just do it?

He jerked away from the kiss, staring at her. "I wouldn't do that."

"Give me one good reason not to." Why did she hope he had one?

The pale emerald green of his irises almost glowed in the darkness. No wonder he wouldn't let her see his face fully before. No one else would have eyes such as these.

No plea, no argument came from him. Could he not think of a single reason to save his own life?

She pressed the blade until blood beaded up around it. "Any last words?"

A smirk pulled up at the corners of his mouth. A *smirk*. Layala almost jerked away at his strange reaction. Did he wish to die? Why wasn't he afraid when she held his life at the point of her knife?

Eyes sparkling in the starlight shining from the

skylight above, he searched her face. "If you kill me, you'll die, too."

Her hand flinched, but she steadied again. "I'll be out of here before your guards even know you're dead."

"Indeed you might slip away, if you weren't already dead on top of me."

Her eyebrows furrowed. Was this a trick? Some sort of strategy to live? "Speak plainly, *High King*." She spit his title like a curse. The light sweat on her palm made the blade handle slick. She needed to end this before she slipped up and was forced to use her magic.

"Our lives are linked, Layala." She hated when he said her name. It made him more likable, harder to kill. "If I die, you die." His tone held no malice, as if they were speaking about the spring weather over a cup of tea.

"You're lying." He must be. The ritual mate spell that was supposed to force their marriage wouldn't include that. Would it?

"I'm not." His voice held strong, not a single waver or inflection of untruth. His large hand wrapped around her wrist that held the knife, but he didn't push her away. Yet she knew he wasn't about to be put down like an animal. He would fight back.

They stared at one another, waiting to react, to make a decision. Was he lying or not? She would never get a chance like this again. He wouldn't leave himself vulnerable to her attack a second time. In fact, if she let him go now he'd have her locked up in a cell or perhaps chained to her room to keep up appearances. It wouldn't do to have his betrothed in the dungeons. He'd poison her to keep her magic at bay forever. She'd be a caged bird. It was now or never.

A heavy knock slammed the door three times. Layala's pulse thrummed as she pressed down. Thane pushed, bucking his hips and tossing her over him onto her back. The full force of his weight pressed her into the bed, and his legs wrapped around her outer thighs. One hand held her left arm against the pillows and the other pushed against her knife hand. She fought with all her strength against him, willing the blade to end him, but he was a force much like the tearing winds of the Sederac Mountains. His muscles were taut, veins bulging in his bare skin. Grinding her teeth with the effort, her arm trembled from fatigue.

"Fennan was right about you needing to be tamed."

"Piss off." She pushed even harder, fighting him with all her strength. He slammed Layala's hand into the headboard. She yelped and dropped the blade; the clang of it hitting the floor echoed.

Three more booming knocks. "Highness, your betrothed is missing."

Thane glanced at the door. Layala threw her forehead into his chin. His teeth clacked together hard, and he reared back. "*Missing* is she," he growled. She shoved him in the chest and slid out from under his weight. Rolling off the bed, she stood, knees bent, hands up in a fighting stance. With her chest heaving up and down, she glanced about the room looking for another weapon. A candlestick was the closest thing, but it wouldn't get the job done. She'd have to get to the other side of the bed and around Thane to get the knife.

"Sire, are you well?" The guard's voice grew in concern.

"I'm fine. I'll be out in a moment to look for her," Thane shouted at his guard, and slid off the bed.

She took a step back... Look for her? Why not bring his guard running in here to grab her? He swiped for her. She ducked, drove her fist up then punched him in the side of his cheek. Head snapping to the side, he turned back with a snarl. "Don't you dare do that again."

She kicked hard at his shin; he stepped back and grabbed her left wrist. She slammed her elbow down, breaking his hold and kneed him hard in the upper thigh, barely missing his male parts. His nostrils flared, and he took a few steps back. His eyes trailed down her form then back up, assessing her.

"You know how to fight." They slowly started to circle one another in the small space.

"Of course I do," she bit out, fists up. "I've had the threat of *you* looming over my head all my life. The prince and king who would use me as their *weapon*. Well, I won't be used by anyone." Layala darted for the bed. Ducking under his swooping arms, she dove onto the covers. He grabbed her ankle and she kicked to break free then slid across the mattress and picked up the knife.

From the other side of the large bed, he smiled as if this was but a game. "Put the knife down."

She raised the weapon, taking aim for his heart. With a snap of her wrist the blade soared for Thane. He leaned to the side and it embedded in his left shoulder. *Damn...* she only succeeded in angering him. With a grimace, he reached up and tore it loose. Blood spilled in a small stream down his arm when he charged her. "That was a mistake."

She backpeddled until she hit the wall. On the table to her left was the candlestick. She flung it as he advanced; his forearm blocked it, and it hit the ground with a thunk. Heart crashing into her ribs, she threw up her forearms and braced herself for a blow that was sure to come. She closed her eyes but instead of a hit she felt big hands wrap around her wrists. She took the chance he'd given her and went for the groin, only to hit his knee. He flung her around and threw her on the bed and was on top of her in a breath, pinning her down again with his weight. Gritting her teeth, she clawed at his face and raked her nails across his cheek. He grunted and folded her arms across her chest and pressed down hard, pinning her fully.

"Stop," he commanded.

Squirming and struggling, Layala wanted to scream, but it wouldn't do her any good. No one would take her side. They'd punish her for attempting to assassinate their king. She had no other choice now.

The hum of her magic cooled her skin as she readied it to curl the ebony tendrils.

"I'll make you a deal," Thane said.

She stilled her body and magic, the power waiting to escape. Thane breathed heavily. Sweat glistened on his bare chest. "Deal?" she whispered.

Chapter 9

A cool breeze from an open window shifted the light airy curtains and brought the smell of lavender and a chill to Layala's skin. With heat and sweat from struggling against him, the outside temperature felt extra cold. She watched Thane intently, his jaw flexing as he stared down at her, his long dark hair falling around him in a tangled mess. Her nails drew four thin lines of crimson over his right cheekbone, barely missing his eye.

"I won't let you kill me, but if you can find a way to break our mate bond, I'll let you go. I won't look for you, or want to see you ever again. Once the spell is gone."

Throat too dry, Layala swallowed. "I could take your life right now and not have to worry you're lying."

He chuckled quietly, but there was no humor in it. "Even if you were suicidal, it seems to me that you're not in the position to do so."

"You have no idea what I'm capable of," Layala snapped.

"Tenebris believed you would be a powerful mage, but I see nothing before me but someone blinded by hatred enough to kill for the sins of a father."

The pressure against her lightened as he leaned back, and Thane released his hold on her arms but his body was still very much on her thighs and hips. Her eyes slowly traveled over his body she didn't have time to inspect before: defined abdominals, thick obliques to be admired, and chest and shoulder muscles that belonged to a warrior, somehow both lean and large, soft and hard. The Warrior Prince, indeed. The knife wound she gave him bled some, but it did significantly less damage than she thought it would. It was only a small puncture.

Thane seemed to take notice of her inspection of him and cocked an eyebrow. "Are you done perusing?"

"Get off me," Layala demanded.

"Are you going to try to knife me again?"

Layala didn't answer. She was still deciding what she would do once he moved. "No."

He lifted off her as he hopped from the bed. Standing at least six feet away now, he watched her sit up. She set her feet on the wolf pelt and stared at him. "Why? You've been looking for me all my life and you'd let me go now? Let my magic go?"

"I don't want your magic. My father did. But in either case, I don't think you can do it." He crossed his left arm just below his chest, and with his right hand, he rubbed his chin. "No one has ever broken a bond like ours."

So there it was. He thought he was giving her an impossible task, which would leave him to use her against his enemies. "I need some proof you'll keep your word."

"You don't really have a choice but to take my word, do you?" He walked over toward the open window and latched it shut. "You have eight weeks. If you can't break our bond by then, we will marry as planned."

Layala clenched her jaw, taking in a deep breath. "That doesn't seem like nearly enough time for something that hasn't been done before."

"I know you can feel it." He stepped closer, his feet barely making a sound as he padded across the stone floor. Her heart seemed to beat faster with each step he took. He stopped mere inches from her, his body heat emanating into hers like the warmth of the sun. "The darkness pulling at you. Threatening. Seducing. I can feel its call. We are almost at the end of fulfilling the promise of this magic. We had twenty-five years to marry, and guess when that anniversary is?"

She gulped. "Eight weeks?"

"When a spell created by the Black Mage like ours isn't fulfilled, there are consequences, Layala, and we're almost out of time." He paused. "That is my reason for wanting you. It's not your power. We will turn into pale ones if we don't meet the requirements of the spell, so if I must marry the girl who hates me then so be it."

BACK IN THE STARLIGHT ROOM, she tossed and turned the entire night, dreaming of pale ones closing in on her and then a wail came out of her own mouth. The hideous cry of a pale one. *No! No. No. No.* She thrashed around until she sat stark straight, hair damp with sweat, breathing hard.

Heart still beating rapidly, she took in her surroundings. She was in a room at Castle Dredwich, not surrounded by pale ones. But she wanted to see to make sure. Dashing in front of a mirror she stared at her reflection; her skin was still honey beige, not ashen white. Her hair black as ink. She was herself. Even Thane's mention of the potential to change forced her to consider marrying him right away to not risk the consequence.

And yet, she wasn't one of the creatures. The heaviness that seemed to loom over her, had to be the unfulfilled mate magic. But she had time. Eight weeks.

"Nightmare?" a small feminine voice said.

Layala whipped around, ready to fight if need be. "Where are you?"

"Down here." Eyes dropping, Layala found a tiny

humanoid female no taller than a foot, creeping out from beside the bedpost. She wore a soft red hat with a pointed tip. Her brown curls tumbled around her robust chest and belly. Cheeks and lips the color of dusty rose and a bulbous nose nearly as red as her hat. Her dowdy floral dress looked like it was ages old with unmatching patched holes here and there, and her toes sprang from worn brown boots.

"You're a gnome," Layala said, squatting down nearer to the tiny creature. "What are you doing here?"

"A gnome, I am." She put a stubby hand on her hip. "And I live here, unbeknownst to the jumbos. Great food, always a warm empty bed even if I have to sneak about. I've been in this room the longest, see. It's never been occupied before."

A smile tugged at Layala's lips. "Jumbos?"

"Yes. You are a jumbo. Tall, lanky, need to eat a few more meals by the looks of you." She put a hand on her belly. "But I knew you were different when you tried to kill the king. I figured you wouldn't toss me out into the bitter wilderness."

Chuckling, Layala sat cross-legged. "Me being an attempted murderer made you feel safe? Forgive me if I don't understand that one."

"Well, the maids, they'd surely toss me out if they saw me disturbing the royals. The guards, too. But I knew you were none of those. They wouldn't dream of trying to hurt his majesty." Her rich brown eyes traveled over Layala. "And not to be rude but your attire and woodsy smell gave you away as an outsider. I thought you might be one of the woodland jumbos. They like gnomes."

"Fair enough." Layala tapped her fingers against her thigh. "I am a high elf, but I've been among humans for years and have absolutely nothing against gnomes. You're welcome to stay. I'm Layala."

"I'm Tifapine, and my friends would call me Tif, if I had any." She scratched her chubby cheek. "Other gnomes prefer tunneling underground, gardening, being generally smelly but not me. I knew I was different. Mama said I was a romantic and should stick to baking in our hole. But I was meant for more and what better place to be *more* than Castle Dredwich. I have a dream of being an elven lady's maid."

"I think you're in the right place then." Layala stood and stretched. "I need to find something clean to wear before the other jumbos arrive."

Tif snickered and scampered into the closet and Layala followed. She searched for a pair of pants, a tunic, corset, something she was comfortable wearing, but after looking, there were only dresses with tulle and fluffy yards of fabric, florals and lace. She would not be paraded around this place looking like a docile, doe-eyed maiden. Now that Thane knew her true nature there was no need to pretend anymore.

Lightbringer, she cringed at the name her parents had given her, the one that the maids had crooned. Wishful thinking on their part. The power that ran through her was anything but light.

"Anything suitable?" Tif asked.

"It looks like I'll be wearing the same clothes I came in. Although the outfit is dirty." Layala grabbed the clothing off the floor, showing the dirt to Tif. Not wanting to get the bedsheets filthy, she'd slept in her undergarments. "It was a long journey here." She found an attached bathing room with a gold clawfoot tub, a gold sink with a silver pitcher beside it. A vase with black curling branches and peacock feathers in between for decor.

The pitcher was full of water, enough she could wash her clothes as well as her face and arms with the bar of soap. There wasn't enough water to fill the tub. She assumed the servants would have to bring it to her.

Tif somehow climbed up to the lip of the sink and with her hands behind her, tilting forward and back on her tiptoes, she said, "I can wash them for you. It would be my absolute pleasure, Lady."

"Auditioning to be a lady's maid?"

Tif grinned. "If you'd be so inclined as to allow it."

"I would."

When Tif finished washing, Layala hung the clothes to dry on a vine near a window and wandered into the bedroom in a deep purple robe she found in a drawer. It barely covered her upper thighs but the silky fabric wrapped around her well enough. She paced over the cool stone floor, wondering where she would even start to find a way to break the mate bond spell. There must be an archive of the Black Mage's spells, if the one between her and Thane was one of them.

"Oh, I forgot." Tif reached into her belt and pulled out a small, folded piece of parchment. "A bird brought this. I can't read but the bird said it was for you."

"The bird said?" Layala took the tiny note.

"I understand *tweet*," Tif said.

"*Tweet* is a language?"

"Of course."

It was a note from... Evalyn. *I'm safe. Hope you are too. Do what you must then come home. ~ Evalyn*

Evalyn didn't know what Layala did, that she *couldn't* kill Thane. But relief washed over her knowing her aunt and Briar Hollow were well.

A quiet knock made her pause. It hadn't come from the main door. Three more knocks followed. No, it came from behind the fireplace. It took her a moment but there might be a secret door in the stonework.

Tif darted under the bed lightning fast.

Before she could even figure a way to open it, the stone wall moved, rotating to reveal the king's room on the other side and standing in the entry was Thane. She lifted her chin slightly, putting a hand at her hip.

His eyes traveled slowly from her bare legs up to her face. "I heard you—whimpering earlier. Are you alright?"

"I was not *whimpering*." She shrugged trying to feign ignorance to that ridiculous dream. "I don't know what you heard, but it wasn't me."

He was still shirtless, and she had to fight not to look down at all that bare skin the longer he stood there. She was used to it; the men she trained with in Briar Hollow often took off their shirts, but they didn't look like *him,* and she didn't want to give Thane the pleasure of her *perusing* a second time.

"I wanted to be sure someone wasn't in here trying to assassinate you." He smirked as if the attempt had only amused him.

"I'm as well as I can be being attached to you and being forced to come here against my will." Somehow the claw marks on his face were gone as well as the stab wound he should have had in his shoulder.

"I don't want to become one of those monsters any more than you do. You can say it was against your will, but I did you a favor. If I didn't find you, you would be a pale one soon enough. We both would." He paused looking her up and down. "Perhaps a thank you is in order."

She scoffed. "As if I'd ever say thank you to a murdering bastard like you."

"That's rich coming from someone who tried to commit murder not a few hours ago." He stepped closer, his face scrunching with disapproval. "I'm not proud of some of my actions, but they were necessary. And you don't know everything. Only lies and rumors that drifted to your precious Briar Hollow, most of it embellished by their hatred for elves."

"The hate is for good reason, trust me. And necessary?" She ground the word through her teeth. "Is that how you sleep at night? But that would mean you'd have to have a conscience and I doubt that."

He straightened up as if she slapped him. "Get some clothes on. I'll see you at breakfast. Don't keep me waiting."

When the wall closed behind him, she stamped into the bathing room to see if her clothes were dry enough she could put them on. Still damp to the touch, she debated on dressing in one of the plain cotton dresses but instead pulled aside the draping vines over the windows and looked out over the Valley of the Sun. "He can wait as long as I please."

Tif climbed up a vine and perched beside her. "Mama always said when things get heated, get to gettin', and you two are hot."

Layala gave her a sideways glance. She had no idea what that meant, but it made her smile anyway.

Chapter 10

Steam practically rolling out his ears, Thane dressed and made his way to the dining hall. Not only did she have the audacity to kiss him then try to kill him, but she scolded him like a child, scowling at him with those crushing blue eyes. Ruining her striking face with such hatred.

Maker above, how was he supposed to change her mind about him? He had to make her see he wasn't the horrible monster. He didn't understand why she couldn't feel their connection the way he did. Instead, she loathed him enough to try to murder him. He heard her come into the room and waited to see what she would do. It wasn't a complete surprise she wanted him dead after the lies she was told about him, but she was actually going to do it. He saw the fear and determination in her eyes.

Before he came into the pub that night, he guessed she'd have some hesitation at first, given what his father did to her parents, but nothing like this.

"Morning, sire," Fennan hollered.

Thane looked up. He'd been staring at the stones on the floor hardly even aware of where he was going. "Hello, Fen."

"Have you seen Layala since she went to her room last night?" he asked.

Their steps tapped quietly as they made their way to the dining hall. He almost snorted with a laugh. "I've more than seen her."

Fennan lifted an eyebrow, growing a huge smile. "I didn't expect it would happen so quickly, you sly dog. I mean the wedding hasn't even happened yet and I was under the impression she didn't like you but—"

"*Doesn't like* is an understatement." Thane shook his head. "She tried to murder me while I slept. Held a damn knife to my throat."

Fennan's eyes widened. "Truly?" He chuckled. "She's got bigger balls than I would have guessed."

Thane shot him a glare. "You find it funny?" Of course he did.

"Oh, I do. I do." They both nodded to a pair of passing guards. "What happened after that?"

"I told her if she could break our bond then we could go our separate ways. She has eight weeks."

Fennan pulled the heavy ashen oak door to the dining hall open. "That's cutting it uncomfortably close, but so was waiting so long to find her. Do you want the bond broken? She is a mage. She might actually do it."

Thane didn't know what he wanted. He hadn't

entertained the idea of not being connected to her in several years. "Mage Vesstan said it couldn't be done. But I need to buy some time. All she knows is the garbage the humans tell. My reputation isn't serving me well in this case." He once naively thought she might care for him because of their connection.

They sat at the long rectangular table, large enough to seat twenty. Silver candlesticks lined the middle over the crisp white tablecloth. Sprigs and flowers of white and blue sat as the centerpiece. The room's decor had been chosen by his mother, which she changed on occasion. The current fashion was navy blue tapestries hung from the walls, and paintings of abstract art he didn't see the appeal of, although one did resemble an ocean if he looked hard enough with swirls of blue, green and white.

The plants brought life to the space. Some had magical properties, others didn't. Mother placed a Pernus plant with its deep green and crimson red tropical frond leaves in every gathering room. It energized and uplifted the mood. It was the aroma they gave off, akin to lemon but sweeter.

One of the maids came through the doors leading up from the kitchen and dipped into a bow. "Good morning, sire. Are you ready for breakfast or shall we wait for your mother and sister to join?"

"Start by bringing us some fruit but hold off on the main course until they arrive. I'll also be having another guest with us this morning."

"Of course, sire." She hurried through the exit.

Fennan leaned into the high-backed chair. "Your mother will be joining us?" He didn't sound enthused with the idea, and Thane wasn't, either.

"She'll be upset if she doesn't join us to meet Layala. I'm certain the maids have already spread the news."

Fennan scrunched his nose. "We certainly don't want to upset her."

"That we do not or Layala might not be the only one trying to cut my throat."

"The last time I made Orlandia angry, she snatched me by the ear to scold me, and that was only six months ago."

Thane laughed, remembering. "I forgot what you did."

"I said your sister was a nosey little worm and she overheard."

"My sister is a nosey little worm."

"Well, don't tell your mother that."

The double entrance doors burst open and in strolled the pair dressed in gowns fit for a ball. Hair styled in fancy updos, lips painted red for emphasis. They must have assumed Layala would be joining and wanted to make a show of their first impression. Strikingly beautiful were the both of them, but behind those eyes malice and cunning lurked.

"Morning, brother, Fennan," his sister Talon said, taking a seat beside Fennan.

"I hear we have a special guest this morning. Where is she?" Mother took the seat to his right, where he expected Layala to sit as his betrothed. A purposeful move, no doubt. A sort of letting Layala know who the female of this castle was.

"She'll be down soon."

"It does seem rather interesting you were able to find her so shortly after your father passed when he looked for such a long time. And had you told me, I could have already started the wedding planning."

Thane lifted a shoulder, unwilling to give away any truths in the matter. She was more loyal to Tenebris even in death than a dog who loved his master. "One of the spies happened to pass through the town where she lived and spotted the mate rune. Luck. I wish Father could have been here, too." The lie rolled off his tongue easily.

"And where was she hiding?"

"In Svenarum."

"So she was with the humans all this time. Her manners must be atrocious." She tapped a knife gently against the glass in front of her making a pinging sound. "Where are the servants? We should have a full spread by now. You know I don't like to wait."

Fennan and Thane tried not to smile at each other. "They're bringing up fruit until everyone arrives, Mother."

"Must we wait on her more than we already have?"

"It's rude to start eating without everyone seated," Thane said. "You taught me that."

Her lips formed a hard line. "It's rude to make the High King and his family wait. Not a good impression."

"I don't expect she cares to make a good impression," Fennan said, smiling.

"And why not?" Talon asked, pinching her face in outrage. "She should. We are royalty."

"She wasn't exactly pleased to come with us." Fennan shrugged.

Mother scoffed, setting down the knife. "Why I've never heard such a thing. Being stolen away as an infant and raised with the humans, you'd think she'd be glad you saved her from such a wretched life."

"That's just it, Mother," Thane said. "She was raised by them, raised to hate us."

"You better work that charm of yours, Son and get things set right. We need her. I won't have my son turned into a monster because of the way she was raised to think of us. And how could we use her to restore the balance of our lands if she refuses to help?"

"Perhaps we don't *use* her."

His mother gave him a scowl to rival Layala's. "If your father were here..." She slowly shook her head. "She could be the key to restoring the magic to our family, to the elves." She gripped the butter knife in her hand with an incredible amount of viciousness and pointed the tip of it at her son. "We will not give up now. You win her over. Do whatever it takes."

Thane forced a smile, thinking of the knife pressed against his throat. He could almost feel the ghost of the pressure now, the sharp edge biting into his flesh.

He severely underestimated her absolute detest for him. "I'll do my best."

After the fruit had been eaten and menial talk went on for far too long, Thane sighed, tapping his fingers on the tabletop. "Fennan, go get her. She will be joining us whether she likes it or not."

Chapter 11

The two maids, Reina and Pearl, stood before Layala, arms crossed. "You must wear a dress for breakfast with the High King," Pearl said, pushing a strand of loose orange hair out of her face.

Tif hung out of view on the vines draping from the ceiling and shrugged at her. Layala pulled the robe tighter around herself. She argued with these two for the last five minutes. They came up with every reason she needed her hair in a certain style, fancy braids and updos and pins everywhere. She preferred hers free flowing unless she was training, in which case, she wore a single braid down her back or a tight bun. They said she needed her lips stained with more color, blushed cheeks, and some sort of contraption that was supposed to make her waist look smaller and breasts larger. The many ties and loops in the back were intimidating enough. They called it a corset, but the one she wore wasn't tight. It was mainly for looks and worn on the outside of her top. "My clothes are almost dry. I'll wear them."

Reina shook her head. "Traveling attire is not proper. Don't you wish to impress your betrothed? Your *mate*? His mother and sister will also be present. They'll expect a certain fashion."

Not only did she have to endure breakfast with Thane but his family, too? "I don't wish to impress anyone."

Both looked like they'd been slapped. Even Pearl's mouth hung slightly ajar. "My lady, please. You will make us look inept if we don't dress you properly."

She'd hate for them to lose their employment here because of her. Combing her fingers through her hair, she sighed. "Fine. The simple blue one will do."

They both beamed and started tugging at her robe. "Excuse me, but I can undress myself."

"Oh, you don't need our assistance?" Reina asked.

"No, I don't. I'm not incompetent." Her voice came out sharper than she intended, but these two needed to learn boundaries. She actually liked that they brought her meals. Who wouldn't want food cooked for them and not to even have to clean up? And the hot bath she soaked in earlier was soothing and much needed, but she didn't require them to do *everything* for her.

"We meant no disrespect, Lady; it's just the royals like the help. It's part of our duty."

Tif nodded furiously and mouthed. "*It is.*"

Pearl stepped back and held the dress over her arm. "And next time we can help you wash your hair."

They'd brought her water to bathe, but she insisted they leave while she did so. "I don't need help with that either." They truly looked devastated at her comment. "Thank you," she added, hoping they would cheer up a bit. "I'm not trying to be rude. I have lived in a simple cottage, and I'm used to doing things for myself. Normally, I bathe in a river."

Pearl stifled a giggle and Reina's eyes grew about as big as saucers. Apparently bathing in the river wasn't done around there.

Three knocks on the door and Reina's hand flew to her chest. "Good *gracious*, you're not even decent."

Layala snatched the dress from Pearl and slipped her legs through the neck and pulled it up.

"A moment, please," Reina hollered.

When her arms were through the sleeves, she nodded to Reina who pulled the door open.

"Oh, Sir Fennan. What brings you here?" Reina asked.

"I've come to fetch Lady Layala. The family is tired of waiting and them being hungry doesn't help the matter."

"Oh dear." Pearl held a hand over her mouth. "The queen—you must hurry. Quickly, quickly." She pushed Layala toward the door. "She'll not be pleased with us."

"I don't have any shoes," Layala protested. Pearl shoved a pair of silver slippers in her hand. Layala put them on and walked beside her escort. All she had to do was play the part until she could get this bond broken and separate her life from Thane's.

Fennan was taller than Thane by an inch or two. He must have been at least six feet six inches. "Just for a bit of a warning, the queen and princess are ... challenging."

"I got that impression from the maids, but I can handle my own." She dealt with hard-to-handle people over the years. Even Aunt Evalyn could be a nasty piece of work when things didn't go her way. Layala had to earn respect from the men at the training yard, and until she did, they ridiculed her for being different, for being small, for thinking she—a female—could even get in the arena with them. They called her "pointy ears" or simply "pointy" for years if not *elee*. Of course she was only twelve when she started fighting with them. Fifteen when she could kick all of their behinds. The queen couldn't be worse than some of the men there.

A line appeared between Fennan's black brows when he gave her a hard stare. "I heard."

"Did he tell you?" For some reason she expected Thane to keep her attempt on his life quiet since he hadn't alerted the guards.

"I'm impressed you made it into his room and even got close enough to put a knife to his throat, but you know he let you, right?"

"Let me?" Layala balked.

"There's no way he didn't hear you enter his room.

I don't take kindly to anyone threatening my king, Lady, even if it's you. Don't do it again."

"I don't plan to, especially since our lives are linked."

Fennan smirked. "Tricky little bastard, the spell, isn't it?"

"Yes," she acknowledged begrudgingly. "I need to know more about our mate bond. Where can I learn about it?" They descended the large staircase with suits of armor set into the wall on either side every five steps or so. The armor was bronze and their swords pointed up. The intricate designs carved into the metal of the chest plate made them the most beautiful pieces she'd ever seen. Poetic even.

"Thane can give you answers."

That was out of the question. She needed to see something in writing. Something original. "Surely, there is another resource. How would I know he isn't lying?"

"He's not."

"And how do I know you aren't lying?" she challenged. "You must understand how I feel. Trust is earned, and so far, I don't have much to go on but what I've heard about him."

"I do see your point of view and how scared you must be. It's not my place to speak of the details, but Thane means well. He is a dangerous person but not to you. He only wants to keep you safe. And he doesn't want to turn."

"He wants to keep me safe because our lives are connected?"

"Partly." He stopped before two dark oak doors with beautiful whirling tree designs carved into each of them. "Give him a chance. At least speak to him, ask him questions without your preconceived notions. He is not Tenebris."

Her mind flashed back to his easy smiles at the Smoky Dragon, their flirtations, even the way he disarmed her when she tried to murder him. He didn't use aggression or malice in retaliation, and his lovely green eyes. Maker, she *kissed* him... but she found it hard to believe that someone who went with his father to towns and villages, killing along the way, could have a decent bone in his body. And if he was not like Tenebris then why did he follow his father's orders for so long?

When they stepped inside, the High King, queen, and princess all stood and watched her. With the glare the queen cut, and the just as glacial look her daughter gave, Layala wanted to step back out and eat breakfast alone in her room. Not because she wasn't up for a pissing contest, she enjoyed little squabbles and light banter, but these two looked like they wanted to set her on fire for arriving late. She couldn't guess how they'd react when she refused to marry Thane, or had he told them she tried to kill him the night before?

Her gaze locked onto Thane's. Part of her wanted him to defend her against these vipers, but why would he? He must hate her after what she did. She was out of her element here. In a looming castle, in a populous city full of elves not humans, who expected her to do Maker knows what, and in a room full of royals who would anticipate certain behaviors and mannerisms, both of which she likely didn't have. Why did what they might think even bother her? After what she was prepared to do last night, she couldn't let these royals intimidate her. For the first time in her life, Layala felt truly alone. Even among the humans, she at least had Aunt Evalyn and the boys. Now, she dined with the enemy.

Fennan walked by and took a seat; all the while Layala simply stood in the doorway. Where should she sit? Next to the queen? On the other side of the princess?

"Good morning, Layala," Thane said. His hair had been combed and his clothes of black and forest green pressed and perfect. He was the epitome of a High King from the gold crown on his head to the shiny black boots on his feet. "Please join us." He placed his hands behind his back. "Mother, will you move down a seat? As my betrothed, Layala should be seated beside me."

"Oh, I'm to be replaced so easily? And after she made us wait nearly an hour."

"Never replaced, Mother," he said, softly.

Some of Layala's bite faded. She might need them to find a way to break their bond. "Thank you." Layala took the seat, and Thane helped her scoot in, then he settled in his own chair. Almost immediately, the servants brought in a spread of meats and cheeses, scrambled eggs, fruit, rolls, cubed potatoes; a banquet enough for the entire town of Briar Hollow, it seemed.

Silently, they started eating. The queen and princess openly glared. The blatant disregard for her was a little surprising considering they wanted to use her. One would think they'd be nice, but the room was heavy with tension, and it felt as if it could explode at any moment. As if Layala walked on hot coals on the verge of burning skin.

"So you've been in Svenarum with the humans," the queen started. The glittering blue jeweled crown on her head was wrapped in pieces of her dark hair, somehow braided around the sides of it. The shimmering, pretentious crimson gown she wore seemed a bit much for breakfast. She even had red lips to match.

"Yes," Layala answered and took her glass of deep purple juice. "In a small town." She took a long drink savoring the sweetness of the berry liquid. She thought about spilling it on herself so she wouldn't have to endure this any longer, but she didn't want to run from this situation anymore. Instead, she admired the painting on the wall. It reminded her of the ocean. She went a handful of times as a girl and the swirling blue-green with white-crested waves held a spot in her memory.

"How quaint," the queen said and lifted her hazel eyes to the princess.

"Forgive me," Thane said. "This is my mother Orlandia, and my sister, Talon. And call me Thane."

Layala wanted to keep addressing him as High King. It was more formal, less intimate. If she called him by his name it made them appear as friends, at least in her mind.

"Well, hopefully Castle Dredwich isn't too much for a small-town elf to navigate. It's probably overwhelming for someone like you," Princess Talon said with a smile. "Do all the females wear their hair like that in Svenarum?"

Without thinking, Layala touched the soft tresses resting against her chest and waist. Her hair curled at the ends but was otherwise straight. "It's how I prefer it." She never took the time to learn the complicated hairstyles these two had. There was no need for it before.

"Interesting," she said and took a bite of her food. Her hair was tightly done up with small braids and loops and all sorts of nonsense.

"Is there something wrong with it?" She didn't want to think they were belittling her, but they were. What else should she have expected though from the Athayel family?

"No," Thane said quickly. "Your hair is perfect."

Layala's mouth twitched, but she forced back a smile. She didn't expect him to defend her against his family. He somehow held her gaze with his brilliant green eyes and smiled for her.

"Perfect is a strong word, dear," Queen Orlandia said. "She'll need to learn proper fashion."

"Must we truly get into a conversation about hairstyles?" Thane snapped. "As if it matters at the moment. You've *just* met her."

"She doesn't even know which fork to use," Talon cut in. "And I can see dirt under her nails. You expect me to call her High Queen?"

Thane's nostrils flared as he glared at his sister. Blushing, Layala looked down at her hands. There was a little dirt she'd missed under her left pinky nail. She tucked her hands under the table and glanced at the door. If she got up and left it would let the enemy win, but could she sit here and take their ridicule? And there were three different forks that all looked very similar. Was there a correct one? Why did it matter?

"How about we discuss the wedding then?" Orlandia said. "It should be *soon*. And she'll have to learn our fashion and how to bathe properly if she is going to marry you, Thane. And that is most certainly only the beginning of the training she'll need. She'll be High Queen of Palenor for Maker's sake."

Why were they talking about her as if she wasn't in the room? Like she was but a statue... maybe because she was acting like one by taking their ridicule in silence. "*If* I'm going to marry him?" Layala finally cut in. "As if you gave a choice in the matter when you bound us together as *children*."

The queen, sitting directly beside Layala, shot her a scowl. "No, you don't have a choice, but you should feel privileged. How ungrateful of you. Any other she-elf would be more than happy to be born with magic and have the honor of marrying the High King of

Palenor. My son rescued you from squalor, and this is how we are treated by you?"

Layala clenched her teeth. "It's not a squalor."

Fennan had a hand over his mouth as if he was hiding a laugh. He thought this was funny? He found humor in Thane's mother belittling her? Or was he laughing that Layala had the gall to argue back?

Thane rubbed his chin. "Enough, Mother."

"She needs to be told what she has, apparently, not been taught. That someone of her status should hold her tongue in the presence of the king's mother."

"And sister," Talon added.

"Of *my* status?" Layala started. "Which is?"

"A low-born orphan elf who got my husband killed searching for her!" A vein throbbed on Orlandia's temple, and she gripped her napkin so hard her knuckles turned white.

The room was tensely silent. Layala leaned away from Orlandia, who stared at her with white-hot rage. "Need I remind you why I am an orphan? Don't expect me to feel remorse for your *husband*." Layala pushed her chair back and threw her napkin on the table. She wouldn't sit here with these people any longer.

"They were executed because they couldn't follow a simple order, you ungrateful little-"

"I said, enough!" Thane boomed and shot up. The chair he'd been sitting in hit the ground with a thud. "How dare you bring up that day." Thane gently wrapped his hand around Layala's upper arm. She suddenly regretted that she hadn't gone into the queen's room first last night. There was no bond to keep her from murdering that evil wench. Without a fight, she let Thane lead her from the dining hall. When the door slammed behind them and they stood alone, he released her. "I apologize for their behavior. My mother is not always so rude. My father's passing has been hard on her."

"You're truly apologizing after what I tried to do to you last night?" Layala asked, bewildered. His mother was indeed rude, but what Layala had tried to do was much worse, and she hadn't apologized to him. "Why do you defend me against her?"

"I should think that was obvious."

"It isn't to me."

"Layala, I've been defending you for nearly all my life."

Chapter 12

Defending her all his life? And he knew where she was for years... had he watched her from a distance? The thought made her shiver. Layala stared at him a moment, trying to decipher his meaning. Aside from his mother and sister's wicked tongues, what could he have been defending her from? They'd been hundreds of miles apart, and if she guessed correctly, they were further apart in idealism.

He tilted his head as if to say, *follow me*, and she cautiously started walking beside him, tense and ready to defend herself if need be. She couldn't let her guard down around him. All this niceness could be an act to draw her in.

With a guarded expression, he said, "Whether we chose it or not, you're my mate, my betrothed. I will defend you against anyone."

She didn't want to believe him but had he not

done just that? He stood up for her against his own family. But she hated the mate word. Hated what it meant and that she was branded with the symbol of it. And he said it so casually, as if she belonged to him already. She *belonged* to no one. "I tried to kill you and you're my *mate*." She anxiously picked at the dry skin around her nails.

"Clearly we have different ideas of how to treat one's mate. But it wasn't the first time someone attempted to slit my throat. I can hardly hold a grudge." He smiled and she snapped her eyes away. He thought her attempt was laughable at best. "Although I am curious what you planned to do after you killed me?"

This conversation was amusing to him? Did he enjoy talking about her attempt on his life? As if it was nothing but entertainment for the evening, something to liven up his night.

She didn't want to admit to her other plans, then he might lock her up. "Leave." All she wanted to do at the moment was get away from him and get to her task.

He arched a dark brow. "And where would you have gone? You would have had to kill Piper, Fennan, and Aldrich to be able to go back to your home. And my mother would hunt you until the end of her days."

She glared at him. "I wouldn't have left any loose ends."

"Vicious she-elf."

"I wouldn't say I'm a vicious person."

"What would you call it then? I'm dying to know a more fitting word for the murder of several people who haven't wronged you."

Layala rolled her eyes. "Haven't wronged me? You and your sister may not be responsible for making me an orphan as your mother so nicely put it, but she was there that day, standing at your father's side. And your friends are just as responsible for abducting me. Besides, it would be self-defense."

"I'm confused. Who came into whose room and held a knife to whose throat?"

"Don't act so self-righteous."

"Now you presume to know my motives. You must be a mind reader." He shoved open the double doors that lead down a set of stairs to blooming flowers, a large pond with six pillar fountains, three on either side. She scarcely paid attention to any other details.

"When I say I've been defending you, I mean I had to keep you away from my father. He's the one who would have used you." He paused and let his green eyes roam over her face. "I don't trust my mother or sister, so keep this little detail between you and me."

Layala stopped at the top of the staircase and stared at his broad back as he went down the steps. Her heart slammed against her chest, her throat tightened with anxiety. What if she'd been wrong? All her life she'd trained for this time, thinking of the ways she could make Thane and his father suffer. Thought of Tenebris dying to rid the world of his tyrannical leadership, to stop them from using her for their nefarious motives, to get revenge for killing her parents, and she'd never once thought Thane might care about anything other than himself.

If he was telling the truth, she'd severely misjudged everything. But if he wasn't... This changed nothing. He could be lying, could be trying to get her to fall for him so he could take advantage of her power. It could all be a lie to stop her from breaking the spell between them.

He stopped halfway down the steps and turned back, looking over his shoulder. He was more beautiful than any male; *anything* should be to her, as if it were some sort of sadistic joke from the Maker to have her attracted to the elf she hated.

"Are you coming?" His attractiveness made her more wary of him. Sometimes the most gorgeous things were the most deadly.

Recovering, she lifted her chin and slowly made her way down the steps, wishing she had her daggers on her person. She felt safer with them. She had so many questions for him, like why hadn't he been on his father's side, if he indeed wasn't? Why choose a stranger over family? Why didn't he come for her sooner? Why, why, why... but she didn't trust him to give an honest answer, however, so she asked nothing at all.

"Where do I start with removing the mate rune?" she asked.

"That's for you to figure out. You're the one who wants it undone."

"You don't?" She felt stupid for asking. Of course, he didn't. He needed her. She didn't believe him when he said he would simply set her free in the end. This alliance they had at the moment was only temporary. She had a feeling she'd have to kill him to get away.

"I haven't thought about that in a long time."

Eyebrows furrowing, she watched him skeptically, "I'm surprised you've even thought of it."

"When my father beat me for not being able to find you despite our connection, yes, I wanted to be rid of it. But now... how could I want someone as stunning as you gone?"

"Does that line typically work for you?" She all but rolled her eyes again. And yet she pictured the blond king she'd seen portraits of hitting a small boy and anger bubbled in her. Even if Thane was grown now, no child should be beaten.

He offered a sly smile, and Layala gritted her teeth. That line or one similar probably had the females ready to drop their dresses, given who he was. He needn't any lines at all. He could have anyone he wanted.

"It's only a *line* if it isn't true. You are stunning."

Every man at the training yard in Briar Hollow loved to tell her how beautiful she was once she hit about nineteen. The creative lines they came up with became ridiculous. It was a game to them after a while. Compliments meant little now. She needed to get back to the main goal here. "Is there anything about the spell in the library?"

"There is a copy of the spell. You're welcome to look at it."

"I'll start there then." They paused on the far side of the pond between short hedges and stared at the water. A few frogs sat on the lily pads. Their ribbits and the water spilling into the pond from the pillars were pleasant, relaxing sounds. The smell of jasmine and eucalyptus filled her nose. This environment could put her into a trance. She needed to get out of there before she caught any feelings besides the bitter ones she harbored at her core.

"I'll show you where it is."

She shook her head, taking a step away from him. "Given that you are leaving it up to me, I can go alone." Someone could give her directions. A guard or maid. She could find Reina and Pearl.

"You're free to go where you'd like within the castle. With an escort. But stay inside."

Her eyebrows furrowed as she tried to decipher his placid expression. "Why can't I go alone? And why can't I go outside?"

He lifted a shoulder, but she saw worry through his mask of calm. "Number one: I don't trust you. Number two: I don't trust everyone within these walls or outside them as previously stated. And number three: you don't know where you're going."

"And I suppose *you'd* like to be my escort?"

"I do have other things to do, you know. I am High King. But I can make time. Unless you'd prefer Piper."

"I would prefer Piper." She folded her arms. Why was she standing here still? She should walk away even if he'd follow.

He smirked. "She is pretty..."

"I didn't mean in *that* way."

"So you do prefer me."

She cleared her throat. "I'd like my weapons back."

He rubbed his chin, grinning. "After you tried to kill me, you think I should give you weapons? Should I hand over my balls on a platter as well?"

"As if you have any."

"Vicious, like I said."

"I'm not going to try to kill you. That was before I knew it would kill me, too."

He laughed with real humor. "At least you're honest. But no, you won't get them back. I know I'm not the only one you'd like to kill. As you said, no loose ends; that could be a rather long list now. I hope I don't have to give you the katagas serum again."

Her cheeks flushed with anger. "I haven't used my magic against anyone, and I don't plan to. There is no need to threaten me."

"And why haven't you? You didn't even attempt to use your power when you came into my room."

"That's none of your business." Balling her hands into fists, Layala tore her gaze away. She should have kept her mouth shut. She turned and strutted off having no idea if she was going the right way to the library or not. He was at her side so fast it startled her. Shivering, she kept her eyes forward, not giving him the satisfaction of looking. They didn't travel far before Piper rounded a corner.

"Sire," she said, dipping her head. "There are emissaries from the dwarves of Fang Peak here to see you. As well as two male elves from Calladira."

He nodded. "Piper, please escort Lady Lightbringer to the library."

"Of course, sire."

As he started walking away, he looked over his shoulder, "You'll join me for dinner, Layala."

Layala found it difficult not to spit a nasty comment about him ordering her around. She'd never taken orders from anyone well. "So your mother can ridicule me more?"

"No." He met her stare. "It will only be you and I tonight."

THE WALK to the library was spent in silence. Layala didn't know for certain if Piper was upset with her but the frown and angry line between her brows as she stomped was proof enough. Thane and Fennan might have taken her attempt on Thane's life with a grain of salt but would Piper?

When they stood before an archway with a sign

carved into the wood "knowledge is power" she knew they had arrived at the library. There were many staircases, some swirling to upper shelves, some leading to the next levels and the next. Plants sat in blue and silver vases. One she recognized; when held, it helped retain information. Yet most of the plants here she couldn't name, though they were familiar. Maybe something she saw in Aunt Evalyn's plant diary.

Books filled the bone-white shelves. To the left, a small rock waterfall spilled into a pond. Piper led her by it. Layala peered inside to see various colorful fish swimming among the water plants and rocks. They stopped in a small room with nothing in it but a single high table with a scroll rolled open on top.

Piper gestured toward it. "Don't touch it. It's old and must be handled properly."

Annoyed with more orders, Layala strutted by and stared down at the parchment. It was torn in some places and yellowed from time. A brown stain splattered over the bottom corner. The script was old elvish, a language no one she knew spoke anymore. She understood a couple words; "binding" and "eternity". Good heavens, was she bound to Thane for eternity, not even until death? She couldn't even get away from him when she died. The idea made her stomach ache. The mate rune on her wrist was marked at the bottom of the page.

She turned back to Piper. "Can you read it?"

"No," Piper answered sharply.

Layala stared at it a while longer. Aunt Evalyn

taught her some of the old language but not much. "Is there a book in here that will translate the words?"

"I don't know. Why do you want to read the spell anyway?"

"I'm curious."

"Your *mate* could read it to you. He's been schooled in the old language."

"I'm curious if there is a way to undo it, and he won't tell me." Maybe that would give her some motivation to help. After what Layala did, Piper would be glad to be rid of Layala.

Piper's stiff posture didn't change. She gave Layala a lazy glare. "You should be more concerned with the war at our southern border against the pale ones than trying to get out of something that cannot be undone." Her eyes narrowed. "I know what you did to Thane."

Frowning, Layala turned back to the parchment. It's not as if she could deny stabbing him. "Life force bonded," she mouthed. So he wasn't lying. Not only could she not kill him, but she was stuck at his side. It was truly break the bond, marry him, or turn into a pale one. She held a small amount of hope that he'd lied and she could still get away.

Taking a steadying breath, she read "Magic-coupling" but wasn't sure of the second word. Maybe it wasn't coupling or magic. If it was then wouldn't that mean both of them would need magic? No, she must be mistaken. Layala was the only elf mage born in recent history. She searched the shelves looking for a book to translate so she could do more than pick out a few words, while Piper sat in a chair, chin resting against her fist. She looked bored to tears.

After a few hours of scanning the shelves, searching for a book on the Black Mage or runes, she found nothing. The library attendant said that such books were illegal, and any rune spell books by the Black Mage had been taken to a secret location that only the High King knew. Any old Elvish books were written in that language and there wasn't a manuscript to translate it, at least in the castle library.

Piper had dozed off, mouth hanging open with her head leaned back into the chair. Layala tapped her shoulder and then headed for the exit. Piper jumped up, rubbing her eyes and was quickly at Layala's side.

"I'd like to go back to my room," Layala said. Without speaking to each other, they made it through several hallways and up two sets of stairs. While passing a window, Layala stopped. From here she could see the bridge and it was full of elves. The guards didn't allow them in. "What's going on out there?"

Piper leaned against the frame on the other side. "You're the mysterious child with magic no one has seen in nearly twenty-five years. There are shrines in your name around the city. There are also those who think you are dangerous and should be killed because of the sign at your birth. The dark sign... some said it looked like black smoke circling around you with poisonous black lilies." She paused. "Both groups want to see you."

Layala stared at her trying to decipher if she lied

but all she saw was the truth. Layala had no idea that all of this went on. Shrines? How disturbing. And they lined up to see *her*? Now Pearl and Reina's reactions to her didn't seem so odd. "That's why he said not to go outside," she said more to herself.

"And you better listen. Your life is connected with his. If you're in danger, he's in danger and that cannot happen."

A chill ran through her body as she moved away from the window. When they arrived at her room, she left Piper outside and dove onto the soft bed. She'd never felt silken fabric so soft. Even the feather pillow was like lying on a cloud. A part of her could get used to this luxury even though she always lived with meager things. She stared up at the ceiling, peering through the vines and sheer ivory fabric that dominated the center above her. Through that, she gazed at the midnight blue mural with silver and white splashes that looked like stars. The Starlight room, Thane called it.

The only useful thing she got out of the trip to the library was seeing for herself that nothing in the spell said how to undo it as far as she could tell. "Binding for eternity" said it well enough. The words "magic-coupling" nagged at the back of her mind. Did that mean Thane would be given access to her magic once they were wed? Thane said they must finish the magic by getting married or they'd turn into pale ones. If he could access her power, he wouldn't even need her to comply. That must be why the former king wanted them bound in the first place.

And the war Piper spoke of… Layala knew there were constant skirmishes with the pale ones but had something changed? She didn't want any part of the war, or of the elves clamoring outside the gate to see her. Feeling antsy she stood, wandering around the room. A shelf on the wall held a set of statues, carved from a marbled white-gray stone. A female with long hair and a flowing dress and the male counterpart opposite of her, both reaching toward the other. As if they wanted to take hands but something kept them apart. Beside that was a fertility fern; she thought about tossing it out the window. There was absolutely no need for that thing. It made her wonder if this room was always meant for Thane's mate, for her.

She tried to focus her mind on anything but him and his words, this thing between them—his beautiful face haunted her. Where was Tif to distract her? Instead of conversing with the missing gnome, her thoughts drifted to what he said about always defending her. Why would he have any sense of loyalty to her? He hadn't chosen her himself. They didn't know each other, and yet, she was supposed to believe he cared for her. Her gallant mate set on keeping her safe. It sounded like a farce.

A knock at her door made her jump.

"Lady, it is Reina and Pearl, here to dress you for dinner," Reina said.

She lost track of that much time pacing and pondering? "Come in."

They entered one at a time, Pearl with a huge smile, Reina more demure. "Good evening, Lady," Pearl said with a dip of her head.

"I suppose you'll want me to change my dress for dinner."

"It's customary to change clothes for each meal." Reina went into the closet and returned with a glittering rich-blue gown over her arm. "We would have gotten you for luncheon, but the High King said not to bother you in the library."

Her stomach growled as if to tell her she indeed missed a meal. She eyed the dress Reina held up. "Will this do?" she asked.

It was floor length, fitted at the waist and perhaps slightly loose around the hips and thighs. It looked more like a dress for a fancy ball, not that she'd ever been to one but she could imagine. "It's a bit much, isn't it?"

"For dinner with the High King?" Pearl put a hand to her chest. "If he'd asked me to dinner I'd find the most beautiful gown I could. This is certainly not too much."

Spending a casual week on the road with Thane and fighting with him the night before took away how spectacular one might see dinner with the King of Palenor.

Tapping a finger against her lips, Reina said, "Perhaps not good enough."

"No, it's beautiful. I'll wear it." She didn't want them to come up with something even more audacious.

After slipping out of the cotton dress and stepping into the sparkling evening gown, she stood in front of the full-length mirror. It was without a doubt the most stunning thing she ever put on. She wanted to hate it, wanted to complain and say she'd rather wear her pants, but the way it hugged her curves, and brought out her eyes, she reveled in it. She looked like royalty. The V neckline hit at just the point where a slight bit of cleavage showed. Her shoulders were covered but barely. Pearl handed her a pair of white silky gloves. She slid them on to just past her elbows. They added to the elegance.

"You look marvelous," Reina said. "Can I do your hair?"

Layala slowly nodded. "Yes."

When Pearl and Reina were finished, her hair was half up in a braid crown while the bottom was left to tumble down in curls. As a final touch, Pearl opened a black velvet box to show her a necklace with a blue teardrop surrounded by diamonds on a silver chain. "A gift from his majesty."

"The king told you to give that to me?" Layala asked.

"He did, Lady. Isn't it beautiful? A perfect gift for a future queen."

Layala turned and headed for the door. "Put it on the shelf over there." She couldn't wear a gift so precious from him. It might be seen as wanting to accept their bond... she tried to murder him for Maker's sake.

"But my lady, it matches your dress." Pearl looked genuinely confused. "Won't you wear it?"

"No but thank you." Layala pulled the door open and stepped out to find Piper waiting. "Did Thane assign you to watch me?"

"Yes."

"All the time?"

"You won't be allowed to go anywhere alone after the stunt you pulled last night and rest assured the servants' entrance to the king's room isn't accessible anymore." She faked a smile. Her eyes fell to Layala's chest. "Where is the gift King Thane sent you?"

"In the room."

Piper said nothing more as she led the way to the dining hall. When they stopped outside the door, Piper turned to her before reaching for the handle.

"Let me guess, I should give Thane a chance?" Layala drawled. She didn't need Thane's friends telling her what a great person he was. Of course they were on his side.

"Actually, I was going to say Queen Orlandia was right."

Layala's brows pulled down. "About?"

"About you being an ungrateful wench." She jerked the door open and then stepped back. "Have a wonderful dinner."

She turned and stalked off before Layala could

even muster a retort. Layala glared daggers at her guard's back. What did they truly expect of her? To be thankful for everything? To be grateful her parents were murdered and she was bound to a male she didn't even know? With her fists tight at her sides, she stepped inside the dining room. She hated that the sight of Thane made her nervous.

Chapter 13

Thane stood upon seeing Layala. He clenched his jaw to keep it from falling open. How beautiful she truly was. He always thought so, but tonight, in that dress, was there ever anyone to match her? He moved her chair back and motioned for her to sit opposite of him. He had the servants remove the large dining table to replace it with a small square one set for two.

With her chin slightly raised, she made her way to the chair. Once he was seated, the servants appeared, bringing in a plate of salad for each of them and two glasses of white-berry wine from the woodland elves. It was the best, though he hated to admit they made better wine than the high elves.

The two candles on top of silver candlesticks at the center of the table gave off a soft glow. The pastel-blue curtains lay open to reveal an evening sun, bathing the room in orange light. The way it made her skin illuminate made him shift a little. "You look lovely," he said as soon as the servants cleared out.

She stared at him for a moment then picked up her fork and stabbed at the lettuce as if it was a foe in need of impaling. The open windows let in the sound of a breeze rustling the oak trees and a few songbirds filled the silence between them. This would be a long dinner.

Thane picked up his glass of wine and took a drink, draining nearly half. When he set it back down, she still hadn't looked up at him. She speared another vegetable and shoved it into her mouth. Thane nearly laughed at her seeming hostility. "You must have a quarrel with salad."

Her stunning blue eyes lifted, the color of the sky on a cloudless day. "What?"

"It is only salad. I dare say it hasn't wronged you."

She set her fork down and glared. "Do you have a problem with the way I eat? Or maybe I'm using the *wrong* fork."

"No. I could watch you all day in fact. With any fork."

"Pig," she murmured and went back to her meal, angrier than before.

"I hope you don't hold grudges against venison. It's the main course tonight."

No reply. Thane tapped his foot on the ground and took another drink of wine. Before she went to the library they were at least able to have a conversation. Now she would hardly look at him. As if the very sight of him disgusted her. "I presume you had no luck in your research at the library this afternoon then." Very few people could read old elvish and even if she could, the spell would have only told her what he had. That there was no way out of it.

"No," she said between bites, eyes fixed on her plate.

"I can't say I'm upset. I'll get to see what's under that dress if you don't succeed." He knew *that* would get her attention. Her head snapped up, fury smoldering in her eyes. He thought she might very well leap across the table and attack him. Some reaction was better than nothing. It was almost laughable how easy it was to rile her up.

Instead of flying at him, she took a deep breath and sat up a little taller. "Well, I've already seen most of what's under your attire." She shrugged as if she wasn't enticed.

He couldn't hold back his smile. "Don't act like you didn't like what you saw. We both know you did."

"That must be why I stabbed you… You're not as impressive as you think you are." She grabbed her wine. "I'm sure the lower half," her gaze flicked down a moment, "isn't anything grand either. You know what they say about male ears; the smaller the tip the smaller the lower bit." She tapped her left one. "Yours are on the petite side."

Thane licked his lips trying not to laugh. "That's not a thing, but I guess you'll have to see for yourself in eight weeks."

"Even if I don't manage to succeed, I'm not remotely interested in your male parts." She brushed her hair over her right shoulder. "That role in our would-be marriage will never come to fruition. We'll simply be two people bound by a curse."

"I wouldn't be too hasty with the word *never*. Never is a long time. You might come to like me—crave me even." He leaned in slightly on the table.

She scoffed. "Hardly."

"Your eyes betray you, dearest, in the way that you can't seem to look away from me."

"That's most certainly wishful thinking on your part. Besides, you won't have to worry. Soon our bond will be broken and, if I allow you to live, you can find a nice elf to settle down with. Piper perhaps."

Thane chuckled. What a wicked thing she was. "If you allow me to live? Part of our deal was me living, as was me letting you go."

She tilted her head. "Was it?"

"If you don't like our bargain, I can have the date moved up and we can wed tomorrow. I'm already doing you a courtesy by allowing you precious time. Time that is waning for the both of us."

Her haughty expression dropped and she squirmed in her seat. "You can't force me to do anything."

"It's not me that is doing the forcing. It's the magic. You think I would have chosen you as my bride?"

She stiffened. "Not up to par, am I? I suppose I'm

not pretty enough as a *low-born* elf, or is it my manners that offend?"

He watched her for a moment, gauging her reaction. Why did it bother her that he said he wouldn't have chosen her? It's not as if she should care. She wouldn't have chosen him. She was actively not choosing him, in fact. "You might be the most beautiful female I've ever seen, which I told you the night I met you by the way, but I suppose I'd have chosen someone who doesn't despise me. How cruel, I know."

He thought about every wretched thing he did because of her. How much pain and suffering was thrust upon him because of this bond. "No, if I had gotten to choose it wouldn't have been this." He tapped his wrist where the mate rune resided.

Yet after everything he endured, he didn't think he could ever be happy with anyone else. He'd fought so hard, done so many things for her before he even met her. She carved a special place in his heart before they ever spoke a word. Through their bond he felt her, knew she was there even when he couldn't see her. Sometimes her pain or happiness transferred to him like a tug or pull at his heart. When he felt alone he knew he wasn't. She was out there somewhere.

He would catch glimpses of what she saw, flashes of what she heard. Her lovely voice filled his dreams. He knew who she was the moment he stepped into the pub in her hometown. He wanted to simply stare at her, enthralled by actually seeing this lovely being he was connected to. To behold her face for the first time was like marveling at the sunset for the first time.

He assumed she felt their connection too. He *knew* she would be as excited to see him as he was her, but Maker above, he was met with a rude awakening. She thought he went around murdering people, and believed he was like his father. He couldn't think of anyone worse to be compared to.

Often he led his own "search" parties to appease Tenebris, knowing the whole time Layala wasn't near. His soldiers, the Ravens, would arrive in a town of Palenor, eat and drink, ask around but never hurt anyone. There *were* small skirmishes with the woodland elves of Calladira, where he killed more than he liked to think about but it wasn't as if it brought him satisfaction. The discrepancies over land never seemed to end and usually came to bloodshed.

In recent years when his father grew more desperate. Thane heard stories of Tenebris's escalating brutality in his searches for Layala, the last mage. Tenebris tried to keep it hidden, claiming he never hurt anyone, but rumors abounded. To see if they were true, Thane accompanied his father once... he was horrified. His father's soldiers killed their own people of Palenor in a small northern village, who knew nothing about Layala. He wanted to murder Tenebris right then and there for his cruelty, for his abuse of power but to his everlasting shame, he didn't. He couldn't bring himself to do it.

"If you don't want me then help me break our

bond," Layala said, pulling Thane from his thoughts. "If you truly meant what you said and you don't want to use me for my magic, you would help."

"It's more complicated than what I want or don't, Layala." He took another pull of wine. "With time running short, believe me, I've looked for alternatives. There isn't a way."

"I don't believe that."

"I'm sure you don't. The news is new to you."

"I mean, I don't believe you've truly looked for a way out." Her blue eyes widened with her frustration. "With your arrogance you probably thought I'd drop to my knees, begging you to take me to your bed."

Thane cocked an eyebrow. "If you knew what you were missing out on, you would."

She picked up a fork and with remarkable speed, launched it. He snatched it out of the air in front of his face, twirled it around his fingers and set it down. "I don't know if I've ever met someone so hostile. And keep in mind I've been in countless battles against pale ones." So why did part of him like it? He supposed it was because everyone wanted what they didn't have, and as High King, he had pretty much everything he could want, except her.

The door creaked open and the servant Alfrend came in pulling a silver tray with their dinner, silencing both of them. Alfrend set Thane's plate before him and removed the lid. "Enjoy, sire."

"I appreciate it. Thank you, Alfrend." The smell of the roasted meat filled his nose and his mouth watered. He looked at Layala. "Did you not like the necklace I gave you?" There couldn't be any talk about breaking bonds in front of the servants.

"It was gorgeous. But I don't want any gifts from you."

Alfrend gave Thane a long look of surprise then set Layala's plate before her.

She nodded. "Thank you."

Thane gave him a quick wave, telling him to ignore her rudeness, and he pulled the cart out the servants' passage.

"Would it be so bad to accept a gift from me?"

Layala cut into the meat on her plate and then set the silverware down. "What I want from you is your help in setting me free. Setting us both free. So we can go back to our lives." Her eyebrows furrowed. "How could you even want me? I tried to kill you." She took in a deep breath, "You want to know what I was doing in that pool in the woods? Poison. I retrieved Gaudrey's root and I planned to—poison you and the others so I could get away."

He lightly chewed the inside of his cheek. She felt guilty. He sensed that now. She was confused and angry with herself. When she said she didn't know what to think of him, she truly meant that. Thane took a bite of venison and savored the salty flavor, and thought for a moment. "I'll take you to Mage Vesstan and he'll tell you what I already have. We'll leave in the morning."

Her answering smile hurt him more than it should.

***

Later that evening, Thane wandered the halls of Castle Dredwich alone. He stepped out onto a balcony to enjoy the warm evening air. The stars winked above and the moon shined bright, illuminating the stone balcony. He glided to the edge and leaned against the railing. At this hour most of the light in the houses in the city below were out save for a few, but the light from the stars and moon reflected off the roofs of the homes, a sight that lit up the city even at night. He loved his home, this place. Even if there were bad memories within the walls of the castle, the Valley of the Sun held a special place in his heart. He would do anything to protect it and the people within.

He picked at a callus on his palm, thinking about the war in the south, about how he should be there defending Palenor, not sitting within the safety of his high walls. The war with the pale ones had gone on for hundreds of years now. Whenever they thought they'd beaten them back enough that the enemy couldn't regain strength, somehow there were always more. Thane had even watched some of his own turn. Somehow resurrected on the battlefield.

His mind drifted back to a couple of months prior....

"Thane," called Osric. "You're not going out there, are you?"

They sat on the backs of their horses, behind a skirmish with the pale ones. Thane's father was up north and in order to get away from him, Thane came to oversee the latest battle.

"Oh, why not. I could do with working out some frustration on the creeps." He held one of his swords across his lap, a tether of arrows on his back.

Osric smiled. They'd been best friends since childhood. Fist fighting and wrestling as kids to see who was tougher. Fennan was usually the mediator, getting in between when things got too rough. The three of them learned the sword together, and that turned into a competition which made them all better. They battled every chance they got until they were teenagers, then they stopped fighting each other and teamed up against everyone else who wanted a go at them.

"What did Tenebris do to piss you off this time?" Osric asked.

"He said he got a tip that Layala was somewhere up north and demanded my accompaniment. She's not there, thank the Maker."

Osric patted his horse's neck. "He'll never give up, will he?"

"No. He won't."

"And you'll never give her up." Osric knew that Thane could find Layala if he wanted to. But Osric's loyalty was with his prince, not his king. "It seems this will go on for eternity, but I suppose it can't? You're running out of time, Thane. You must get her soon. Even if you do it in secret."

"In secret? You think I haven't thought of that? My father would send spies after me. They watch me even now. He suspects I know where she is even still."

"Then it's him or you. If you won't kill him, I will. You should have done it a long time ago."

"He's my father."

"He's an evil tyrant."

Thane kicked Phantom onward raising his sword high; he let out a roar that burned his throat. Phantom plowed into a row of pale ones, crushing them under his weight. The soldiers rallied around him, growing in enthusiasm to end the battle. Thane slashed and hacked furiously. He lost count of how many he cut down. Their horrid screams echoed in his ears. The cries of his own like a terrible melody one can't shake. He'd lost track of Osric during the fight. When the battle ended, he looked around. "Osric!" his voice echoed across the grassy, rocky plain but his friend didn't answer.

He rode Phantom all around the battlefield. Over bodies, mostly pale ones but elves too. The smell of decay and death made him want to retch after a while. He asked his soldiers if anyone had seen Osric. No one had or they didn't know who he was. "Osric!" he roared. When he spotted his friend's horse grazing off in the distance he raced over. The pounding of horse hooves matched his heart. Osric's foot was caught in the stirrup, and he lay unmoving on the ground.

Thane slid down and crouched beside his friend. Pushing his mass of dark hair out of his bloodied face. "It's me. It's Thane."

Osric groaned.

He grabbed him around the middle and set him on Phantom. "I'll get you help. Hold on. Don't you die on me. Don't you dare."

When he made it back to camp, he carried him into the healer's tent. It was full of injured soldiers, not a single bed open. "One of you will come with me now."

A healer he didn't know followed him to his own tent and he set Osric on his cot. "Help him."

The healer knelt beside Osric, inspecting for major wounds and stopped at a jagged bite mark on his calf. It was red and inflamed with black streaks stemming from it up his flesh. The healer, a female with light hair, jumped up and backed away. "He's been bitten by a pale one." She nearly stumbled on her way to the tent flap. "Prince, get away from him." She covered her mouth and nose with a cloth. "You must cut off his head. You will be doing him a favor."

Thane's stomach twisted into knots. His friend's lips already looked purple, as he grew closer to death. His pale skin had a sheen of sweat. "If we could catch whatever turns the pale ones by nearness, we would all die or turn on the battlefield. Now do something. Save him."

"I can't. If he's been bitten it's a sure sign he will turn."

Thane growled and threw a bottle of brandy from a nearby table on the ground, smashing the glass into a thousand pieces. "Get out!" he roared. As soon as the flap closed behind the healer, he dropped to his knees and sobbed into his hands.

Thane was drawn from his memory when Fennan stepped up beside him. "How did dinner go?"

He cleared his tight throat. "Not well I'm afraid." His voice had more emotion in it than he intended.

Fennan ran a hand over his hair. "That bad? Could it have been worse than her trying to kill you?"

Thane chuckled and turned away from the city leaning his back against the railing. "We've moved onto threats but not real ones at least. Unless you count trying to spear me with a fork."

"So what will you do?"

Thane ran his hand over the smooth stone of the railing. "We're going to see Mage Vesstan in the morning."

"Shall I pack my things?"

"No, it will be only her and me this time. We'll take the portal so it's only half a day's ride from there."

Fennan folded his arms. "I don't like you two going alone. I can hang back if you want time alone with her, but allow me to come in case something goes wrong. Like if she tries to kill you again. We don't know what she's capable of with magic."

"She won't try to hurt me. And you know I have my own defenses."

Fen's mouth twisted. "I still don't like it."

"You don't have to like it, Fen." He patted his shoulder. "I'll see you when I get back. Make sure my mother doesn't do anything rash and don't tell her where I've gone."

"You're leaving me in charge of your mother?" He shuddered.

"She likes you." Thane smiled and walked inside. "You're like the second son she never had."

Chapter 14

Layala tossed and turned and couldn't get comfortable despite how soft the bed was. She stared at the ceiling for a countless amount of time. She punched the pillow trying to make it a little flatter. Pulled the blanket higher, then shoved it back down, then up again. One leg out then it got too cold, so she tucked it back in. Groaning, she rolled over and screamed into the soft bed.

Tif sat on the pillow beside her. "You know, screaming to get out one's frustration has been proven to help with anxiety and aggression."

"Has it now?"

"It's true. I used to do it when the birds tried to scoop me up in their talons. They scattered as their aggression went away."

Slowly shaking her head, Layala didn't have the heart to tell her the screaming *scared* them away. It didn't even make sense that someone else's screaming would help another. "Well, I do feel a little better."

But she couldn't stop thinking about her conversation with Thane and the impossibility of breaking their bond. She wished Aunt Evalyn was there for advice. Evalyn became a mother to her, one of the only people Layala trusted with her whole heart. And now she was alone with no one.

It was strange Layala wanted to go to Thane's room. *It must be the mate bond,* she thought, *making me think stupid things.* The rune on her wrist tingled again as if willing her to go. He was right on the other side of the wall. A part of her wanted to apologize for throwing the fork at dinner, and for lashing out in general... Wasn't he trapped as much as she was? What if he wanted to be free of her but he truly thought it was impossible?

Planting herself firmly in her bed, she rolled over and pulled the blanket over her head, determined to fall asleep. Eventually, she did.

IN THE MORNING, dressed in the clothes she came in: her black pants, boots, long-sleeved blue top and black corset around her waist, she paced her room waiting for Thane. She opened the windows and looked out over the castle lands. Guards walked the paths below, chatting and laughing. The river that ran in front of the grounds appeared higher today, the waterfall cascading down the rocks to the far right, louder and more intense.

Reina and Pearl had already stopped in to dress her for breakfast, but she refused to change into a gown. So instead, Reina brought her bread with butter and some cheese. She ate quickly so she wouldn't be hungry on the way to see the Mage. Nervous-excited flutters filled her stomach. She had never seen a woodland elf or been anywhere near their lands. Would they look different? Act differently? The high elves of Palenor thought of themselves as superior but she never knew why.

"You seem on edge," Tif said sitting on the end of the bed. "Might I make you some calming tea? It's made from the calming tree leaves."

The sound of Layala's feet lightly patting with her steps, resounded in the room. "No, thank you. I am a little on edge though. I'm going to Calladira."

"Oh, how I wish I could go. It's a dream of mine to explore the wild terrain of the woodland elves. I hear they like to run in the nude under the moonlight." She sighed. "I'd like to do that too."

"Maybe another time," Layala said with a chuckle. She didn't want to have the responsibility of taking care of her out on the road or worry about her wanting to stay so she could run in the nude.

"Will it be dangerous?"

"I don't know."

"I have trained with swords some. Not jumbo size

obviously but I can still be deadly. I can cut off an elf ear quite easily. I did it once."

Shocked at the admission, Layala paused her pacing to look at the gnome. "Why would you do that?"

"The jumbo kept stomping on my parents' home, caving in our entrance. So, I followed him and cut off his ear and said if he ever came close to our house again, I'd cut off something he'd miss much more."

Laughing, Layala continued around the room, checking the fireplace every so often for movement. "You surprise me, Tif. In a good way."

"I hope so." She folded her arms and kicked her tiny legs rhythmically over the edge of the bed. "If you want me to cut off something from you-know-who, I could do it."

Shaking her head, Layala held up a palm. "No, leave you-know-who alone, please. I need him." A few moments later Layala said, "Have you ever seen any— sacrifices of young maidens here?" That was another rumor she needed to put to rest, the most horrid of them all.

"What?" Tif's eyes widened.

"I heard rumors."

"Oh," Tif tapped a finger against her lips. "Can't say I have. And I'm sure on my many ventures I would have noticed something so terrible. Even King Tenebris wouldn't do that, in the castle at least. He liked to keep up appearances. I can't imagine King Thane would ever do anything like that. He has a sort of kindness in his eyes his father most certainly did not. When I saw King Tenebris it was like his soul was—gone. I almost wet myself just looking at him."

Layala nodded. "I can't wait any longer. I'll see you when I get back." She jerked her door open. Piper leaned against the far wall standing next to another guard. The male wore short sleeves and a gray leather chest plate with the three weapon high elf sigil on it. He held a large wooden staff in his right hand. Piper wore something similar to Layala which made her wonder if she wasn't an actual guard. That or she didn't have to wear a uniform because she was friends with Thane.

"Morning, Lady Layala," the male elf said, grinning.

Piper nodded. "Do you need something?"

Layala waved a hand at them. "No, thanks." She strutted over to Thane's door and knocked.

"Lady, you can't bother the High King," the male guard said, taking a step closer to her.

Layala shrugged. "Well, I just did."

"She doesn't follow rules well," Piper mumbled.

When Thane didn't answer the door after a minute or so, Layala knocked again. She turned to the guards. "Is he in there?"

"He's not come out," the male said. "He's probably sleeping. He was out late."

Layala turned the handle and both of them screeched, "No, you can't." She pushed the door open and walked inside. With a quick wave at the guards and a devious smile, she shut them out. Dallying all day left an opening for Thane to change his mind about taking her to see the mage.

Her gaze fell to his freshly made bed. Flashes of her kissing him and the struggle that followed quickened her breath. She swiveled to the right where there looked to be a bathing room and her heart lurched a little. What if he was taking a bath? She thought of how they said he bathed in blood. That seemed so ridiculous to have believed now. He may be a killer, but she couldn't see anything in his nature that made him so sadistic and savage. She listened for a splash or any noise, staring hard through the doorway.

"Do you have any knives I need to worry about?"

Layala jumped and whirled around. He stepped through the tall curtains moving in the breeze. He must have a balcony off his bedroom. She scanned his bare chest, all his glorious muscles and perfect skin. He looked as good if not better in the daylight than he had in the evening shadows. With a sheepish smile, she lifted her hands to show her palms. "No, knives. I came to see if you are ready to leave."

He had a mug in hand and took a sip of the steaming liquid. "I'll be ready soon. Would you like some bramble tea?"

Brambleberry leaves were said to aid in breaking into the minds of others with their magical properties. It was extremely rare and coveted and he was offering it so casually. "Whose mind do you wish to know?"

He smiled but didn't reply.

"Mine?"

He let out a low, bedroom chuckle and took another sip, and a shiver slithered down her spine. "As if it were a mystery what you think of me or what you want?" He set the mug on his dresser top. "Brambleberry doesn't do that. The berries themselves are sweet and awaken the mind to be alert. The leaves help read others' minds which I don't often drink. Most people's heads aren't worth looking into."

She wondered if *his* head might be worth browsing, then she could know if his intentions with her were true or ill. "No, but thank you for offering. I'm plenty alert today."

"Wow... she says 'thank you'."

Layala couldn't help her smile. "I have *some* manners."

"When it comes to me, they seem to be lacking. You threatened to cut off my balls the very first time we met after all."

"And at the time I didn't even know it was you." She paused. "Why did you come into the Smoky Dragon that night?"

He pulled a drawer open and rifled through the clothes inside. "I thought perhaps we could get to know each other a little and I'd tell you who I was, and you'd willingly come with me. Maybe even be happy to. But I was obviously mistaken."

"And your backup plan was showing up in a hideous mask and dragging me out of my trashed cottage?" Such a stark contrast from the first attempt.

"It's customary for the High Elf King of status to wear a mask for ceremonial purposes as I told you. And I needed to remain hidden." He tapped near his eye. "This emerald color runs in my family's blood, my father's. I was surprised your aunt didn't know who I was right away given that she knew him."

"She'd been drinking ale," Layala murmured. "Why would you think I'd be willing?"

He stared at her with those emerald eyes he spoke of, face unreadable. "I thought... never mind. I thought wrong, so it doesn't matter."

Layala pressed her lips together. She wanted to know. "You thought what?"

He pulled a black long-sleeved shirt out of the drawer. "If you don't mind, I'd like to finish dressing alone. I'll come to get you when I'm ready."

Dismissed. She didn't blame him after the way she treated him.

Layala turned without a word and left the room. Piper and the other guard looked anxious when she stepped out, but they said nothing as she went to her own bedroom. It felt like an eternity before the knock sounded at her door. She jumped up from a padded chair, and hurriedly opened it. Thane stood on the other side dressed in black and blue, somewhere between a warrior with the swords on his back, the forearm guards, and a wealthy elf lord with the silver embroidery down his chest and around the collar.

His hair was pulled back accentuating his striking features. "Shall we?"

They silently made their way down the stairs. Across the massive entry and out the heavy front doors, passing several guards who watched her with curiosity and awe. It made her uncomfortable the way they stared. She followed Thane along a stone path out to a huge white barn and matching stables. There must have been room for fifty horses in there. Out to pasture were around twenty-five of the regal animals of various colors.

"How far is it? Shouldn't we have packed more?" she asked as they stood waiting for the stable master to come forth. She didn't bring extra clothes or food or anything but what she had on her. She assumed that it would all be brought for her but yet again it looked like Thane preferred to go without a host of guards.

"There is a portal not far from here. It will bring us into Calladira. Mage Vesstan's residence is close by."

"Will you give me a sword at least since we won't be bringing guards?" She glanced behind her to make sure they were indeed alone. "Why *aren't* we bringing guards? I find it odd that a king would travel alone, especially when he fears his mage companion will be stolen."

"Guards draw attention. If we go out like this, we likely won't be recognized by anyone. We're simply a pair of elves, not the High King and his mate."

"I thought your eyes were recognizable."

"They are but only by those who bother to know the trait. You didn't." He tilted his head toward her.

"As far as weapons, you have magic if the need arises, use it."

"I—" she cleared her throat, "I can't. Not without consequences." Honestly it had been so long since she used it; she didn't even know what would happen.

That piqued his interest; his eyebrows lifted. "And what sort of consequences are they? Hopefully not like Mage Vesstan's."

"What happens to him?"

Thane lifted a hand in greeting to the elf making his way toward us. "You'll see."

Layala fidgeted with her hands. He needed to know the danger in case she had to use them. "My power draws the pale ones to me when I use it. It's as if they can sense it. And before you accuse me of anything, no I didn't use it while we were on the road. I had nothing to do with them following us."

She could tell he was trying not to look shocked, but it wasn't working. When he trained his expression flat, he said, "And you know this because…"

She told him of the encounters she had with them each time she used her magic as a child.

"So, you haven't used your magic in more than fifteen years…" His mouth hung open momentarily. "Is it rune magic you use—spells? Or do you have an inherent ability?"

"The only rune I know is this one." She tapped her wrist. "My magic is much more raw. Wild… dark," she whispered the last word.

He pursed his lips but said nothing further on it

and Layala was relieved. What if Piper was right about some elves wanting to kill her due to the nature of her magic?

The elf approaching bowed before Thane. "Good day, sire. Will you be going for a ride?" He looked at Layala and bent at the waist. "You must be Layala Lightbringer. Word spreads quickly in the castle."

She blushed at the attention that name brought. "I am."

"Please ready Phantom for me." Thane turned to Layala. "And for the lady, I think Midnight will do."

The male elf smiled, putting a fist on his hip. "Ahh, Midnight is a monstrosity and rare beauty." He raised his eyebrows at Layala. "Sibling to Phantom."

A monstrosity? Phantom was one of the tallest horses she'd ever seen. Was Midnight as well? She wasn't all that experienced with horses and the description made her a little nervous. "Phantom is a lovely horse. I'm sure his brother is as well."

"I've always preferred to ride Midnight myself. He has a calmer countenance. Phantom likes to run, and charge into battle, although both were bred for such a cause. War horses. Afraid of nothing but a bit on the wild side." He nodded. "Right, I'll be back swiftly, sire." He bowed again and hurried off.

"So, you're actually allowing me to ride my own horse today. How generous." Having not done much riding in her life she was glad to hear the horse was calm. She'd always loved them but neither she nor Aunt Evalyn ever owned one.

He gave her a half smile. "I'm not going to keep you prisoner here. You know the consequences now if you should leave."

The heavy weight, the feeling of impending doom, was stronger today.

The horse master came back swiftly as he'd promised, leading the two tall black horses, one on each side. *Midnight* he was indeed, muscled shimmering onyx fur with a white star on his forehead. That's where the two horses differed. Phantom was entirely black, not a stitch of white.

Midnight wandered straight up to her and shoved his nose in her hand. Layala giggled and stroked between his eyes. "You are a monstrosity."

"He likes you," the horse master said.

Midnight bobbed his head up and down as if to agree. "Hello, Midnight," she said quietly. Running her hand along the soft fur of his neck she stopped and reached for the horn of the saddle. He was too tall and she couldn't quite grab hold of it. She struggled to get her foot to reach the stirrup, missing it by a few inches. She supposed if she got a running start, she could make it up but that was embarrassing.

"Shall I grab a step?" the horse master asked.

Thane appeared behind Layala and tapped her leg. "No, I'll help her. We won't be able to bring a step with us, so she'll need me anyway."

Trying to keep a blush from overtaking her entire face, she took a deep breath and put her boot in Thane's waiting hands. He lifted her as if it was effortless, and she threw her leg over, settling in. Thane got up with ease and then tilted his head. "Follow me." He waved at the horse master again. "Thank you. We'll likely be back this evening. Hopefully before dinner."

Layala nudged the horse's sides and he trotted ahead, prancing up beside Phantom. She couldn't help but smile. It had been so long since she rode alone and had the control and joy of her own horse. She patted his side and held the reins with the other hand. "I didn't know there was a portal between Calladira and Palenor. I thought you didn't get along well with them."

"It's very old and few know of it. As far as our relations with Calladira, I hope to improve them. I have a meeting set with their ruler Lord Brunard next month. Hopefully we can find some peace if not an alliance. I bought a lot of their wine recently to try to break the ice, so to speak."

"Why don't you get along?" Having lived in Svenarum all her life she didn't know details of feuds. Aunt Evalyn said it was because the High Elves of Palenor called themselves "high elves" and the woodland elves didn't like that Palenor thought of themselves as above.

"Mmm," Thane rubbed his smooth chin. "That is a tough question. But much of it is over land and because they have left us alone in the fight against the pale ones. We are the sole kingdom who must take the losses, train soldiers to be elite, and provide for a large army. We've been on our own in keeping the creatures in the Void, which protects everyone in Adalon, not just Palenor. My father cut off all trade with Calladira a hundred years ago because of their refusal to help and the tensions have only grown since. They tried to work deals out but never could."

"Why won't they fight?"

Thane shrugged. "Why don't the humans in Svenarum or Vessache? I know Palenor has a reputation for brutality, but we don't have a choice. The Void touches our southern border which makes it our direct problem. The pale ones can't go through the desert or mountains into Vessache but our land is wide open. We've been forced to become a brutal warrior kingdom. Everyone else has been spared because of our strength. They would only have to fight if we were overrun, and the pale ones invaded their lands."

It suddenly made much more sense why Tenebris wanted her as a weapon. The elves of Palenor died every day to defend this land.

They entered the bridge over the river. It had been cleared of the elves who gathered there the previous day. Layala risked a glance down. The height and distance to the water below made her eyes hurt. The waterfall was far enough away she could see the top easily but still close enough that light sprinkles of mist hit her face. The bridge looked to be the only access to the castle grounds. The rockface the castle was built into appeared impossible to scale down, with the sheer smoothness hundreds of feet high. Once they crossed the river, Thane turned right, away from the city.

"Does Calladira know we are coming?" Layala asked.

"It's too short of notice to arrange it. My meeting next month was the soonest they'd allow me, and I've been king for several weeks now."

"But don't we need permission to enter their territory? I thought they kept their borders as tight as you do."

Thane lifted a shoulder. "Only if they know we're there."

"And they won't?"

"As I said, the portal is concealed. It won't be guarded. We should be able to slip into Calladira easily."

Midnight was content to follow behind his twin as they rode on a narrow dirt path. Trees and boulders littered on both sides of the trail. Many with rune engravings carved in the bark and stone. One moss covered rock the size of a molehill was painted purple and had a yellow flower growing on the top. At its base was a tunnel. A pixie fluttered out from underneath with an arm full of mini rolls. The pink glitter trailing behind her brought a smile to Layala's lips. Pixies didn't reside in Svenarum although she saw a handful in her life. The only reason she included them on the list of banned races at the Smoky Dragon was because if a pixie came, they were always with an elf companion.

The pixie whizzed by, mumbling about being late. The many weeping willows swayed in the breeze, interspersed with great towering trees with white trunks and small green leaves. As if curious, squirrels and other small furry critters seemed to be following them, leaping from tree to tree. Up the hill of the valley they rode, and down the other side until the city below disappeared, neither of them speaking. Layala didn't know what to say, and it seemed Thane was content. He peeked over his shoulder occasionally; part of her wished he would say something, though she didn't know what. After so long the silence between them felt strained, as if either spoke it would be some sort of win for the other. As if staying quiet was the game.

At first it was easy to watch the surroundings and listen to the nature around her, but after he tried so hard to get her to talk to him last night, disappointment crept in. She hated herself for it. Why should she want to talk to him? Why should she care? She hardened her jaw and looked everywhere but at the elf in front of her.

Then Midnight nipped at Thane's horse as if he were bored too. Phantom turned his head with teeth bared. Midnight bit again and in return his brother kicked, nothing too violent but a warning. "Woah, no biting," Layala said as Midnight danced backward then without provocation, he trotted up beside the other two, despite Layala tugging back on the reins. "Is this normal behavior?"

Thane smiled and shrugged. "A little healthy competition never hurt."

A few more steps and the black horse's trot turned into a canter, and he took off, apparently wanting to lead. "I thought the horse master said you were the calmer of the two," she moaned as they tore down the somewhat uneven path. Her hair fell loose from the bun Reina and Pearl had done and it whipped wildly. She looked back and Thane was racing up behind her, grinning.

"So, it's a race you want?"

"It's not me doing the wanting!" Layala shouted, pushing her weight up in the stirrups and holding on tight. Phantom's head reached near his brother's shoulder, breaths coming heavy.

Thankfully the path widened to allow for both of them side by side. She felt like she was flying, and a laugh escaped her; this time they weren't running for their lives. It was exhilarating. The beating of the hooves like drums, the whirl of the wind an instrument of its own. The trees became a green blur as horse and rider tore across the land. She glanced at Thane, gaining the lead. "Come on, Midnight," she whispered. But she tensed, catching sight of the fallen log up ahead in the path. "Wait, slow down," she said, tugging back lightly on the reins. The horse kept going at nearly full speed. He wanted to win too. She squealed as he leapt over it and crashed hard into the saddle when they landed.

Thane was right beside her. "You're going to have

to pull back hard if he's not responding. Show him you're in charge. We need to get off the path at that dead tree ahead."

Layala cocked an eyebrow. "How about we see who gets to the dead tree first."

He answered with a grin.

She kicked Midnight's sides and he went even faster. The loneliness she felt the night before faded, filled by the rush of the wild speed, the thrill of competition. It looked like she was ahead by a nose when they ripped by the white-washed rotting tree.

Layala tugged back, leaning into it and Midnight slowed to a walk then a stop. His heaving breaths moved beneath her. After a moment, he dropped his head to nibble on some grass.

"I suppose I should have warned you that Phantom and Midnight tend to test each other," Thane said, brushing his fingers through the wild stray hair springing up around his face. "I think you beat us, and not to brag, but Phantom always wins."

Midnight whinnied as if he didn't like being told his brother always won. She patted the horse's smooth neck, grinning at him. "Did you hear that boy? You won." When she lifted her head, Thane was staring at her. She peered back but after a few beats, she shifted uncomfortably. "I know I'm wonderfully beautiful and you can't help but gaze; however, you should do something useful instead and lead the way," she drawled.

"I was admiring your smile. You haven't smiled much since I met you."

Layala thought of snapping a rude remark: why would she smile, given that he'd stolen her away? But the resentment she held for him even a day ago wasn't there. She knew now why he took her. Perhaps they could be allies in breaking their bond. Two elves with the same goal. "Maybe I needed a reason to."

"I think I'll take that as a challenge: find ways to make Layala smile." He tugged his reins to the left and started off into the knee-high yellowing grass. "Come on. It's this way."

Chapter 15

Hidden deep among twisting and gnarled trees of wood she didn't think existed on a map, they came up on a stone circle structure overtaken by draping vines, and moss that covered most of the gray surface. Deep red and purple roses surrounded its base.

"You weren't joking when you said it wasn't well known." Layala slid down from Midnight's back and made her way over to touch the surface of it. It was both cool and somehow warm at once. It lightly vibrated against her touch, as if the power within was barely contained.

The thing whispered, "Who are you?" in an eerie voice and she jerked back. Losing her footing on a vine, she started to fall until Thane grabbed her around the waist, steadying her.

"What's wrong?"

She liked the feel of his warm hands on her more

than she'd ever admit and tugged away. "Did you hear that?"

Thane's eyebrows lowered. "Hear what?"

"It—it spoke when I touched it. I think we should go back."

A serpentine smile. "Did it ask what color of underwear you have on or something? You seem shocked."

Her skin prickled at the thought of that voice, or was it his question? "This isn't a joke. How can a stone circle speak?"

He lifted a shoulder and tugged Phantom by the reins toward it. "Your guess is as good as mine. It was created by our Mage ancestors and, as I'm sure you're aware, we don't know how they did these things. The Black Mage was the only one of his kind to create rune spells. Mage Vesstan knows how to perform them but doesn't have the ability to create."

Thane touched the circle and the runes at the top began to glow with a bluish light. He whispered something Layala couldn't hear and then the middle shimmered to life, swirling what lay on the other side into a blur. "Thane Athayel," a voice whispered, tasting the name like a lover who had long awaited him. "Who is your companion?"

The voice projected all around them, not coming from a single source.

His green eyes flicked to hers. "A friend."

"Touch the stone," the voice cooed. It didn't sound

male or female, and it was both deep and light, with almost a hissing element to it.

"It must grant you permission," Thane clarified.

"Is it a test?" she took an involuntary step back toward Midnight. She placed her hands against his shoulder for comfort. "What if I don't pass?"

Thane didn't look worried when he said, "I don't know. I didn't fail."

She glared.

"Worst case scenario is it won't allow you to pass through and we'll have to take the long way which is three days ride, and that would present us with the task of sneaking past their border patrol."

"That's the worst-case scenario?" She nibbled on her bottom lip. "What if it finds me unworthy and sends me"—she didn't want to say it, it sounded absurd but it was a real fear—"to the Void? You said yourself you don't know how it works." With her dark magic, she didn't trust an ancient relic to judge her.

Thane gave her a placating look. "Then it will have to send me, too. I'll hold your hand when we pass through, and I won't let go."

She swallowed hard, trying to fight the ever growing nervousness. "You would do that? But if you went to the Void—"

"I'd likely die or turn into a pale one, I know. And if I stayed without you, the same would happen. But I'm not worried and you shouldn't be."

She nodded slowly and lifted her chin. She wouldn't be a coward. Hand hovering over the stone structure, she felt that hum again. Then before she could talk herself out of it, she stuck her hand to the portal.

"Hello again," it whispered. She almost stepped away but rooted herself there. After a moment an inner pull seemed to tug through her hand as if the portal was taking something from her. "Magic," the voice purred. "Beautiful, twisted, wild."

"Can we pass?" Thane urged.

"Yes," it said, "but you know what I require."

"Take it from me, not her."

"I've already had yours."

Layala looked back, still holding steady. "I think, I think it's taking magic…"

Thane rushed forward and jerked her away from the portal, arms wrapped around her middle and swung her behind him. The voice let out a hissing laugh and said, "You may proceed."

He swore and released her. "Come on, quickly before it closes." They both took hold of their horses and Thane held out his hand, palm up. Layala looked at it briefly, and convinced herself that her racing heart was only for fear of stepping into a portal. She set her hand in his, and his fingers closed around hers. With her pulse drowning out the noise of the forest, they stepped through.

When they came out on the other side, they were in another wood, but much different than the one they left; it even smelled distinct. Wetter, as if it had rained recently, and hints of pine. The warm-toned tree trunks were massive, wide enough to fit three elves across with arms spread wide. The leaves were varying shades of reds and yellows and greens all mixed together as if the season changed but she suspected that they stayed colorful permanently. Some pine trees were mixed in with their sharp evergreen needles.

The portal closed behind them leaving the stone circle appearing as lost and ancient as it did on the other side. The difference was this one didn't have roses at its base but a rainbow of wildflowers.

"See, we're not in the Void," Thane said, dropping her hand. "But we are in a different land so keep your guard up."

Midnight dug at the ground and then took a mouthful of flowers. Layala tugged him forward away from the portal and that creepy voice. What did it take from her to cross? It said it required something. If it had stolen some of her magic...

Thane held out a dagger, a twelve-inch blade if she had to guess; the handle black onyx crisscrossed with jade stone. "Take it." He pushed it closer.

She desired to snatch it up like a hungry beggar would bread, but composed, she reached out and grabbed hold. "Thank you." She slid it into her belt and a wave of comfort cascaded over her. Weapons were her safeguard, her shield against danger.

"We'll walk beside the horses until we reach a clearing," Thane motioned for her to follow. Tree roots jutted up all around, rocks and uneven ground with no path in sight. Easy to trip or lose footing. Layala nodded and pulled Midnight. It wasn't long before they came upon a path winding through the thick woods. Thane helped her to mount Midnight and then they set off, riding side by side.

"Do the elves here truly live in the trees?" she imagined with the large circumference of the tree trunks one could live inside.

"They carve out the center, cut windows, use the leftover wood for stairs, doors, furniture, the like. The trees continue to live too. They enjoy providing shelter for the elves."

"I would love to see it." She heard stories of the treehouses, and always thought it would be interesting to visit. A child's dream.

"We won't be going anywhere near the city. And Mage Vesstan lives in a regular cottage." He looked her over. "Another time, perhaps."

Hearing the mage's name made her wonder why Thane was helping her. Maybe he already knew the mage wouldn't tell her how. Had he commanded him long before now not to? "Why did he come to Calladira? I thought he was a high elf."

"He is," Thane's mouth twisted. "You'll have to ask him why, but I suspect it's because it's so peaceful here. Something I wish for Palenor."

"But the Valley of the Sun is peaceful, isn't it?" It was enchanting, at least.

"In some ways, but mothers know at some point their sons will have to go off to war. They train from a young age to fight pale ones. That's not peace."

They reached a clearing in the woods and at the center was a small thatched-roof cottage. It was painted yellow with white shutters and a rich brown front door. Potted lily flowers sat on either side of the entrance. Shrubs lined the well-manicured front path. A male dressed in a light green robe held a silver watering can in one hand and with the other, he shielded the sun from his eyes.

Thane waved at him, and he returned the gesture. A wooden post hitch waited at the start of the path. Thane slid down and tied Phantom to it. Layala quickly followed and hurried to catch up to his side. She knew instantly what the consequence was Thane talked about. Mage Vesstan's knobby, crooked hand barely gripped the pail. His skin wrinkled and spotted as if his hundreds of years showed as it would in a human. Silver hair and thick white eyebrows matching his beard. The use of magic aged him. It must be it. Elves could live thousands of years and not show the penalty of time.

Mage Vesstan dipped his head as they approached. "My, my, I wondered when I'd see you again after..." He trailed off and Layala didn't know if he forgot what he meant to say or if he didn't want to finish. "You've grown much." He turned to Thane. "Young prince, it is good to see you."

"I am High King now." He didn't say it in a bragging manner, simply stating a fact, but with that statement came implications. The mage worked for Tenebris for many years.

A white eyebrow ticked up. "Word doesn't travel fast out here I'm afraid. Come inside. It seems we have much to discuss." Painstakingly slow, he hobbled his way toward the front door. Layala wanted to take his arm and help him, but she didn't know if he'd find it offensive; after all he lived out here alone. But Thane didn't have the same hesitation. He slipped his arm through Vesstan's and helped him up the step and over the small hump to get inside. "Thank you, sire."

The first thing Layala noticed about the small cottage was the smell of mint leaves and lavender. She gently closed the door behind her while Thane guided Vesstan to a padded rocking chair. The inside was simple, a small kitchen with two cabinets, a sink, a black stove and an island, a living room with a wooden table, and a set of chairs with it. A slender but full bookshelf, and the single rocking chair he sat in with a tiny table with several books stacked beside him. She suspected a closed door to the right led to a bedroom.

Letting out a sigh, he said, "Ah, I should make some tea."

"Allow me to do it." Thane went into the kitchen. He opened a cupboard, pulled out a teapot then walked outside.

Layala hovered near the door, unsure if she should sit or wait to be invited to sit. "Now, Layala Lightbringer," Mage Vesstan said, shifting to look at her. "I suspect you have questions for me."

She stepped forward, her light feet creaking on the floorboards. "I have one, mainly."

His knobby hands lightly bounced against the armrests. "Just one?"

She decided to grab the dining table chair and set it in front of the mage and sat down to face him. "Yes. I need to know how to break the mate spell between Thane and me."

His bushy eyebrows shot up, wrinkling his forehead further. "Oh dear." He stared at her for a moment. "I'm afraid you can't, although I don't know why you'd want to. Thane has—" the door squealed open, and Thane stepped back inside.

"The well water is as delicious as I remember."

"Oh yes," Vesstan nodded. "Quite refreshing. It's what keeps me alive."

She prepared for him not to give an answer so easily. "Rune spells can be undone, can't they?"

That brought his attention back to her. He closed his eyes, and for a moment she thought he fell asleep. Until he took a deep breath and his eyelids fluttered open. "No. No spells created by the Black Mage have ever been undone unless he was the one to undo it. He was clever in that. It's how he was able to create so many pale ones, you see. If his spells weren't fulfilled or the price not paid, they'd turn. He was meticulous in making certain that there was no way out of it once done."

Her stomach dropped. "What price must be paid?"

"Thane hasn't told you?"

She twisted around to see him setting the kettle on

the burner. He didn't look up, but she knew he heard. What else did he keep from her?

"You must finish the spell and be wed."

"He told me that. Is that all?" she prodded.

His rich brown eyes searched hers. His weathered face took on an air of distress. "My dear, that's the part that worries me." He swallowed and started rocking slowly. "It's not a price per se, more of a stipulation but... you must—"

The hot water hissed and squealed, Layala jumped a little. How did it come to a boil so quickly?

"Tea is ready." Thane poured three small white teacups full. Steam rose up from each bringing with it the smell of lemon citrus. "What Vesstan was about to say is we must be wed under a full moon, which is a little less than eight weeks away. It happens to coincide with our deadline, well, a day earlier."

Vesstan's gaze held Thane's for a moment. Layala found something odd about the exchange, but then he nodded in agreement. "Yes, that's what worries me. Waiting until the day before you turn into a pale one is frightening. If something should go wrong..." He gave Thane a stern look. "He waited too long to find you."

A full moon rose the previous night, which meant they missed that opportunity. "Isn't there anything else we can do? A counter-spell or an object or something?"

Thane handed him a cup of the steaming liquid, and the mage shook his head. "Not to my knowledge." Layala accepted hers but didn't drink just yet. He took a sip of tea. "Very good, sire, thank you." He stared off for a moment. "Although there may be something."

Layala's heart thudded loudly. *I knew it*, she thought. Thane swore as his teacup and plate clanked as he nearly dropped them.

"Are you alright?" Vesstan asked.

"I'm fine." He shook his hand. Layala suspected it spilled over and burned his fingers. "It's just," he paused with a sharp look at Vesstan, "when I asked you some years ago you said there was absolutely no way out of it and when I asked you six months ago you said the same thing."

"Well," he took another sip, likely buying some time, "*I* don't know of a way, and what I'm thinking is probably not worth looking into but there is a Drakonan sorceress who worked with the Black Mage. It's rumored she is still alive, living in the Sederac Mountains. If anyone knows, it's her. I fear we are in desperate times now."

She wasn't sure what he meant by desperate times. Did he want them apart? "A dragon shifter sorceress?" Layala asked.

Thane stiffened. "We don't go into dragon territory. And if this shifter worked with the Black Mage, she'd try to kill us before she would help us."

Knowing Thane was correct, Layala inhaled the sweet scent of citrus, hoping it would uplift her mood. "I want to go." Both Thane and Vesstan stared at her.

"You'd rather die than marry Thane?" Vesstan asked. "Because that is the risk you're taking and there is no guarantee she would have an answer or would be willing to give one if she did."

Of course, she wouldn't rather die, but she could get answers. A part of her training was inflicting pain to get people to talk. Layala set the cup on the plate in her hand. "It's worth risking at the very least. I need to know. I want to go home." If she didn't at least try, she'd be angry with herself forever. She couldn't be tied to this king without exhausting every option. She couldn't be connected to the family that murdered her parents and killed in her name. She heard the stories from drifters who came into Briar Hollow, telling how entire towns were burned. Children ripped from their mother's arms to be thrown into a prison cart while their parents were cut down, and everyone knew Thane was one of the king's best warriors. It didn't matter how cordial he was now. Anyone could pretend to be a certain way for a short period of time.

"This is worse than I thought," Vesstan mumbled. He sat up a little straighter and smiled at Layala. "Will you go out to the well and get an old man some cool water, please?"

"Of course." She stood and set her cup on the kitchen island. Even if he just wanted to get rid of her so he could speak to Thane alone, he had that right. "Is there a particular glass?"

"In the cupboard, any will do."

She grabbed the first one she saw, a simple jar with a handle and headed for the door.

"It's just around the back of the house," he said with a wave of his hand.

She stepped out into the temperate air, the sun warming the skin of her face. For a moment she closed her eyes, and basked in its glory. If she was to go to the Sederac Mountains, she'd be exposed to frigid temperatures and would miss this warmth that filled her with an energy only the sun could. After walking around the cottage, she spotted the well and followed the stone path to it. Lowering the bucket, it dipped into the water, and she tugged the rope hand over hand pulling it up until it reached the top. She took the bucket in her hands and a drink from it. The water tasted almost sweet and more refreshing than any she'd ever had before. In moments she felt lighter, happier. With another gulp, she smiled, and a tingle went through her body. She felt like she could run for days and not tire. No wonder the stuff kept the old elf alive.

Sitting on the edge of the brick well, she watched butterflies and pixies and birds of all kinds flutter around the clearing. When she felt she'd given them enough time to talk, she headed back, but she paused outside the door, listening.

"This is not something to trifle with," Vesstan said. "You waited too long. Now I fear you have no other choice but to find a way. And perhaps you should tell her the truth."

What is he keeping from me?

"There is always a choice. I'm not giving up." His

footsteps padded across the floor. "And to see this dragon shifter? Bringing her straight to the enemy's hands isn't only a ridiculous idea. It's not an option. Period."

"Better to have a backup plan than to be a pale one. Besides you have skills I think should be made known now that you are king and have found your mate. You could handle this dragon sorceress."

What skills did he hide? And why did they need a backup plan? They honestly thought she'd still refuse to marry him if she couldn't find a way. That was the one thing that could force her into marriage with Thane. She'd be his wife before she was a pale one.

"And you're sure your father is dead?"

"He must be," Thane said.

"But did you see it? See him die with your own eyes?"

Silence. Layala leaned in a little closer and the wood creaked beneath her feet. She swore, *no sense in lingering now,* and pushed the door open.

"Ah, there she is." Vesstan pushed himself up and stood. "Did you have any trouble?"

"No trouble." She handed him the glass then looked to Thane. "So, there's a chance your father is alive."

Chapter 16

Thane didn't know how much she heard, but if that was her biggest question, she didn't hear anything important. He stuck his hands in his pockets and shrugged. "If there is a chance it's so minuscule it doesn't even need to be thought of. If he was alive, he'd have shown up by now."

"Pearl and Reina said he died in battle."

"And that's all anyone will ever know."

"But that's not the truth?"

Thane didn't want anyone else to know the truth of what happened to Tenebris. It was dangerous information. There were only three people who knew: Fennan, Thane and now, Vesstan, and that was more than there should be. Fennan only knew because he was there.

He leaned a shoulder against the wall and folded his arms. "It doesn't matter how, as long as he's gone." Clearing his throat, Vesstan gave him a subtle nod. The old mage wanted him to tell her, as if it would help anything. "Are you ready to leave? You got your information."

"You're glad he's gone." She stated, staring at him in a way that made his insides squirm. "Why won't you tell me how he died?"

"I don't trust you."

"And the truth requires you to trust me?"

"Yes."

She tore her gaze away from him and offered a half smile to Vesstan. "Thank you for speaking with me and for the tea."

She turned on her heel and started for the door. Thane pushed off the wall and nodded to Vesstan. "It was good seeing you. I'll try to make it out here again soon to check on you."

"Oh, don't worry about me. You have enough on your plate." He held up a hand as if he wanted to catch Layala's attention, but she had her back to them. "Layala, for what it's worth, I am sorry for everything that happened. Your father and mother loved you very much. I hope you know that."

She whipped around, with a glare so cold it chilled Thane's bones. He felt a wave of power, the same as the night she tried to stab him. Like a gentle wind at first, tickling his skin and then it was filling the room, bearing down on him as if someone clamped every inch of his body. A wild living thing. His body tensed; she refused to use her magic before, even when being chased by pale ones, and she chose now to unleash it?

"Don't speak of my parents when you did nothing

to stop them from being murdered. I wouldn't be surprised if you helped."

Vesstan stepped back at the venom in her voice, the power he no doubt felt weighing on him. "I didn't hurt them. I wish I could have saved them. I think about that day sometimes and wished I would have argued harder against it. Your parents were good people."

That pressure lifted, but only slightly. Thane didn't know if she was doing it on purpose or not. The wrath he felt coming from her through their connection would say so, but she almost seemed afraid of her magic before. Perhaps it was an act.

She shoved a finger at them. "Maybe you should have refused to do the spell in the first place. What sort of mage would bind children when there was even a chance we could be turned into pale ones."

"At the time, I didn't know the consequences," he stammered. "I—If I could take it back, I would."

Thane took a step forward, sending a gentle push of calm toward her. He'd done it before through the magic binding them. "Vesstan was following orders from my father. He is not at fault," Thane said gently. Vesstan was there for Thane and always treated him and others with kindness. He was a guide his entire life, the father Thane should have had. He didn't deserve ridicule.

"Following orders is not an excuse for the atrocities committed. You had a choice." She didn't stay long enough for further arguments. She might never let go of the crimes his father Tenebris enacted. She wanted someone to blame, and Thane was the easy target. And he understood how she felt and why. He hoped one day she could see past the pain and anger.

The door slammed hard on her way out. The pressure sucked out of the room like a deep breath and Thane calmed his own magic he held ready to use to shield against her. Mage Vesstan trained him, but it wasn't common knowledge that he was a mage. His friends and family knew, and some guards and servants, but they kept it quiet. He used it sometimes but usually no one noticed. He didn't want the attention it brought. He watched what Mage Vesstan went through. People constantly begged him to help them, even when he couldn't.

His father didn't want anyone to know. When he was young, Thane believed it was kept secret because the pale ones might come for him too, the way they wanted Layala, but when he was a teen, he realized that wasn't the true reason. His father was jealous and didn't want anyone to know his son was magical when he was not. He also discovered Tenebris mated Layala and Thane to not only keep Layala around, but it was a backup plan. A possible way to get himself magic should his other plan fail. Vesstan wasn't capable.

Vesstan shuddered. "I said it the day of her testing and I'll say it again. I've never felt power like that. There is something dark about it. Something unruly. Yours is certainly comparable in strength, but the sign on her day was concerning."

"Do you think they're right?" Thane's throat was dry, his voice coming out strained.

"Mathekis and the pale ones?" Vesstan slowly shook his head. "If they can use her to bring back the Black Mage, he must have left some sort of safeguard, a way to return. Why it's her they can use, and not you or I, is a mystery to me."

Thane encountered Mathekis several times on the battlefield. They'd never faced off one on one, but the leader, the second to the Black Mage, was cunning and intelligent. Unlike many of the others, who seemed like mindless beasts only searching to hunt and kill, Mathekis was strategic. He gave orders like a general and was obeyed as such and even after hundreds of years he held onto a fraction of his magical power. Thane met with him once when both sides were at a standstill, and the killing and bloodshed too much.

Mathekis told him during that meeting that if Thane could only give him Layala, they would leave Palenor alone. They wouldn't attack again. Thane didn't believe it and wouldn't have given her over even if he did. "Why do you want her?" he asked.

"My master wants her."

"Your master is dead."

"His body may be gone but his essence lives."

That sent a chill through Thane. "You will never have Layala."

"We will. It is only a matter of time."

He shook his head, clearing the memory. "She said they are drawn to her when she uses her magic."

Lifting a shaky hand, he reached toward his staff in the corner, and it flew to his hand. He leaned against it. "That is troubling. All the more reason you must never let them have her. You've done well, sacrificed much to make sure she wasn't found. But with her bitterness like that, I truly think you might consider going to find that sorceress. I don't know if you'll be able to fulfill the obligations of the mate spell ever, let alone by the twenty-fifth year coming up so soon. She hates you."

He knew that all too well. Thane finally tore his eyes from the door. "I'll have to weigh the risks. It would take us weeks to get there."

"Not if you convince the portal to deliver you."

Tapping a boot on the floor, Thane narrowed his eyes at Vesstan. "You've kept secrets from me."

"You never asked. And you've never needed to go to the Sederac Mountains."

"Will the portal take me anywhere I need to go?"

He lifted his shoulders briefly. "If a returning portal has been set up at the location. There is a possibility it could spit you out anywhere and then you'd have to return home the long way. I've never tried it, however."

"And how would I even find this dragon sorceress? The Sederac Mountains are vast."

"That you'll have to figure out on your own." His staff tapped on the floor as he hobbled to his rocking chair. Once seated, he placed the smooth, wood cane across his lap and rocked. "I'm sorry you've had this burden, Thane. Layala is right. I should have never done the spell, even if your father would have killed me for denying him."

When Thane stepped outside, he was relieved to find Layala standing in between the two horses, feeding them out of her palms. That power she pressed upon them was gone. The anger she felt before disappeared with it. He sensed she was still a little upset but either his calming settled her, or she let it pass on her own. "Shall I be expecting any pale ones?" he asked as he approached.

She brushed her hands together. "Why would you be?"

"After what you did inside."

She rolled her eyes and attempted to grab hold of the saddle horn. Thane smiled at her struggle. Some small part of him enjoyed that she needed his help to mount the horse.

"If I'd used my magic, believe me, you'd know. I didn't."

He moved closer, holding out his hands for her to use as a step. "It felt like you wanted to crush me."

She stilled and slowly turned her head, her eyes meeting his. "I didn't use my magic." She put her foot in his waiting hand and he lifted her.

"But you didn't have it hidden. You weren't actively forcing it down, willing it to the deepest part of you."

She adjusted herself in the saddle and blinked several times before saying, "How could you know that?"

If he was going to get her to trust him, get her to care, he had to allow her to know things about himself for her to do the same. She was guarded and with good reason. He didn't want to give up on her, on what they could be. If there was any part of her that could care for him, he must try, even if it was about as impossible as breaking their bond. "Because I keep my power tucked away, too."

Chapter 17

Layala stilled in surprise. "How is that possible? It would have shown at your testing day." And she wouldn't be the only mage so many sought after. She wouldn't have shrines in her name or be expected to destroy the Void because she wouldn't be the single born magic child in hundreds of years. And yet when she thought about it, she did suspect he possessed some sort of power. He seemed to heal quicker than most. There wasn't even a blemish on his face the day after she drew blood with her nails. She assumed it was healing flora but nothing she knew of completely healed wounds overnight without leaving a trace.

"True, it would have," Thane said, nudging Phantom into a walk on the path leading into the thick woods. "Except my father knew I was a mage before my testing day, suspected anyway. He forced Vesstan to test me before the official presentation. When it came to showing me to the kingdom, he placed another child on the altar while I slept in the castle nursery."

"So, I'm not even the last mage as so many say. Why keep it a secret? And why did he want me if you have what he wanted?" Thane was quiet, as if debating on telling her or not. Layala nudged Midnight closer. "I won't say anything to anyone."

"I keep it quiet because I don't want the attention it brings. And for my father's part, I asked myself why he wanted you when he had Mage Vesstan at his disposal, as well as me." His eyes flicked among the canopy of trees then landed on her. "But then I realized it wasn't simply someone with magic he wanted. I spied on him one night when he talked into a crystal ball. He and Mathekis think you are the key to bringing back the Black Mage because of the sign on your testing day and the lily's mark on your arm. Tenebris planned to give you to Mathekis, the dark general, and in return my father would be granted the gift of magic when the Black Mage rose."

Her head began to pound, a low dull ache. She knew the pale ones were after her, drawn to her, but never knew why. It made sense now. Her birthmark took the shape of vines with lilies. She always knew there was something wrong with her magic and that confirmed it. Sweat prickled all over her body, a sheen that wracked her with a shiver. It was suddenly hard to fill her lungs. If only she could bring back the Black Mage, *she* was evil and all this time she thought it was Thane. No, it was her. She *killed* Novak. She got her parents murdered. She did that...

Chest tightening, she clutched at it. White spots erupted in her vision; she was too hot, too cold, the world spun.

"What's wrong?"

His voice sounded far away, as if she was underwater. She looked at him through blurred vision, and thought she was going to be sick. She felt herself sliding from the saddle but couldn't get a grip before she slipped into complete darkness.

Light trickled in, as if she lay at the bottom of a well so deep the sun could barely reach her. "Layala, wake up," a deep voice commanded. "Layala. Layala." His muffled voice became clearer every time he said her name. "Layala, please wake up."

She peeled her eyes open to see the forest of so many wonderful colors. The brightness hurt for a moment, but her vision adjusted. Regaining control of her body, she turned her head to look into Thane's frustratingly glorious face. She realized with sudden acuteness he knelt on the ground, and she was cradled in his arms.

"Hi," he said softly.

It took great effort to lift her arm, but she placed her hand over her forehead. It still ached. "Hi," she said back.

"What happened?"

"I don't know. I guess I fainted."

"Have you ever done that before?" He still held her like she was something precious and rare.

"No." She struggled to sit up until Thane pushed her. "I don't know what came over me." A lie. She knew exactly what: panic, sheer panic, anguish, and the truth.

"Are you sure? I thought I felt you panicking." He took her by the hand and guided her to her feet.

"Felt me panic?" She said each word slowly. "What are you talking about?"

He pursed his lips and reached for her, pulling a leaf out of her hair. After he tossed it aside, he rubbed the back of his neck. "Can you not feel it?"

"Feel what?" she demanded.

"The magical bond between us allows me to feel your emotions sometimes. If it's strong enough." He watched her carefully as if he was afraid she might pass out again. "Sometimes I see what you see, hear what you hear. You don't?"

"No," she snapped. "I-" she slammed her mouth shut. *Maker above, I have.* So many times, and all the while she thought it was a side effect of her magic or that she was delusional. The voices, holy Maker, this was why she thought Piper, Sunshine, Fennan and Thane felt familiar, *sounded* familiar. The flash of the field of wildflowers the night he showed up at the Smoky Dragon. She knew that field because she saw through his eyes the night when he was on his way to get her.

"That's how you knew where I was. You could... sense me."

"Yes."

"And you never told *him*. You never told your father." Even when Tenebris threatened him. Even when he beat him as a boy. He kept silent to protect her. He held her gaze as he slowly shook his head. "I don't know what to say other than... Thank you."

Riding in silence, Layala stared at the back of the horse's head, her vision going in and out of focus. Going to the Sederac Mountains where dragons nested and hunted would be dangerous. They had a taste for elf or so she heard. Swords and regular arrows would be useless against them. She would no doubt be forced to use her magic which made her stomach turn. But something shifted in the atmosphere, stealing her thoughts away. Birds quieted and she sensed they were being watched. Midnight's ears twitched, moving back and forth.

Thane already drew one of his swords from the scabbard on his back, resting it across his lap. "We're being followed," he whispered.

Was it another vulture or something worse?

Her only reaction was to let her eyes scan the area. She didn't want to give away their awareness. Would it be pale ones? When the portal stole her magic did it send out a pulse? The colorful trees stilled, as if even the very wind hid. The massive trunks could easily conceal several assailants. The quiet groan of a bowstring being pulled back flared her magic. The power humming in her blood tingled all over her body. As far as Layala knew, pale ones didn't use bows and arrows which meant—

"We are within our rights to execute trespassers." Three light-haired elves stepped out from the trees, blocking their path.

Her stomach flipped and she pulled back on Midnight. Turning, Layala found three more behind them, all with arrows knocked back and ready to release. They wore various shades of greens and browns, matching the surrounding environment. The attire was more practical with no fancy designs, but she did note their necklaces made of bones intermixed with raw cut colorful stones. Their brown cloth boots reached above the knee, a style she wasn't accustomed to.

Midnight either felt Layala's tension or that of the elves around them; he shifted about and knickered loudly. Layala held the reins tight. She didn't want him to run lest she be shot in the back. Thane lifted his hands in a show of surrender. "We came to see a friend. We mean no harm. If you'll let us go—"

"Let you go?" the center elf questioned with a sneer. "You either die here or come with us."

"I'm afraid we can't go with you. Dinner plans, you see," Thane said. He was so calm Layala could hardly believe it. Her heart beat so fast and loud she had difficulty hearing anything else. She kept looking back at the group behind her making sure they didn't make any sudden moves. A simple slip and the arrows would fly. Wrapping her hand around the pommel of the dagger Thane gave her, she readied herself to throw it and take out the leader.

"Get off the horses," the leader commanded with his arrow pointed at Thane's chest.

"We're not your enemy." Thane lowered his hands.

Did lowering his hands mean he wanted to fight? Her arms tingled, and she loosened the damper on her power, letting it trickle through her blood. Maybe that alone would be enough to scare them off. They looked at each other confused and took a couple steps back.

"Who are you?" The male to the left's voice beheld a slight tremble but none of them lowered their weapons.

"Someone you don't want to anger further," Layala said and squeezed the reins as hard as she could, fighting the magic to stay inside. It never liked when she was threatened.

"I ask that you allow us to leave before things become bloody," Thane said, calmly.

The leader's eye twitched and as if in slow motion,

she watched his fingers loose the arrow. The twinge seemed to echo in the forest. The arrow headed right for Thane's heart. Layala threw up her hands and unleashed her magic's hold. Thick black vines ripped free of the dirt, growing at rapid speed. The roar of them snapping through tree roots and bark and solid ground. A thorny vine blasted up in front of Thane taking the arrow's hit that could have killed him. More arrows released. Layala grew more wild vines, but an arrowhead grazed her arm. She hissed from the sting.

Thane sprang from the horse and drove his sword straight through the chest of the leader. Blood gurgled out of his mouth. Layala gasped at the suddenness of Thane's action. When he turned and slashed his sword at another elf, a head hit the ground moments later. The eyes stared at her accusatory as she froze in horror, as if she'd been the one to do it. She fought down rising nausea when blood pooled at the base of the severed neck. She couldn't believe how much. She killed pale ones, but their blood was black; the crimson staining the forest floor now was like her own.

She jerked around to the sound of the elves behind them reloading their weapons. One raised his arrow and met her gaze. The arrow flew straight for her chest —it dissolved into dust inches before it struck her. The debris carried away in the wind. Layala blinked several times and the elf who shot at her looked just as confused as her.

"That was your *last* mistake," Thane said and

marched toward the elf with an unnerving calmness. Layala directed her magical barbed vines to twist around the remaining enemies like boa constrictors, growing thicker and taller until the stalks were nearly a solid wall. She kept the three woodland elves' faces free, but their bodies were completely immobilized, wrapped entirely in the vines. Midnight purple lilies bloomed, beautiful but deadly if she allowed them to spray their poison.

"I warned you." Her voice was low and venomous.

When she glanced at Thane, he was smiling. *Smiling*. He killed three elves and watched her wild magic explode and yet he smiled. She thought he'd be terrified, and recoil away from her like she had a plague. And yet he appeared to enjoy it.

"You're *her*," one of them said.

Thane swaggered up to the male who'd spoken. "I bet you're wishing you would have listened to the lady." He glanced back at Layala. "Should we kill them, too?" He pulled a knife from his belt and slowly drug it down the side of the male's face.

His eyes went wide; blood seeped up and dripped, plopping loudly on the ground below.

"No, please," they started to beg simultaneously. "No."

They were trapped and defenseless now, but they'd tried to kill her and the High King of Palenor. Could they honestly let them go?

"Please, your highness, let us live," he said in a shaky voice

"Ah, so you *did* recognize me, yet, you still tried to kill me? And that means you must know who she is." Thane rested the blade against the elf's cheek; the pressure caused a light indentation in his skin. Blood poured even faster.

"I didn't at the time; we didn't," his voice wavered. "I—I see it now. I sincerely apologize, High King. I beg your forgiveness."

"And you expect I, the High King of Palenor, should be merciful? You injured my mate. You specifically. You tried to kill her."

Layala glanced down at her arm. The wound was superficial, but a couple inches over and she might be dead.

The elf's chin trembled but he didn't speak. Wetness pooled at his feet, seeping out from under the black vines. The few moments of silence were like watching dark storm clouds waiting for lightning to strike.

"Please, most High King, mercy." A glint of metal beamed between the two of them; the elf begging for his life held a weapon and somehow he got his arm free.

"Thane, he has a knife!"

Thane shoved his blade through the base of the elf's throat. The elf's dagger clanked to the ground. The elf let out a dying groan, his eyes wide. When Thane turned toward the other two, they started to beg for their lives as well. This was the exact reason he earned the reputation of brutality, and yet, she wasn't upset. Shocked at the suddenness of it but not angry. That elf did try to kill her, would have killed him. Her heart still pounded from the attack.

"If anyone touches her in any way, death will come swiftly. And I am the reaper." Thane wiped the blood on the collar of one woodland elf, and tucked the knife in his belt. He took a step back, looking at the piss collecting near his boots then climbed up onto Phantom. "If you get out of your trap, take the message back to your Lord Brunard." After his gaze fell to her injury, he said, "Let's go," then nudged his horse into a trot.

Layala looked at each of the living elves before she followed. If they had luck, the pale ones wouldn't come and finish them off before they could escape.

Chapter 18

They rode hard until they reached the portal. Thane hopped down, placing his hand against the stone circle. It didn't ask her to touch it this time or demand her magic. When it activated and swirled, he held out his hand to her. She took hold and they hurried through the portal and came out in Palenor. Layala felt a wave of relief to be back in high elf territory.

Thane turned to Layala, grinning like a schoolboy. "That's what you've kept hidden? It's absolutely marvelous. I understand your fascination with plants now. The vines are spectacular. The way they wrapped around those elves, and tore out of the ground—incredible. You saved my life."

Trying to understand his reaction, Layala fidgeted with the reins. He was so used to killing that he could be excited in this moment? Her magic came in handy, but she still wished she didn't have it. "And you saved mine—that arrow dissolving—that was you."

"Yes."

Layala lightly chewed on the inside of her cheek. "My magic might be incredible if it didn't bring the pale ones to me. If I wasn't hunted because of it."

He mounted Phantom once again. "You could easily take out a countless number with power like that."

Her eyes found the forest and the gnarling and twisting trees all around them. The wood here was such a stark difference from the serenity of Calladira. Something about it put her on edge, but she couldn't quite say why with no immediate threats. This place was spooky with the near-black bark and trees so thick they nearly blocked out the sunlight. She focused on the squirrels and other small furry creatures peeking down at them, anywhere but Thane.

She was afraid of what she was, of what her power meant. She never could embrace it. It was the reason so many she loved were dead. She hated it although, somewhere deep down, she loved it. Delighted in what it felt like to unleash that power and control and let it rip through the ground and coil around those helpless elves. She stopped their arrows with barely a thought. And that's the part of her she was afraid of. What if she was like the Black Mage.

Her gaze lifted to Thane now. He promised death to anyone who *touched* her. And she didn't know how to feel about that.

"They'll tell their Lord Brunard what happened and I expect he'll be pissed as hellfire. I've fought against the woodland elves on a few occasions and none of the battles were pretty. I'm sorry you had to see that." He reached down and stroked Phantom's smooth black coat.

"Why didn't you just kill them so they couldn't tell?" Strategically, it's what she would have done if she were High King, although she might very well see that detached head staring at her in her nightmares for a long time. She was sorry those elves had to die, but they brought their fate upon themselves.

He raised an eyebrow. "You're more ruthless than I thought."

Her cheeks warmed. "If they couldn't tell then you could have a chance of peace with them. Now you won't."

"The message they'll take back is more important than peace."

Layala sucked in her bottom lip. That death would come swiftly to anyone who touched her. "When did you fight them before? Was it because your father wanted to find me?"

"There were three times I fought against Calladira and all occasions were over land. Twice they started it, and once our side did, but I finished all three."

She sat in silence, wondering if he was to be believed.

"The only killings I've committed in your name were against pale ones. I didn't ride with Tenebris. I didn't even know what he was doing for a long time. I have my own battalion; the Ravens." He glanced at the portal. "We should go. It will be dark soon." He kicked Phantom into a gallop without looking back.

When they returned to the castle, he left her at the door to the Starlight room and went inside his own chambers. She assumed he was changing for dinner since a moment later Reina and Pearl showed up seemingly out of nowhere. Pushing her way inside the room, she took off her boots and fell back on the bed. Her backside was sore after riding all day. Using her magic seemed to make her ravenously hungry. That or because she hadn't eaten but a few bites at breakfast and it was now dark.

"Will you bring my meal to me? I'm tired and I'm not up for dinner with Orlandia or Talon." She was exhausted, but mostly she didn't want to have to talk to anyone. She mulled over what Thane said for over an hour: he never killed in her name, well except a few hours ago. He didn't ride with his father. Only fought Calladira over land. He never told his father where she was even though he knew. Even as a young one, he took a beating rather than give her away. It couldn't be a lie; Tenebris would have come for her.

Aunt Evalyn pounded into her head that the Athayels were monsters, Thane included. Now Layala found it difficult to believe that about Thane when the truth seemed to be staring her in the face. He killed that elf for his attempt to end her. And even when she punched him in the jaw—*stabbed* him, he didn't hurt her or lock her up. After admitting she planned to poison him and his friends, he didn't speak of it. He treated her with respect when she came here expecting to be subject to torture if she didn't get away first.

"I don't wish to speak ill of her majesty, but she is somewhat difficult. It's understandable," Pearl said, then the maids exchanged a glance and Pearl nodded. "I'll go get you something."

"Can I help you bathe or get you a change of clothes?" Reina asked after the door closed quietly behind Pearl.

Layala let herself relax, sinking further into the bed and closed her eyes. "I'll be fine for now. I just want to lay here a while."

She didn't realize she dozed off until she heard the tray being carted in. Pearl left it at her bedside and was gone before Layala even sat up.

Thane didn't request her at dinner or visit her that night. The next morning, she went to knock on his door, but the guard said he was gone already. She expected to talk about how and when they'd leave for the Sederac Mountains to find the dragon sorceress, if he planned on going. As the day dragged on and she didn't see or hear of him, she wondered if he was avoiding her.

She wandered the castle with Piper in tow, always several paces behind. Layala peeked inside grand ballrooms with high ceilings and ornate fixtures of silver and gold. Large windows showed off the view of the castle grounds which were vast with orchards of blossoming trees, and statues of warriors and maidens and creatures. Beautiful stone fountains, and ponds with swans gliding over the water.

After meandering the halls, looking at paintings and other works of art, and saying hello to servants and guards, peeking into rooms to see if Thane was inside, she gave up. Night came and still no word from him or about him. Where could he be? She paced by the fireplace, touching edges, wondering how the thing opened—just in case she needed to use it of course, not because she wanted to go see him...

Layala rubbed her face; they get attacked in the woods and then he disappears? No one would tell her where he was or if anything was wrong. Nothing the next morning, either. "He's busy," was the only response.

So Layala started collecting food, hiding it from the maids so they wouldn't report it, and made plans to leave to find the sorceress on her own. Tif helped. She was good at smuggling things, even if she was too small to carry much at once.

Thane might very well avoid her until the time was up and she wasn't going to stick around like a fool hoping he wanted to break the bond too. Over a few days, she stole a map from the library when Piper's back was turned, found a leather bag in her closet, and filled it with a set of warm clothes, gloves, an extra pair of boots, and a coat Tif dragged in for the cold in the mountains. Tif also brought packets of tea for energy and warmth. But she needed at least another couple of days to collect more food without drawing suspicion. Thane said she wasn't a prisoner, but she wasn't allowed anywhere alone, for the safety of others more than her own, she suspected. He didn't trust her not to hurt anyone.

That evening, there were more servants than usual in the castle. Several of them hurried about moving furniture, changing decor, and more food whisked around on trays than ever before as if they readied for an event of some kind. If that mad queen was prepping for the wedding, Layala would put a stop to it.

"What's going on?" Layala turned around and asked Piper. Their relationship didn't change over the past few days. Piper didn't spare words and Layala didn't have much interest in speaking with her either, but she was getting bored and even Red might be worth conversation.

"It's the Summer Solstice celebration tomorrow."

The longest day of the year where the elves celebrated the sun and symbolized it as a triumph of light over dark. They recognized it as a sacred day and made offerings to help them in their fight against the pale ones and the Void. Even though Aunt Evalyn wasn't an elf, she still taught Layala all their traditions. In Briar Hollow, the town recognized the day but didn't celebrate. It was only seen as a day they could work longer or stay out to have fun later before dark.

"Will there be a party?" she asked.

"We call it a festival, but yes."

Layala found a window that overlooked the back grounds. Servants set up tables and decor outside.

Strings of flowers and lights bobbed in the air and on the pond water. As much as she wanted to leave for the mountains, she didn't think she could miss this. It would be her first elven festival. The first time celebrating anything with her own people.

There were also gatherings of large groups, who couldn't be servants. Mostly males but females too, in fine dresses.

"Is Thane going to be there?"

"He wouldn't miss the most important day of the year," Piper answered as if it annoyed her to speak.

"Where is he now?"

Piper walked up beside her and peered out the window. "He had some business to attend to."

The guard finally broke her silence. Layala smiled. "What kind of business?"

"The fighting in the south kind." Piper let out a long breath. "It never ends. And on our celebration day the pale ones always attack with more force. They know it's a day we cherish and want to ruin it. So, the High King had to make certain our forces were ready."

A rogue thought crept in: *I should be there fighting. I should be there for my people...* Another side of her argued back, *but they're not your people. Aunt Evalyn, Ren, Forrest, and Briar Hollow are your people.* She wondered if that's what her mother would have wanted. She touched the willow necklace gently. Her mother's last words: *someday she will have to fight too,* stuck with her. Evalyn said she meant to fight the High King and his hunger for power, but what if her mother simply intended for her to fight evil. And yet if the Black Mage returned because of her, it could be the end of freedom and life, not just in Palenor but for the whole continent of Adalon. The Void only grew further when the Black Mage was alive, infecting good land with its sickness. Infecting people. It could spread everywhere if he was allowed to return.

When Piper carried on further, Layala was a little surprised. "I know what Tenebris did to your parents, and I feel for you, I do. He was an unjust, terrible king. But I know the consequence hanging over yours and Thane's heads. Being a pale one would be much worse than being married to him. You have to see that. You can have a life of luxury, if you'll accept Thane with it. I know you don't care for him, but you have to marry him for yourself at least."

Layala ran her fingers over her scalp and slowly nodded. "If it comes to it, I will. We have to wait for the full moon anyway, so I have time."

Piper narrowed her eyes. "Full moon?"

"Thane said part of the stipulation of the mate bond spell was that we had to be wed under a full moon." She shrugged. "Perhaps the magic requires the strength of it. I don't know rune magic." It crossed her mind to tell her about the dragon sorceress in the mountains, but she thought better of it. The less anyone knew the better. She was going to have to slip Piper's watchful eye too if she couldn't convince Thane to go. At the end of the festival when everyone was distracted would be a good time.

Rubbing her arm absently, Piper shifted staring at the ground momentarily as if lost in thought. "We should get you back to your room so you can be ready for dinner, and if Thane allows it, the games tonight."

"Games?" Layala wondered about Piper's sudden change in demeanor but followed her without asking.

"Yes, the night before the Summer Solstice we have challenges and games with elves from all over Palenor."

"That sounds fun."

After bathing, Pearl combed through Layala's long hair while Reina rifled through the closet. Tif still wasn't brave enough to come out in the open with the other "jumbos" around, even though Layala said she'd protect her. She built a little nook among the vines above the bed that she hid in when they came. "We need to find you the perfect gown for the Summer Festival tomorrow. I'm thinking something burnt orange in color, thin straps, flowy. The queen and princess usually wear yellow, and we want you to stand apart from them."

Yes we do, Layala thought. "Will they be at dinner this evening?"

"I believe so," Pearl answered. "And the princess

wanted to meet with you. She wants to get to know you a little better."

"Joy," she mumbled.

"Princess Talon is nice once you get to know her," Reina yelled from the closet.

Continuing with her hair, Pearl rubbed in some lavender-scented oils to the ends and tied her hair high on her head into a loose bun. She added a dusty rose-colored lip balm to Layala's lips but otherwise left her natural. Reina helped her into a rich purple floor-length dress for the games tonight with a jeweled waist belt.

"You're stunning," Reina said, holding a hand to her chest.

Layala smiled genuinely. "Thank you, Reina."

Pearl gathered a handful of dirty sheets. "We'll leave you be. I'm sure someone will be up in an hour to fetch you."

An hour? She was growing bored of sitting in her room waiting for others. The two maids left. Layala sat on the bed for a moment then glanced at the servants' passage entrance. It wouldn't hurt to go exploring by herself. There were still many places she hadn't seen, but the dominant part of her wanted to find Thane.

Pulling open the shelf against the wall, it easily moved, and she slipped inside. A cold breeze swept through from a crack somewhere in the walls. She quietly walked past entrances to rooms, hoping she wouldn't run into any servants. Most rooms were silent and seemingly unoccupied. She paused at one when she picked up on deep voices, but she didn't recognize them, and they weren't saying anything interesting. When she went down a set of stairs onto the main floor, she stopped at a notable door with gold painted trim. Curious as to where it would lead, she slowly pushed the sliding door aside and peeked her head out. Blue tapestries hung directly ahead blocking the view of the room.

"It isn't wise to come into my kingdom, in my castle, and accuse me of anything." That was Thane's voice. Deep, resonant, and commanding. He somehow sounded bored and yet at the same time like he might order the execution of whoever he spoke to.

Interest piqued, she slipped out of the passage and taking in slow deep breaths, she grabbed the edge of the velvet tapestry and risked a glance. The hall was absolutely massive. Up above white stone archways loomed. Sunlight cascaded in from the colossal windows on either side of the red carpet running down the center. Two wide doors with hand-carved designs in the mahogany were shut. A stone altar was placed before the long steps up to the throne, where the children must be tested for magic. Where she was once tested. Her eyes searched the steps for stains of blood on the light gray stone. Her parents' lives were cut short in this very room; dejection welled up in her imagining their last moments and how scared they must have been.

Finally, her gaze landed on Thane, sitting on the very throne his father ordered her parents executed...

or was it? It wasn't white like the paintings depicted. It was solid shiny black stone. Large enough to seat two people but he somehow dominated it. Casually sitting with his legs spread, leaning on his elbow on the armrest. *Arrogant swine,* she thought and smiled reluctantly.

He stared down at three elves dressed in the same style they wore in Calladira: the green and brown garb. The knee-high cloth boots. She shifted nervously. No one stood guard in this room. Thane, the High King, was alone with three potential enemies.

"Witnesses put you and your betrothed in Calladira where you murdered four of ours. She used magic on our patrol, seriously injuring one of them that survived," the center elf said. "It isn't an accusation. It's a warning to stay out of our land. The Athayels are not welcome there. And our lord no longer wishes to meet with you."

Layala tensed at the woodland elf's tone with Thane, a harsh one that wouldn't be taken well. What would he do now?

"Is that all?"

Another smile tugged at her lips. This completely unphased him, as if he'd expected it. Although, she couldn't help but feel this rift was partially her fault.

The three woodland elves glanced between one another. The middle elf again cleared his throat, but stammered now, "If-if you or your betrothed—"

"If we what?" He sat a little taller and curled the fingers on his right hand. The elf clutched at his throat, suddenly gasping. His mouth hung open and his skin grew redder with each passing second. Was Thane choking him somehow?

"Your highness, please," the elf on the right begged. "You're killing him."

"If we what?" he asked again. "I couldn't quite hear you."

The elf choked and wheezed, trying to pull in a breath. It was disturbing on so many levels but mostly because nothing touched him to cut off his airways. It wasn't as if Thane clamped a physical hand around his throat. He was several yards away.

"Your highness, I beg you to show restraint," the other elf said gently.

With a quick wave of Thane's hand, the choking elf sucked in a deep breath and dropped to his hands and knees. "Before any of you make threats you can't take back," he shoved to his feet, and the air seemed to draw out of the room replaced with a heaviness that weighed down the atmosphere. "You better remember who you're talking to. I will go wherever I please with whomever I please and there is nothing any of you can do to stop me. I guess my message wasn't clear enough before. Do tell your lord if he wishes to threaten my mate in any way, he will find me as a shadow at the foot of his bed. It will be the last thing he ever sees." The three elves stood there seemingly stunned. "Now, do you have anything else to say?"

His fierceness in protection of her made Layala's

heart beat faster. Before it may have scared her. Now —wrath looked good on him.

All three stood silent.

"I didn't think so. Get out."

Without hesitation, the three turned and although they walked, they may as well have run. The heavy mahogany doors flew open then slowly closed in their wake.

Thane's attention flicked to where Layala stood, and she ducked behind the tapestry. As she held her breath, she hoped he didn't see her spying. She felt dirty for eavesdropping even if she wasn't doing anything explicitly wrong. With slow steps, she quietly made her way toward the servants' passage.

A warm hand slid around her waist; she sucked in in surprise. She knew who it was before she saw him. Like she could feel his very essence. When he gripped her shoulder and spun her around to meet his intense eyes, Thane backed her into the wall. "It looks like I need to post a guard in the servants' entrance to keep a certain little spy in her room."

Chest rising and falling rapidly, Layala pushed his hand from her waist. The heat of his touch lingered much longer than it should have. "I wasn't spying, and I thought I wasn't a prisoner here. I'm to be locked in my room now?"

"I said you could go wherever you'd like *with* an escort."

"I won't hurt anyone. I promise."

Ignoring her comment he said, "If you weren't spying then why are you skulking in the shadows?"

"I wasn't *skulking*. You make it sound like I'm some creature from the swamp." He laughed and she went on. "I was looking for you. Where have you been? It's been four days and I haven't seen or heard from you."

His eyes flared for a moment. "I didn't think you'd miss me."

"I didn't."

"Sure, you didn't. I felt your longing to be with me. Especially at night."

She blushed. "You're getting your feelings confused with mine... And you killed those elves then just vanished on me, leaving me wondering what the hell was going on." She risked revealing her magic to him, and used it for the first time in years to defend him. He'd killed, potentially starting a skirmish with the woodland elves to protect her. In a way, they bonded in that moment. Their lives were literally tied in the other's and that thought made it impossible for her to not think of him and his safety. Things felt a little different now—less rigid, at least for her part although she didn't trust him fully. If he was avoiding her, it was because he didn't want to break this bond.

He smirked and inched back, gesturing to the great hall behind him. "And because of those dead elves, I've been busy. There's always some threat I must defend Palenor against. I thought you'd be glad I wasn't around to annoy you."

She pursed her lips. "Will they make a move against you?"

He lifted a shoulder. "I doubt it. Although they may, to test me as I am the new, young High King."

"But those emissaries were obviously scared of you."

"Their lord is also young. A rival of mine you could say. I killed his father in battle two years ago. He's been itching to get back at me."

"Yes, I heard. That you killed him anyway. I also heard you killed his two daughters."

Thane narrowed his eyes. "I never touched his daughters. I don't kill females. And as far as I know, they're both alive and well. There are many rumors about me as you well know, most are hardly true. I'd hoped you'd have seen that by now, or do you still believe I mark my flesh with my kills and sacrifice young maidens for Maker only knows why?"

How did he— "I never told you about that..."

"I have excellent hearing, my dearest."

Her cheeks flared with heat. She saw him shirtless on more than one occasion and knew for a fact his skin was flawless. Not a single scar. "I—no, I don't believe those things." She quietly cleared her throat, lifting her chin. "What will this Lord Brunard do? Is he scared of you?" She would be if she were his enemy. Her eyes flicked up to the top of his head. It was driving her crazy that his crown was slightly crooked on his dark locks.

"He has a healthy amount of fear but not overtly so. He is not weak in any sense of the word."

Unable to stop the urge, Layala reached up and adjusted the silver crown. He blinked a few times in surprise. "It was crooked," she said, tucking her hand behind her back. "Now, about the mountains—"

The doors to the hall crashed open and Piper frantically ran in. "Thane! She's gone, she's—" she stopped, staring at the two of them partially hidden by the tapestries.

He stepped out with his hands behind his back. "She's right here."

Layala followed after him and gave a small wave at Piper. The guard shot Layala a scowl. "You're making me look incompetent."

"It's fine, Piper." Thane sauntered toward his throne. Layala watched his every step, amazed at the grace with which he moved. She was around humans for so long she didn't realize the difference in a simple gait. When he sat, he tapped his foot slow and methodically. "I'll be up for dinner soon. We can talk about whatever it is you came searching for then."

"Now seems like a good time. You're here. I'm here." Layala waited long enough already to find out if he would help her go north so she could go home. Or if she'd have to escape and do this on her own. No matter what he said, she knew he wouldn't allow her to leave alone.

With a playful twist of his mouth, he sat a little

taller. "I have another meeting. I put off most of them to retrieve you."

She worked hard not to roll her eyes. *Retrieve me?* He made it sound like she'd willingly and happily joined him. "About dinner... I would like to go outside instead. I've been locked in this castle for days and I heard there are games tonight before the Summer Solstice."

"You wish to see the games?"

"I do." It was better than dinner with his family or wandering around with a grumpy Piper.

"Alright. We'll go to the games. I'll come to get you when I can."

The double doors opened by a pair of guards and in walked five very human-looking men. Piper tilted her head toward the exit. "Come on."

After watching the men in light armor with the sigil of Svenarum on their chests, she followed Piper out. "What are they here for?" She held pride and allegiance to Svenarum given that was where she lived her entire life although she never met the king or any of the royals.

"Each ruler in Adalon will send diplomats to meet with Thane since he is the new High King, both as respect and to see if he will differ from Tenebris. Thane hopes to repair the damage his father did with the other races."

Layala glanced back one last time. Thane stood with a big smile on his face and descended the stairs like he was meeting with old friends. The difference between how he was with the elves of Calladira and the humans was... interesting. When the guards closed the doors Layala turned to Piper. "Must we wait for Thane to go to the games? I'm bored."

"That is what he said," Piper answered.

"And do you always do what you're told?"

Piper shot a sidelong look. "When my king is doing the telling, yes."

Chapter 19

When they rounded a corner on their way out of the Hall of Kings, Sunshine leaned against the wall as if he'd waited for them, and since his leg bore the full brunt of his weight it must be healed. He smiled as big and bright as the day she gave him the nickname. "Good Evening, ladies. You clean up well, Layala."

"Thank you. Glad to see your leg is better," Layala said.

Sunshine pushed off the door frame. "As much as I'd hate to interrupt your stroll, Princess Talon wishes to meet with you in one of the sitting rooms."

She groaned internally. "I guess I have nothing better to do."

She hesitated a moment then followed Sunshine down the corridor. Their conversation along the way consisted of the upcoming festival and to her surprise, he didn't say one word about Thane or try to convince her to marry him. It was refreshing to talk about normal things. Like desserts they hoped to eat or songs they wanted to hear performed. She didn't know many elvish songs, but she couldn't wait to watch the elves at the Solstice dance during sunset. She wished she knew it so she could join in.

When Sunshine opened the door to the sitting room, he bowed and left with Piper at his side. Layala walked in to find Talon sitting with her legs crossed and holding red liquid in her high stemmed glass. She stood and smiled. "Oh, dear soon-to-be sister. I wanted to apologize for the way my mother and I treated you at dinner the other night. We haven't seen you since, and I realized the error of my ways."

There was something off-putting and disingenuous about her apology that got under Layala's skin. And she was calling her *sister*? "Well, thank you."

"I'd love to help plan the wedding. Mother wants to do it all of course but I said we must include you." She swirled the contents of her glass and then took a sip.

Lifting an eyebrow, Layala deadpanned. "How thoughtful of you."

"We can discuss that later. I want to get to know you. Lady talk." She brushed her dark curls over her shoulder. "Like have you ever kissed anyone? Do you play any instruments? That type of thing." Her green eyes almost sparkled when she said, "Has my brother tried to make a move on you yet, you know, romantically?"

Technically she made a move on him when she

planted a kiss on his full lips before she tried to stab him, but that was neither here nor there now. "I can hit a target with an arrow from a hundred yards away. I like to throw knives, fight, and drink ale. How's that for 'lady talk'?"

Talon spat a mouthful of wine back into her glass and reached on a nearby table for a napkin. After dabbing her mouth, she said, "You fight for *fun*? I thought only males did that type of thing."

Layala almost laughed but kept her composure. "On occasion. Although it's not really for fun. Training is to keep up my skills and endurance." Something she needed to do soon. Her last sparring session was over two weeks ago, unless tumbling with Thane in an attempt to kill him counted.

"Don't tell Mother any of that. She already thinks you're barbaric and in need of lady's lessons. But my father, he would like you. If only he were here." She gestured toward a table with a wine bottle and a glass. "Care for a drink?"

Bristling at the mention of Tenebris, Layala picked up the glass and poured herself red wine. She wanted to tell Talon that Tenebris wouldn't have liked her when she drove a blade through his heart, but she sipped her wine instead. It was lightly sweet, velvety smooth and fruity. "What about you?"

She smiled as if she'd been waiting for Layala to ask. "I love to play the flute. My friends are great company, you'll meet them soon. We walk through the gardens and pick our favorite flowers and talk about boys. I love chocolate," she licked her lips. "Who do you think is more attractive, Fennan or Aldrich?"

"Aldrich?"

"Thane's friend and personal guard. The one who escorted you here."

"Oh." *Sunshine.* Layala lifted a shoulder. "Um, they're both attractive. I can't say I favor one over the other."

"Good answer. My brother would be insane with jealousy if you chose. Are you a virgin?"

Was this conversation a test? Is that why Talon truly wanted to meet with her? "I don't think that's any of your business."

"So, you're not."

Layala arched an eyebrow. "Are you?"

"Of course, I am. I'm a high lady." She smirked. "Waiting for my husband, whoever he may be, is an absolute joy."

"You're being facetious."

"As far as anyone around here knows, I'm as innocent as a wee lamb."

This princess must be far from innocent, whether or not she was a virgin. "Don't you find it frustrating that males can do whatever they want without repercussions but a female's virginity or lack thereof, can be used to destroy her?"

Talon sipped her wine. "I like you. But not all males do whatever they want. Some wait for their fair maidens, whom they love and will marry, or so I hear."

"Perhaps, but a rare male indeed."

They were both quiet for a moment. Talon stared at Layala's birthmark on her shoulder. "You know my father believed you would save us. I believe you can too."

"And how might I go about that?" Layala drawled. "Your father must have had some idea if he took the measures he did to find me. More than an inkling, surely." She believed Thane when he said Tenebris planned to give her over to the pale ones, but she wanted to feel out Talon's intentions, see whose side she was on.

"It was for the good of us all." She licked her lips, briefly looking out the window. "I find it uncoincidental that Thane found you only weeks after our father died. Almost as if he knew all along. Almost as if..." her eyes were fixed on the window's ledge like it suddenly became interesting.

"As if what?"

Eyebrows drawing close she said, "Was he in contact with you previously?"

Layala's face scrunched at the idea. "Certainly not. And I doubt he knew my location before he stole me from my home." She kept at ease so as not to give away the truth. If she said too much it would sound like she was covering for him.

Talon half smiled as if the idea was entertaining. "Stole you?"

"Yes, they forced me into a carriage and dragged me here," Layala said. She set the glass of wine down on the window's ledge, and challenged Talon with a look to say otherwise. "And I'm now trapped here because of your father forcing a mate bond on us."

"I'm impressed. Dragging a beautiful elf maiden from her home, especially his mate, seems out of character for Thane. My brother can be a brute if put into the right situation, don't get me wrong. Everyone knows how good he is at killing, but I thought he was a softy at his core when it came to females." She paused. "Guess I was wrong."

Layala took a long swallow of wine after that. *She's impressed by that?* "Speaking of your brother, he doesn't seem to know or won't tell me how your father thought my power might save us. Frankly, I don't know rune magic and have no idea how to destroy the Void."

Tapping her finger against her glass, Talon smirked. "Oh, my father didn't know the way for certain; he simply had faith. I have a feeling you'll find out soon enough. The folk of Palenor have been praying for you to come forth. Praying for our magic to be restored."

She almost snorted at that. "You act like I'm some sort of goddess." Layala shifted on her feet uncomfortably. "Using words such as faith and prayer in regards to me. I fear you're putting me on much too high of a pedestal."

"It's not you we pray to, but you're the answer. You're the tool."

Layala didn't like being referred to as a tool and didn't want to take it as nefarious, but this was the daughter of the king who murdered her parents after all, and if Layala had to guess, she was on her father's side. "What does that mean?"

She giggled. Perhaps she drank too much wine. "I just think that you'll find a way, that's all." She practically skipped toward the door. "Let's go to the games. Maybe I'll find a husband of my own." She turned back to wink.

Thane was right. Layala watched the elven princess prance from the room. Talon couldn't be trusted.

Chapter 20

No one waited outside the doors for Layala. Not Piper or Sunshine or Fennan. Layala found it odd but fell into step beside Talon. She paused only a moment; Thane told her not to go outside, but what harm could there be? There was a guard around every corner it seemed.

Talon chatted on and on about how fun the games were in previous years, and how many foreign nobles always came. Talon couldn't wait to find a certain male she stole a kiss from the last gathering but didn't know the name of.

They stepped outside onto a dais with several waiting guards. The guards dipped into shallow bows as they passed. A long stone staircase lined with an intricately designed railing, led to the waiting crowds and bustle of the games below. Everything was so green, from the grass to the trees to the hillside in the distance. It was beautiful. The regal swans both white and black, slipping over the nearby pond added to the enchantment. They started down the stairs when a smooth voice cut in, "I thought I asked you to wait for me."

Talon and Layala both turned to find Thane with his arms crossed, and leaned up against the doorframe. Talon rolled her eyes and then raised her hand high, waving wildly. "Oh, look, it's my friends. I better go."

Layala sighed and shifted toward Thane. "You did ask. I simply didn't listen."

He cocked an eyebrow. "I asked as a courtesy from you so we could arrive together. Besides, I'm much better company than Talon and her gossipy friends." Thane stepped to her side and looped his arm around hers and started down the steps.

Layala weakly tried to tug away from him, but the guards stared at them, and she stopped struggling. "What in Maker's name are you doing?"

"Taking the arm of my betrothed. I should think it was quite obvious."

"I know what you're doing. Why are you doing it? We're not actually betrothed."

"Oh, but we are, whether you like it or not. Or are you angry I haven't gotten down on one knee?"

"Would you? Get on your knees for me?" she drawled, holding back an eye roll.

"For you? Oh, absolutely," he purred.

She glared up at him. "When are we leaving for the mountains?"

He cleared his throat. "I thought you wanted to see

the games. There is a tug-of-war match over there." Thane pointed to the left. A group of maybe a hundred elves gathered with much shouting and grunting rippling from the area. Through the throng of people, she spotted thick twisting rope being fought over a pit of mud. "But there are also archery tournaments, sword matches, horse races, and the team sport of Vandastu. I think there might be a drinking contest, as well. Mother thinks that should be outlawed because it's in her words, 'disgusting'."

"I'm not going to drop the issue."

"I promise we'll talk about that later."

Why was everything always on his time? "Fine. What is Vandastu?"

Thane pointed to the right to teams lined up opposite of each other wearing different color sashes over their chests. One red, one green. "The basics of the game is to hit the ball past the two posts there, only using the stick. It can't be moved by hands or feet. It can be rather violent. They're not allowed to outright punch each other but many elbows are used and lots of hip checking."

"Do females participate in any of these?" After looking around, she couldn't find a single girl doing anything other than peacocking in their gowns and spectating.

"Occasionally one or two will compete in archery, but it's not common."

"And do you compete in anything, High King?" her tone dripped with sarcasm. She doubted he'd lower himself to mingle with the common folk or risk getting his boots dirty. "Or is there a cushy chair somewhere reserved for you?"

"I sense some challenge there." He grew a slow smile, tucking dark hair behind his ear. He wasn't wearing his crown anymore and his hair was half pulled back again. "What would my lovely betrothed wish me to participate in so I can win her fair heart?"

"It would take much more than a game to win my heart." But Layala lifted her hand toward tug-of-war. What she would give to see him face down in the mud, but she knew he wouldn't participate. "But if you wanted to make me laugh, tug-of-war would be entertaining enough."

"I don't think I've heard your laugh, so I guess I can't pass up on the opportunity, can I?" He steered her toward the tug-of-war match.

Her eyebrow raised in surprise. "You're actually going to do it?"

"You'll find backing down from a challenge isn't in me. Actually, challenges give me life. That's why I enjoy your company so much. I never know what you're going to say or do. You might stab me or kiss me." He turned to her with a wicked smirk.

She narrowed her eyes. "Bastard," she murmured. There was no need to remind her that she'd kissed him and stabbed him.

He chuckled in that way that made her spine tingle. They passed groups of gathered ladies in their extravagant gowns and hairstyles. She noted that each of them either beheld a blind disdain for her or they'd all eaten something sour. The looks of jealousy, shock, and frustration clear on their faces. Many whispered behind their hands to one another but they weren't quiet enough.

"Who is *that* with the High King?" One girl's chocolate brown hair contrasted with her porcelain skin in a bright, yellow dress.

"I don't know, but it looks as though you have some competition, Vyra," the other replied.

Another said, "The king never openly courts anyone."

"Who could she be?"

"I thought he'd pick someone prettier," one girl sneered.

"And thinner. You can tell she likes sweets."

"Maybe he likes her big breasts."

Layala glanced down at herself. She never considered herself big breasted or overweight, but she wasn't as thin as many of the she-elves she now saw. She had hips and soft curves to her frame. Her arms and shoulders showed light muscle definition from training, but she thought it was normal for a female. Was it fashionable to be so frail?

Thane leaned closer; his lips grazed her ear and sent a jolt down her body. "Don't listen to them. You're the most beautiful female here by far. And... I do so adore your breasts."

Layala smacked his arm gently and would have hit him harder if they weren't in public for everyone to see. "You shouldn't even be looking at them." The females were jealous she was the object of the king's attention, but their comments still stung, despite what Thane said.

He chuckled, "They're hard to miss."

"They aren't even that big." She couldn't believe they were having a conversation about her breasts.

He looked at his open palm and then to her chest, then lifted his eyes to her face. "I think they're the perfect size."

"I'm not above punching you in the face again."

He grew a feline smile and swung around the crowd toward where a group of seven males gathered, waiting to take up the rope. They turned and stared when they saw who approached. Some dipped into bows and many, "Greetings, your highnesses," trailed in their wake. They didn't appear to be surprised he was there.

A brute-looking elf slapped Thane on the back. The sun, moon, and stars tattooed on his face, among others, made him stand out, as did his fire-red hair tied into braids. His deep-brown skin brought out his light-blue eyes like stars. The mud up to his knees and a fair amount on his hands and splattered on his chest said he competed already. "Who's the lady?"

"A friend," Thane said and dropped Layala's arm to grasp the forearm of the elf. She liked the brown leather bands on his wrists with rune marks etched into them. They were different from the typical gold or silver. The sleeves of his deep red tunic were rolled to his elbows showing them off.

"Oh, a friend?" He looked Layala up and down. She couldn't quite place his accent, but he had more roll to his "r's". The other elves nearby examined Layala's form as much as he was. As if she was a prized horse on display. Were they inspecting her because she was with the king or because they just liked to ogle females? She shifted a little, uncomfortable, but raised her chin to meet their stares. She was used to staring down large males after so much time in the training yard with the men.

"Well, if she's but a friend, you don't mind if I—" the elf reached for Layala's backside and Thane knocked his hand away as fast as a snake strike.

"I'll break your hand if you try that again, Leif." Thane was firm but not overly aggressive. Were they friends?

The burly elf burst into laughter and grabbed Thane's shoulder. "She's a lovely one, I'll give you that. Looks rightly proper for a High King. Child-bearing hips, too."

Layala rolled her eyes and looked him up and down as he had her, so he would know what it was like to be inspected. She frowned a little. "You're lucky it was your king that stopped you from grabbing my ass or you'd have a broken nose as well as a broken hand."

Thane glanced down at Layala with a smirk. Leif and the other males, also with brown skin and tattoos on their faces, looked amongst each other and then they all laughed. "I don't think I've ever heard a lady use the word 'ass' before, at least not outside brothels," Leif said.

"A place I'm sure you frequent since you'd only be able to get a lady to touch you if you paid for her, no doubt."

Leif furrowed his brows at her and he let out another bellow. "She even makes jokes. You better wife her immediately, King Thane or I might."

"I'd leave her be or you really might end up with a broken nose. Unpredictable that one," Thane said, rolling up the long sleeves on his black top. He pushed through the group to take hold of the rope at the very front. "Let's get on with the match. You rabble from the west are lucky I'm here or you'd surely lose against Dynadar."

"We've won three matches in a row," Leif boasted and picked up the rope behind Thane.

The Dynadar team smiled as if the king joining the other side only encouraged them further. Thane's team appeared confident until an ogre, at least eight feet tall with a potbelly, wearing only a brown loincloth and vest came from behind a tent. He grinned, bearing his huge, crooked yellow teeth and grabbed the end of the rope. Many in the crowd gasped and murmured, pointing at the huge creature. Layala saw an ogre once while out traipsing around the Redcrest Woods behind her home when she was thirteen. It was terrifying then and even now she wanted to reach for a weapon, the dagger she had strapped to her thigh. Since when did high elves commune with lesser creatures like this? And was he allowed to compete in this game? Thane and the males from the west with tattooed faces all laughed.

"You must have an ogre on your side to win?" Leif mocked.

"They're afraid of a little dirt on those pristine uniforms," another on Thane's side shouted, and the crowd laughed. The other team did have clean matching uniforms of white and navy blue. More white than blue. They must be confident.

Thane looked over the massive ogre. "Last I checked it was against the rules to have any race besides elves compete, but I'll allow it." He looked along the crowd. "Makes it more interesting, doesn't it?"

Many shouts of "yes" and more laughter ensued. Layala stepped back in the front row with the other spectators. "You must want to get dragged into the mud." She was surprised that Thane picked the front given that he'd be the first in the mud pit.

"You underestimate my team and me, sweetheart. Mostly me."

Layala folded her arms, wishing she hadn't spoken. Now everyone looked at her again. And although he said "sweetheart" in a long drawl, the term of endearment wasn't lost on anyone in the crowd.

Leif shoved Thane lightly in the back. "His highness is a beast trapped in a tiny elven body."

The elf beside Layala cackled.

They really put on a show at these events, Layala thought.

"Tiny?" Thane shot a glare behind him. "Is that what you call six foot four and two hundred thirty pounds of pure muscle?"

Leif looked to Layala as if she was the only spectator. "He likes to boast, too."

"As well he should!" someone from the crowd shouted. "He is our Warrior King!"

A massive burst of cheers and whistles rose up from the spectators. She didn't know why but she was surprised at how well-liked Thane was. They appeared to adore him and if he was such a terrible elf, they wouldn't. If he only ruled by fear like his father before him, he wouldn't receive such high praise.

Thane only offered his devastatingly handsome smile this time. Both teams took a firm grip on the rope. The ogre in the back raised one massive fist in the air and let out a booming roar that sent a smelly gust of wind rushing past Layala despite being several yards away from him. *Disgusting.*

An elf off to the side let out a whistle. The jerking and tugging started, both sides grunting with their efforts. Layala expected one big wrench from the ogre would send Thane and his team soaring into the mud, but... it didn't happen. Neither of them gave an inch as they pulled, faces scrunched with effort.

"Pull harder!" Leif hollered.

The team was clearly pulling hard. Now it seemed it would be who tired first. The ogre bellowed. Thane's forearms bulged with veins and taut muscles. He also mouthed a steady stream of curses which brought a smile to her lips. As much as she wanted to see Thane flat in the mud, she couldn't help but silently root for him and his team. *Come on. Come on, Thane, pull!*

The crowd around her shouted and cheered on their side. Getting caught up in the enthusiasm, Layala stuck her fingers in her mouth and let out a shrill whistle. "Come on, Thane! I thought you were a beast!" she shouted, and then slammed her mouth shut, astonished she actually said that out loud. She laughed at herself; after she despised him for so long, now she encouraged the elf king. Rooted for him, even.

Then suddenly the momentum shifted, as if Thane's team caught a second wind. He took a step back, and then another and his team followed. The ogre's side was wide eyed in surprise; the crowd grew wilder. They were actually going to pull this off. She knew Thane was strong from how easily he picked her up, and how he handled her the night she attacked him, but could he be the factor to win against an eight-foot-tall ogre? The creature must weigh four hundred pounds, and add seven other elves to that. It should be impossible for Thane and his side to win.

The first elf in the white uniform slid into the mud, shin deep. Then the next. When the ogre let go of the rope the whole team toppled to the pit on top of each other and Thane's team fell backward in victory.

Layala laughed and clapped along with everyone else. Thane rolled onto his side and found her in the crowd. "A laugh, as promised." She read his lips more than heard with the cheering so loud.

She ran a hand through her hair. He did get her to laugh. Slowly shaking her head, she started for him. A flash of yellow passed by her, something snagged around her ankle and Layala tipped forward, heading straight for the mud pit. She almost caught herself but then she was pushed on her back and fell hands and knees into sticky, thick mud.

The whispers and gasps from the crowd around her made her face burn with embarrassment. If she was home in Briar Hollow, she might laugh and start a mud fight but here, that wouldn't be acceptable. The silence of the crowd said enough. A few giggles and snickers followed as she struggled to get up in her fancy purple dress. When she got the courage to lift her head, one of the girls she saw earlier stood with her arms crossed wearing a smug smile. The one in the yellow dress called Vyra.

A black boot sunk into the mud beside her, and a big warm hand wrapped around Layala's arm. She looked up to see Thane above her. The mud squished loudly when he tugged her up. "I didn't see what happened. Are you alright?" He didn't laugh like some in the crowd. He looked embarrassed for her, angry even.

"Someone pushed me." Her fiery gaze shot toward the yellow bundle of joy.

"Who?"

"I didn't see." It wasn't an outright lie. She truly hadn't seen, but she knew who did it and it was something she could deal with later on her own.

"I'm sorry. That shouldn't have happened." With everyone staring after them, whispering, Thane led her to where the team was gathered around a trough.

She dipped her arms into the water scrubbing off the mud. Leif handed Layala a towel. "Sorry your pretty dress got ruined."

Layala patted her arms dry and brushed at the mud on her dress. "Reina and Pearl will be more upset than me." Leif and the others looked confused. "My maids."

Thane scanned the crowd around them. "Did the girl in the yellow dress push you?"

How did he know that? Layala patted herself with the towel. "Why do you think that?"

"Call it a hunch."

"And if she did?"

"Then she'll be dealt with. You are the future Queen of Palenor. No one touches you. Ever."

Leif's eyebrows raised. The other males on the team stared at Layala like she was some rare jewel. "So, she *is* more than a friend," Leif said. "And would your name be Layala Lightbringer?"

Layala fidgeted with the towel in her hands. There

was a connotation with that name and the way he said it. Lifting her head, Layala met Leif's stare. "It is."

"The last mage," one of the males said, and they glanced between each other.

Thane grabbed Leif's bicep and then looked around at the others. "Keep quiet about it. I don't want to draw any unnecessary attention for now."

"Of course, sire," the group muttered one after another.

"By unnecessary, you mean dangerous, don't you? Because there are groups of people who want me dead. For the sign at my birth. That's what Piper said."

Leif rubbed the back of his neck and found other things more interesting. Thane set his jaw and those green eyes pierced hers with unnerving connection. "Yes. But you don't need to be afraid. I've taken many precautions on who is allowed on the castle grounds. Any who have shown or are connected to the fanatics will not be permitted past the gates."

"I'm not afraid." She knew he would protect her. His life depended on it.

"Come. Let's get us a change of clothes and dinner. I'm hungry after that match. It wasn't easy to battle an ogre even if I made it look so."

Chapter 21

After changing and washing, Thane and Layala entered the dining hall to find Talon and her friend Vyra already seated, giggling. He heard part of their conversation before the door opened. They laughed at Layala's struggle to get out of the mud pit. The hairs on the back of his neck stood on end, but he must keep his cool and not overreact even though he wanted to. He felt Layala's embarrassment like it was his own when everyone stared at her and no one moved to help.

He didn't know whose side his sister was on. Talon never spoke about whether she knew their father meant to give Layala to Mathekis but he suspected. Of course, in open conversations around the dinner table, they only spoke of Layala as a way to destroy the Void because that's what good monarchs do for their people, but that's not what anyone in his family truly wanted. They wanted magic, and they'd get it by any means necessary. Either by destroying the Void, which wasn't a guarantee to bring magic back to the elves, even if Layala knew how, or somehow help the Black Mage rise once again. It didn't matter to them. His father bet on the Black Mage. Thane wasn't sure about his mother and sister.

The irony that Thane was the only one in his family who didn't care for magic and was born a mage, wasn't lost on him. Why was he chosen? Why had he been paired with Layala to top it off? Was this a plan of the Maker, or the old gods even—did fate decide this? These questions kept him awake at night for years. He was happy to fight with his swords and do things the old-fashioned way. He rarely even used his magic after he saw the envy in others.

"Brother, why do you look so glum?" Talon moved her arm, waving him to sit. Her drink nearly sloshed over the side as she did. She always had a taste for spirits, but she was particularly fond of Calladira's wine. "Never mind, don't answer that. You're always glum."

Vyra giggled and then met Thane's eyes. The girl had pursued him since she was fifteen years old, and now at nineteen, she only tried harder. He made the mistake of kissing her one night after too much wine, and it gave her hope when there was none. Enough to push Layala into the mud, he suspected. But since Layala wouldn't say and he didn't see, he wouldn't punish her for it.

Thane stood a little straighter, and his mouth

twitched in irritation. "My sister is so endearing, isn't she?"

Breaking into a knowing smile, Layala sat and scooted her chair in. She opened her mouth to speak when Talon cut in, "Oh, your mate and I had a rather nice conversation, actually. *Maker above*, how unromantic of you to force her into your carriage and drag her here. You could have started by asking. Father would be disappointed."

"Yes, sire, you've always been more of the grand gesture type. At least with me." Vyra batted her eyelashes with a coy smile.

Grand gesture type? When had he ever done anything to try to impress Vyra? He was simply kind to her, and she took it the wrong way, apparently. Thane leaned back into his chair casually, trying to feign like his sister and Vyra didn't annoy him. Of all people, Talon thought their father would be disappointed in his actions? Tenebris would have burned Briar Hollow to the ground and bound Layala's hands and feet so she couldn't run. And once they arrived, he'd have locked her in that room until he was sure she wouldn't leave. "What can I say? I was eager to get her here. We also had a group of pale ones on our tail."

Talon swirled her wine and giggled. "Ooooh, pale ones. I'm shaking."

Vyra snickered and took a sip of her wine. Layala sneered at both of them, annoyed as he was. He was surprised she kept quiet thus far.

Hot anger trickled down his spine. "You've never

seen what they can do. You've never even seen one up close, so laugh all you want, but you're an ignorant child for doing so." Tenebris doted on Talon like the spoiled princess she was. She never saw the war. Never saw the rotting corpses of elves she knew, or had the putrid smell invade her senses. Never saw their soldiers fed on by a pale one or watched a friend turn. She didn't know what the sickening crunch sounded like when a sword cut off a head or broke through bone.

She painted portraits of wildflowers and gossiped with her equally childish friends, and pined after males she had no business entertaining. She tried to lure Fennan into her bed recently, thankfully he had sense enough to turn her down. Drinking excessive amounts of wine was typical, and she snuck off castle grounds to party with commoners often. Their mother didn't know much of what Talon did. She was too busy gossiping and drinking wine herself. Mother enjoyed making plans to ruin elven lives, especially among her own circle. Spies employed by her found dirty secrets about her friends or their husbands and exploited them.

Thane didn't have the luxury of being so free as his sister. Sure, he drank until he couldn't stand a time or two, but he had too much responsibility to be so careless. And the idea of making other people miserable for his own entertainment repulsed him. Not that he had time to consider such nonsense anyway, he was training for war, in a battle, or making sure his people had necessities and were safe.

"Pale ones are certainly nothing to laugh at," Layala said.

Talon set her glass down and grabbed a garlic roll from the center of the table. "Here you were acting like you didn't even like my brother, and you're taking his side." She tore off a piece and popped it into her mouth.

"I'm on nobody's side but my own. But you've clearly never come face to face with one," Layala said, picking up her glass of wine and giving his sister a challenging look, one eyebrow raised, a slight tug on the corner of her mouth. "And it shows, Princess."

Thane wanted to grab her face and kiss her for not backing down to his sister like so many females did. Before he even went to get her, he worried he'd have to constantly protect her from his mother's wicked tactics and his sister's lashful tongue. He watched his sister belittle she-elves a thousand times and she'd met her match.

"And *you* have?" Vyra practically spit.

A cruel smile. "Of course, I have."

"I wouldn't brag about that." Talon's face went cold. "You're a low-born elf raised by humans, no less, and it *shows*. It only proves that I am better than you. I would never need to face a pale one." Her expression softened and turned into an almost feline smile. "See, males go to war for *me*; they fight for *me,* because I am a prize. A true lady. You may have magic, but that's all they want you for. You're filthy and tainted. You will never have the qualities a male truly desires, least of all our High King. Vyra should be at my brother's side, not you."

"Talon," Thane snapped. "Apologize and then leave."

Layala held up a hand, seemingly not affected at all. "No need. But the difference between you and me, Talon, is I can protect myself. I can fight for myself, and I don't need nor want a male to save or desire me, and that's how I like it."

That blow hit Thane like a punch to the gut. Perhaps Mage Vesstan was right about going to find this dragon shifter after all.

His mate and his sister stared each other down, a lone wolf who was used to fighting her own battles and a lioness who ran the pride through viciousness. "And if you want to compare male desires," Layala said, "well, they all want me, but at least it's not to pleasure themselves. Who would care for a spoiled, helpless, brat beyond looking for you to warm his bed."

That did it. Talon shot to her feet and threw her wine glass at Layala's face with blurred speed. Thane reached out with his magic and halted it mid-air, inches from breaking and cutting up her delicate skin. With remarkable calmness, Layala grabbed hold of the glass and then took a sip from it.

Talon sneered at both of them and left the room,

slamming the door hard enough to shake the wall. Vyra kept her head bowed.

"You're excused, Vyra," Thane said.

She quickly got up and chased after Talon. Thane let out a long breath and his tight muscles relaxed. He didn't even know who he should apologize to at this point. Both of them had made some deeply cutting remarks, even if Talon had started it. As a much-needed distraction, one of the servants entered and quietly refilled their glasses.

"How did you do that? Stop that glass," Layala asked, watching him carefully.

"With magic."

She deadpanned. "I know, but how?"

How could he explain it more than she could her power? "It's how my magic works. I can manipulate matter. So, for example, I can stop things in motion by manipulating the air around it. I can make water boil or freeze or move. I can bend fire at will, but I can't create it from nothing. I can bend and move trees... Mage Vesstan thinks I'd be able to make plants and trees grow if I took the time to learn."

"Lucky." Layala took her first bite of the chopped tomato on toasted bread appetizer. "So, when do we leave for the Sederac Mountains?" Layala asked, completely unfazed by the argument with Talon. Didn't she want to talk about what his sister said? *He* wanted to talk about some of the things Layala said, like if she meant she didn't want any male to desire her or if it was simply that she hated *him*.

He meant to speak to her about finding the sorceress, but he simply didn't have time with preparations for the battle that would come on the Summer Solstice and the celebration itself. His mother and other advisers handled all the actual planning of it, but he made sure the security was tight. Elves from within the city were only allowed in with an invitation and his guard was always doubled on this day. He made sure to triple it this time with Layala present.

He tapped his fingers against the hardwood table. "I don't think it's worth the risk." She opened her mouth to argue, but he said, "Hear me out. Even if we were able to find this dragon sorceress, how would we be able to trust her information, if she didn't try to eat us first? She could do something that would make the situation worse. How could we trust that what she told us would actually break the spell and not, say, accelerate our becoming pale ones? She may use you right then and there to resurrect her master."

"If we bribe her properly, I'm sure we can get her on our side. Everyone has a price."

Not everyone. Some people were loyal no matter what. Even if she could be persuaded, she would certainly want something in return, but they wouldn't know what that was until they found her. And bringing Layala to this sorceress was practically handing her to the Black Mage and his followers over on a platter. "No. I won't trust anyone who has worked with the Black Mage, especially not when it comes to you. I don't think you understand what you are to the enemy."

She sucked her bottom lip between her teeth. "I didn't think you would go anyway."

He narrowed his eyes. She was giving up way too easily. "That's it? No 'you're a bastard' or anything?"

Silence.

"You'll have to look for another way."

She glared. "You don't get to dictate my life."

"I do when it comes to this." He didn't mean to snarl, but he was growing restless with her self-indulgence. Everything she did was for her own selfish reasons, because she didn't want to be with him. He had enough on his damn plate as it was. "If they get their hands on you it could be the end of us all. I know you don't like it—like *me*, you've made that painstakingly clear, but I will not allow the enemy to use you. Period. You can hate me all the more for it, although I doubt you could loathe me more than you already do." He pushed up from the table and started for the door, his normally quiet feet slamming hard with each step.

The legs of her chair scraped against the floor with a groan. "You expect me to do nothing? To accept this when it's not what you or I have chosen?"

He whirled around. "I don't expect anything of you. I know something of duty and honor, but you? You should do what you do best and hide, doing nothing for your own people like you've done your entire life. Honestly, you think my sister is a selfish brat? Try looking in the mirror. You would watch all of

Palenor burn so you can be free of me. You'd risk bringing back the Black Mage and becoming his slave for the chance to go back to your hovel with the *humans*, while I have sacrificed my life to keep you safe. You have no idea the unforgivable things I have done to make certain they never have you. So go ahead and throw away our safety on some off chance this sorceress will help you rather than condemn *all* of us."

Real hurt trickled into him through their bond. That lovely face of hers showed something other than anger or distaste for once. Tears filled the rim of her eyes and a single droplet spilled down her cheek. He turned and threw the door open slamming it hard behind him.

Chapter 22

With tears burning her eyes, Layala slipped into the servants' door. She didn't want Thane or Piper or anyone else to follow her and she certainly didn't want to go to her room with Thane so close. It wasn't her responsibility to help anyone but herself. She wasn't a king or a ruler. Her magic wasn't owed to anyone; it was hers and hers alone. So why did his words cut so deep? She didn't have to destroy the Void or do anything. It was her choice to be free of their bond, and she wasn't wrong for wanting that. All she wanted was to go home, go back to her life and be with people she cared about and trusted.

The torches provided plenty of light for her to maneuver through the damp, cool stone. There were no windows and being inside the servants' halls was like walking through underground tunnels, a little claustrophobic and maze-like. Being inside brought back the memory of waiting outside Thane's room with the intent to kill him. She felt it was wrong then and even more so now. Yet she hadn't apologized.

She blinked, clearing away the tears and lifted her posture. She hoped to find an exit to the outside soon. Fresh air and open space were much needed. After passing several doors, one of which sounded like the kitchen on the other side with clanging dishes, and shouting servants, she came to a much heavier one at the end of the hall. It had a heavy metal latch which she shoved up and hooked against the wall. Stepping outside brought the warm evening air, the scent of fresh-cut grass, and the hum of nature. Clouds covered the sun but the colors of pink and orange still bloomed behind them.

Everyone she passed stared at her like she was a pale one, but she didn't give them a second look. She wandered the stone path far away from everyone until she found a willow tree. It was a symbol of safety, the ghost of her mother's arms that had been stolen away. Leaning her back against the trunk, she sank to the ground and grabbed her mother's golden willow necklace. She brought it to her lips and gently kissed it. *Mother, please, help me. Help me know what to do. Give me an answer.* Everything was still, quiet. More tears poured down her face. *I'm begging you. If you can hear me, I need help. I need you.* A breeze picked up, and long stringy branches swayed until a few lightly wrapped around her shoulders as if to comfort.

She sat in the silence and the sun peeked out from the clouds. Its warm light kissed her face. She closed her eyes, rubbing her temples. She was so sure about everything until she came here. So sure she knew who the enemy was but Maker above, she was wrong. She knew *nothing* before she arrived. She didn't even know Tenebris and Mathekis wanted to use her to bring back the Black Mage. She didn't know Thane had been protecting her all her life rather than searching to find her and use her. He wasn't a monster at all. An arrogant prick at times but not what she once believed.

She sat there until the sun dipped below the mountain in the distance and night fell. Thane was right. She was being selfish. Her mother said she'd have to fight, and maybe it was time. She wiped her tears and pushed to her feet. She must speak with Thane.

When the morning came, Layala stood at her windows, watching elves pour in through the castle gates. Many lined up on the bridge and waited alongside the river that protected the grounds. The females wore gowns in shades of yellow, orange, and red, colors that represented the sun. The males dressed in white and light blue, representing the daytime sky. Their gathered movement in the brilliant colors was as if watching a school of tropical fish, shifting and dancing in unison.

Reina and Pearl had already been in to dress her.

The two-piece burnt orange gown wasn't as extravagant as she expected it would be given what they forced on her for dinner. The top was covered in lace and hung off her shoulders. It left a two-inch gap at the bottom, revealing a little skin. The skirt dragged on the floor, hugged around her navel, and was made of fine silk. It was good for twirling. As soon as her maids left, she spun around, watching the fabric flow around her like the wide-open petals of a flower. She left her hair free to tumble down her back despite their protests.

Reina said this would be an all-day event. The elves set up stations for different interests such as music and art or animals and magical flora. Tables and booths of food lined both sides of a cobblestone path and went deep into the castle grounds. The aroma of sweets, hearty meats, and baked goods drifted to her already.

The bag she'd packed for her journey to the mountains sat on the bed mocking her. Should she stay and marry Thane, so she could help her people? So she could fight? She wouldn't have to be with him the way a wife usually did. She couldn't. They could simply be partners in their plight against the pale ones. There was still her fear of the pale ones capturing her, but she didn't want to live the rest of her life afraid of being taken. She didn't want to hide anymore.

"It sure does smell good," Tif said, staring longingly outside. Her tiny arms hugged the vine she leaned against.

"You should go down there. Taste some of that delicious smelling food."

"Oh, I would sooner stick my hand in boiling water. The jumbos would chase me away with a broom and I'd surely die of shame."

Layala patted Tif's head gently. "I would never allow that. You're my lady's maid now. You're important."

Her little heart-shaped face lit up. "I got the job?"

"I prefer you over Reina and Pearl honestly. They're so pushy. Nice but pushy."

"I am honored, Lady. And I do like your hair down like that," Tif added. "Even if they don't. You're most beautiful. Like a flower."

"Thank you."

"But I still can't go." Her shoulders sagged and she leaned against the glass. "I'll sneak some food from the kitchen."

"One day you will be brave enough to show yourself. Brave enough to be free."

"I hope so." She was quiet for a moment. "You'll take me with you, won't you? If you go to the mountains. Although, I think you should stay."

Nibbling on her bottom lip, Layala wanted to say no. "I don't know what I'm going to do, and it would be very dangerous."

"I don't care. I would brave the mountains with you. You are my friend."

"But not a few jumbos?" Layala gestured toward the outside festival.

"That is different. Plus, there are thousands, not a few down there."

A knock startled her. She quickly shoved the bag under the bed. Tif climbed out of sight, and Layala met Sunshine and Fennan at her door. She hoped it would be Thane. There were things she needed to say, starting with an apology.

"If you want to see the festivities, Thane asked that we take you," Fennan said, with an overly dramatic bow.

Layala snickered at his gesture but couldn't help her disappointment. "Oh, where is he? And where is Piper? She's usually out here."

Sunshine folded his arms and leaned against the door frame. "She is with Thane. He had meetings and correspondence all morning."

A small part of her was bothered that they were together, but she shoved that away. He was only her mate through a spell. "Have there been attacks?"

Thane's crushing words the night before still hurt. She knew that with power like hers, she could save so many elven lives. She might turn the war in their favor if she fought. But all her life she hid. And she still had no desire to fight pale ones in a war. She killed them when they came for her or to Briar Hollow, but she didn't want to seek out the confrontation, the risk. It terrified her to think of being surrounded by them, especially when they might not just kill her. They wanted to capture her and use her for their dark purposes.

"There are attacks regularly in the south," Fennan said. "But today has been bad, yes. Although, nothing we can't handle, don't worry."

She nodded slowly, a pit growing in her gut. She needed to choose her focus. Would she head to the mountains or stay? "I would enjoy going to the festival. Thank you." She stepped into the hallway and started for the stairs. The males walked on either side of her.

"Do you like sweets?" Fennan asked. He wore a light blue tunic with beige pants. He put effort into his appearance for the festival, when usually he looked like he'd come off a week on the road. His black hair was cut shorter, and he didn't even have a spec of dirt on his hands or face.

Layala smiled. "Doesn't everyone?"

"You must try the brambleberry cream pie. It's the best thing you'll ever eat," he bragged and licked his lips. "It's sweet and the purple berries are plump. Oh, and the creaminess. Not to mention the energy kick that comes with the berries is a bonus… Mmmm, I wait all year for it."

"It is rather good," Sunshine agreed. "But I prefer the chocolate-dipped pastries. You'll have to try both and tell us which *you* like best."

"Fennan did a better job at selling the pie, but I'd be more than happy to try both and give you my thoughts." She imagined for a moment that Ren and Forrest were beside her instead. They'd love a big festival like this. They'd drink and feast and dance with as many pretty maidens as they could find. She missed them.

When they stepped outside into the sunlight, light music drifted on the air, drums and wind instruments. It was somehow wild with the thrumming beats, and yet calming. Tents of many colors were erected nearby. Strings of tiny faerie lights hovered above stretching from flowering trees and the tops of booths, and would look marvelous at night. The aroma of sweet and savory food lingered heavier in the air now that she was closer.

Most of the elves they passed were locked in conversation with one another, too busy to notice her between her tall guards, but soon eyes began to drift. They watched her as if they could sense she was different from them. She checked to make sure her birthmark was covered with the sleeve, and it was.

She spotted Leif and his gang of tattooed friends. They waved and carried on. Fennan and Sunshine laughed at a male who fell into a barrel of wine and then hit the ground. The drink soaked his face before he rolled over and burped. "Is he drunk?" Layala asked. She'd seen many drunkards, but it was early in the day and for some reason, she expected more from the elves, especially from a race who called themselves "high".

"For certain," Sunshine said, then went over and dragged the elf to his feet. "Best go find a spot to sit for a while."

The elf chortled and swayed on his way to a bench.

"How long have you two known Thane?" Layala asked. If she was going to try, if she was even considering staying, she had to give the elves a chance and get to know those closest to her.

A little girl ran up and handed her a bright red wildflower. "Thank you," she said with a smile. The girl giggled and darted into the crowd.

"I was under his command at Zendora six years ago," Sunshine answered. "He saved my life, chopped off the head of a pale one right before it could take a bite out of my arm. I insisted on thanking him since I owed him my life and made him a pledge to be at his side. And here we are."

Layala shuddered at the thought of getting bit by a pale one. "I don't understand how you can fight so close to them and not—turn."

"We've found that if you're bitten you're certain to turn but otherwise, you won't. Some fear being close to them still, but those of us who have fought them in the war know that catching it like a sickness is a false belief." His dark blue eyes stayed on hers a few beats. "The other way is if a spell isn't completed."

"I'm all too aware," Layala mumbled. She turned to Fennan. "And you?"

"We've known each other since we were children. My father is a high-ranking general who worked closely with King Tenebris for years."

"Yes, Osric, Fennan and Thane were quite the trio,

or so I hear," Sunshine added. "Menaces, if you ask their nursemaids. Always running amuck and getting into trouble."

Layala smiled. "Who is Osric? I haven't met him yet." Fennan and Sunshine went suddenly quiet. "What's the matter?"

"He's dead." Fennan cleared his throat. "He turned after a battle, and well, that was not long ago."

"Oh." She couldn't fathom watching a friend turn. She wondered if Talon knew and still mocked her brother. Even Layala wouldn't do that to him. "I can't imagine how much that must hurt you all. I'm sorry."

Neither of them responded. She didn't blame them for not wanting to talk about it. She didn't want to talk about the loss of Novak even still and he died two years ago. Osric's death was fresh, a wound that would send shocking tendrils of pain if prodded. "Will you two dance at sunset?"

"We must," Sunshine said as if the question shocked him. "The blessings from the Maker help us through the year. Didn't you celebrate in Svenarum?"

"Not like this." Layala twirled the flower's stem between her fingers. Goodness radiated from the flora. She wasn't sure what it was or what mystical properties it possessed but that little girl meant to give her a favor of some kind. "I'm afraid I don't know how to dance the Kenatara."

"We must teach you then," Sunshine said with a huge grin.

"After she tries some of the food. I can't teach

when hungry." Fennan hooked his arm around hers and dragged her presumably toward the brambleberry cream pie booth.

For the next hour they tried food from every vendor. The brambleberry cream pie was as delectable and rich as Fennan described, and the chocolate-dipped pastries were a close second. They ate exotic fruit tarts and cheeses, breads with flavors from buttery garlic, to cookies mixed with cinnamon and topped with vanilla frosting. After the final bite of a pixie-sweet red apple, she was so full she couldn't eat any more and couldn't fathom how her two companions wanted more. Her stomach was already stretched beyond its usual capacity.

After they dragged her to listen and watch the music performers, and then visit the different flora booths, she found herself looking for Thane. Shouldn't he be here? Was their fight the night before his last straw? Maybe he was done with her. After how horrible she was, she didn't blame him.

"Come on, we need to show you the Kenatara," Sunshine said, nodding toward an open area, thankfully with a few luminor trees for cover. Layala didn't want everyone watching her try to learn a dance that she should already know. On their way over, the princess, with a group of four friends, walked toward them in a line, forcing others to move out of their way like they were a stampede. Layala immediately stepped closer to Fennan who might be enough to block her. She could only imagine Talon would be more bold with her gaggle of females.

"Oh, look, it's my soon-to-be sister!" Talon cooed; she took the hands of the friends beside her and pulled them ahead. One of them was Vyra, who wore a wicked grin. Passersby gave Layala long looks. If the princess was announcing a soon-to-be sister, then they knew what that meant. Layala had never wanted to be able to turn invisible more than that moment. She could already see elves talking behind their hands, watching her with distinct curiosity, more so than before.

"Maker, why me?" Layala moaned.

Sunshine and Fennan both stiffened at her sides, as if preparing for a crowd that might get unruly. "I told you she was difficult," Fennan murmured even as he stopped and greeted Talon with a bow. Sunshine dipped his head and winked. Talon's smile grew tenfold.

"Hello, Fennan." She said his name with deliberate affection. "Aldrich." Her stern gaze fell to Layala. "And my dear, sweet sister. Can I call you that?"

"I'd prefer Layala."

"Layala Lightbringer," Vyra said unnecessarily loudly and clutched at her chest. "The long-lost mage." She and the others giggled but like the rest of the ever-gathering elves around them, watched her with a sort of fearful reverence. She was the lost magical child after all. "Are you enjoying your time?"

"I am," Layala answered, nervous at the circle growing around them.

"Blessed, are you truly she?" The male elf practically charged her until Fennan stuck his arm out bringing the elf to a jerking halt.

"You will not touch her or come any closer." Fennan gave him a light shove back and the elf adjusted his tunic, but his eyes fixed on Layala like he might risk a second try.

That made the chatter louder. "It's truly her."

"Look at how beautiful she is. Absolutely stunning."

"I want to see her magic."

"We're saved! She is here to save us all from the pale ones!"

"I don't have to send my son to the war now!"

"How do we know it's her for certain?"

"If this is the High King's mate, where is the High King?"

"Should we bow to her?"

Someone ran off yelling that Layala Lightbringer had been found and was here.

Layala wished she could sink into the ground and cover herself with dirt. No wonder Thane said he wanted to keep who she was quiet. Her eyes darted around, searching for a way to escape but the circle only grew tighter, more compact. The buzzing and whispering and questions grew louder. The bright sun even seemed to get hotter, burning her skin.

Talon smirked as if this was her plan all along. "I

hope you have a wonderful evening, but I must be off with my friends." Talon strode straight at the crowd which parted for her without hesitation.

Layala noticed the queen nearby surrounded by a group of ladies, with a terrible grin. She lifted her glass at Layala then turned away. Did she send Talon over to do this?

Sunshine and Fennan's shoulders pressed against hers. "We need to get you inside," Sunshine took hold of her arm and waved his other hand. "Make way!"

"But we want to hear from her! Is she going to save us?" a female yelled.

"Yes, we've waited almost twenty-five years! Let her speak!"

Layala's heart slammed into her chest. This wasn't a situation she could fight her way out of; she couldn't hurt them for only wanting to see her. But she had to get away, had to break through into the open. She needed to run but that would scare them, and would they chase her? She'd never seen this many gathered in one place, let alone surrounding *her*. More questions were hurled at her. The bright orange and yellow gowns began to hurt her eyes as they melded together. The drumming music and the loud chatter, the distant laughter of children rang in her ears, threatening to overwhelm.

Her throat seized up. She made speeches in Briar Hollow at town meetings when she prepared for them, but none where they expected her to be a savior.

She stared up at Fennan, silently pleading with

him to get her out of there. He gave a curt nod. "Layala will not be speaking as of now," Fennan shouted. "Now please, give us some room before we have to call the castle guard."

Not a single elf moved. They pushed to draw closer. Arguments started. A male shoved a female; she yelped, and a fight broke out. First it was two males then a whole group because someone bumped into a wife, or another got hit by accident. Fists flew, screams echoed, curses and groans erupted.

Leif hollered, "Get out of here! With haste!" He and his tug-of-war team joined the fighting, only adding to the chaos.

"We have to get inside!" Fennan snarled at Sunshine. "Damn Talon, damn her. She did this on purpose."

In the chaos, elves grabbed at Layala, pawing her hair. A few even tore out some strands, holding them high like it was a prize. Others tugged at her skirt, or caressed her arms. Anger and fear and disgust ripped at her as she shoved hands away, "Don't touch me!" she shouted with venom. She wanted to scream to scare them like Tif had her birds. A male grabbed her hand and jerked her closer, dragging his tongue across her wrist. Tears of rage and revulsion burned her eyes. She wrenched herself free and punched him hard in the nose. "How dare you!"

Fennan shoved the assailant back until he tumbled into the crowd.

But they kept coming. Kept pawing her and

begging. "Blessed, please help us!" a female in yellow said, wrapping her hand around Layala's other wrist. In reaction, Layala jerked away and shoved her down. Another tripped over the lady and she cried out in pain.

"Where is the guard? This is out of control!" Fennan shouted. He and Sunshine tried to form a barrier around her, but many reached around them as if touching Layala would make them *blessed*. The fighting group fell into them, Sunshine caught an elbow to the jaw, and he growled, shoving his foot into the back of an elf. Layala's magic began to trickle through her veins, warm and cool at once. *Let me out*, it seemed to say. *I will free you from this... No no no no.* She shoved it down, down until it was in the depths of some deep darkness, locking it in a cage. If it exploded here, they'd demand her death surely.

"STOP!" a deep voice boomed, laced with power, the kind only the High Elf King possessed.

Chapter 23

Guards shoved their way through the crowd until a tunnel opened up to Thane at the other end. His silver crown sparkled in the sun, his large stature a beacon of power. He wore no weapons, but he didn't need them to be feared. "You will not touch my mate!" he roared and it was enough to cause every one of the elves to step back several feet without the pressure of the guards.

The panic welled up in Layala turned into relief. Lifting her skirt, she moved toward him, walking at first and then her pace quickened. She could still feel where the hands of strangers groped her, and pulled her hair. She felt dirty, and was upset she was helpless to stop them. She burst into a run, scared they were right behind her, reaching for her until she slammed into him. She wrapped her arms around his body, breathing hard as she pressed her forehead into his chest. Holding onto him was the only thing keeping her knees from buckling.

He placed a firm hand on her back. "Today is our most sacred day. We are here to celebrate the Summer Solstice and ask the Maker to bless us. I hope this abhorrent behavior hasn't cursed us in our plight against the pale ones. You must all do your duty and dance the Kenatara well tonight. Now go, have fun. But do not make the mistake of coming near Layala again. I will not tolerate it a second time."

Layala peeked out to watch the crowd disperse. Once they were far enough away, it struck her that she was still holding him and she didn't know if it was because his wonderful scent drew her in, or if it was the comfort of a strong male she didn't want to admit she missed. She hadn't held a male like this since Novak. Pulling back abruptly, she ran a hand over her hair and smiled in embarrassment.

"Um, thank you. For rescuing me. I remembered what you said about the shrines and everything, but I didn't expect *that*."

"Are you alright?" His gaze traveled down her form then back up. "I apologize I wasn't out here with you sooner."

"I'm alright." She nodded. "You don't need to apologize. You have other things more important to worry about than me."

His tense face softened. "No. I don't."

She held his gaze until Fennan and Sunshine stepped up, drawing Thane's fierce eyes. "What happened?" His voice was harsh but calm. A king reprimanding his soldiers, not a friend. They both spilled like a couple of lady's maids. Talon got most of the blame, but they took the brunt of it when he snapped at them for not seeing the signs sooner and removing Layala from the situation. They took the rebuke in silence.

With Thane at her side, Layala walked without anyone daring to come near. Several guards trailed them including Fennan and Sunshine, but it wasn't them that kept the onlookers at bay. They respected Thane. Their wariness of him was as clear as mountain river water.

"Would you like to go back inside?" he asked.

"No." Layala folded her hands behind her back. "I want to enjoy the festival. It was fun until the incident. Fennan and Sunshine—I mean Aldrich, were about to show me how to dance the Kenatara for this evening."

He glanced over his shoulder. "Were they?" Something about his tone said he wasn't pleased.

When Layala looked back the two seemed to shrink a little as if Thane lashed them. "Is that a problem?"

"The Kenatara is a divine dance and shouldn't be taught by those who don't know it well. I've seen the pair of them dance it and they always miss a few steps, usually several. Practically throw off the entire thing." He smiled despite his words. "They didn't take their lessons seriously as children."

"Maybe I should sit it out. I may offend the Maker."

"But the dance doesn't require perfection; it's the

effort that matters most or those two wouldn't be allowed. We have time before dusk. I'll show you."

He brought her to a stone gazebo where vines grew up the eight pillars and covered most of the gold-domed ceiling. Tiny white flowers that resembled roses grew all around its base and within the vines. The black marbled stone floor was pristinely clean and shiny. She was amazed that not even a speck of dust seemed to be found. Their feet lightly tapped as they stepped inside. The guards waited several yards back and turned around to give them privacy. Nervousness bloomed in her belly when Thane stood opposite of her and dipped forward from his hips. "First we bow."

"Is this a couple's dance?" she breathed, heart beating faster.

"It's a partner dance where you'll mainly be with a single partner but switch a few times throughout." He lifted an eyebrow and his right hand. "Put your right palm up to mine but don't touch it yet. They'll hover about an inch apart, and then take three steps to the left." She followed. "Good. Now we switch hands and take three steps to the right." Layala rotated and counted her steps, then waited. "Now for the fun part."

They stood face to face, and he held out his hand. She stared at it for a moment. "Am I supposed to—" Without waiting for her to finish her question, he grabbed her wrist and pulled her close, leaving almost no space between them.

"That's better," he cooed. "Now it's four basic

movements. Simple so even children can do it, which goes to show you how much Fennan and Aldrich don't pay attention to the finer things in life."

"I see. And do you pay attention to the finer things?" There was an electricity between them, humming and alive, she swore it. Like the charge of thunderclouds before lightning lit up the sky, before thunder cracked. It only grew more intense when his hand glided over her hip and settled on her back.

"You'll find out here in a moment." A smile twitched at the corners of his mouth. "The basic steps are forward, sidestep, close feet together, back, side, close, repeat. With a few spins here and there."

It sounded simple but she figured it would be more difficult than that. "You lead."

He stepped and she followed. After stumbling and stomping on his toes a few times, she started to get it. She focused on her feet watching each step, thinking *forward, sidestep, feet together, back,* until he put a finger under her chin. "Up here." Their eyes met, the moves flowing easier when she wasn't staring down. He carried her around the gazebo with ease. Warmness blossomed in her chest and trickled throughout her body the longer she stared into his face, into those unique green eyes.

"I'm sorry," she said quietly. His eyebrow ticked up. "I'm sorry I came into your room that night and held a knife to your throat. I—I'm sorry I tried to kill you." Confessing the last bit was almost like chewing on sand, hard, gritty and difficult to swallow. "I'm sorry I've been so rude. I misjudged you then."

"And now?"

"I'm not sure, but you're not what I once believed," she confessed. "But I think you hide behind a mask of brutality."

"I don't hide. It's one of the many faces I must wear being High King. I am brutal when I need to be against the pale ones, against those who would wish people close to me and my kingdom harm, but it's not all of who I am." He spun her around in a circle and gently tugged her back in. "And I appreciate your apology, though I've already forgiven you." He spun her out again and said, "This is where you would take the hand of the male to your right and do a single round of steps and then he will spin you back to me."

She nodded but didn't care about the dance just then. "I can see that you forgave me, but why? Why do you put up with me when I've been horrible?" She was glad he wasn't who she thought but with the way she'd treated him, she thought it would have pushed him away. And yet she knew it hadn't. Even as they slowly danced, holding onto each other's bodies, their connection burned, an invisible force willing them together, basking in their closeness. Her mate rune tingled with warmth. As if taking notice of the sensations building between them her heart picked up, thudding loudly. Could he hear it? "And don't say it's because I'm your mate."

"Two years ago," he started. "I felt something break in you. It hurt me like my own wound, nearly dropped me to my knees. Your pain was so sharp and profound I first thought someone had injured you mortally; it scared me. But I realized it wasn't physical pain. I don't know what happened, and you don't have to tell me, but you were crumbling. Where you were once colorful, you became gray in my mind's eye. I wished I could go to you then, but it wasn't the right time. I swore when I did come for you, I would put back those pieces no matter how long it took. I would make those once bright colors shine again."

The lump in Layala's throat thickened and her eyes prickled with threatening tears. She stared at the golden whirls on his sky-blue tunic. He wanted to put her back together? He spoke of when Novak died. The agony of Novak's passing broke her; she hadn't even fully smiled in a long time. But that wasn't the reason for her emotion now—she wished she could fall in love. Thane was this charming, beautiful elf king, who wanted her, almost needed her. He was someone who could have swept her off her feet if there wasn't the terrible past. But falling in love with Thane was dangerous for him, for them both.

"I think I've got the steps now. Thank you." She tugged out of his arms and turned her back, holding her hand to her mouth. Walking to the edge of the gazebo, she put her palms on the stone and stared out at the elves in the distance, flocking from stand to stand. A white butterfly fluttered around her hands a moment then landed on her wrist. Its small wings slowly opened and closed.

"That's a Pieris butterfly." Thane leaned against the gazebo beside her. "They say if one lands on an elf, she is brought luck for a year."

"Is that true?" Layala asked, eyes fixed on the creature.

"I've never had one land on me so I can't say from personal experience."

The butterfly lifted into the air and flew toward the sun, now hanging low in the sky. She hoped it was true. Before things grew serious again Layala blurted out, "Did you know there is a gnome that lives in my room? Her name is Tifapine. I've taken her on as my lady's maid."

Thane smiled. The sight of it made Layala's heart beat faster again. "I did. She sings when she thinks no one can hear."

"You knew and let her stay?"

"I have nothing against gnomes and she's only one. It's not as if anyone was using the room before you arrived and when you came you didn't seem to mind."

"I like her. She's become a friend. My only friend here it seems. Your sister is the one who started the spectacle earlier, you know. And her friend."

Thane frowned. "I'll have a talk with both of them later. What happened earlier was dangerous, not a silly game."

"I can handle her." Layala started thinking of ways

she could retaliate. Nothing too damaging but she'd get what was coming to her. She wondered if there was anything between Thane and Vyra. Was there a past there? Talon said her friend should be at Thane's side.

Chuckling, Thane said, "I think Talon should be afraid, but please don't kill her or her friend."

Layala half smiled. "I won't. Will you take me to the south? I want to see the battles." Perhaps if she saw them with her own eyes, it would make her feel more for her own people. She still couldn't connect with the elves. They still didn't feel like hers the way Briar Hollow did. Maybe they never would. The need to help them wasn't there, but she was capable of it.

Shifting uncomfortably, Thane's lips formed a hard line. He still leaned against the pillar, but his casual body language had noticeably stiffened. "I don't know if that's a good idea."

"I can't stay here forever, Thane. I know you worry about the enemy getting me and so do I, but I need to see the war for myself. I don't want to hide. I want to help our people."

He lifted his chin and looked out. "I should never have said that to you. Staying away from my father and living among the humans was the best thing you could have done. There is no obligation for you to fight. That belongs to me." His gaze flicked back to her. "And what of your quest to break our bond?"

Clenching her teeth together, she brushed her

fingers through her hair. If seeing the war didn't change her mind about wanting to help and fight for the elves, she would have time to go to the mountains and find the dragon sorceress. "I'm still working on that."

His jaw muscles twitched. "There is someone down south who might know more about our bond too. We can leave tomorrow. It's a three to four-day ride." Squaring his shoulders to face her he said, "But you will not go anywhere near the battlefield. You'll watch from afar."

The rebellious side of her kicked in. "My *mate* is giving me orders?" She practically growled the word. "I'm well trained, you know. I'm probably a better fighter than most of your soldiers and you've seen what my magic can do."

"No, your High King is giving you an order." There was no room for argument in his tone. "You want to compare yourself to a soldier then listen like one. I've never seen you in battle, and just because you can throw a punch and a knife doesn't mean you can go sword to sword with a pale one. You've trained against humans, not elves which is starkly different so I truly don't know if you can fight well enough. Your magic could draw a horde of pale ones that may overwhelm my soldiers. When we are down there you must listen to me, Layala. I've never lost a battle because I know what I'm doing."

She would never admit it but when it came to large

battles, she was naive. Besides, fighting wasn't entirely why she wanted to go south. "I trust your judgment," she relented, although the words tasted bitter.

He stared at her a moment, seemingly stunned. "As you should," he said with a growing smirk.

Layala stepped out of the gazebo and said over her shoulder, "Don't let it go to your head."

For the rest of the afternoon, they went around to different booths. Thane sampled a variety of foods which delighted the merchants. Layala took an interest in a small potted tree with thin twisting trunks wrapped around each other sprouting green, pink and white leaves. She'd never seen one like it. Aunt Evalyn would be impressed. "What is this called"? she asked the maiden merchant.

"It's Drivicus Dendium. The white leaves induce invisibility for a time when ingested."

"I didn't know that was possible. I've never heard of it." She could have used it earlier when the mob surrounded her.

"It's yours if you'd like it." She smiled. "A gift from me to Lady Lightbringer."

"Allow me to pay you for it," Thane said beside her. "It must be rare."

The lady shook her head. "No, no. I insist it is given as a gift."

"Thank you," Layala beamed, knowing what a treasure the plant was. Aunt Evalyn would love it. Perhaps she could bring her here to the castle one day. "That is very kind of you."

"It's my pleasure." She bobbed her head and smiled at an approaching customer.

Fennan took the plant to Layala's room, so she didn't have to carry it while they enjoyed the evening. Layala and Thane were lost in conversation about whether Fennan or Aldrich would win in a fistfight. Layala bet on Fennan, as did Thane, which made the two males threaten to start a match right then to see for certain.

When the sun was on the verge of dipping below the horizon, all the elves gathered together near the musicians. "The dance! We're going to miss it!" Layala exclaimed.

Smiling, Thane took Layala's hand and pulled her into a run. "We can make it."

"I don't even have a partner!" Fennan shouted behind them.

"That's lucky for the ladies," Sunshine retorted.

They stepped into one of the lines of elves. Piper came out of nowhere to dance with Fennan, and Vyra snuck up and took to the spot opposite of Sunshine. Slow drums started. Thane bowed and Layala copied him. They held up their palms and she counted her steps one way and then the other. He smiled at her all the while and she couldn't stop her lips from tugging up. And then she was in his arms again, spinning around and somehow everyone else faded away and it could have just been the two of them moving to the steady booms of the drums. The energy vibrating between them was much stronger than before, as if the music added to it, as if the drums were a living thing. Her skin flamed. She glanced at her arms to make sure she wasn't glowing. Did everyone feel this way? She could get lost in this intensity blooming for hours.

Maker above, he was truly beautiful, sinfully so, as she once thought. She didn't notice the small braids in his dark wavy hair until now or that the slight bronze on his cheeks reminded her of a summer day.

When he spun her out a second time and Fennan grabbed her hand, it broke the connection. While she followed the steps with Fennan with her feet, her eyes were set on Thane. When she glided under Fennan's arm and back to Thane, she hated that unwanted desire flooded her insides and her mate rune seemed to pulse as if it was willing them to stay close.

When it was over, all the elves kissed the inside of their fingers and held their palms to the sky. "May the Maker bless us. May light defeat the dark," they said in unison. Then a thunderous boom followed by a shimmering gold light that burst in the sky for a brief moment. Golden trails rained down all around them and then everyone cheered. Layala whistled and threw both her arms up. *May the light defeat the dark.*

An elf in full battle armor approached, breathing heavily as if he'd been running a while. The dirty face and dried blackish-blood on his hands made Layala shift back nervously.

"Sire," he said, bowing before Thane. "The pale

ones have overrun Bogg's Landing," he took in breath, "many are dead; I don't know the number, they are gathering to take Doonafell."

CHAPTER 24

Being on the road this time was much different than the long carriage ride from Briar Hollow. Layala wasn't trapped in a carriage. She rode Midnight and was given a sword, and her daggers and throwing star back. The ground shuddered with the steady march of a battalion of five hundred and sixty. Armor and weapons glinted in the sunlight. Layala swiped at her eyes when dust billowed up from the stamp of horse hooves. All around her, wagons full of supplies creaked and groaned. In the front and back, soldiers held the blue and white flags of Palenor. The air around her was tense; no one had to say it, but they were all nervous and angry. Bogg's Landing was a small swampy town closest to the Void. A couple hundred elves lived there, among other creatures such as centaurs, gnomes, sprites, and a handful of rogue dwarven families who left the mountains, or at least this is what Thane told her the night before. But Doonafell was what worried Thane. She saw it in his eyes.

Thousands of elves lived in the southernmost city. If the pale ones got to them, not only could it be a massacre, but they could turn a vast number into the horrible creatures.

Layala, Thane, Fennan, Sunshine, Piper, and to Layala's dismay, Talon, rode in the center protection of the troop. Talon whined to Thane all morning, insisting she go since they'd ridiculed her for never having seen a pale one. Tifapine hid in the folds of the bag strapped behind the saddle. Apparently whining worked because Layala gave into her protests as well.

"This is so amazing." Tif poked her head out enough to see everything. "Look at all the jumbos. And the gleaming weapons and uniforms and wow, it's like a painting."

After what happened the day before, Layala was nervous about being surrounded by so many elves. But the soldiers were different from the common folk. When she mounted Midnight and rode up beside Thane, the males in their gleaming uniforms all dropped to one knee. Not a single one dared step forward. Either they feared Thane or respected her, perhaps both.

Now as they rode out together, already hours on the road, her uneasiness faded. No one bothered with her. There was enough on their minds, like the possibility of dying in battle, being eaten by a pale one, or worst of all, turning into one. Many of the soldiers joked with each other, and carried on conversations about menial things, no doubt to take their minds off the worst. Thane and Fennan were to her right and they both started laughing so hard they almost fell off their horses. She was sad she missed the joke.

"It is pretty amazing," Layala agreed. "You should come out of that bag and sit where you can see better."

"Nope, nope, nope," Tif said, dipping back in. "Too many, too many. And if I fell off the horse it would surely be my end. I'd, at the very least, break every last bone in my body and then you'd have to kill me out of pity and bury me in the middle of this orange poppy field. Although it is a beautiful and poetic place to be laid to rest, I'm too young to die. And you'd never forgive yourself for it, and I can't have that on my conscience even in the afterlife."

"I think you'd get a few bruises and be just fine," Layala retorted. "And no one here wants to hurt you. The High King knows you live in my room. I didn't even have to tell him."

"I don't believe it. If he knew he'd have thumped me with a broom and whooshed me out a window where my tiny broken body would have been left to rot. The guards would walk by as if I was nothing but trash if they didn't point and laugh at my demise. I don't know what would be worse."

Layala sighed. Such a dramatic little thing. "Tifapine, King Thane and the rest of us elves have more important things to worry about. And the king doesn't hate gnomes. This is some made-up notion you have in your head. Certainly no one would laugh if you fell out a window. How morbid."

"Mama told me high elves have no love for gnomes and I believe it."

Yet she chose to live in Castle Dredwich and had dreams of being an elven lady's maid. Rolling her eyes, Layala said, "What I can't believe is that you were brave enough to cut off an elf's ear, but you won't even come out in the open, when you know I will protect you."

Tif peeked up a little. Her red hat and brown curls moved in the gentle breeze. "That was under the cover of darkness. I was an assassin in the night, using but the meager light of the moon to guide me. It's high noon. The sun is enough to blind a gnome at this time," she hissed. "I might very well wither away under the harsh rays before any other elves notice me."

"You're impossible," Layala drawled.

"We notice you, gnome," Piper said from Layala's left. Her rich brown horse nickered as if to agree with her.

Tif gasped and slammed the bag over her head.

"She talks a lot for one so small," Piper said, running her hand over her thick red braid. "But I suppose her size doesn't mean much in regards to that."

"She could talk to a wall for quite some time I think."

Piper chuckled. "Interesting friend you've made." Piper looked directly at the bag. "We ladies need to stick together, even the small ones. There aren't many of us here."

Tif's eyes gleamed in the shadows as she slowly moved the bag open. "I think we are the only three." Her head emerged fully, and she smiled at Piper. "I'm Tifapine, but my friend calls me Tif."

"Piper."

Layala noticed they were surrounded by mostly males, but such was to be expected when it came to the military. So few she-elves wanted to fight and they weren't expected to. She wasn't even sure if many of them trained in self-defense or not. Layala did but she had reason to. What would she have done if her parents were never murdered, and she didn't have magic? Would she be like Talon, playing dress-up and trying to attract male attentions? Would she have learned to sing or spend her days painting? She liked to think she would grow and scavenge for magical plants like she did with Aunt Evalyn. "Don't forget about Princess Talon," Layala murmured. The princess was talking to Fennan, staring at him like he was the only male out there. It annoyed Layala that they acted like nothing happened. Like the evil wench hadn't caused a mob to surround her the day before. "How did you become a soldier anyway, Piper?"

"My parents have been friends with the Athayels for centuries. When I was young, they brought me to play with Talon. But I grew bored playing with dolls and didn't have an interest in gossiping or walking around in pretty dresses in hopes of catching someone's eye when we became teens. So, I started watching the boys spar and fight outside." She grew a smile. "After a few weeks of spectating and never saying a word to any of them, Thane dragged me over and shoved me in the fighting ring with Fennan. I was in a dress and my hair was styled like a lady and I knew if my mother saw she'd faint. But then Thane tossed a sword at my feet and said, 'let's see what you've got.'

"I expected them to jeer and make fun of me, but the group of both young and older males simply watched. And when I bent down and picked up the sword, they started to cheer me on and even started shouting instructions. Obviously, Fen took it easy on me because I had no training, but I loved it. And every day I went back for more."

"That sounds like me," Layala said. "Although, many of the human men ridiculed me relentlessly at first, especially about my ears, but some took special care to see that I learned. The guard master Hanzen took me under his wing so to speak. He had an eye for my Aunt Evalyn. He became like a father to me in many ways. Protective and a guide. He showed me how to be lethal." Layala's eyes dropped down to the saddle horn. She'd trained all those years with one thing in mind; kill the royal family when they came for her and now, she rode beside them.

"I can't imagine living among humans," Piper said with a shudder. "No offense."

Her mind dipped back to slinging mud at Novak,

Forrest and Ren when they were children and then jumping into the river to wash the grime off. The three boys would always dunk each other and Layala would laugh. Aunt Evalyn always said it was unfortunate that the only kids close to her age in Briar Hollow were boys and she was fighting in the mud and used sticks as swords rather than playing with dolls, although she had dolls of her own. "I've had a good life with them. Even if there have been some tragedies."

Thane cleared his throat and bumped his leg into Layala's. "I need to go and talk with some of my soldiers but when we stop tonight, I have a surprise for you," he said, teeth gleaming in the sun from his big smile.

Her stomach did a little flip. She had no idea if that was good or bad. Eyes narrowing, Layala asked, "What kind of surprise?"

"One I think you'll enjoy."

When the stars and moon were the only light, the battalion stopped and set up camp. One side of the terrain, in the not too far distance, were the Ranaheim Mountains rising high with snow-capped tops, and on the other side of the road were open flat fields of crops as far as the eye could see. The distance held torch-lights and homes. Piper said it was a town named Bendbrook.

Within their camp, fires roared with roasting meats that made Layala's mouth water. Once horses were secured and tents were set up, lines formed for food. The sound of many elves talking at once filled the space. They laughed, some shouted, one man danced with some unique footwork while his spectators jeered and threw things at him. Layala thought he was a good dancer and didn't understand the food throwing. She bit into an apple while sitting on a log next to a fire. Some of the soldiers walked by watching her, whispering as they passed. One worked up the nerve to wave at her, she returned the gesture.

"They don't know how to act around you because you're their High King's mate," Piper said, taking a seat beside her. "They don't know if they should bow to you or stay as far away as possible, but they will fight to the death for you."

"Because I'm his mate or because I'm me?"

"Both, I think," Piper answered. "But you have no idea how much these elves respect and admire Thane."

Thane walked among the soldiers like he was simply one of them and not their High King. He stopped and talked with different groups, making sure everyone had what they needed. Before they left, she believed he would ride away from them while on the move, and sit in his tent and only allow visitors of high rank. Maybe it wasn't just his skill that made it so he'd never personally lost a battle. He made them feel like they couldn't lose. She heard some of the things he said, "With soldiers like you we'll tear them apart" or "The pale ones will shit themselves when they see the Ravens coming. They always do."

Layala turned to Piper. "What are the Ravens?"

"That's what we are." She gestured all around with her hands. "This particular group of soldiers was hand chosen by Thane to fight for him when he goes south. We come in when the enemy has gotten too bold and needs to be reminded that this is our land, and they can't have it."

Layala smiled at Piper's obvious pride. "Why Ravens?"

"Ravens are an omen of death," Tif said, climbing up on the log and sitting between Piper and Layala. "Quite a clever name in my opinion. Although I think plain old 'death bringers' or 'blood letters' would have been better. No misunderstanding that."

Layala chuckled. "True. And I'm glad you finally emerged from the bag."

"Well, it's dark now so no one will notice me except the two of you." She patted both Layala's and Piper's thighs.

A couple servants brought over plates of food and even a small one for Tif. The gnome jumped to her feet and scrambled behind Layala's back where her nails dug into the skin as she clung on to hide. The servants left the plate on her spot on the log. "I told you we see you, gnome," Piper said and then bit into her roll.

Twisting around and pawing at the gnome, Layala said, "And get off me." She finally caught her leg and dragged her out from behind and sat her on the log. "They brought you food. Now eat."

"Oh, well, it does look rather delicious. I suppose I can eat a little." Tif grabbed the roll which was half as big as her and chomped into it, tearing a piece so large, Layala thought it would take her several minutes to get down. She ate it in seconds.

When Thane's looming shadow cast from the crackling fire fell on them, Tif squeaked, knocked her plate into the dirt and darted into the shadows behind the log. Layala rolled her eyes and then stood as did Piper.

"Would you like to sit, sire?" Piper asked, waving a hand at the log.

"For a moment, while you two finish eating." He sat down in between Layala and Piper where Tif had been. Layala leaned back and searched the shadows, but the tiny gnome scuttled off somewhere.

"So, you said you have a surprise for me," Layala said, and then took a bite of the salty meat. It was juicy and flavorful, and only a few bites filled her belly. She wondered if they added something to it to make it more satiating. After all, there were a lot of elves to feed.

"I do."

"And what is it?" Layala set her plate aside. "You've kept me waiting all day to find out. Not very polite, High King."

He turned his head with a pointed stare and a growing smirk. "*You* want to speak to *me* on the topic of politeness?" Piper snickered on his other side.

"I've been very polite," Layala said and couldn't hold back her smile at the obvious lie. "Down right cordial, even. Probably the sweetest elf you've ever met I'd wager."

Thane laughed and slapped his leg. "Hmm, are you willing to put your money where your mouth is?"

"I'm fond of a good wager but not in games I know I'll lose." Layala stood and stretched her arms over her head. "Like cards. I'm terrible at any game to do with cards."

Thane rose to his full height. "Perhaps you'll get to play a different game. Come on." He led them through the camp; soldiers nodded, said their greetings, and a few stopped to shake his hand. Layala smiled and tried to look amiable. Some of these elves wouldn't come home after they fought the pale ones and she wanted to be as kind as possible. Loud cheering from somewhere nearby and small groups of elves heading toward a huge orange light pushed Layala to her toes to see better. What could be going on over there?

"Is that the surprise?" Layala asked. "What are they doing? Fighting trolls?"

Thane chuckled. "No trolls but fighting..."

Layala's heart picked up a little speed and a zing of energy coursed through her veins. When they stepped around the last tent, they came upon a large circle of elves cheering on a pair fighting in the middle. They grappled on the ground, rolling and grunting like animals.

Thane put a hand on her back and pushed them through the soldiers, who moved once they saw who approached, until they reached the front. "You said you knew how to fight. I want to see for myself."

"You want me to fight with your soldiers?" Layala asked, staring at the pair now punching each other in the face.

"Only if you want to. I thought you might want to train since you haven't for a while."

After blood leaked out of one elf's nose and the other had a split above his eye, an abnormally tall elf stepped in and called the match. The pair shook hands and walked out of the circle with their arms around each other's shoulders, throwing compliments about how great the other was. Layala rubbed the back of her now sweaty neck. She missed training with the men in Briar Hollow and most of them stopped being a challenge for her years ago, but stepping in the middle of a ring with the High King's hand-picked fighters was a little intimidating. Another pair stepped in the circle and bowed to each other then pulled out swords.

"Um, couldn't you and I train somewhere a little more private?"

The corner of his mouth ticked up. "You want to tumble around in the dirt alone with me? I'm intrigued."

"And what if I did?" She knew exactly what he inferred.

"I don't think you're ready."

"I'll be the judge of that."

He chuckled. "If you want to spar with me, Layala, you have to earn that privilege. I don't step in there for just anyone."

She faced him and put a hand on her hip. "And here I thought you'd be jumping at the chance. I'm hardly 'just anyone'. I'm your mate that you seemingly can't stop thinking about."

His eyes narrowed. "Now you're admitting it?"

"Sounded like it, didn't it? Although I still haven't seen you on your knees." She wanted to get under his skin for once and it appeared to be working.

He flashed white teeth. "You're teasing me. Who is this new Layala?"

"I've always been this Layala. You just had to work to get past my hard outer shell." She laughed when he rolled his eyes.

"I bet you can't take one of my soldiers, let alone me." He paused briefly. "It would be a repeat of what happened in my bed, although I must say I didn't mind you on top of me, even if you had a knife at my throat."

Flashbacks of that night warmed her cheeks. "I'm sure you didn't. But what are the stakes? Because I'm fully willing to take that bet." If Thane wanted to test her, so be it. A thrill went through her at the thought. She'd win this no matter what.

"Oh, let's do something fun." He paused. "If you lose, I'll ask you a question and you have to tell me. If you win, you can ask me anything and I'll answer. And not something trivial. Something real."

What did he want to know? It didn't matter anyway. She wouldn't lose. "Fine. Do I get to choose my opponent?" Nervousness and excitement ran through her equally. She started thinking of what she wanted to ask him. What deep dark secret might he have?

"I daresay you'd have to since I doubt any of my soldiers would volunteer to spar against Layala Lightbringer."

The two fighters' swords rang and clanked. They grunted and groaned when they pushed against one another. A musty, sweaty odor was like a cloud with all the soldiers gathered so close in the warm summer air. Watching them carefully for weaknesses, Layala didn't catch many. The two were well matched and didn't leave many openings to strike. She glanced around the ring at who she might choose. Every one of them was taller and broader than her. They'd also have elven strength and although she'd never sparred against an elven male, she assumed they were stronger than human men. Thane certainly was but he was different.

Piper would be a good match, size wise, but Layala wanted to prove a point to Thane and picking her would be predictable. "And do we choose if we want to use weapons or not?"

"Yes," Thane answered. "If weapons are used then the fight is stopped when one gets the other in a life-ending position. If it's hand-to-hand then it's stopped by him," he pointed to the tallest elf there who stood off to the side with his arms crossed. "We don't do this to hurt each other; it's to test and refine skills, and keep the soldiers in shape, and to get their minds off the coming battle. It also builds bonds."

She would definitely choose a weapon. Although she could fight hand-to-hand well enough it would be risky and she didn't want to get punched in the face, even if she thought none of them would dare. "When do you train?"

"Most mornings right as the sun comes up."

"And you've never asked me if I wanted to join?"

His green eyes sparkled in the orange firelight. "To be fair, you don't seem to like or want my invitations."

"Well, I would like to join you."

"Alright," he said, and she could tell he was trying not to smile.

The crowd around them burst into a cheer as the match was called. "I knew it!" someone nearby shouted. "You owe me a bottle of wine when we get back."

Layala's eyes snapped to the ring as the two shook hands. She missed who won. Thane put a hand on her back and guided her forward. Everyone fell silent. Their breathing, the night insects chirping, the crackling fire seemed loud now. A few whispered about what was about to happen. Thane stopped them in the center and said, "Layala is sparring next. She will choose her opponent."

The hush of the soldiers was eerie as the hundreds of eyes stared. Her gaze swept across them. She could almost hear their thoughts of "Don't pick me" from the worried looks. The only ones that made eye contact with her were Sunshine and Piper. "Aldrich," Layala said using Sunshine's real name. The soldiers let out an "Ooooo" as he stepped forward, grinning.

When he reached them, he stuck out his hand and Layala shook it. "It's an honor to be chosen," he said. A look passed between Thane and Sunshine. She wished she knew what they were silently communicating.

"I choose swords."

Aldrich nodded and pulled his weapon from the holster on his back and stepped away swinging it around to warm up. Layala gripped her sword's leather-bound handle and tugged it loose. Thane backed her up a few steps. "If at any time you—"

"Don't placate me." Layala stared him in the face. "You'll be consoling your friend soon."

Thane smiled. "Confident. I like that." Once he was to the side, Layala marched at Sunshine with determination. She wasn't simply proving herself to win a bet or to show Thane she could fight. This was to verify to the Ravens she could contend with them, the High King's hand-picked warriors. Her breaths moved in and out in steady trained motion. Her grip on her sword tightened as she brought it up and stepped to the side with a quick strike. Aldrich blocked it but his blade came dangerously close to his face, and his grin dropped. He may have thought this would be easy, that he would toy with her a while so as not to embarrass her, but she was by no means someone to be toyed with. He underestimated her strength. She swung again with her elven speed, the clink of their blades slamming against one another echoed off the Ranaheim mountainside. Then again and again, they circled, striking, blocking over and over, high and low. He favored his right side heavily.

Sweat beaded on her brow. Her steady heart was a calming sound as it pounded in her ears. They hit again but this time they pushed in a battle of strength. Her arms and legs screamed with the effort, and she sidestepped when he overpowered her but used the momentum and shoved him in the back.

The circle of elves started shouting, some for Aldrich, some for Layala. "You're allowing a female to best you!?" one of them yelled.

"Knock his ass into the dirt!" Piper bellowed.

He turned around and came at her with quick strikes. She blocked everything he threw at her, then dropped low and swung her leg out. It caught his foot and he stumbled backward into the elves behind him but didn't fall. *Damn it.* They shoved him forward and Layala struck with a downward hack and again at his ribs and it got through, smacking into him hard. She expected him to block it and didn't pull back enough and it cut into his side. He cried out; she jerked her sword back and dropped it. The clang of it reverberated loudly in the silence.

She gushed, "I'm so sorry."

Holding his side, Aldrich slid his sword up to her neck, the cold metal like ice against her flesh. "Don't ever drop your sword."

In her haste to see if she'd hurt him badly, she did the one thing she never should have, but this wasn't a real fight. Against a pale one she never would drop her sword. "How bad are you hurt? I don't care about who won right now."

Aldrich's face blanched white and he put his arm around her, forcing her to bear much of his weight. "I'm fine. It's a scratch."

"I don't think so," Layala murmured. After he broke his leg not long ago against the pale ones, she felt bad to hurt him again, even if magical plants could heal him quick enough.

Others ran forward and surrounded them, shouting about the outcome. "Layala won with that blow. The fight would have been stopped," one soldier argued.

"No, she dropped her sword before it was called," another argued.

"We all know who was going to win either way," Piper barked. "Layala."

Thane stepped in and tugged at the fabric of Aldrich's top. "It's not that deep, but get him to the medical tent."

Aldrich pulled his arm from Layala and took a few slow steps into the grasps of Fennan and Piper.

"Sire, who won?" a stout blond elf asked.

He gave Layala an apologetic look. "According to

the rules, Aldrich since Layala dropped her sword and he put his blade to her neck before it was called."

A bunch of the elves booed. "She whipped his ass. He was on the defense the whole time," someone in the crowd shouted.

"She's as skilled as any of us," another said.

"Layala Fightbringer," the fire-haired Leif shouted, and many laughed. He put his arm casually around her shoulders. "You think she's a Raven, boys?"

"Caw, Caw!" Then they roared with cheers. The chorus of deep voices all around made Layala's arm hairs stand on end. She was accepted into the group and didn't know how much she wanted that until right then.

Thane smiled at her with pride. "I think she is." Then Thane lightly shoved him in the chest and pulled Layala to his side. "Now back off. She's mine."

Layala rolled her eyes as everyone laughed.

Chapter 25

Just when Thane didn't think he could find Layala any more attractive, she went and proved him wrong. She proved she could fight. Her magic was impressive but her talent with a sword against one of his best fighters was even more so. A skill like that took years of practice, dedication and fortitude. He pulled her by her hand through the horde of his warriors. They patted her on the back, smiled, fist pumped, cheered her on as they passed by. She'd earned their respect and been accepted by them, which wasn't easy for any elf to do.

When they came upon his five-pole tent, gray in color and thick enough material to stop the wind or insects from getting in, he pulled the entrance flap aside and gestured for her to step in. She hesitated. "I planned on sleeping in a tent with Piper."

Why did she always think the worst of him? Did she honestly think he would try to take advantage of her? Maybe he shouldn't have claimed her like that in front of everyone, technically she wasn't *his*. The mate spell wasn't even complete, and she hadn't chosen him. Maybe he pushed her away by doing that. And she was finally starting to lighten up after their last argument. "I expected you would. Can we talk for a while first?"

She lifted her chin, straightened her shoulders, and stepped inside. After she glanced around at the makeshift bed of sheepskin furs, a single wooden chair, and a heavy black trunk full of his belongings, she said, "I thought there'd be more."

"I like to travel light on the road."

She toyed with the dagger at her belt for a moment then claimed the only chair. Thane sat on the furs and began to unbuckle the sword sheath latched on his chest. "So, since you lost the fight, you owe me an answer."

Her mouth dropped. "You know I won that fight. Losing on a technicality is horseshit."

He licked his lips and set his sword on the bed beside him. He slipped his weapon belt off, placing it in the dirt and then laid back into the soft blankets, wrapping his hands behind his head. "You impressed me by the way. I expected you to have skills, but nothing like that."

"Thank you."

"So as a consolation, how about a question for a question then?"

Her eyes held him steadily. "I suppose that's fair. I

won't be making the mistake of feeling sorry for your soldiers when I beat them again. Ask away."

"What happened two years ago when it felt like your heart shattered?" He'd been dying to know this for years. It haunted him knowing how much pain she was in, and he couldn't be there. He had his suspicions, but he wanted to hear it from her.

She tore her gaze away and stared at her hands on her lap. "Ask me something else. Anything else."

He frowned. "Why don't you ask me a question then?"

She sat a little taller. "How did your father really die?"

He knew that was coming. After taking in a deep breath, he said, "I killed him." Her eyebrows significantly raised but he continued, "I knocked him unconscious, tied him to a horse and sent him into the Void. The last time I saw him, he was being dragged down by pale ones." He expected her to be surprised but there was something else there, something he couldn't quite understand. "Are you disappointed?"

"No, I'm glad he's dead. I'm just surprised you'd do that. Not just because he's your father but elven law states you should be executed for your crime, not take his place as king."

Assassinating kings simply wasn't done by the elves. It hadn't ever been done to his knowledge. His grandfather who ruled before, died in the last war with the Black Mage, and before that, his great grandfather stepped down after reining a thousand years. Prior to that, wars shifted and changed leaders but never was there an inside killing. Never had an heir killed to take his father's place.

"Which is why I didn't want to tell you before. The people, as well as my mother and sister, would demand my execution."

"I won't tell anyone, and not only because our lives are linked."

"I pray that you don't. And I hope you take my honesty as an offering that you can trust me."

The flickering candle on the small table at his bedside danced in the quiet. Layala stared at the flames for a moment, as if trying to figure out a puzzle she didn't have all the pieces to. Voices of soldiers walking by drew their gazes to the tent's entrance. If any of his Ravens happened to overhear what had been said, Thane didn't think they'd tell anyone. They cared about him more than his father, but it was still dangerous information. When the voices were gone, she spoke again, "So why did you?"

He tsked his tongue. "If you want me to answer another question you have to answer one."

Her chest heaved as she took in a deep breath. "Someone I loved died that day."

"Someone?" Thane questioned. She stayed silent. Thane stared at his deep brown boots getting drawn into his memory. "My best friend Osric died two months ago. We'd been in battle, and he was bitten by a pale one." Thane drew in a steadying breath. It still hurt to speak of him, and it would hurt even more so to say aloud what had happened that day. "There was nothing the healers could do to stop the change. And when he turned... I didn't have the strength to end it before he could turn. So, when he woke with skin white as snow and hair that once was warm turned alabaster, and lips as black as coal, I hoped that he would be able to see reason. That some part of him was still there. And part of him was. He knew me." Thane stopped talking as his throat tightened and tears burned his eyes.

"You don't have to tell me any more," Layala whispered.

Thane's heart thundered at the flashbacks, at the images of Osric laughing as he pulled a sword and tried to skewer Thane and then tried to bite him. Swallowing down the lump in his throat, Thane went on, "Anyways, it wasn't him anymore. I—I killed him, and something in me snapped. I knew I'd have to kill my father, I'd known it for years but I was a coward. I couldn't do it. I kept thinking he would change. I kept reasoning that he wasn't as bad as he was, even when he was set on bringing back the Black Mage and using you to do it. After I killed Osric, something in me died. Maybe it was my compassion, I don't know, but I went after my father the next day. And then a few weeks later, I showed up in Briar Hollow because with my father gone, you would be safe. Palenor would be safe. At least that's what I rationalized."

"I can't imagine how much it must have hurt you," Layala said. Even if Tenebris was an evil tyrant, he was Thane's father. "In both cases you were right. You shouldn't feel any guilt." She looked away briefly. "But I wish you would have let me kill him. I wanted to."

Truth was the guilt ate away at him, a little more each day. Every time his mother or sister talked about Tenebris. When the people held a huge memorial service for him. He knew what his father was, hated him even, but it still left an invisible wound because he loved his father too. Despite everything, he loved him. But putting down Osric was the hardest thing he'd ever done. It nearly ripped the heart right out of his chest. "Well, it's done now."

"His name was Novak," Layala said without any prompt. "We had known each other since we were children. He was a few years older than me, so we didn't get along until I was about fifteen. I think before that he always saw me as an annoying little child. For years we were friends, and we trained at the yard together, and we walked the woods behind my house, picked berries, and hunted for plants for Aunt Evalyn. Then his younger brother Ren kissed me one night after a night of drinking. It was very unexpected I assure you, and Novak punched him for it. I never knew that either of them had feelings for me. But I loved Novak and he loved me and when he died—he almost took me to the grave with him."

Thane was quiet for a moment, trying to find the right words. "A part of him will always be with you. I am sorry you lost him," Thane said, and he truly was.

He could feel the ghost of that pain even now through the magic between them. "How did he die?"

Layala shot to her feet and hurried for the tent flap. "I'm done talking about it."

Damn it. Thane shoved himself up off the furs and darted in front of her, blocking the path. "I won't ask again."

Layala pushed him aside and stomped into the night. Thane sighed and watched to make sure she made it into her own tent adjacent to his, and when she closed the flap behind her, he sagged a little. How was he supposed to know that the way the man died would be worse for her to talk about than him actually dying? It must have been traumatic, but it couldn't have been worse than when he had to cut Osric's head off. Or worse than when he had to carry Osric's broken, changed body, and slam the shovel into the ground over and over while he sobbed so he could bury his best friend in a shallow grave. Or worse than when he told Osric's parents what happened. Obviously, he shared a different kind of relationship than Layala did with Novak, but he loved Osric like a brother.

When he went back to his bed, he removed his boots and shirt, and curled up under the blanket. After he couldn't fall asleep for a while, he opened his trunk and pulled out his folded leather that contained medicinal flora. He took out a dried, azure, slumber berry and popped it into his mouth. Hopefully it could calm his mind. Eventually, he fell asleep.

The next morning, he awoke and dressed. Hesitating outside Layala's tent, he paced for a moment. She said she wanted to train with him but after the way she left the night before he didn't want to ask and get something thrown at his head.

Ah blast it. He shoved through the flap. Layala still slept, as did Piper. One of Layala's long legs poked out of the blanket and her tangled hair half covered her face. He nudged her foot with his boot. "Wake up dearest. We're training before we head out."

Layala slowly sat up and pushed her black hair out of her eyes. Half of her blue button-down shirt hung off her shoulder. She yawned and tugged her shirt up. "It's still dark out."

"We leave soon after sunrise which means if we're going to train, we have to do it before."

Piper rolled over and covered her head. Tugging the blanket off her, Layala revealed her bare legs. She wore nothing but that shirt and thin silky emerald-green underwear. His eyes were drawn to the length of her thighs and the curve of her hips. "I'll be waiting outside."

"You sure you don't want to stay and watch me dress?" she teased, picking her trousers up from a neatly-folded pile beside her.

"Is that an invitation? Perhaps you can take some more off instead."

Piper threw a pillow at Thane. "Ew, save your bedroom talk for when I'm not around."

He tossed the pillow back and laughed on his way

out of the tent. When Layala emerged a few minutes later, her hair was tied back in a braid, her weapons were strapped on her hips and back and she looked as grumpy as ever. "Do I at least get a cup of energy tea and something to eat first?"

"And here I thought you'd be glad I woke you to train. I can let you sleep next time instead." Thane tossed her an apple. "The cooks should have tea brewing."

"I am glad you woke me." She yawned. "But I didn't sleep well. There was a rock jabbing my back the entire night and Tif decided she wanted to snore on the pillow next to me. I wanted to smother her with it."

"So vicious," he said playfully.

"I'll show you 'vicious' in a minute."

They stopped at the cook's tent, the only other elves awake at this time, drank down some energizing tea and ate a couple biscuits. He didn't like to be too full when training, but he needed something to fight off the ache in his belly. He led Layala to a clearing far enough from camp that they wouldn't be bothered but close enough they could see everything. The stars were still shining brightly but to the east light peaked over the hillside, giving them enough to see each other clearly.

Briefly glancing at some of the tents in camp now being pulled down, Thane said, "I don't know what you do but I start with a run, push-ups, pull-ups on a tree branch if I can find one, practice sword moves and then spar with a partner."

"How about today we follow your training and tomorrow, I'll show you mine?"

"That's fair." Thane started off at a steady pace, jogging toward the massive gray-faced mountainside, soon they'd be close enough they wouldn't be able to see the top. The grass grew vibrantly green, and the atmosphere smelled of wind and rivers and pine trees; the needled trees bunched in pockets around here. Thane followed a thin goat or perhaps a centaur trail. The soft dirt below his feet was pleasant to run on unlike rocky, ankle-breaking paths.

"How old were you when you started training?" Layala asked.

Was she actually trying to make conversation with him? He wondered what caused her change in attitude the last few days. Ever since the festival she'd been amiable, even to him. His mind pulled up the memory of the day his father sent him into the training yard with a sword that was much too big. He remembered that although it didn't feel heavy, it was long, and the blade dragged on the ground as he carried it. His mother patted him on the head and gave him a little push when he hesitated to meet with his master trainer, Jorgon. The trainer had a scar down the side of his face; tall and thin he looked like a giant to the small child. *"I'll be watching the entire time, my love," his mother said smiling.* Thane peeked over at Layala. "I was six." Shortly after

Jorgon got a proper sword for a boy, the training started.

"That seems a little young, doesn't it?"

Thane lifted a shoulder. "They didn't expect much of me at the time and they weren't hard on me until I was older. It was more technique and mindset training. Learning to get up and follow a routine, I suppose. And you?"

"I started at twelve. Which means you have about nine years on me." She gave him a shove that sent him stumbling off the path. "But I bet I'm still better." She propelled ahead into a sprint.

Thane shook his head, smiling, and dashed after her. She was fast. He'd give her that. He was at his body's full running capacity, his arms and legs pumping hard, before he caught her. They weaved between boulders and trees as they raced across the grassy landscape. He had a feeling he'd be chasing after her for a long time, maybe always.

"It's nice to run with someone who can keep up!" she hollered. "No one in Briar Hollow could."

"You're in Palenor now. Everyone can." Thane jumped up and swung from a tree branch, catapulting over a small stream, and landed clear of the water on the other side. Layala leapt over, her boots splashing at the edge. She grinned at him and reached back, the rub of metal on metal *chinged* as she pulled her sword. Waving it slowly in front of her, she tapped her boot lightly. "Let's see what you've got, High King."

Maker above, she looked good with a weapon. He

thought he might prefer her like this over fancy dresses, but she was beautiful either way. When he took out not one sword but two, and weaved them in front of himself to show off, she started laughing.

"You wield two swords," she mused. "I didn't know that. I thought you simply had a backup."

"As if I'd ever lose either one," he said with a wink.

"No matter, I can contend with a cheater."

"Cheater?" They clashed swords; the clang of metal ricocheted off the sheer weathered rock to their left. "It's a skill like any other. It doesn't make me a cheater." She knocked one sword aside and then blocked his other. *Ping, clank, grind,* their blades slid off each other. She jabbed straight at his belly, he darted around and ran up the trunk of a tree and backflipped over her head, landing lightly.

"He's got moves," Layala purred.

"I have other moves I'd be more than happy to show you sometime."

She narrowed her eyes in a predatory gaze and swung right at his very important male appendage. He sucked in a breath and blocked the strike with both swords. "Woah now, that was a little too close."

"You practically asked for that."

They carried on for a while, both easily blocking every attack, although he wasn't trying to get through and he could see that she wasn't either. Soon he found himself laughing and he couldn't even say why other than he was simply having fun. It was enjoyable to train with someone who wasn't trying to prove themselves to their king or worse, trying not to hurt him so they blunted their skill. She was at ease and that put him there too.

After they were both breathing heavily and sweating, he backed up and dropped his arms to his sides. "Shall we call it for the day?" He hadn't even realized it was fully light out and they were meant to leave soon after sunrise. "They're probably waiting for us back at camp."

Layala sheathed her sword. "That was fun. I'm excited to do it again."

"As am I."

"Shall we run back to camp? I think we got pretty far. At least a mile." She climbed on top of a large, rounded boulder and peered with her hand shading her eyes. "Yep, the camp is taken down, except maybe your tent. Although it looks like they're sparring in small groups, so not entirely bored."

Thane strutted casually ahead. "It's a good thing I am High King, and we go when I say we go." He jogged on, expecting a remark from her about his arrogance but it never came. When he didn't hear her footsteps behind him after too long, he turned. She wasn't on the rock which now looked small because he'd gotten so far away. She wasn't anywhere. He turned in a full circle. "Layala?" Was she playing a game? "If you're hiding, it's not funny. We need to go." Nothing answered but the wind. The steady thud of his heart quickened. He ran back to where he left her to find a wide area of flattened grass where she may have jumped down, but would she have fallen and then rolled around?

There were several trees around she could have climbed and a few scattered boulders a ways off but the stone dropping in his gut told him she wasn't hiding. His walk turned into a jog when he looked up into the canopies of the nearest trees to find them empty. On the side of the Ranaheim mountains there was a dark crevice that looked like a jagged scar on the gray rock. He stilled himself and closed his eyes, reaching out for that gentle line that connected him to her. His mate rune itched like a healing scab. Close, she was close. In his mind's eye a lavender cloud directed him toward the mountain, toward the crevice. His eyes shot open when *her* panic hit him with full force. "Layala!"

Chapter 26

Layala's head throbbed, and her vision was so blurry everything looked like dark blobs of paint around her. She thrashed about, fighting whoever held her legs and upper body. It smelled like a carcass mixed with a musty aroma of moss and pine. Water trickled and the feet of her captors quietly splashed in it. Were they in a river, a stream? She'd been near one when sparring with Thane. Where was he? Did they get to him too? She bit at the cloth tied around her mouth, but it would take much too long to chew through it.

The moment she climbed down from the boulder, she was knocked on the temple with a rock that dropped her to her hands and knees. Black spots took the place of the scenery around her. Although she didn't completely lose consciousness, she was dizzy and disoriented. Immediately after, someone wrapped a rope around her upper body and jabbed a barb into her arm. The effects of whatever poison it had been laced with seeped through her veins quickly and rendered her magic completely null. She couldn't even feel its fight to get out, let alone release it now.

She blinked several times, finally clearing the blurriness away and got a good look at the captor holding her legs. A pale one; the inky black around her eyes and lips, the pure white hair and skin. Layala screamed, fighting even harder. She kicked so hard it sent the dark female flying back into a cavern wall. Her feet fell into the shallow water and hit her calves. They'd carried her into a *cave* and Maker above. What did they plan to do? The one holding her upper body gripped her harder. His fingers dug in on her arms enough to leave bruises.

"Calm down, sweetness," his gravelly voice sent shivers down her spine. "Master just wants to talk. If I wanted you dead I'd have skewered you already for a nice juicy kabab. I bet you'd taste good."

Layala drove her head back, catching him on the chin hard enough he let go. With her legs bound she couldn't run so she worked to loosen the ropes around her arms to get the dagger at her belt. Arms wrapped around her again and the pale one put his lips to her ear. "Mathekis wants to see you. Stop fighting or I'll bite you right now and that pretty black hair can be as white as mine."

Her blood chilled enough to freeze her into stillness. His mouth was dangerously close to her, his breath smelled like death, and she forced a gag down. The female pale one pushed herself up and balled her hand as she charged and drove her fist into Layala's gut. The pain had her gasping for air as she bent over. She gagged on the cloth in her mouth and forced herself to breathe through her nose. The creature may as well have had a brick in her hand. It landed so hard.

"Master said not to hurt her."

"She'll be fine. You're the one who threw the rock." The female grabbed Layala's face, squeezing hard enough that jagged nails bit into her flesh. She forced Layala to look up and meet her black eyes. She could still hardly drag in a breath. "You're what all the fuss is about?" The second she released her hold, a fist clopped Layala's cheek from the other side and sent her crashing to her knees, and shortly after her face hit the water. She was jerked up within seconds; the pain radiated down her body then throbbed where the impact hit. Water streamed down her face and neck.

"That's enough!" the male screeched, his voice echoed loudly off the walls of the damp cave. He held her firmly against him. "Mathekis will know it was you who marred her face, not *me*."

"A few bruises never killed anyone."

"And if you killed her, it would be both our heads. Now stop fooling about and help me."

Finally, Layala got her hand on her dagger and angled it to saw at the rope. The female abruptly started screaming and slammed her hands to the sides of her head. "Ahhh, make it stop! Make it stop!" She threw herself into the wall with a sickening thud and dropped to the ground. A whistle and a glint of metal shone just before a knife went through the dark female's temple.

Layala jerked her head to the cavern's entrance and there stood Thane in all his raging glory. His swords glinted in the light; his hair billowed in the breeze. His face was onyx shadows and furious seas. The pulse of his magic hit her like a tidal wave. He unleashed its hold and although it was powerful, it oozed over her like warm honey. A protective shield of some kind.

The pale one holding her trembled. He must have felt something different.

Threatening.

Wrathful.

Layala finally cut through the rope pinning her arms down and drove the dagger into the gut of the pale one behind her. She stabbed wildly over and over as he howled. Swinging around, she slashed the blade across his neck.

Thane grabbed Layala's arm and pulled her away from the pale one as he fell to the side, gurgling black blood. "Are you hurt?" he asked frantically. "Did they—"

"They didn't bite me," she finished, which made her wonder why. He had every opportunity.

Thane jerked her into him, and wrapped his arms around her in a tight squeeze. "I thought you were gone."

Layala melted into him and returned the embrace. "I'm still here." Something flowed into her; foreign emotions she always repelled not knowing what they were. Thane's relief flooded her like a broken dam.

Scowling, he pulled back and looked around. "Are there more?"

"I've only seen two, but he mentioned bringing me to Mathekis." She frowned. "I never realized they were so aware, so intelligent. I thought of them as mostly mindless beasts following their instincts. More like an animal than like us."

Thane moved for the cave opening. "They don't lose their cognition when they turn but their instincts to kill, maim, and feed are strong. I think what they lose is their conscience. They're emotional intelligence of right and wrong. Osric didn't care that I'd been his friend for all our lives. He wanted me to be like him."

When they stepped out into the daylight Layala's eyes burned with tears. The stark contrast from the darkened cave to the brilliant sun hurt. "But these two didn't want to kill me. They were following orders."

"The older ones have more control. Osric was freshly turned. If I had let him live, he would have found others like him and eventually he would have been able to follow orders." He glanced over at her as they ran back toward camp. "And why didn't you use your magic? I know it could draw more but if your life's in danger like that you must. No hesitation."

"They dosed me with katagas. I can't feel my magic right now." Pulling up her sleeve revealed a swollen red mark on the flesh of her left forearm.

"It's only temporary." His eyes lingered on her a beat longer than usual. "You need to see a medic."

"I'm fine." She reached up and touched her cheek; it was sticky. She thought the wetness she felt was from the stream but when her fingers came away bloody, her stomach ached. The rock that knocked her down must have done some real damage or when the female punched her in the same spot.

"You're not fine."

"I don't want anyone to see me like this. I don't want them to know how close the pale ones got." A worrisome thought stirred in her. "Somehow, they keep finding us. I don't trust your soldiers. I hate to say it but one of them may be leaking our location."

Thane shook his head. "No. No way."

"Do you have another explanation? How did they know where we were after leaving Briar Hollow? Or if they were the ones to trash my house, how did they know it was mine? It wasn't anything I did."

Thane's mouth formed a hard line. "You're suggesting that one of the three people closest to me in the world betrayed me. That's not possible."

"Did anyone else know where you'd gone?"

Thane shook his head. "Not unless we were followed."

"Piper, Aldrich, or Fennan might have told someone without malicious intent, or one of you could have been overheard. Tifapine may not be the only gnome or small creature hiding within the castle."

Layala clenched her teeth. *Either way someone is a traitor.*

He darted around a tree and then swept back to her side. "Anyone in the city could have seen you leaving with us. It doesn't mean it's my friends or Ravens."

"That doesn't explain the first encounter with pale ones outside of the Brightheart Forest. That wasn't a coincidence. They had a leader. The one who spoke to me called me a dark mage. He knew what I am just as these two did."

Thane went quiet until they reached camp. Most of the elves were sparring in pairs or talking in groups on one end, allowing them to slip mostly unnoticed into Thane's lone standing tent. A few sentries dipped their heads as they passed but they weren't stopped.

Throwing the tent flap aside Thane stepped in and held it open for Layala. Holding her now-throbbing head, she slipped inside and plopped in the chair. Thane opened his trunk and dug through it cursing and grunting as he did.

"What are you looking for?" Layala asked, closing her eyes, and leaning back. Her head felt like it might split in half.

"Ah, here it is," he said. Layala opened one eye to see he held a brown satchel. He flipped open the flap. "It's my med kit."

She sat taller and held out her hand. "Just give me a cloth and I'll clean myself up."

After setting the bag down, he drenched the tan

cloth with whatever was in the green glass bottle he had in hand. "Do you *ever* allow anyone to help you without pushback? Pearl and Reina have told me stories."

Traitors. Letting out a huffy breath, Layala snapped, "You literally just helped me in the cave. I didn't complain."

He shot her a scowl. "That's different. And you haven't seen the cut. It needs stitches to stop the bleeding, and healing balm."

Layala stood and stepped closer to him. "Then give me a mirror and I'll do it."

He shoved the cloth against her wound and held it there firmly. "Sit," he commanded.

Much to her chagrin, she complied. She gripped the wooden handles of her seat as he pressed and dabbed the cloth. It smelled strongly of plant oils, perhaps peppermint and pinegrout which smelled similar to lavender. It also burned with astringent, but the pain began to subside. She stiffened when he slowly and carefully wiped down her neck. His concentrated face was inches from hers, and Maker above, had she stopped breathing? Although she knew he didn't mean for it to be, the gesture felt sensual. The hairs on her body prickled when he gently sponged the blood that stained along her collar bone.

His eyes lifted to hers and the intensity that passed in those brief moments sent a tingle down her spine. He pulled his hand back and cleared his throat. "I got most of the blood but there's still some in your hair.

You'll have to wash in a stream," he tugged on the collar of her top, "and there's blood all over this too."

She didn't realize she stared at him like a doe at the other end of an arrow until she dropped her gaze to her shirt. "That's more than I thought."

"Exactly as I've been saying." He held a needle in hand. "Now this part hurts the worst, but you must hold still."

The cut was near her eyebrow, a sensitive area. She gave a curt nod and an unnatural wave of calm filled her. Grabbing his wrist before he could press the needle into her flesh, she asked, "Did you do that?"

"What?"

"It *is* you," she breathed, heart stuttering a beat. "How do you send that calming feeling to me?"

"I do it through our magic bond."

"How?"

"I don't know how it works entirely." He bent to eye level with her wound. "I just know I can connect with you, in the same way you send your emotions to me without meaning to I suppose."

So, she sent him all her bad emotions while he tried to calm her. This connection between her and Thane was more intimate than she ever thought.

With her teeth clenched, she dug her fingers into the chair as the needle pinched over and over until the wound was sealed shut. After dipping his fingers into a tin of balm, he rubbed it over the wound and lightly over spots on her other cheek where the pale one's nails had dug in.

Thane began placing the items back in his satchel. "You should be healed up by tomorrow."

"Thank you." She lightly brushed her thumb over the smooth pommel of her dagger, admiring Thane for a moment more. He really saved her life back there. She slowly pushed up from the chair, waiting for him to say something more. He didn't. She nibbled on her lower lip. "Well, I'm going to put on a new shirt and if anyone asks, I fell during training." She hurried out of the tent before he could respond. The tent she slept in the night before was gone and with it her belongings. A group of five soldiers walked by with their horses in tow.

"Good morning, Fightbringer," said the one with dark hair and a crooked grin.

"Morning," she said with a quick wave. "Do any of you know where Piper is?"

Since she was one of the only females there, they'd know exactly where she was. "She's over by that tree," the soldier closest to her answered. "Are you alright? Looks like you got injured." He tapped his temple.

"Oh, I'm fine. Thanks." She turned before they could ask more.

Jogging over to where Midnight and Phantom were tied, she found Piper and Tif sitting nearby under the tree. Midnight greeted her with a nicker and was already saddled with her belongings.

"You two have held up the entire company for an hour longer than usual." Piper stood and brushed the dirt off her pants. Her demeanor changed when she asked, "Why is there blood all over your shirt?"

"I hit my head on a rock. We were sparring and I tripped over a tree root." Layala gestured toward the stitches.

"I didn't take you as clumsy," Piper said skeptically.

"I'm not."

Waddling over with a handful of berries, Tif popped one in her mouth. She looked up at Layala. "That sounds like one of those things abused wives say when they get beat by their husbands. I know you don't have a husband, but you have a king who is notorious for being ruthless."

"The *king* didn't hurt me."

"Now *that* didn't sound like a lie," Piper said with a smirk.

Tif went on as if nothing had been said, "Although I do have a feeling, and don't ask me why, but I bet he has gentle hands too. Sweet hands. Can you imagine them running through your hair?" She twirled a lock of her rich brown curls around her chubby finger. "Or rubbing your shoulders? Or—"

Layala grinned. "Are you in love with the High King, Tifapine?"

"Of course, I'm not. That's the most ridiculous thing I've ever heard in my life." Her cheeks turned as red as a ripe strawberry. "More ridiculous than a squirrel loving a horse."

"If you say so," Piper teased. "He is nice to look at though, isn't he?" Piper gave a quick wink at Layala.

"Oh my goodness gracious, he is so handsome. The most-handsomest elf I've ever seen," Tif gushed, holding her hand over her heart like she might swoon. Layala and Piper burst into laughter. "Hey, you tricked me into saying that," Tif whined. "I only said it because I didn't want you to tell him I think he's as ugly as a bridge troll. Never mind his muscles and those shiny green eyes and the fact that he looks nothing like a troll."

Layala dug into her bag and pulled out a clean shirt. After setting it on Midnight's back, she tugged off her sword and holster, unbuckled her corset and tugged her dirty top over her head. She peeked over her shoulder hoping none of the soldiers were watching. Midnight blocked most everyone from even getting a chance at catching her changing. "Why is it so hard to believe I tripped anyway?" She slipped the fresh shirt on quickly and finished dressing.

Piper bit into her apple. "Because the she-elf I saw fight last night against Aldrich would be aware of her surroundings."

"He's better, by the way," Tif said. "I saw him this morning. Up and walking around like you didn't bust him in the ribs with a sword."

"His pride is hurt more than anything," Piper said with a shrug. "But Talon and Fennan kept him entertained while the healers fixed him up."

"What's the situation with those three?"

"I don't know. Talon liked Fennan for a while, but she gets bored easily. Aldrich has been spending a lot of time with her recently, but I never thought anything was there. But I could be wrong."

She couldn't see the attraction between them. Aldrich was bright and funny while Talon was cunning and vindictive. Fennan was too smart to fall for her wiles. But after what Talon did at the Summer Solstice, she still owed her retaliation and perhaps she'd use Sunshine or Fennan to do it.

Layala stepped on a raised tree root which gave her enough height to reach the stirrup and mount Midnight. From there she got a better view. Most of the soldiers were on their horses and lined up. She didn't see Thane anywhere, but his tent was being taken down by a small group of servants. They didn't wear uniforms like the soldiers but rather various traveling attire. "We better get going. It looks like we're moving out."

Piper lifted Tif up and set her behind Layala. She untied Phantom and her golden horse and took hold of their reins. "I'll meet you over there."

As if a sign from above, Sunshine and Talon crossed her path. "How are you two love birds?" Layala called and both of them turned as if they'd been whipped.

Chapter 27

"Love birds? That's probably an offense to the princess. She could do much better than me." Aldrich chuckled and ran his hand over his dirty blond hair. "Nice fight by the way. You sure can swing a sword." He patted his side where she cut him.

Layala caught the quick subject change which meant she might be on the right track. "So can you. Sorry about that."

Talon cut her a glare. "Well, if it isn't the wayward low-born again. How did you enjoy the festival? It looked like you had such a good time with your adoring devotees. It was so nice of you to give them pieces of your hair."

Wench. "I did have a good time, actually. Aldrich is a good bodyguard."

The princess tightened her grip on her horse's reins. "I'll be sure to pass on to my brother that you have a thing for Aldrich and your body. Maybe you want him to touch it."

"Woah, woah," Sunshine said, holding up a palm giving her a confused look. "Don't pass anything remotely close to that to your brother. That's not—just no. Hard no."

Poor Sunshine had to be wrapped up in the squabble. "She won't because she knows it's not true. She's just angry I outrank her now. Poor princess."

"You should learn to keep your mouth shut, Layala, or you might find yourself in a shallow grave."

Does she know that her brother's life and mine are linked? She wasn't afraid of Talon either way, but the princess might be crazy enough to try if she didn't know.

"Princess," Sunshine snapped. "Do not threaten her. She is under our protection, *my* protection. She is set to be your queen in but weeks."

"Maybe yours." She kicked her horse and rode ahead. "Not mine."

When the troop moved on, Layala found her place in the center. She'd tugged her hair loose from the braid and let it flow freely to cover the injury near her temple. Since Piper didn't believe the story, she didn't know if anyone else would and she didn't want to tell the lie over and over again anyway.

Although she was safe in the center of hundreds of

elven soldiers, she found herself searching for pale ones among them. Scanning the outskirts for them lurking among the shadows of trees or hiding in the tall grass for an ambush. She found none but it didn't mean they weren't there, waiting—watching. Was Mathekis near? Even his name forced a chill down her spine. Did he not want her turned? She assumed she couldn't be a pale one for their purposes or that creep would have bitten her. They would have turned her to get her on their side. At least she lucked out where that was concerned.

Thane rode close beside her, looking over frequently as if he worried she might suddenly vanish. Now that she could distinguish his emotions and allowed them through their connection, she knew his anxiety.

She watched Thane for a moment, admiring the profile of his beautiful masculine features, and she thought of the way the pale one screamed out of nowhere, crying out in pain and threw herself into the wall so hard, it might have killed her. Did he do that? If anyone could save the whole of Adalon it had to be him. He was a strong leader, and he knew what he wanted. Perhaps it was *his* magic that could destroy the Void, not hers. What if she was the darkness and he was the light? What a cruel act it was for fate to have bound them together.

Thane peeked over again, worry etched in his face.

"I'm not going anywhere," Layala said with a half-smile. "You can stop worrying." It would have scared her too if Thane had been captured. If he died, she died. It was strange to think that her life was tied literally in the body of another elf.

His face smoothed out and he relaxed his tense posture. "I'm not worried. You're so beautiful I can't seem to look away."

"Liar." She pulled her boot from the stirrup and gave him a little shove on the thigh with her foot. Phantom looked back and whinnied as if to tell them to stop messing around.

"Must I hand you a mirror so you can see yourself properly?"

"You're dodging."

"Maybe I learned that from you."

"Sire," one of the soldiers called back. "We have a rider approaching. Looks to be one of ours."

"I'll be back." Thane nudged Phantom into a trot and made his way to the front. Layala tried to sit taller to see who it was, tried to listen for what message was brought, but the clop of hundreds of horse hooves, and wagons shifting and creaking, and chatter from all around prevented that. She couldn't even see Thane over all the soldiers ahead of her.

Thane didn't return. She and Piper and Tif speculated on what news kept Thane. Had the pale ones overrun Doonafell? Had the city been burned down? Were there refugees on the road trying to get away? Layala wanted to ride ahead and find out.

"When Thane wants us to know, he'll tell us,"

Piper said. She was better at following orders than Layala.

Nightfall came and the Ravens stopped. Tents went up and the aroma of cooking food filled the air. It smelled of ham this time and seasoned vegetables. Probably more bread if it hadn't gone stale. Although they only got one meal a day, besides nuts or other small snacks they brought with them, she couldn't think about her stomach.

Layala paced by the fire, waiting for Thane. He had to come to his tent to sleep at least, didn't he? "Where is he? Did he leave?"

"I don't think so," Piper answered. "You're awfully nervous for someone who claims to dislike him."

"I'm worried about the city and the people there."

"Uh huh," Piper said, leaning back into her rolled up sleeping bag.

Fennan and Sunshine were nowhere to be found so she assumed they joined him. If he went ahead and didn't tell her—"You know our lives are linked right? If something were to happen to him..." Layala drug her thumb across her neck.

"You sure that's what you're worried about?" Piper pulled the plaits of her braid loose. "He's fine. He's fought many battles and is still alive, isn't he?"

"So, you think he went ahead and is fighting?"

Piper sighed. "No, he would have told us, or someone would have. I'm fourth in command here, you know, after Fennan."

Layala dipped her hand into her pouch of nuts and

grabbed a handful. "Then why weren't you invited to do whatever it is he is doing? And where am I in this chain of command?"

"Because my first assignment is to watch you." Piper crossed her ankles. "You're second."

Layala froze and slowly turned on her heel to face Piper. *Second? Second!* No, that must be a mistake. "That doesn't make sense. Wouldn't it be some general or Fennan or something?"

"By law, as his mate and betrothed, even if you are not yet wed, you're higher ranked than any of us. Even above Talon which is why she hates you so much. In the line of succession, she's fourth, and when it comes to military movements, she has no say in what goes on here while you and he are alive."

"But—but..." Layala couldn't even come up with words. That couldn't be correct. Everything in Palenor was done officially. If they weren't married, then she wasn't technically queen. Thane even said that himself. "We aren't married."

"No but most would agree that being bound as mates is more official than a wedding. With marriage the only thing that shows you are together is a signed document. Mates are just as legally binding. You aren't the only two to ever be bound, Layala. Mage Vesstan secured many with mate runes on their wedding day in his years. It became the fashion, if you will, after you, the magic child, and Thane the Prince of Palenor. It is seen as a true commitment since it can't be undone. They even think it's poetic because if their mate dies so will they."

Anxiety welled up in her. Why wasn't she told this before? "But the spell hasn't been completed for us."

Piper rolled onto her side and stared into the fire. "As we all well know."

Layala rubbed her forehead, struggling to comprehend that she was second in command and in the line of succession for the throne of Palenor. "And what happens when it is completed? What else is there?"

"For you two? I don't know." She shrugged. "Everyone else is bound on their wedding day; you two were children so it could only be partially done because you must both agree. Maybe nothing will change. Maybe all that's left is the time limit."

Breaking the tension, Tif showed up dragging a canvas bag of goods larger than her with a huge smile. "I got snacks."

They ate while Tif prattled on about her run-in with a pixie who tried to steal the sack of berries she picked. Always with the dramatics and this tale wasn't lacking. "She punched me straight in the face!" Tif crooned. "I bet I'll have a purple shiner here soon. Battle wounds for the prize. I hope you two are happy I'm willing to share the spoils. These berries be blood berries."

"You're not even bleeding," Piper said.

"She was," Tif said with a wicked grin.

Layala popped one of the berries in her mouth and nodded but her mind was elsewhere. She watched every soldier who appeared in the firelight hoping it was Thane or someone coming to bring news. Why wasn't Piper more concerned? Even when a light drizzle of rain dampened her clothes and hair, she waited outside. The fire still burned but the wetness brought it to near embers. When Piper and Tif both moved inside the tent and fell asleep—Tif's snores were proof—Layala walked back and forth between her tent and Thane's. The clouds above blocked the stars and moons, creating an eerie black night. Every movement, every snap of a branch or deep voice nearby brought out instincts to pull her sword. Only the very wisps of her magic came back and the lack of it put her on edge.

A tall, cloaked figure appeared in the glow of the barely visible orange light. Before she even saw his face, before he even spoke, she knew it was Thane. Something in her recognized the essence of him. "Thane," she tried not to sound too desperate with relief, but she failed. Layala darted in front of him before he could enter his tent. "What happened?"

He tugged his hood back revealing the dark circles under his eyes. He pushed his hand through his hair and stepped around her and into his tent. She followed without being invited. *It must be bad.* While he rummaged through his trunk of belongings she waited quietly by the exit. He took out a bottle of wine and pulled the cork. *It must be really bad.*

"Half of Doonafell burns. They're trying to evacuate the city and save as many ladies and children as possible, but they also have to make sure that the innocent aren't being followed to be slaughtered on the road." A low growl rumbled in his chest. "The fact that we even must do that is disgusting. They would kill our children and eat them." He shuddered.

Her stomach ached at the thought. "Have the pale ones' numbers suddenly grown? Are we lacking soldiers? I don't understand why they're breaking into Palenor now when they haven't before. Palenor has held them at bay for hundreds of years."

"They have broken through plenty of times but not for long and not far. They've never reached Doonafell in any large number. As you know some stragglers get through from time to time but they aren't a huge threat." Thane dropped into his chair and took a big gulp of wine. "Their numbers *have* grown but that's not what drives them now. I suspect it's because now they know where *you* are, and they are fighting harder. I sent some of the Ravens ahead. If they ride through the night, they should be there in the morning."

"Shouldn't we all ride through the night then? How many soldiers have been lost? How many civilians? The children on the road..." Images of small children screaming and running, of their mothers dying to protect them flashed across her mind. She shook her head trying to clear those horrible thoughts.

Thane gave her a long look; she couldn't quite read his expression. "I'm surprised you care so much," he finally said.

That stung a little. She didn't believe he meant it

as a dig at her character but after the way she treated him, she deserved that comment. Truthfully, she didn't realize she cared so much either, but how could any person with a heart not care about dying children?

He went on, "And we need some fresh fighters when the others are tired. As far as numbers lost go, too many." He tilted his head slightly to the side and held out the bottle. "You want some? I'm sorry I don't have a glass for you."

"This is all because of me," Layala whispered. She gripped the handle of her dagger on her belt for something to take the brunt of outrage and fear and anxiety pulsing through her. "They're dying because of me. If I didn't exist, then—"

"Don't. Don't go there." He rose up and in two strides was in front of her. "The pale ones existed to slaughter before you were even a thought. This is the Black Mage's fault, not yours. This is what he and they want you to think. Mathekis and the pale ones want you to doubt. They want you to fear them because they know *you* don't know how strong you really are yet. But when you find out and let go of thinking you're but a pawn in this game to be used—when you realize you are the *queen*, the most powerful chess piece on the board, they will fear *you*." He shoved the bottle into her hand. "Now have a drink."

Layala gulped and brought the bottle to her lips. After a slug of wine, she murmured, "Thank you," and she didn't know if she was thanking him for the speech or the wine, but both warmed her chest.

Chapter 28

After Layala passed the bottle of wine back to Thane, he gestured for her to have a seat in the lone chair while he removed his wet cloak. "Are you cold?" he asked. "Your clothes are wet."

"No." Although it was drizzling, the temperature was warm enough. Layala tapped her feet on the ground. "Do you still wish me to stay out of the fight tomorrow?"

He stilled while removing one of his boots and lifted his eyes. "Unless it's absolutely necessary, yes. And it has nothing to do with your abilities. I know you're a good fighter."

She expected that answer, especially after she was captured by a pair of pale ones. As long as the battle went in their favor, she'd stay out of it. More than anything she needed to learn how Thane strategized troops and what it took to defend a city. She fought well one on one, but this was more than just her.

"Will you stay back, or will you be on the front lines?"

He tossed his boot and then rested his forearms on his thighs. "That all depends on how things play out but keeping you safe and out of their hands is more important than anything else."

On one side, the pale ones believed she was a tool to bring back their master. On the other, the elves thought she was a tool to destroy the Void; either way she was a tool. Almost nothing more than an object in their eyes. But if Thane was right, she wasn't a pawn. She was a queen, and she could move anywhere on the board. "Do you play chess?" Layala took another long drink of wine and passed the bottle back to Thane.

He brought it to his lips. "I do. Mage Vesstan taught me. He said it would sharpen my mind."

"I played it with my Aunt Evalyn every week. We had tournaments in Briar Hollow monthly. Guess who is the reigning champion?"

He smiled. "You?"

"Unfortunately no, Aunt Evalyn is." Layala thought back to the last tournament and how Evalyn had got her with a knight. "She always seems to be one step ahead of me. I've beaten her in the game but it's rare."

"This is the woman who raised you?"

"Yes, she was my mother's friend." Layala toyed with the willow necklace. "They made wine together and ran an apothecary in the valley. My father was a sword maker. I wish I had one of them, something that he touched."

Thane was quietly staring at his hands clasped between his bent knees. His long dark hair hung like a curtain, covering most of his face from Layala's view. She wished she could know what he was thinking rather than emotions. Although she couldn't feel anything from him.

"I remember you said Briar Hollow was your town. What did you do there?"

"I trained almost every morning since I was twelve and when I was nineteen, they promoted me to Briar Hollow's vice chancellor. It's the position just under Master Guardsman, who is in charge of policing and making laws. Basically, if there was trouble, I handled it. And everyone came to me with their problems although it wasn't part of the job description."

"What kind of problems?" Thane lifted his head and sat erect, giving her eye contact.

"Oh, like when Laurena thought her husband was cheating on her, she came to me. I followed him for a day and found out he was going to the next town to sell his bushels of apples for a higher price so he could buy her a ring. They'd been so poor when they got married. She only had a piece of twine wrapped around her finger." She crossed her legs and grew more comfortable. Thane was easier to talk to than she expected. But then again, she'd never really given him a chance to speak openly with her.

"At least it turned out well," Thane said leaning back into his pillow. "I expected the story to have a different outcome. Would you have told her if he was cheating, like she thought, even if it broke her heart?"

"I would have felt bad but yes. It's better to know the truth than live a lie."

"I planned to offer my sister's hand in marriage to the young Lord of the Woodland Elves, in hopes to unite us." He sighed. "At the very least make us allies rather than squabbling over small pieces of land. I can't afford to lose any more soldiers over something so petty when we have an ongoing war with a real enemy."

"I think you should give Talon a choice." Layala bit her bottom lip. "A choice that you or I never had."

"Ah yes." Thane's mouth twitched. "I should have known you'd say that. I wouldn't force her if she was entirely against it. But she's ambitious."

Layala shook her head. "Is there something between her and Aldrich or Fennan?"

"They both know exactly what she is so no, I don't believe so. They're close but over the years I've never seen anything romantic between her and Aldrich or Fennan. They treat her more like—a sister. All of us are like family."

Talon was cold and snake-like, nothing like how Layala would treat family. Layala watched her direct the servants like they were imbeciles and barely worthy of cooking her dinner or washing her clothes. At the castle when Layala eavesdropped a few times, she heard Talon say horribly mean things about her so-called friend as soon as she left the room. Her exact words were: *"Her voice is ghastly. I don't know why we allow her to speak at all."* The others giggled. *"And did you know her mother was a low-born elf? The daughter of a horseshoe maker. Can it get any worse?"*

"Why are you so different from her?" She hadn't a chance to eavesdrop on Thane, but she watched how he treated everyone from his mother to the stable master and it was all with respect.

"You think we're different?"

"I know you are."

Thane smiled at that. "I suppose it's because she was spoiled, and I was not. I had to work hard, and she didn't. My father loved her; I don't think he ever loved me." He went quiet. The drizzling rain pattered on the tent. The lone candle flickered creating shadows under his already heavy eyes. "I suppose I am better for that," he said so quietly she almost didn't catch it.

Instinctually, Layala almost said she was sure his father loved him even if he didn't show it, but she caught herself. This was Tenebris they were talking about. There was no point in placating him with lies. He'd also recently killed his father and she wasn't sure how he felt about that. It was intrusive to ask; she wouldn't even know how to phrase the question without sounding insensitive. Maybe Thane loved his father even if his father hadn't loved him. Maybe it nearly killed him to do what he'd done... for her. "What about your mother? I think she's been avoiding me."

"My mother has always been there for me. And

probably is avoiding you," he said with a smirk. "I can't for the life of me fathom why. You're always so *sweet*."

Layala rolled her eyes. "Must I apologize again? I'm trying my best to..." what was she trying to do?

"Your best to..." he prodded.

"To be cordial. Our lives are tied together for now. There's no reason I need to make us both miserable." She thought about Piper and how close she and Thane were. She was curious about his relationship with her. "Has there ever been anything between you and Piper? I won't be offended so don't worry."

Thane's lip curled. "Me and Piper?" he asked, almost laughing. "No. Not that there's anything wrong with her but she knows I've only had room in my heart for one. Besides, I think she likes Fennan but she won't admit it."

And that one was *her*. Layala's skin tingled, and she quickly added, "Fennan? Interesting. Does he like her?"

"Fennan likes many females. He's not ready to settle down. Piper knows that." He held out the bottle of wine to her. "Mage Vesstan said we could possibly convince the portal to take us to the Sederac Mountains."

Her eyes widened and she took the wine. It would make the journey weeks shorter. "Why would you tell me this? You forbade me to go." She remembered quite clearly every word he said to her that night.

"It's not entirely my place, although as our lives

are connected, I think I should have some say. I've told you before I'm not keeping you prisoner, but I did kill my own father to keep you out of enemy hands." His jaw muscles twitched. "You know what you risk going there. I hope you find another way."

He hopes I find another way. He wants out of this. And somewhere deep inside a small ache protested at that. "You said you know someone in Doonafell who might be of help so there may be another way. I should let you get some sleep. You look tired." She finished off the wine and set the glass bottle on the table at his bedside.

"There's room in here for one more," he patted the bed. "You know, if you get scared and need me to chase away the nightmares from that pretty head."

She flipped her middle finger at his wicked grin on the way out of the tent.

When morning came Thane did not wake her for training. She woke to find Piper packing up her things and the sun already up. With a frown, she pushed out of bed and dressed. After rolling up her sleeping mat and blanket, she nudged Tif. "It's time to go."

Tif shot up. Her wild curls looked like a bird's nest on top of her head. "Go?"

"Yes, we're leaving soon."

She rubbed her eyes and yawned. "I'll make sure your things are packed. I gotta do my job lest I get kicked back to the mound."

"Thanks," Layala said with a smile, even though she had already packed on her own. She stepped out into the dewy morning air. The rain clouds from the night before cleared away to bring forth a brilliant sunrise. Already the dampness was lifting. Layala made her way to Thane's tent and stood outside fidgeting with her dagger's handle. *Should I call his name? Peek inside?* She couldn't knock. "He's not in there," Fennan said from behind and Layala jumped.

She whirled around as if she'd been caught stealing. "Oh, um, alright." She cleared her throat. "I thought you went with the group who left last night."

"I was going to, but Thane asked me to stay to help guard you."

"Ah, of course he did." She tried to not sound annoyed, but she was. She didn't want to be what kept some of the best fighters away from the innocent people who needed help in Doonafell.

"It's not just about you, you know," Fennan said. "If something happened to you, we would no longer have a king, and since he has no heir and no uncles or brothers, that would leave Queen Orlandia as ruler. We'd be overrun by pale ones within a fortnight if she were left in charge. She has no interest in running Palenor, let alone doing a good job of it. It would be chaos."

That hit harder than he likely even meant it to;

Layala tried to kill him before. She had no idea the fallout his death would have caused. She assumed someone would step up in his place and everything would work itself out. "She can't be that incompetent. And surely some military leader would step up. You perhaps."

He smiled crookedly. "I would do what I could, but without a strong king or queen to look to, I fear the high elves would lose hope. This war has gone on for so long, Layala. We're tired. Tired to our very bones. Even the souls of the newborns must be."

She seemed to feel that tiredness in her lineage. "Do you think I was born to destroy the Void?" Layala asked tentatively.

"I think your life has been steeped in sorrow and anger."

His heavy-lidded eyes found hers. And for the first time Layala saw that bone-deep tiredness in him. He hid it behind a smile but what atrocities had he witnessed in his life?

"But I think only you get to decide what you were born to do. Tenebris wanted to use you but, having met you, I don't think he ever could have." A smile tugged at the corner of his mouth, "Fight-bringer."

"Is that to be what I'm called now?"

"Among the Ravens? Oh yes. In public, Lady Layala until you marry my High King."

"If I marry him," Layala corrected.

"You're not the first to have an arranged marriage,

certainly not the last. Most just accept it and learn to live with their partner."

"This is different." For more reasons than he knew. Novak's pale face with open lifeless eyes flashed in her mind. It wasn't simply because of who Thane's father was.

"Is it?" Fennan drawled. "I think you're convincing yourself it is."

Layala turned away and trudged to find Midnight. Fennan's footsteps followed behind. When she got to the horse, she picked up the saddle and then Fennan took it out of her arms and lifted it onto Midnight's back. "You're the king's mate. This task is below you."

Layala threw her arms up in frustration. "Why do you all act like I'm incapable of work?"

"We all have jobs to do. Would you put the horse hands out of work because you want to prove a point?" He reached under the horse to grab the belt. "What about your lady's maids? Would you rather see them out on the streets than allow them to help you?" He tightened the saddle with a jerk.

She never thought of it that way. "No."

He handed her the reins. "Good. Now put your armor on. Today is battle day."

"But I don't have any."

"Sure you do," Fennan said. "Ask Piper."

Layala found Piper close by, buckling a deep gray body plate of armor on herself. The outside had a layer of black leather, but she guessed underneath was metal. It had the Palenor sigil of three weapons engraved over her chest. Her shoulders, collarbone area, and arms were covered in smoky black scalemail. The small pieces glittered in the sunlight. On both sides of her helmet a metal wing protruded. "You look good," Layala said.

Piper smiled. "So will you." She pointed to a wooden chest. "Yours is inside."

Lifting the lid, Layala found a matching set to Pipers. When she slid it on it fit snuggly and wasn't exactly comfortable, but it was meant to protect. She waved her arms and found she could move freely. The scalemail was pliable and she wondered what metal it was made of. Also, in the chest she found gloves, thigh armor that buckled in the back, shin guards and the same winged helmet.

Piper folded her arms upon inspection. "Now you look like a Raven."

Layala looked down at herself and grinned. She never wore armor before. She never needed to. As much as she was impressed with the pretty dresses she wore back at the castle, this topped them. This felt like who she was meant to be. A warrior. "Is everyone's armor the same?"

"Yes, the Ravens are. Other soldiers don't have scalemail or winged helmets. The scalemail is expensive. It is replicated after dragon scales."

"I thought my arms and shoulders would be stiff and hindered with it but they're not. It's almost as if I don't even have armor on them."

"Your only weak points are your neck, and the back of your legs. Guard them well."

When they set off, Layala rode beside Piper and Fennan. Thane and Sunshine were nowhere to be seen. Fennan insisted he was still with the troop and didn't go ahead. The entire day she was nauseous. A haze of smoke dusted the horizon. The soldiers grew unceremoniously quiet. Horse hooves clopped, tails swished, wagons creaked but no one talked. The smell of acrid smoke infiltrated her senses. She couldn't see the city yet, but she knew what they'd soon find. Heading in the opposite direction, they passed groups of female elves and children on the road and a few soldiers leading. Layala's throat tightened. They held only a few possessions in their arms, their faces tear streaked between the soot. One little girl held a doll in her arm, staring at the ground holding her mother's hand. She never looked up. Had she lost her father? Did they have anything to eat?

When the city came into view, Layala's hand flew to her mouth. More than half was burned to the ground with skeletons of blackened wood still standing. Screaming and shouting, and metal clanging presented a terrifying tune. The soldiers ahead of her started their horses from a steady walk into a gallop. Midnight followed. Thane's voice carried over the drumming of hooves, shouting orders, directing the Ravens. They split into two lines. One going east, the other west around the city. Layala planned to go right to where she could hear the most fighting. She turned the reins and then Fennan reached over and grabbed hold of Midnight bringing them to a stop.

"You're staying back here with me."

Tif tugged on the back of Layala's top. "Please stay. I don't want to be pale one food," she whispered.

Piper rode on and the soldiers behind split around them like river water around a rock. "But Fennan, we can help. I can't even see what's happening from here."

"You know what's happening. You don't need to see it up close," he said sharply. "It's horrible, Layala. It will infect your dreams. You don't want to see it."

Princess Talon stopped on the other side of Fennan, putting a hand to her chest. Her horse nickered and threw its head. "I can't believe this has happened. My father would be horrified. This never happened while he was our High King."

Layala frantically searched for Thane. She heard him moments before but where did he go? Did he ride in with the others? "We can't just sit here."

"Yes we can," Fennan said. "Your High King gave you an order. You will stay."

"Don't act like you're so special that you're needed down there," Talon droned. "Do as you're told and sit here like a good little she-elf. Or better yet, go down there and get yourself killed. You'd be doing us all a favor."

Cheeks burning Layala glared. As much as she wanted to rip the princess off her horse and beat her face in, she held still. Now was not the time.

"Shut up," Fennan snapped. "I don't need you causing me any more trouble."

"Excuse me," Talon croaked, wide-eyed with shock. "You do not speak to me like that, Fennan. I am your princess. Apologize or I'll have you whipped."

"This is war. You can take your niceties and threats elsewhere. You are under my command while we're out here."

Talon snapped her low-hanging jaw shut and stared ahead, clearly fuming.

Heart thundering, Layala listened to the screams and the flames as they roared like a dragon, reaching more buildings. She gripped the reins until her hands ached. Her magic scorched in her veins, threatening to escape. More people evacuated the city, crying as they hurried past Layala and Fennan and Talon. The fighting happened on the far side of Doonafell so she couldn't see it, couldn't see if the Ravens were beating back the pale ones or not.

"You need to rein in your magic," Fennan said quietly. "I can feel it."

She whipped her head around to find Fennan staring. She risked a quick glance at Talon, who wore a worried expression, and it wasn't because of the battle. She pushed her magic down, down until it was nothing but a spark. After the sun moved to the other side of the sky, and she listened to Talon prattle on about her worry for Sunshine and her brother, how horrible it must be down there, moaning about all the people dying, she slid down from Midnight. It was enough to make Layala's stomach twist into knots. "I can't sit still any longer."

Tif peeked from the bag and whimpered. Layala paced for a moment and then froze. Coming from the trees to the left were a group of seven pale ones chasing a mother and two children. She held a baby, no more than one year old in her arms and pulled the other, who couldn't have been more than four along at her side. Her face was pinched in horror as the pale ones drew closer.

Layala jerked her sword out. "Fennan!" she didn't wait for him to give her permission. She ran, sprinting until her legs burned from the effort. She pulled the throwing star out of her pocket and launched it. It whipped past the mother's head and lodged in between the eyes of the pale one only feet behind her. Horse hooves rumbled behind her and Fennan bellowed out a war cry and rode down a pale one, chopping his sword at another. Layala nodded at the mother as she sprinted by and drove her sword straight into the gut of the first monster she came to. She jerked it out and blocked a downward hack coming from another. The jagged-edged blade grated against hers as he pulled back. He swung at her again with greater force, enough to knock her a few steps back.

"Come on, sweetness," the pale one said with an eerie grin. "You wanna play with the big boys, you better be prepared."

She heard a *whoosh* behind her and dropped into a

crouch; a blade passed over her head. Diving out from in between them, she faced the two pale ones as they prowled closer. They were huge, and muscular, much bigger than any she'd seen before.

"Layala, run!" Fennan shouted as he swung at his own two opponents.

But she would never leave Fennan to fight these beasts by himself. She tore the dagger from her belt and flicked it. It soared for a throat but was knocked aside. The one on the left stepped up and swung, she dodged it and stepped to the side and sliced into the back of his thigh. He hissed as the other jabbed his sword straight for her belly. She knocked the blade away; he hit her with a punch straight to the jaw that sent her twirling to the ground. A low growl rumbled in her chest as the metallic taste of blood filled her mouth. She spat and looked up from her hands and knees. *That's it, you son of a bastard!* Her magic roared to life; black thorned vines as wide as her torso tore out of the ground like the tentacles of some great sea monster. They crashed through the surface and wrapped around the pale ones, squeezing the life out of them. She barely heard their muffled screams at the vines closed around them like a tomb. She rose up and with a slight motion of hand more ripped from the ground, a vine tore *through* the one opposite of Fennan, until the monster's body was split in two and rose up as the vines grew taller. The other was crumpled into a tight ball. Dark purple lilies bloomed along the trailing magical plants.

With his sword arm hanging at his side, Fennan gawked at Layala. "What was that?!"

"Holy horseballs!" Tifapine exclaimed standing on the back of Midnight, holding his reins as they sauntered over. "Your magic is something special for certain. And look at me. I'm riding all by myself."

Layala wanted to smile at her and at Fennan as they were clearly impressed, but she stared at the burning city. "Now they'll know I'm here."

Chapter 29

Thane cut the head clean off a pale one, and then brought his blade down across the chest of another charging at him. Warm black blood sprayed his face, but he kept going, hacking and slashing, anger roaring in him like a wild beast. They'd tried to take his city, murdered and feasted on his people. *Kill them. Kill them all*, he chanted in his head. If his magic had a price, it was that it made him beast-like, a wraith in need of the kill. A king of no mercy.

He clenched his teeth as he drove his boot into the gut of the enemy and jerked his sword free of the pale one's chest. With only a look he focused on a trio surrounding one of his soldiers; his magic flared, and the pale ones screamed as the blood pumping through their wretched bodies began to boil, and their skin oozed with black sores. They clutched at themselves, clawing at their own skin, screeching, wailing until they fell dead. Falan gave Thane a quick nod of thanks and chased after a pale one who turned and ran.

The pale ones were on the verge of retreat. Many began to turn and flee. His Ravens brought a force that not only outnumbered the pale ones but with skill they couldn't contend with, as always. And then something strange happened. Every pale one in sight suddenly looked north. Even the ones on the run stopped and whirled around. A horn blew, a deep bellow that sounded like it belonged to a cave troll, and as one, the enemy gathered in a single group and marched north toward... Layala. Thane snapped out of his raging oblivion to slaughter the enemy.

"Do not let them by you!" Thane shouted at his warriors. "Hold them back! Fight! Kill every last one of them! Do not let them flee!"

He searched for Piper and Aldrich and found them fighting back-to-back. With each other he felt confident leaving them.

The smell of smoldering flesh and structures alike burned his nose. The first time the putrid scent hit his senses, he vomited, but after years of this chaos, it no longer turned his stomach. He flicked a dagger through the back of the skull of a pale one and sprinted for Phantom. The horse lifted his head up when he saw his master coming and whinnied. Launching onto the gelding's back, Thane kicked him into a gallop. "Go! As fast as you've ever run, Phantom!"

The horse seemed to sense his urgency and they

flew through the burning streets, passed his soldiers, dashed by citizens hunkering down in shadowed alleys. He leaned and hacked at any pale ones or used his magic to boil or freeze their insides along the way. *This was a mistake. I have to get to her. I have to get to her!* The slamming of hooves matched the throbbing of his pulse. *I shouldn't have left her.* Horse and rider tore through the opening in the stone wall that was meant to guard the city, out into the open. At the top of the hill, he saw those black twisting vines taller than any tree in sight. *Maker, please let her be here. Let her be safe.*

As soon as he came upon the magical vines where dead pale ones lay about, some killed by weapons, one hung in pieces from thorns, he jumped off Phantom. "Layala! Fennan!" he shouted, searching for signs of them. "Talon! Damn it, I should have had them wait back further."

"Layala!" He put his foot in the stirrup and swung his leg over his horse. He calmed himself long enough to follow the trail of their connection. It went east. The Void was south. If the pale ones captured her, they wouldn't head away from their home. He followed the instinct, the pull guiding him toward her into the Lanvore Woods. The further he went, the thicker and closer everything grew. Moss-covered vines stretched from hunkering yew and mangrove tree to tree. A spider's web hit him in the face; he fought it off. When ferns and rotting stumps and protruding roots got too much, he hopped off Phantom and tied him to a branch. "I'll be back."

Ducking under a branch with a hissing snake, he held his sword ready in case it wanted to strike. The connection grew stronger the further he went. Sweat trailed down the side of his face. Was it that much hotter in here? It was stuffy, with no wind. The point of a blade jabbed into his back, and he stopped, skin prickling with a warning.

"I could have been a pale one and you'd be dead, and consequently so would I."

He turned to find Layala standing with a hand on her hip. Fennan stood beside her, arms crossed. "Sire, did you think I'd let anything happen to her?"

Layala scowled at him. "As if it was you who did all the work?"

"I'm glad you're safe." He glanced around. "Where is my sister?"

Talon pushed herself out from behind a bush pulling sticks from her wild hair and wiping something off her arm. She looked so beyond out of her element it was almost comical. "Here."

Finding them safe pushed down the anxiety that had nearly eaten away at his nerves. "Good. I hope you learned something today. Pale ones are no joke."

Talon blushed and looked down. That was a good sign. He turned back to Layala. "The pale ones, they must have sensed your magic. They started gathering to charge this way."

Slowly bobbing her head, Layala said, "I figured as much, so we hid in here."

"Now that I know you weren't captured, I need to

go back." He took hold of Layala's hand and tugged her along beside him. "And you're coming with me."

She pulled out of his grasp and sheathed her sword. "You should have brought me with you in the first place."

"I have to agree," Fennan said. "She can fight, and her magic is destructive. You should have seen it, Thane. Those vines took them out in seconds."

"Even I was impressed and that's saying something," Talon said, trailing behind them. Her dress snagged on a branch, and she cursed as she tore it free. Then screeched and slapped at her head. "A lizard! Ugh, disgusting!"

Thane tried not to smile at his sister's struggle. "I have seen Layala's magic." Having her in the middle of the fighting was too risky. All she asked was to be brought here so she could see the plight of the high elves. Now she'd seen it. She gave him her word she would listen to him if he brought her here. As much as Layala didn't want to admit it, she was the greatest risk to Palenor, to all of Adalon, excellent fighter or not, magic or not. He didn't envy the burden placed on her through no fault of her own, but it didn't change anything. "But my job as High King is to protect Palenor at all costs, which means keeping her away from Mathekis."

"Of course, sire," Fennan relented. "I apologize."

"You don't need to apologize."

"And I have no say in this?" Layala asked.

He looked at her. "You should be more worried

about making sure you aren't caught rather than fighting in battles. My Ravens and our soldiers are capable. Until we know if your powers could potentially destroy the Void, your number one goal should be to protect yourself."

"I have no desire to be taken captive, but you said I wasn't a pawn, and yet you're treating me like one. If you want to keep referring to chess, the queen protects the king."

He shot Fennan and his sister a dangerous look.

"We'll, uh, be scouting ahead," Fennan said, and dragged Talon away with him. Talon grumbled about wanting to stay to see their argument, but Fennan pulled her even faster.

Thane looked down at Layala. Maker above, she was beautiful and infuriating. His fingers itched to caress that arrogant set to her jaw. "In this case the rules are changed."

"You can't change the rules in the middle of the game."

He walked at her, backing her up until she bumped into a tree trunk. His body felt tight and electric. The adrenaline from the battle and from his fear of her being captured still raged through him. With her chest heaving up and down, she stared up at him, not with anger but guarded curiosity. Thane placed his arms on either side of her, palms flat against the tree trunk. "I've had enough arguing with you. As your mate, you are *mine*. You can deny it until you have no breath, you can fight me and hit me and call me every filthy name you can think of, you could even try to kill me again, but I'm not going anywhere. You are mine and I am yours, and I will destroy anyone who gets in my way." His eyes dropped from her wide blue eyes to her full lips. He'd never wanted to kiss someone more. The urge was almost overwhelming. He wanted to feel something other than the consuming outrage from what he saw in that city. "And as much as I claim it's all for Palenor, for the good of our people, it's *not*. Because if I was being honest with myself," his voice dropped low, "I would sacrifice too much if it meant you were safe."

She didn't look away, didn't try to hide her feelings. He thought it would be disgust or fury, given how she reacted to him before, but her yearning enveloped him thick and wonderful. Intoxicating. It both calmed and excited him.

"I can't give you what you want," she whispered and her feeling of desire slowly retracted, pulling away like bait on the end of a hook. He was the fish trying to catch the treat, chasing the need for it. "Your duty to help me must be about Palenor. Only Palenor."

Maybe his head still wasn't clear after the battle, but he leaned closer, his body brushing close to hers. "I said one day you'd love me, and you don't yet." His lips grazed her ear, and he felt her tremble. "But I know you want me. I can feel it."

"I can't." She firmly put a hand on his chest, but she didn't push him away. "I can't," she repeated as if the words wounded her, but that desire in her flared again, overwhelming him.

Giving in to the urgency, he smashed his lips against hers. A warm pulse cascaded down his body. His lips moved against hers with a need he hadn't known was so strong until this moment. Then with a shove and a *whack,* Layala's palm smacked his cheek, snapping him out of his drunken hunger for her.

"How dare you kiss me!" she slammed her hands into his chest and pushed him back again. Then she went to smack him a second time.

He caught her wrist. "*Don't.* Hit. Me."

"Don't kiss me!" she fired back swinging her other arm, but he caught that too. He pushed her back against the tree, pinning her arms down, and they stared at each other both seemingly breathless. Her eyes were wild, more animalistic than elf. "Let go of me."

"Calm down first." That only made her more frenzied to get free. She wriggled and kicked and got one of her arms loose, grabbed a fistful of his hair and after one heart beat... two... she jerked him down to her mouth and kissed him. It was full of built-up passion and anger and confusion. He wrapped her in his arms, pulling her hard against him. She moaned and it sent goosebumps over him. After feeling like his lips were swollen and he needed a breath, he pulled back.

Breathing heavy, they sat in the quiet and then she pushed out of his arms, leaning into the tree trunk. "I can't do this."

He shoved off the tree and turned away briefly, confused about her choice of words. "What does that mean? You don't want to or you *can't*?"

"Can't."

His eyebrows pulled down. "Did you make some sort of vow? I don't understand. It's one thing if you just don't want me but to say you can't is another."

"Yes, I made a vow. Trust me, you don't want me, Thane." She pushed by him, but he grabbed her wrist whirling her around to face him.

"Explain, *please*." His teeth clenched so hard his jaw began to ache. She tried to jerk away but he held fast. Her anger was building again but he wanted to know what could stop her from caring for him, from wanting him; their lives were on the line here. The deadline for their marriage might not have been at the forefront of his mind the last couple of days but he hadn't forgotten. He would never be a pale one. He'd kill himself first. After what felt like an eternity for her to answer, he groaned. "Tell me."

"Forget it. It's better this way."

She twisted away, jumped on top of a fallen log, and hopped down, marching the path out of the woods. He took a couple deep breaths, and it took everything in him not to chase after her and demand an answer.

THE BATTALION of pale ones was slaughtered by the time they made it out of the Lanvore Wood. More heartbreaking was the aftermath. The Ravens went around the city looking for survivors and helping the wounded. More forces were sent south to look for any remaining pale ones. He would need to pull off-duty soldiers from around Palenor to the border for security, and he and his Ravens would have to stay here to help rebuild and secure for at least the following week. The enemy couldn't be allowed to infiltrate a second time.

Squatting at the side of a stream, he dipped his hands in to wash the black blood from his arms. Staring at his reflection in the water, he saw the black splatters on his face for the first time. Scrubbing it away, his mind flashed back to the delicate female in a bloodied pink dress being fed on by a pale one until he chopped its head off. So disgusted and filled with fury, he lost control and kept hacking and hacking until the monster was unrecognizable and then he turned with a roar and went wild, slicing and chopping any pale one near, letting his magic roam free and tear apart the enemy. Not only had their blood boiled but so had their skin with sores that eventually curled their pale skin away from their bones; he'd never done that before, didn't even know he could. That's when they started running at the sight of him: the Warrior King. He usually kept count of his kill number, but he'd been so lost in the wrath for his people, for the city, that he lost his head until that horn blew. He was crazed until he realized they might be going for Layala.

If many considered Thane powerful and ruthless, the Black Mage was ten times what he was. The fact that the Mage created the pale ones was proof of that. As was his ability to trap elves within his magic even hundreds of years after his passing. Trapped just like Layala and Thane, on a steady path to becoming the things Thane hated most in the world. He was a fool to think she would ever want to be with him. An utter fool. Deep inside he was the monster she thought he was. They should never have called him the Warrior Prince. He was the Bloody Prince. The Bloody *King* now. He may not regret killing pale ones, but he'd killed many of the woodland elves because his father ordered him to. He slapped the water, ruining his reflection and stood.

Phantom munched on the thick foliage alongside the stream until Thane tugged his reins and pulled him along. Servants set up the tents and cooked in the clearing behind Doonafell. Many of the citizens sat in small circles, crying, hugging, and consoling one another. Servants brought them bowls of soup and he hoped that would help. The sorrow was palpable. His eyes burned and it wasn't from the smoke still billowing from crumbling buildings a half mile away.

Wordlessly, he handed Phantom off to one of the horse hands. "Shall I unsaddle him, sire?" Thane nodded with a heavy heart. Many of the elves bowed to him as he passed.

"Thank you, High King, for coming to help us," said an elf with black soot smears across his face. Many murmurs of thanks continued, he simply nodded but he had to get away. This happened on *his* watch. The pale ones never destroyed a large elven city when his father ruled.

He went into his tent, grateful that it was set up for him, a place he could find a little respite. He tugged off his bloody top and weapons then collapsed on the sheepskin furs, hands and body slightly trembling as the rush of battle faded. Staring up at the canvas of the tent for an unknown amount of time, he tried to block out the groans and cries all around. Thoughts of Layala fought for his attention, that kiss was all-consuming and he craved more, but he also didn't want to think about her. Didn't want to dwell on the fact that she didn't or *couldn't* give into him, whatever that meant. Was it all her vow to see him and his father dead? Had she not let that go even now? Even after knowing what she knew. After a while he drifted off into a restless sleep.

When he woke up it was evening. The sun hadn't set but it would soon. No one disturbed him or sought his counsel. He felt Layala nearby, but he didn't want to see her. Correction, he desperately wanted to see her, but he was confused and angry... and yet a warm sensation filled his belly. She kissed him back. And what a stark contrast it was to the first time she kissed him in his bed a couple weeks before.

Changed into fresh clothing, he stepped out.

Aldrich stood from the chair he'd been in beside the tent opening. "Thane. All the remaining pale ones are dead, and our scouts haven't found any nearby. If Mathekis was here, he's gone. For now."

"Good." Soldiers walked by in pairs, nodding at him. Many people were still being brought into the camp to be treated. Food was served, and although the crying settled, there was a heavy sadness. "And how are the survivors?"

"Some are doing better than others. The uninjured are going to see what is left of their homes or searching for loved ones. So far... three hundred and seventy citizens dead. Thirty-eight soldiers and we lost fourteen Ravens. Kaden, Marcon, Emerin, Dallen..." he continued, naming each one.

"Damn it." The pit sitting in his gut grew heavier. Not only for all those people but for his soldiers. He knew all his Ravens; personally chose each one of them and their deaths always hurt. He was grateful it wasn't more. It could have been, but it was still fourteen of *his* warriors' lives gone.

"Over a thousand homes and businesses burned."

"We'll be here for probably at least two weeks helping rebuild and secure then."

Aldrich ran his fingers through his dark blond hair. The black blood of pale ones stained one side of his head. "I figured so."

"Are there any bitten?" The hardest part of all was ordering his soldiers to drive a blade through the heart of the bitten before they could turn.

"No Ravens. A handful of soldiers however, and we're still searching among the people. So far there have been three civilians with visible bite wounds. We're... allowing them to say their goodbyes." He cleared his throat.

Thane shifted, watching the elves around with a closer eye. "There may be more. When I was fighting within the city many of the pale ones were freshly turned elves. They had no weapons, and wore elven clothes, not pale one armor." He didn't want to say it, but they were easy kills. "Have the soldiers start asking if anyone has been bitten and have them check the skin. I want all wounded and civilians in one area and guarded overnight. It only takes a few hours to turn. We'll know by nightfall if there are more."

Thane's eyes searched the area, knowing exactly who he was looking for, but he didn't want to admit it. Although there was no real reason he shouldn't. It was his duty to watch her and know where she was to keep her safe. But that's not why he looked for her now; he knew she wasn't in danger.

"She's with Piper," Aldrich said. "They're tending to some wounded children. She's a decent healer, and the kids find her amusing." He paused. "She does better with them than adults. The children don't see her as a Mage—as the Lightbringer. They are glad for a warm smile and someone to ease the pain."

He finally saw her, kneeling beside a boy and girl. He rubbed at the flutter in his chest. "I know how she feels."

"Yes," Aldrich said. "High King. They see you for what you are, not *who*. A heavy burden, I'm sure."

"Speaking of me being High King. I need to go into the city and see what I can do." He stared at the back of Layala's head and as if she sensed his gaze, she looked back, meeting his stare. He should bring her with him. It seemed like every time he left her something bad happened. "Tell Layala she's coming with me and get Fennan. You need to clean yourself off before you go anywhere." He marched to find his horse, feeling a hot sensation on his back; he knew Layala watched him walk away.

Chapter 30

"There, all better," Layala said as she finished bandaging a cut on the girl's arm, trying to keep her eyes from following Thane as he walked away. The girl said she scraped it when her mother and sister ran out of the city. They'd been hiding in the Lanvore Woods. She was six with a missing front tooth that made her cuter.

The child beamed. "It doesn't even hurt anymore. What did you put on it?"

"It's a special tree leaf in the balm. It should be all better by tomorrow."

"Thanks." She hopped up off the log and ran to her mother. The mother nodded her thanks. Layala stood and stared after Thane. Why did she want to go chasing after him? He forced a kiss on her... but she'd done the same bloody thing to him. Her head was still whirling with how much she enjoyed his lips on hers. Before Thane, she hadn't kissed anyone since Novak and never wanted to. What came over her?

What was still over her? Her pulse quickened watching him leave. Her traitorous body ached to be near him again, tangled in his arms against the trunk of a tree.

Fennan strutted over with a confident swagger. His black skin was clean of the dirt and blood of battle and his curly hair bounced with his steps. He dipped into a shallow bow and smiled. "The High King requests your company."

"Requests or demands?"

"When it comes from Thane, they are one and the same, aren't they?"

Too true. Layala groaned but it was more for show than anything. She couldn't deny her desire to go with him. She turned to Piper who wrapped a small boy's hand. "I'm going with Thane and Fennan. Keep an eye on Tif will you? She's still hiding over by the horses." After Fennan and Layala fought off the pale ones, Tif wouldn't come out of her hiding spot in Layala's bag. And she probably wouldn't come out until it was night, and she could go unseen.

Piper nodded. "Poor thing was scared before. Now she's downright terrified a pale one is going to get her."

Walking beside Fennan, they passed soldiers herding groups of civilians. "Please, we're asking everyone to gather in one spot so we can help," one soldier said. Most of the elves complied without complaint. A few looked worried but moved from their spots and followed the soldiers. It made sense to have them all in one area rather than scattered throughout the camp.

"Are these all the people without homes?" There had to be several hundred wounded, but more and more elves came in groups from the city or walked back from the north when they evacuated the day prior.

"Some," Fennan answered. "Many of them are waiting for us to tell them it's safe to go back inside the walls. We're running patrols to make sure that every last pale one is gone and none are hiding." Those walls hadn't done them much good in keeping out pale ones. They had to be at least ten feet tall but the walls to the south must have been battered down.

"Is that what we're going to do?"

"We'll see when we get there."

"You mean we're going into the city?"

Fennan nodded. The smoke still seared her senses, and carried the sickening odor of burning flesh. Curious that Thane wanted her to go with him when the city had to be more dangerous than out here. After walking around tents and through more groups of displaced elves they found Thane patting Phantom's neck. He was saddled and ready to go for a ride. Layala left Midnight tied to a tree next to Piper's and Fennan's horses at the north end. "Should I have brought my horse?" Layala asked and ran her hand over the smooth coat of Phantom's hip.

Thane shrugged, put his foot in the stirrup and pulled himself up with ease. She was a little envious that he was tall enough to do that without assistance. He stared at the city and his shoulders sagged a little. He'd never looked so... defeated before.

One of the horse keepers led over a roan mare. He was young, maybe fifteen at most with smooth pale skin and beautiful warm brown curls. "I only readied the two horses. I can go find Midnight if you wish. It will only take me about a half-hour."

Layala shifted looking north where she left Midnight. It took at least twenty minutes to walk there.

"I don't want to wait. One of you can ride with me." Thane grew a smirk. "You two can fight over who gets the honor."

She glanced at Fennan, who said, "As much as I want to squeeze that hunky body, and feel all those muscles, sire, I'll let the lady."

The horse keeper laughed, handing Fennan the reins to the other horse. Thane cracked a smile. "How kind of you to relent such an opportunity, Fen."

She didn't know if he truly didn't want to wait or if he just wanted to be close to her again. More nervous than ever before, Layala grasped Thane's hand and his touch sent a pleasurable trill pooling in her middle.

"Front or back?" he asked without his usual snark. "Although I think I can already guess."

Never one to be predictable, she said, "Front."

His eyebrow ticked up, but he stayed silent as he pulled her up and she settled in front of him. She was hyperaware of his body pressed against her this time.

His thighs straddled hers, his solid armored core a wall against her back. He closed his arms around her to grab onto the reins. Layala's breaths became uneven, and she closed her eyes for a moment; a memory flashed to his arms around her hours before. Again, the warmness bloomed in her. Maker, her body suddenly reveled in being close to him, touching him. She blamed the mate magic.

He cleared his throat and his voice vibrated against her when he said, "Just so you're aware, you're going to see a lot of dead bodies."

They rode through the opening in the wall around Doonafell, met by an eerie silence, devoid of the bustle a city should have. Only the light crackling of dying fires made a sound. It smelled worse the further they rode along the streets. Heavy smoke burned her throat, mixed with the sulfuric odor of the rotting pale ones. She put a hand to her mouth and nose for a moment suppressing a gag. Buildings smoldered in piles of ashes. Bodies scattered, some burnt black, some stained with blood. Others looked as if they might sit up at any moment, if it weren't for the pallor of death to their skin. A small boy of maybe three lay next to an adult male she assumed was his father, both with their eyes wide in an endless stare. Her throat constricted and she turned away, trying to stop the threatening tears.

"I'm sorry you have to see this," Thane said. Soldiers led a horse-drawn wagon. None of them spoke as they stopped and picked up a body, tossing it in. They weren't uncaring in the way they handled the male, but it wasn't the manner a loved one would pick him up and set him inside. "I didn't want to leave you back at camp in case..." he trailed off.

"In case what?"

"Fennan and I are worried that some of the citizens have been bitten and are hiding it. I've seen it before in other towns. The pale ones usually take the bitten with them to add to their forces, but I want you close to me."

She felt queasy before but now she was downright nauseous. "That was why you put them in one area." She stared at the body of a pale one. Its head was three feet away from the body. "But if someone turns, they could easily kill those close by."

"And if they're separated, they can run wild throughout the camp and kill. At least if they're in one place we'll know they've turned right away and can end it. I have my soldiers watching closely. They should be able to see the signs early. Their hair will start to change first." He adjusted himself in the saddle a little, moving even closer it seemed. "Sorry my leg was falling asleep."

"Is it because of me?" Layala tried to scoot forward but there was no room. She tried to adjust herself another way without much success in gaining space.

He lightly cleared his throat. "No, but rubbing against me is helping."

Layala scoffed, twisted around, and smacked his shoulder. "Don't be disgusting."

"I was kidding," he said with a smile. "You don't have to do anything to turn me on."

Her jaw dropped. "We're surrounded by the freshly dead and you're making wildly inappropriate jokes."

Fennan laughed. "Wildly inappropriate jokes are how we are able to keep our sanity in the midst of all this."

"Don't encourage him."

"I don't *need* encouragement," Thane said and slid his hand around her waist until his palm was flat on her belly. "You seemed a little off balance. I don't want you to fall."

"I'm not off balance," she shot back but didn't push his hand away. She let his touch linger and tried not to think about the fact that she liked it. "I'm not clumsy."

"Certainly not. You're quite agile and capable."

Was that a genuine compliment? "Thank you."

"Qualities I'm sure I'll enjoy on our wedding night. The way you move with a sword in your hands—"

Layala smacked him on the shoulder again, harder this time. "Ha, our wedding night would be a cold, Layalaless bed for you. Your hand would be your only company."

"Ouch," Fennan coughed and then couldn't recover and laughed so hard she thought he was going to fall out of his saddle.

"And besides, talk about what happens in a wedding bed for *most* couples isn't appropriate in front of a lady."

"Oh, I'm sorry, is talk about me and my *hand* appropriate? Are b*alls* in the vocabulary of a lady? How about prick? Bastard?"

"Your *balls* are in danger right now."

"Fine, dearest, I'll keep my fantasies to myself."

"Maker above, please do."

Fennan kept it going, "You got some strange fantasies if it involves your lady with a sword in bed."

"What if I meant a different kind of sword?"

Layala rolled her eyes. "Ugh males. There *will* be a sword involved if you try anything."

"First of all, I wouldn't *try* anything unless you wanted me to." He leaned a little closer to her ear. "But it would be intriguing to see you with *only* a weapon."

Layala tried not to smile as she shook her head in disbelief—disbelief that she was actually entertained by this banter. "I'm sure it would be, but you never will, except in your imagination."

"I doubt that. Like I said, one day you'll love me. Then you can tell me about all the ways you've imagined me... Against a wall, in a field of wildflowers, my bed."

"I've imagined you in a grave. Does that turn you on?"

Fennan laughed again. Thane hugged her tighter. "That was before—I know your fantasies are different now."

"You sure about that?"

"I've never been more certain about anything."

She swallowed hard and turned around; with their

faces so close she fought the urge to kiss him again. "Maybe you should focus on the task at hand."

He lifted his arm to a square. "I will, on my honor. No more dirty talk involving swords."

"Good."

"For at least the next hour, possibly two."

"You're unbelievable."

They entered the section of the city that hadn't been touched by fire. There were a few people wandering the square stoned streets, wide eyed and shocked expressions as if they'd just come out of their homes. "We'll start checking buildings," Thane said. "I want them all cleared before we tell the people it's safe." He dismounted and Layala slid off after him. Here the homes were close together, only about ten feet in between each. Most were made of beige brick and looked almost identical. The doors were painted various colors, the only distinguishing feature from another.

Fennan peeked in the window of the first building, and said, "I can't see anything. It's too dark."

Thane slammed his fist on the door. When no one answered, he tugged a sword loose from his back and shoved the door inward. "Hello?" he called looking side to side and stepped in. Layala gripped her sword handle, heart beating faster with the anticipation of what could be hiding inside. She followed and Fennan trailed behind her. Everything looked to be in place. They cleared the living room, Layala peeked in the kitchen; pots and pans hung in the center. An ordinary black wood stove was on the left, a sink full of dishes beside it.

Thane and Fennan had gone down a hallway and came back. "It's clear."

They continued down the street checking each home. One had a family hiding in the backroom, but the others had been empty. It was almost dark, and they'd gone through several streets with the aid of other soldiers and some male elves who volunteered to help, and it appeared that the pale ones were indeed gone. And if any of the people were going to change, they'd be showing signs by then.

"One more and then we can head back to camp," Thane said, stepping inside what appeared to be a pub. Layala's boot crunched over broken glass when she walked in.

Round tables dominated the room. Some were overturned. A few chairs lay broken and splintered. It smelled of spirits; cracked bottles dripped over the bar top.

"Either they were in a hurry to get out, or there was a struggle here." Layala high stepped over a chair that had its legs snapped off.

"My money is on a struggle," Fennan said.

Thane led the way through a back door that opened into a kitchen. Layala peeked around Thane. Food was scattered all over the floor, pots and pans too. There didn't appear to be anyone in sight. She turned to her left and placed her hand on the door handle. It was probably a closet. When she tugged it open a shriek pierced her ears and white hands came out of the dark and took her to the ground. Layala screamed as the pale one's heavy weight pinned her down, his teeth snapping at her face. The smell of his breath almost made her gag. She barely held him off her, arms aching as she pushed him back. Her magic curled from her fingers, vines wrapped around the pale one's neck and choked him until he stopped moving. Layala scrambled to her feet, shaking, to find Fennan on his back, on top of a table stabbing the pale one hovering over him in the gut. Thane fought two; his sword slashed across the chest of one and lopped off the head of the other. It all happened in a matter of seconds.

Magic humming, Layala frantically looked for more. Four pale ones hid in that closet. When it looked safe, she stared at them dead on the ground. One wore a dress, the other three had on tunics and pants. These had been patrons.

Thane touched her arm. "Are you alright?"

"I'm fine." But she shuddered. "You?"

He smiled and they both turned to Fennan who brushed a towel over his armor chest piece. "Got some blood on me. We were lucky that this was the only place with pale ones."

Thane picked up a bottle from behind the bar and popped the cork. "Let's hope when we get back to camp that is also the case." He took a drink and then scrunched his face. "Damn that's strong."

Fennan hurried out. "Well give it here then." His face soured when he took a drink. "You weren't lying."

Layala held out her hand. "I'll be the judge of that. You two are used to wine, aren't you?" After spending many nights drinking the men from Briar Hollow under the table, she expected this wouldn't be a challenge.

"I'll give you a ruby if you can drink that without making a face," Fennan said, shoving it into her palm.

"You hear that? Your guard is offering to give me jewelry." Layala arched an eyebrow at Thane.

He gave her a feline smile. "*If* you can accomplish the challenge, which I highly doubt."

The smell of it pierced her nose before she even touched the bottle to her lips. She braced herself and the bitterness rolled over her tongue, and burned like fire down her throat. She tried to hold her face steady but shook her head and hissed. "Good Maker, what is this? Troll piss?"

Thane and Fennan laughed. "Perfect description," Thane said. Then he took the bottle from her hands. "Now good little she-elves don't drink vile stuff like this."

Layala rolled her eyes. "Neither do wise High Kings. We'd all be flat on our asses with a few more drinks of that."

"Thane wasn't joking about your filthy language." Fennan folded his arms. "Piss, asses... Did you really call him a bastard and a prick? I've never heard any maiden talk like you. Not even Piper."

"Have you ever met a she-elf raised by a human woman who likes to drink and gamble, or one who grew up in a training yard with human men?"

"Nope."

"I can mold to my surroundings. I was nice enough at the festival. Don't worry I won't embarrass you two in front of polite company."

"And what sort of company are we?" Thane asked, sounding slightly offended.

She smiled. "The kind I hope accepts me for... me. Not as a savior or the Lightbringer or anything else. Just Layala."

Thane put an arm around the back of her neck, and pulled her closer to his side. Fennan gave her a fist tap on the shoulder with a big grin. They didn't have to say anything for her to know that despite everything, they were friends.

Chapter 31

For four days bodies were burned, and funerals administered. Only one person in camp tried to hide she'd been bitten but it only increased the tears and cries and heartache when they had to end her.

Layala didn't know any of the elves here, but their pain was palpable. It permeated the air, and after listening to some of the speeches, especially a young father who had to burn the bodies of his wife and three-year-old daughter on a funeral pyre, tears flowed in a steady stream down her cheeks. She'd never seen a grown male fall to his knees and sob like that. Never seen so many people sad at one time. The father repeated, "I'm sorry. I'm so sorry I couldn't save you," until Layala couldn't take it anymore. Thane put an arm around her waist and hugged her to his side and they walked away. When she looked up, tears glistened in his green eyes, but he blinked them away.

"Let's go."

Layala's throat was too constricted to respond so she nodded. How could she ever walk away from the elves of Palenor now? If she could do something to help, if she could indeed destroy the Void, she had to try. She wrapped her hand around the willow necklace at her chest for comfort.

"I think now is a good time to meet with the elf I told you about. She might be of great help to us."

They walked away from the burned section of the city. "Who?" Some piles of debris still smoked, if only lightly. A child reached under a half-charred door and pulled out a stuffed pony that miraculously didn't have a single mark. He held it tightly to his chest with a smile.

Within minutes the air chilled significantly. Dark clouds rolled in overhead. A summer storm brewed with low rumbling thunder. It smelled of a coming rain.

"There's an old mage tower here. It's a thousand years old at least. Thankfully it wasn't destroyed. She's the keeper." Thane looked up. "And we better hurry or we'll be soaked."

"How far is this mage tower?"

"Far enough that you'll have time to answer some of my questions."

"Questions?"

He pulled a lazy smile. "Yes. What is your favorite color?"

His eyes captivated her for a moment, and she

blurted out, "Green." Although her favorite color had always been purple. "And purple. I like purple."

"Green and purple. For some reason I pegged you for a blue kind of girl."

Cheeks warming, she cleared her throat. "Let me guess, your favorite color is blue?"

"Black."

"Black?" Layala chuckled. "Nobody's favorite color is black."

"Mine is. I look good in it."

"Touché," Layala said. "But I don't think you could guess much about me."

"No?" he smirked. "I think I could."

"Then what is my favorite animal?"

"A horse."

"That was too easy." She tapped a finger against her lips. "What do I prefer to eat for breakfast?"

"Scrambled eggs and fried potatoes."

Layala's mouth dropped. "How do you know that?"

"Because I've watched you eat."

"And you're so perceptive of everything I do?"

"Not everything." He licked his lips. "I don't know how you feel about me anymore. But if I had to venture a guess, I think you want to kiss me again. You just don't want to admit it." A sly smile followed his remark.

"Your ego knows no bounds."

"You liked it when I kissed you."

"Was it the slap in the face that told you that?"

He laughed. "I think it was the way you wrapped your arms around me and kissed me back. Or maybe it was when your tongue slid in my mouth that gave it away."

She thought back to that kiss. It was days ago but she still felt the fire of it. The burn of it still smoldered in her. "That was a mistake on my part."

"You should make that mistake more often."

A raindrop hit her cheek, then another. She stopped to look up and in seconds a downpour hit. The heavy rain pounded, drowning out the sound of the city around them. Water cascaded in tiny rivers down Thane's beautiful face. They both should have been moving, trying to get out of the storm but let it pelt them. As if it could cleanse away the wickedness of what befell the city and the monsters they fought to save it. Thane tilted his face toward the sky, his eyes closed.

"We should get out of the rain," she finally said after they stood there until their clothes were soaked through.

"We should." He started off at a jog, through the street that was very quickly flooding with small streams of muddy and blackened water. They raced past houses and buildings of various kinds. Save for a few soldiers, the roads were empty. Splashing through puddles Layala let out a burst of laughter when Thane slipped, wobbled, arms flailing around wildly and finally steadied himself.

"You think that's funny?"

All the sadness from the day seemed to go down with the water. "Yes." Then she slipped in the same spot and waved her arms to try to get her balance but fell into Thane's chest. He caught her under her arms. She pushed herself upright and then lifted her eyes to find him staring down at her.

After several long beats, he said, "Will you ever forgive me?"

She blinked away the rainwater collecting on her lashes. "Forgive you for what?"

"For taking you from Briar Hollow. For forcing you to come with me." His Adam's apple bobbed. "I am sorry. I should have told you everything from the start. But I—I was scared."

He was scared? Thane Athayel? The Warrior King... "I wouldn't have listened. And I have already forgiven you." She replied, repeating what he once said to her.

Slowly he angled his mouth toward hers, and this time she didn't try to pull away. She didn't want to. She craved the feeling he gave her even though she fought it as much as she desired it. When his breath swept over her lips, he pulled back. "We should hurry. She'll be waiting." When he turned and ran, her heart crashed against her ribs like a fist trying to break free. Why had he pulled away?

A WHITE-WASHED gray spiraling tower overgrown with vines and weeds, and missing a few bricks, came into view at the edge of Doonafell. They passed under a stone archway and pushed through overgrown grass to get to the wooden door. Thane pulled the latch and shoved his shoulder into the door. It slowly groaned open.

Candles lit above from the hanging chandelier, flaming torches lined the walls. A stone stairwell was to the left but the room they stood in now had one large table with ten place settings and ten chairs. Walls lined with shelves, some held books, others, scrolls stacked within the cubbies. It smelled of old paper and dust, although the place was kept immaculately clean.

"Does she live here?" Layala asked and stepped forward. "It seems rude to barge in."

"She does but she won't mind."

"Greetings," a soothing voice called, emerging from the stairwell. "And it's not rude if it's the High King and his mate barging. For I should think they can very well barge wherever they'd like."

How did she know who she was? Her light lavender eyes seemed to observe much more than what could be seen when she stepped into the room.

"Atarah, this is Layala Lightbringer."

She dipped at the waist. "I know, quite a famous name now. I could sense her power. Very distinct in nature. A little unruly, wants to protect its master," she straightened, and arched her sleek dark eyebrow.

"Compatible with," she bowed again to Thane. "Your highnesses' magic. Which isn't always the case, mind you. Sometimes the magic within another is repelling." She gestured to the table. "Not every mage to ever sit here enjoyed each other's company."

Curious, Layala walked around the shiny black table and stopped at the high-backed chair with snakes and lilies carved into the wood. It was cruelly beautiful. Thunder boomed loudly outside, adding to the dark aesthetic of the place. "Were there many mages here at one time?"

"Oh yes," Atarah said. "I sat at this very table with some of the greatest mages of all time. Roelan Cross, Quntius Corvus, Brizelyn Stormfront." She stared at the chair Layala stood beside. "Zaurahel Everhath."

"And you are a mage?" She didn't recognize any of those names, though she thought perhaps she should. In her stubbornness to hide her magic she didn't learn about it or any other mages besides the terror the Black Mage caused. But everyone knew about how he tried to take over the entire continent of Adalon with his wars.

"I was once. Now I am but a keeper of this tower."

"Once?" Layala asked. Had she lost her magic? Was there a way to lose it?

She waved her hand, nearly covered in her draping silver robe trimmed in pale pink. Her warm brown skin was beautiful against strawberry blonde hair. "Let us sit and talk." Layala pulled at the snake chair and Atarah blurted out frantically, "Sit anywhere but there."

Layala jerked her hands back as if those snakes could bite, and looked to Thane. His face was grim when he gestured to the seat next to him. "No one sits there anymore."

As she sat beside Thane and across from Atarah, she wondered who that seat belonged to. Someone revered or despised, although she leaned toward the latter.

"I apologize I didn't mean to frighten you. That was where Zaurahel sat. The most powerful mage in history."

"The Black Mage," Thane clarified.

Dear Maker, she almost sat in his chair. Her skin crawled looking at it now, as if she was tainted for touching it. "Why not burn it then?"

Atarah lifted a shoulder. "I've tried. And I've tried hiding it in closets, and throwing it outside. It returns."

That said all Layala needed to know about the matter. "You knew him. Were you *friends* with him?" She didn't mean to sound accusatory, but her tone was a little sharp.

Atarah lowered her chin and tapped her fingers on the dark tabletop. "I was. He wasn't always the Black Mage, you know. But power corrupts and truly, he had power. Unlike anything I've ever seen and we praised him for it, like he was one of the old gods, or the Maker himself."

"I know he was able to create spells but what else?"

"What more need there be?" Atarah's eyes widened, making Layala feel like she asked a stupid question. "He created rune magic and it was limitless. If he could think it, he could do it. All he needed was to create a rune to hold the spell."

Limitless. Suddenly her magic, though strong, felt inadequate. The praise she received wasn't deserved. "And you could use those spells too?"

"Many elves could then. A thousand years ago there was at least one mage per family, oftentimes entire bloodlines held the power." She slowly pushed her finger around the rim of a crystal glass. "And elves fell prey to the seduction of it. See Zaurahel could make it so that *any* elf could get their wish. But with a price and at first it was for money and precious things but after some years he changed, and the price often claimed your soul and it belonged to *him*. Elves willingly made those bargains, and the pale ones were created. Even after elves knew what the cost was, they'd still risk it, until we were all punished, and our magic was taken from us by the Maker. Mages stopped being born. Elves took sides, wars started. Humans abandoned us. Dwarves hid in the mountains. Dragon shifters stayed in their beast form."

Layala looked at Thane. "Mage Vesstan said he didn't know the consequences when he bound us together. It seems everyone knew." She should have known.

Thane pursed his lips. "He knew. He just thought there wouldn't be a problem with us fulfilling it."

Layala pursed her lips. It's not as if it mattered now. The deed was done and calling Vesstan a liar wouldn't change anything. "How can elves be bound to the Black Mage if he is dead?"

After bringing that crystal glass to her mouth for a sip, she answered, "The Void is him. He is the Void. He is not truly gone until it is. Somehow, he tethered himself to the land. And the more pale ones there are, the larger it grows. It's why they are drawn there."

"But there must be a piece of him within the Void that is connected. Where is his body buried?"

Thane answered this time, "All accounts say it was burned. And we've tried burning the land, but it won't catch flame. No one who enters the Void ever comes back without being turned so if there is a piece of him there, we don't know of its existence."

The candles in the center of the table flickered as if a gust of wind swept through but she didn't feel a breeze. A chill ran down her spine like something caressed her skin. Was there someone else here? She peeked over her shoulder but found nothing but the books on the shelf. "What if we captured Mathekis? We could get the information from him. If he wants to use me to bring back the Black Mage, then he must know how to destroy him."

"Don't think we haven't tried," Thane leaned forward and rested his forearms against the table. "But there is only one being in Adalon I have never wanted to face and that is Mathekis."

Bobbing her head Atarah added, "Mathekis was once called Eldan Avarahim. And he once sat at this very table. He still has some of his power, and its nature is persuasion. His words to many are like bees drawn to flowers. When he commands, most cannot help but follow. He is the most dangerous person in Adalon even if his abilities aren't as strong as they once were." Atarah turned slightly and shouted, "Finnegan Thistle! Get down here with that wine!" Then she faced Thane and Layala again. "My apologies for shouting. My gnome servant is old and slow. Anyway, where were we... Ah yes, we were called the Ten Mages of Magnavallis. For many years kings, queens, lords, and people of all manner would seek our council. We kept the peace between races. Even the ogres and trolls caused no trouble." She took a deep breath. "Until Zaurahel started demanding more than gold or jewels as payment for his magic. He wanted more power. He wanted an army. I opposed him as did six others of the Ten. Mathekis chose his side."

What seemed like a long pause passed. Layala thought she wouldn't continue but she went on, "He betrayed us. He poisoned those who didn't choose his side. Disguised it as a toast to make amends. The only reason I'm still alive is because I didn't drink the wine that night. I pretended to take a sip. I knew something was wrong. After that my magic slowly faded away over a few hundred years as did everyone else's. A few were born after the war: Vesstan, a female named Inara but she's dead, and as you know Vesstan hasn't much magic left. Then you two were born. It is not a coincidence you are together now." The mage lifted her eyes finally to meet Layala's. "Tenebris may have bound you two together with his own selfish motivations but in the end, I think you two will save us because of it."

"Why do they change their names?"

"Zaurahel always wore a black robe, and he had black lilies tattooed on his forearms."

Layala's insides cramped at the realization of the connection. A cold sweat broke out over her skin. She was born marked with black lilies. The very nature of her magic was so relatable to the Black Mage's chair that it now felt encroaching as she stared at it. The serpents resembled her vines, her dark purple lilies uncanny in relation to the carvings.

"He said the poisonous flower that only bloomed at night represented him best. It was quite stark against his light skin. People started calling him the Black Mage. He didn't call himself that. And once Eldan changed into a pale one, he changed his name. Mathekis is fitting for what he has become. It means 'from shadow'."

Layala shivered again, finding it hard to look away from that haunting chair. Did it mean something that she'd been drawn to it? Overwhelming anxiety whirled through her, and she nearly jumped up from the table to escape, when Thane placed a gentle hand on her knee. She whipped her head around to face him and a reassuring smile tugged on his beautiful mouth. He didn't say anything but the warmness in his eyes was enough to calm her nerves.

A further distraction entered: a gnome rounder and taller than Tifapine, hobbled into the room carrying a bottle of wine on his shoulder. His white beard nearly touched the floor, and his brown trousers had patches of polka dot and stripes on them just like Tif's. Layala asked once if she wanted new attire, but it turned out that patches were the fashion for gnomes, as were holes in boots. He grunted when he shoved the bottle into Atarah's hand. He grunted again when he climbed up on a chair and then onto the table. After he took the wine back from Atarah and pulled the cork, he hobbled over to pour the white liquid into Layala's glass.

"Thank you," she said when it was full.

He glared, mumbled something under his breath and poured a glassful for Thane. After setting the bottle down rather loudly and shuffling his boots across the tabletop, he slid off out of sight.

"He pretends to hate everyone, but I've tried to evict him. He refuses to leave so I said if he was going to stay, he'd have to work. I think he secretly enjoys dusting."

"At least you have company," Thane said with a half smile.

Layala took a few gulps of wine trying to work up

the courage to ask if she knew of a way to break the Black Mage's spells. She knew if she asked it would ruin much of the progress that she and Thane had made. It would mean that she still planned to break from him even if they'd become friends.

Thane and Atarah talked about the battle for a while. The gruesome details made her skin crawl, but she listened quietly. Thane explained the nature of Layala's magic and Atarah only nodded. Atarah didn't show any signs of shock or approval. Layala supposed it was because Atarah had seen a lot of mages in her lifetime, but she wondered why neither of them saw the connection she did to the Black Mage. Or perhaps they did but didn't dare speak it aloud.

When some time passed Thane turned to Layala. "You've been awfully quiet."

"Is there something on your mind?" Atarah asked, eyes twinkling as if she already knew the answer.

She gently chewed on her lip. Layala had much on her mind but most pressing, "Um, I was going to ask..." she hesitated. "Is there a way to break a spell by the Black Mage?" She kept her gaze pinned on Atarah to avoid seeing Thane's reaction. She tried to block any feelings that might come from him through their bond too.

Unlike Vesstan, she didn't stare at her in pity or condemnation. Maybe she didn't understand why she asked the question. "The only person to ever break a rune spell was the dragon shifter Varlett. A sorceress. She worked with Zaurahel and was duty bound to him. A rune mark branded her forehead. She is one of the most vile people I've ever known. She released herself from his hold somehow."

"And no one has any idea how or why?"

Atarah finished off her glass of wine. "Your guess is as good as mine. She's clever and cunning."

This was the same person that Mage Vesstan spoke of, and seemingly the only one alive with any answers. "And she's in the Sederac Mountains?" Layala asked.

"Can she be trusted?" Thane interrupted.

"Yes she is, and certainly not." Atarah's eyes moved back and forth between the two of them. "As I said, she's one of the vilest people I've ever met. She drank the blood of elven babies from a hideous gaudy goblet. I faced her in battle once." She tugged down her collar to reveal a thick red scar from the side of her neck, down across her collarbone until it disappeared under her robes. "Left me with this. Her claws are infused with poison. After four hundred years it hasn't fully healed."

Layala sank further into her chair. The one woman with answers was likely the last person Layala wanted to meet. "Why did she break from the Black Mage?"

"I have not the faintest idea. Everyone else who took his side has always been extremely loyal. But even if she is not loyal to his memory anymore, she is as evil as he was."

"Is there another way?" Layala asked.

"Why do you ask?" Layala stayed silent long enough that Atarah answered anyway. "There is the

All Seeing Stone. It would be able to give you the answer but might be even more dangerous than Varlett."

Thane and Layala exchanged a glance. Thane said, "That's rumored to be near here."

"Yes." She nodded. "Where the Void and Palenor meet in the tomb of the one who killed the Black Mage. Many have sought it of course but none have succeeded." She glanced toward a window. "Oh look. The rain has stopped."

Thane stood and the chair scraped loudly against the floor as it pushed back. "Thank you for the wine and conversation. We must go. There is much to do."

"After your mate bond is settled and the risk associated with it is gone, come back and we'll work on a plan to finish off Zaurahel and the mess he made for good." Atarah walked them to the door. "I have kept faith through all these years that someday, somehow, it could all end."

Layala shook her hand. "Thank you for having us. It was wonderful to meet you, Atarah."

"You as well, Layala." She gave her a knowing look. "Fear is the enemy of hope. And you will need hope for what lies ahead."

Chapter 32

Following Thane out the door and over the unkempt path, Layala felt the growing heaviness between them. "Thane," she started but he kept walking without acknowledgment. Quickening her pace, she caught up to his side and tugged on his sleeve. "Are you angry with me?"

"Why would I be angry?" he stared ahead.

"I don't know—you seem different." They walked alone along a muddy path just outside of the city wall.

"I have a lot on my mind, Layala," he finally said. "Things that have nothing to do with you."

"Right." They walked on for several minutes in silence. But she knew it wasn't simply the funerals and the battles and partial loss of the city. He markedly changed after she brought up breaking their bond. "The gnome was funny, don't you think? A grumpy little thing. The bottle of wine was bigger than he was."

A small smile tugged. Seeing progress she continued, "He had quite an impressive beard. I bet you couldn't grow one like that. Not that I'd want you to. I like seeing that fine jawline of yours." He still fought his smile. "It looks like we'll have to capture Mathekis or go into the Void, to find out how to destroy it, which is terrible. The rotten boggs will certainly ruin my boots."

"Yes, I'm sure your boots are your biggest concern. Not that you wouldn't come out alive."

"Oh, I'll survive it. But I might break a nail."

"Heaven forbid that happens."

Layala smiled. "I'm starving."

"I know. I heard your stomach growling. It's like a small beast is trapped in there."

"That's a little exaggerated."

"Is it?" She lightly shoved him, and he laughed. "Was that a fly landing on me? I almost couldn't feel it." Biting down, she pushed him again and his shoulder bumped into the wall. "You're strong for a female."

"I dare you to find out how strong," she said with the intent to rile him up the way he always did when she wasn't speaking to him.

Something primal flashed in his eyes and he advanced on her, unlatching the sword belt over his chest. Layala tensed when he set his swords on the ground and started undoing his weapons belt at his hip. "What are you doing?"

"Let's see those fighting skills of yours. No

weapons, no punches, no magic, takedown moves only."

Layala's fingers shook slightly as she unlatched her own weapons and set them in the grass. Sparring would require them to become *very* close. She was good with hand-to-hand combat but she was much more comfortable with her sword and dagger.

"First you tried to kill me in my bed. Successfully stabbed me. Then you threw a fork at my face at dinner." He stepped so close that she had to look up to see his face. "You slap me and push me whenever you feel like it. Behavior I would never tolerate from *anyone* else."

Her cheeks warmed. "And what? Now you want to punish me?"

"No," he answered. "I'm going to show you why they call me the Warrior King. I don't think you have any idea. After this we'll spar with weapons."

"We have sparred. We're pretty evenly matched."

"If the night you tried to kill me is any indication, you have things to learn. You need to be the best, not adequate. There have been too many times where you've been in danger, and I wasn't there."

More intrigued than she should be, Layala stepped back and readied herself, arms squared before her, knees bent. She did this all the time back at Briar Hollow, but never with a partner so intense or attractive. *It's just sparring practice. You've done this a thousand times.*

He stood stark straight, waiting. She rolled her eyes and kicked at his ankle. He sidestepped, and faster than she thought possible, he had the crook of his elbow tight around her neck and his other arm wrapped around her torso, pinning her arms down. Angry with herself for getting caught so fast, she struggled to break free, but he only gripped her tighter.

"I could snap your neck as easily as I can take a breath. Your arrogance will get you killed," he said in her ear. "And therefore, get me killed."

An involuntary shiver wracked her body. "Get off."

"Escape."

She growled as he clinched a little tighter making her lightheaded. "I can't."

"What was that?"

"I *can't*."

"I just wanted to make sure you knew." He released her, but his hand trailed along her back as he stepped away.

A string of expletives ripped through her mind. "You're such—"

"A bastard? You're getting predictable."

She stepped away and readied herself. "Want to compare magic?"

"I don't want us to die so no," he said with a serpentine smirk. "Again."

Clenching her fists, she took a steadying breath. "You come at me this time."

He tilted his head and in a flash, grabbed her arm and jerked her forward. She shoved her foot at his gut, but he moved to the side, and it grazed off his torso. She swung under his arm breaking his hold with a twist and kicked his knee from behind. It buckled but he didn't go down. Jumping onto his back, she latched on, wrapping her legs around his hard torso. But before she could secure a neck hold, he tossed her over his head. When she hit the ground the air whooshed from her lungs. Before she could suck in a breath, he straddled her, pressing his weight into her thighs and hips, and hovered a knife above her throat.

"Hmm this reminds me of something. Does it you?"

"Pig," she breathed. Unlike the last time he'd pinned her like this, hatred and disgust didn't course through her. Something much different warmed her skin now. An unbidden thought of pushing that damn knife aside and dragging his lips down to hers heated her cheeks. "You said no weapons."

"Just teaching you to be prepared." He lifted the knife away, stabbing it into the ground beside them, but was still poised above her, still very much on her.

Her chest heaved up and down. She couldn't pull her gaze from his bright green eyes. Like he held her under a deliciously sinful spell. All her resistance to him and his charming mouth and otherworldly beauty over the weeks was flickering like a dying flame, and there wasn't a damn thing she could do to stop it. "I don't need you to teach me anything," she said.

"You look good lying on your back under me, Laya."

She ground her teeth. "You really are a pig, you know that?"

He let out a midnight chuckle.

"Do you talk to all your sparring partners this way?" she asked.

"Only you."

"Time for swords, and I swear if you make one joke about *your* sword, I'll cut it off."

He laughed again and Maker, she liked that sound. He finally rose off of her and held out his hand. She grasped it and he tugged her to her feet. "You haven't had enough?"

"Oh, I'm just getting started." Scooping up her sword, she spat in the grass and narrowed her eyes at him.

"You certainly are the epitome of a lady." She flipped him her middle finger and he chuckled, bending down to gather his sword. "I'll even use one sword this time so you can't call me a cheater."

He swung at her first. She blocked and quickly sidestepped, evading another blow. *Whoosh,* his sword cracked against hers and she nearly lost her grip. She parried, slicing at his leg; he blocked, slammed his boot down on her blade, sticking the point in the dirt and quickly brought the tip of his sword to her chest.

"You're not bad, dearest. But I am that good."

"And you say I'm arrogant. Your head is getting so big it won't be able to fit in your tent." *Maker above*, she didn't want to admit it, but he was *that* good. They went at it again. Layala swung with more force and their blades clashed loudly, until he grazed her with an elbow and she fell back, landing halfway on her hip and wrist. The tang of blood filled her mouth as he squatted in front of her. No one had taken her down as easily or quickly since she was a novice.

"I didn't mean to do that..." he frowned and held his hand out to her. He wasn't even breathing heavily.

"Again," she said, spitting blood.

"Layala, I don't want to hurt you."

"Worry about yourself," she said. "And don't take it easy on me."

He sighed and stood. They fought over and over until it was twilight and even their elf eyes had trouble seeing clearly. She had yet to win a bout. He got the better of her thirteen times. *Thirteen*. She was knocked down, smacked with the flat of his blade, kicked, and the calluses on her hand tore open. Each loss stung more than the last, and each made her respect for him grow.

"You're good. Better than most."

"Thanks," she breathed, now laying flat on her back, hardly able to move. Her body ached, her hands stung, as did her pride.

"Are you done?"

"Until tomorrow," she wheezed. He got her good once in the ribs and they must be bruised. She sliced open his forearm and slammed the hilt of her sword into his eyebrow where a small cut leaked blood, so he wasn't completely unscathed. At least she had that.

Before she even knew what he was doing, he

tucked an arm behind her knees and the other around her back and lifted her. "Your will is impressive. Your skills are excellent and will only get better. Sometimes it takes training with one better than you to improve."

She didn't protest as he carried her toward the camp. Resting her exhausted head against his shoulder she murmured, "I'll beat you someday."

"I don't doubt that."

Her chest warmed at his response. "And thank you."

"For?"

"For treating me like an equal." She didn't want to be treated like a delicate flower or she would never improve.

When they arrived back at camp, he set her down in front of her tent's entrance. The small fires all around provided enough light she could see his face clearly. He looked torn and uncertain about something. She wanted to ask but sudden music playing from fiddlers and tambourines close by took the moment away.

"Make sure Tifapine puts healing balm on your hand and wraps it."

"I will." She inspected the slice on his arm she'd given him. It looked as if it was almost healed already. "I guess I didn't cut you as deep as I thought."

He winked. "I heal quickly. Goodnight, Laya."

"Laya?" That was the second time he'd called her that.

With a dangerous smile and a caress of her cheek,

his voice dropped low, "Would you prefer, Temptress? Goddess? My muse..."

Why did each of those words sound so good on his lips? Her spine tingled. "Laya. Laya works. Sleep well, High King." She couldn't pull her stare from his. Why did everything in her want to ask him to come into her tent? To talk, to enjoy the warmth of his body next to her because she couldn't want more. She shouldn't want anything from him. He lingered for a moment and then turned and disappeared into the darkness of his abode.

Every night for a week they trained together. Bumps and bruises became frequent but there was something about pinning each other to the ground that was more sensual than aggressive, and she'd never felt that with anyone else. The pure will to beat her opponent like usual wasn't there. She wanted to improve her skills and she did but with Thane it was much more playful and intense. A blade against her throat never felt so... intriguing.

And each night when he left her outside her tent with a long look, and her mate mark pulsing and a line that seemed to tug her toward him growing stronger, the urge to ask him to stay intensified, but she always turned away without an invitation.

On this night, she lay in her bedroll, staring up at the tent's canvas. Her body ached from working during the day to help the people of Doonafell and the training in the evenings took its toll. But her pulse pounded for no apparent reason. She hadn't been able to fall asleep for hours, like an electric current ran through her veins. Piper was fast asleep, completely covered in her blanket and Tif was snoring, again. Layala got up, feeling a strong sense of urgency. Slipping her pants and boots on, she peeked out the tent flap. A few soldiers patrolled the area, but it was quiet.

What was this anxiety creeping up in her? Was something out there? Her mate line tugged harder than ever, enough to force her feet to follow it to Thane's tent. She stood outside for a moment, contemplating what she would ever say if she went inside. But that urgency and anxiety intensified and with a deep breath, Layala stepped inside.

Thane sat in his wooden armchair, bent over with his face in his hands. A single candle burned on the side table. He was shirtless with a sheen of sweat covering his skin despite the cool night. His breathing was labored and if she didn't know better, she would say he was... crying.

"Thane?"

His head snapped up and his jaw muscles tightened as their eyes met. He wasn't crying but the harsh planes of his face like ice on a cold wintry night spoke of despair. She took a step closer. "Do you want to talk about it?"

They were quiet for a moment. She took another step. Thane stared at his hands while Layala watched his face closely.

"My father," he swallowed hard.

Layala's heart started to race.

"I dreamed about the day I killed my father, and I can't sleep now." He swiped his hand across his sweaty brow. "The way he looked at me as the pale ones surrounded him... The realization of the betrayal–" he let out a long breath. "And then the dream shifted, and I was my father and the pale ones were tearing at my flesh, taking bites out of my body, pulling out my insides. How could I have done that to him?" Thane's hands shook. "Even he didn't deserve that. I know he had to die but I should have killed him swiftly, by my own hand. He was my *father* and I fed him to monsters."

Layala's chest ached and tears welled in her eyes feeling his emotions of regret and sorrow. Not for Tenebris's death, but for the pain this caused Thane. Her quick steps ate up the remaining distance from him. "Oh, Thane." She bent over and cupped the side of his face, beautiful even in the storms of regret. She knew it hurt him, but he'd never been this vulnerable and open before. He'd never let her *feel* how much. And she'd been too much of a coward to ask. "I'm sure it was swift."

He wrapped his arms around her, pulling her on his lap and against him as if she might disappear if he didn't. With her cheek pressed against his, she embraced him, rubbing the soft skin of his back gently. They held each other like that for a while. She didn't know how long, but she listened to the steady pull of his lungs, and the chirping crickets outside. That sharp pain dulled to an ache then warmth and ease like when the sun crested at the first sign of a new day. As if their bodies so close could heal the hurt. When he finally let her go, he took her hand and walked her back to her tent. Morning twilight colored the sky and birds sang happily. He leaned down and kissed her cheek with such tenderness. That playfulness he usually exuded wasn't there, and he didn't smile, but he squeezed her hand gently.

"I have some things to do," he said, his voice more gruff than usual. "I'll find you later." He turned to leave.

She grabbed his arm. "I'm here when you need me."

"Thank you."

Chapter 33

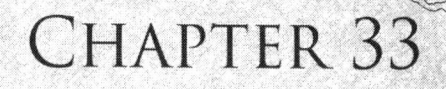

Weeks passed where Thane required all of his soldiers to stay to fortify and help start rebuilding the city. The hard part was watching the suffering of the loved ones of the dead. But everyone was occupied with work: whether it was to feed people, chop wood, hold the hand of someone suffering, sew clothes, patch wounds, or other various tasks.

Although Layala wanted to find the All Seeing Stone Atarah mentioned, she didn't know where it was and Thane was too busy to ask. So, to pass the time she trained with Piper, Aldrich, and Fennan each morning and with Thane in the evenings. He was back to his flirtatious self, and they didn't talk about that night he dreamt of his father's death or the way their arms and bodies pressed together dulled the pain.

Each day Layala was achy and tired, but she also enjoyed the work and the time she got to spend with the elves, getting to know Piper, Aldrich, and Fennan better, and being near Thane. When she wasn't training, she was by his side, helping where she could.

Maker, he was a shameless flirt, and she didn't know when she went from having her guard up to playing into it and wanting it. Wanting him. Although he hadn't tried to kiss her again, he made ways to touch her if only briefly. Skimming her arm or sliding his fingers across her back as he scooted by. She found herself smiling all the time.

To honor his fallen Ravens, Thane ordered a Celebration of Life and the families of those soldiers finally arrived. Their bodies had already burned on a funeral pyre, but the ashes were placed in urns to be given to the families.

The soldiers' swords and weapons were placed next to the urn of their ashes. Layala spent most of the day helping to prepare the event by setting up tables of food and drink, and now weaved crowns of flowers with young maidens for the celebration.

Piper lay in the grass, basking in the sunset but had no interest in flowers or making crowns. Sitting on logs under a yew tree, the three young ladies with Layala giggled when a pair of handsome males walked by. Their mothers were pregnant at the same time and named them after flowers: Rose, Lilac, and Freesia.

Layala shook her head, putting a hand up to shield her eyes from the low-hanging sun, and get a better look at the elves the girls spoke of. She couldn't help the smile spreading across her face. "Why don't you go speak to them?"

All three of them blushed. They were from Doonafell and were lucky that no one in their families had died weeks before. "What's the point? They'll be gone soon," said Lilac, the one with raven curls that cascaded past her rump. Her skin was a few shades lighter than her hair and her eyes were gold.

"You can still have fun with them." Layala raised an eyebrow.

"Lady Lightbringer, it's not proper to speak such things," said Freesia, the one with the lavender eyes and rich tan skin.

Chuckling, Layala tied the crown on her lap with pink ribbon. "I mean dance and laugh and talk, not anything sexual. I hear there will be music tonight."

Rose, with hair so pale it was almost white, lifted her chin. "I, for one, will not be pursuing any males. If they want to dance with me, they'll ask."

"A she-elf after my own heart," Layala said, and the maidens giggled again.

Tifapine plopped a crown on Layala's head from behind. "Now you need a dress to match." Tif walked around her, tapping a finger against her lips.

Layala tugged it off her head and inspected the crown. It was wonderfully done with lavender, soft pink roses and sprays of light green leaves and dark red berries still attached to the vine. "Do all the females wear them?"

"Most *unmarried* maidens wear them at gatherings such as this. It's to show you are available. But you are mate-marked to the High King, so you're not available."

"But the spell is not yet finished, and she's not married," Tif said with a hand on her hip. "So, she can wear it. I spent three hours looking for the flowers and putting it together."

"This sounds like a dangerous game to play," Rose smirked. "I'm intrigued."

"I wouldn't wear it if I were you, Lady Lightbringer," Freesia said. "You might offend him."

"Oh, please do." Rose tucked her pale hair behind her pointed ear. "We could do with something interesting around here instead of the melancholy and tears."

"People died to save you, have some respect." Lilac shot her a glare.

Piper cleared her throat but didn't open her eyes or bother to turn from the sunlight. "If you wear that crown, you better be prepared to get burned by the fire you're playing with."

Lifting an eyebrow Layala found herself itching to put it back on. "It couldn't possibly be *that* consequential. It's just a flower crown."

"Speaking of the High King." Tif lifted her chin.

Layala's stomach fluttered when she spotted him talking with what she assumed was one of the families of the fallen. The revulsion and pure hatred she once held for him was stolen by a spark that ignited every time he was near. He stirred things in her she hadn't felt in years. Things she promised herself she never would again. She couldn't get out of her head that he called her a goddess and a temptress or the way he caressed her face and it had been weeks ago.

His voice was like liquid fire pulsing down her back every time he spoke. In the last week she watched him, riveted with his every move. Somewhere from the time he took her from Briar Hollow to now she saw who he was. Someone kind but fierce. Funny but also compassionate. She fought back the desire to want to touch him. Although many things required Thane's attention, he was never too far. They could be the full camp apart and she still felt his presence like a warm blanket under a cool, open night sky.

"I should go change. They're lighting the torches and the music started." Layala placed the crown Tif made her back on her head. A move that tugged at her gut, but she did anyway. Like Tif said, she wasn't married.

Even though it was out of her way, Layala walked by Thane. Very aware of her heart's sudden rapid succession, she couldn't take her gaze from him. When his eyes snapped to hers, he stopped talking mid-sentence. She was far enough away she couldn't hear the conversation, but when his jaw hung slightly ajar it was tell enough. Inside she was smiling although she didn't let it show on her lips. So, the girls had been right about the flower crown, and he didn't appear to like that she wore it one bit. A dangerous game indeed. She knew she was wicked for it, but she wanted to see what he would do.

Layala tore her gaze away and headed for her tent to change.

Right beside her, Tif said, "I had Piper get a dress for you that matches the crown. It's a lovely maroon color."

"You're the best lady's maid there's ever been, Tif." When Layala stepped into her tent where the dress was laid out on her bedroll.

Blushing, Tif twirled a lock of her hair around her stubby finger. "Ah, you're too kind. But feel free to give me compliments at any time."

Stifling a laugh, Layala slipped out of her clothes and changed into the dress. It reached to just above her knees and the bell sleeves were long, dangling well below her wrists in flowy lace. She strapped a dagger to her thigh and decided to forgo shoes. She liked the feeling of cool grass under her bare feet. "Are you joining the celebration?"

Plopping down on her pillow, Tif shook her head. "I may be able to come out with you around small groups, but I'm still scared of the dark. I'll stay inside."

"Suit yourself." Layala peeked out of the slit of the tent, watching for Thane. He wasn't anywhere near. She wanted him to see her and do something bold. He hadn't even come close to kissing her again. *I shouldn't want him to kiss me. I shouldn't even be thinking about it.* But she couldn't stop replaying the moment he pressed her against the tree over and over, and how much she wanted him to do it again. *You're being stupid. You made a vow to never love again.* She paced back and forth in her tent.

Layala expected Tif to ask her a load of questions about why she was pacing and why she hadn't gone out to the party yet, but the little gnome dozed off. When Layala peered out the slit again it was dark. Night came faster than she expected. The torch between her tent and Thane's was lit and the pale light from the stars and half-moon shone down brightly. She took in a deep breath and stepped out.

Drawn toward the slow beating drums, the light picking of strings and the airy whispering of flutes, she padded across the soft, cool grass. The Ravens danced with many of the young maidens of Doonafell around three large fires. Wine was served out of casks in goblets. She wasn't the only one not wearing shoes either. It was much less formal than the Summer Solstice celebration.

A tug at her chest caused her to look left to find Thane sitting on what could only be described as a throne. It was made of wood but was carved with great whorls and painted midnight blue. His silver crown perched on his dark locks and those predatory green eyes watched her with brutal awareness. It was as if he stripped her bare and could see all that she was. Breath coming shallow, she followed the pull that yanked on her to go to him, then halted. She couldn't give into him no matter how delicious he looked tonight. His black button-up tunic was left open enough to peek at the planes of his muscular chest and his hair was left down, unruly and worthy of grasping. Taking a sharp turn Layala made for the line at one of the wine kegs.

The male in front of her turned around with a smile. She didn't recognize him but there were simply too many elves at camp to know them all. "You are as beautiful as a blooming red rose in winter, Lady."

She smiled. "That's a new one."

He chuckled. "I apologize. It was a terrible line."

"It wasn't too terrible. Unique at least."

"What's your name?"

Layala took the wine offered by one of the attendants. He truly had no idea who she was? Was he not one of the Ravens? "Layala."

"I'm Endafar. From Doonafell."

Layala took a long drink and smiled. "I'm from..." she didn't know how to answer that. "A very small place you've probably never heard of."

"Would you like to dance with me, Layala from a very small place?"

Her eyes darted to Thane whose attention had shifted from her to a she-elf with a crown of white roses standing before him, blocking her view of his face. Jealousy lit within her so hot she had to take another long swig to clamp it down. "I better not."

Endafar's dark eyes danced with curiosity. "And why is that?"

"I think it might cause you more trouble than it's worth."

Thane's words echoed in her mind, *"You are mine.*

And I will destroy anyone who gets in my way." Damn, why did she find that attractive? Why did it make her want him all the more?

When Thane got up from his throne, holding onto the hand of the she-elf pulling him toward the other dancers, she choked on her wine and turned away from Endafar in a coughing fit. Her magic itched at her fingertips, and she couldn't even say why. "I'm sorry, excuse me." Quickly, she started off in the opposite direction with the goblet shaking in her hand.

She paused when she thought she was alone, and took in a few deep breaths. *Stop it, stop it. Thane is free to do what he pleases. You will only ever be mates in symbolism.* But no matter how much she tried to talk herself out of the burning anger building in her, she couldn't. A gentle touch on her arm made her jerk her dagger free and pushed it against—Endafar's neck.

He put up his hands with wide eyes. "I only wanted to make sure you were alright."

She lowered the dagger and shoved it back in its sheath. "Sorry. Reflex."

"What was the name of this small town again?"

"I didn't say." She rubbed her forehead and looked down in her goblet. It was empty. Out of the corner of her eye she found Fennan watching with his arms crossed on the other side of a bonfire with Sunshine beside him. With a smirk, Sunshine winked at her, as if daring her to take Endafar up on his offer, although she knew he couldn't hear. "You seem nice. You should leave me alone." But when she saw Thane smiling down at the maiden he danced with, she gripped the goblet tighter. "Actually, I'd love to dance."

He looked over his shoulder following Layala's stare then turned back with a shrug. "Great."

After setting her goblet on the table beside the wine, she let the young elf lead her in a dance. Her feet moved easily to the upbeat tune. They held hands, spinning in circles, and moving in and out but never too close. It wasn't a song that invited intimacy. She giggled as the wine hit her, feeling lighter and carefree. She caught Fennan giving her a sneer and slight shake of his head. Hypocrite. He wasn't sneering at Thane for dancing with someone else. She stuck her tongue out at him. He rolled his eyes and turned to Sunshine who appeared to be laughing at her. At least one of them had a sense of humor.

Endafar spun her around then let go, sending her bumping into someone. She didn't turn to see who it was, instead swayed to the music caught up in the lovely melody. It felt like castles and pixies, and dragons and mist captured in a wistful song. After a moment of dancing alone, she found Thane with a different elf now. One with long braided brunette hair, completely enamored with him. In the minutes Layala watched them, she didn't take her eyes from his face once. His easy smile made her want to punch him right in the mouth. *How dare he smile at her like that.* She didn't care if it was the wine making her ridiculous; she stamped up to Endafar and kissed him on the cheek. Thane suddenly lost interest in his dancing partner. The muscles in his jaw flexed when she turned away from him. His stare bore into her back causing her skin to tingle in kind. When she approached the wine table again, the girls she wove crowns with earlier circled around her.

"The High King is staring at you," Lilac said and sucked in her bottom lip. "He looks— angry."

"I hope he is."

Rose smirked, tapping her pale fingers against her goblet. "You are wicked. I wish I was you."

"No, you don't," Layala muttered. To be mated to the most beautiful male she'd ever seen and not be able to touch him was a curse so cruel it cut her very soul. To have a secret so dark that it ate away at her more each day wasn't something anyone would wish for. All she was was death for those she cared for. A curse on this realm.

She downed another goblet of wine while the girls chatted about which males they thought were attractive and which they wished would ask them to dance. Why hadn't Thane asked her to dance? Why didn't he want to take her in his arms and touch her and smile at her like he had with the others?

It wasn't long before the second portion of wine left her contemplating confronting Thane. He retook his spot on his throne with Fennan and Aldrich on either side of him, talking as if he had no idea how he affected her. As if he couldn't *feel* it. "I'm going to bed," she blurted out. The girls bid her goodnight as she glided away from the celebration.

She didn't make it even halfway before she heard, "You've had your fun with that poor boy and now you're leaving?" His voice was like that wine, smooth and making her want to do things she shouldn't.

"Like you care, Mr. Dancing-with-every-eligible-maiden-here." She paused a moment thinking about turning to look at him but didn't.

Thane slid into her path, forcing her to stop. "When you put on that crown you gave an open invitation for every male to pursue you. I didn't think you'd care who I danced with."

"It's a silly crown, and I don't care who you have your hands all over. I'm going to bed." She pushed past him. "Alone. I'm sure you'll have plenty of company."

He stepped into her path again, and she balled her hands at her sides. Why did he have to look so good when she was angry? The slight breeze picked up pieces of his dark hair. The moonlight shimmered off the skin of his chest. Those damned green eyes bright even in the darkness.

"I don't want anyone else's company," he said.

"Then what do you want?"

Snatching the flower crown off her head, he tossed it aside, losing it somewhere in the shadows. "It's more than a silly crown to our people." Then he swept her legs out from under her, caught her body in his arms and started toward the gathering.

"What are you doing? Put me down," she protested, although she was silently reveling in his action.

"Doing what I should have done the moment I saw you tonight."

"And what is that?"

He remained silent as he carried her by Rose, Freesia, and Lilac, all three wearing shocked and amused expressions. Then he strutted through the dancers, bumping into Endafar on the way by. His mouth dropped open and his cheeks flamed red. Everyone turned to stare, watching their High King and the Lady Lightbringer, until they reached his throne. After he set her on her feet, he sat. She watched him curiously... what was he doing? Grabbing her waist, he firmly pulled her on his lap. "Claiming what is mine."

Everyone stopped dancing and even went silent as tension seemed to fill the air. As if everyone had paid attention to the drama between them the entire night. Thane lifted his hand, "Get back to the celebration."

His other hand was flat against her belly, and his thumb moved in little circles. Layala's body was on pins and needles, aware of his every curve and muscle against her. She twisted her upper body around to face him. His lips were so inviting, and she didn't know if it was the wine or not, but she slid her hands up his chest and pushed her lips to his. She twisted her body full around, straddling her thighs around him, kissing him harder, slipping her tongue through his teeth. She didn't care that everyone was there to watch them. She wanted them to see. No other girls in flower crowns would approach him again. He let out a low growl and slid his hands up and down her back slowly.

She wanted him enough her body could ignite into flames; it burned for him so much more than it ever did. "I wish I could have you," she murmured against his lips. "I wish you could take me into your tent, and I could have my way with you."

He pulled back with a smile, letting out a sigh. "How much wine have you had?"

Giggling, she lifted a shoulder. "Not enough to excuse saying that I'm afraid." She trailed her finger down his neck then over his chest until she reached his navel and he caught her hand.

"I think you've had more than you're letting on." He intertwined their fingers and kissed the back of her hand gently. "What do you mean you *wish* you could have me?" His eyes dropped momentarily and lifted, locking onto hers. "I'm yours, Laya. I've only ever belonged to you."

Her eyes watered and stung. "I'm cursed." A lump formed in her throat. She could hardly believe she was going to say it aloud, but the secret must come out. "Remember when I told you the man I loved died. He died because of... me. He died moments after we made love. I—I *killed* him. I don't know how. It wasn't on purpose, but my body—my magic is poisonous. So, you can't ever love me."

She'd never told anyone her dark secret. No one in Briar Hollow knew how Novak truly died. Not even Aunt Evalyn. "That day is burned into my mind like a permanent wound. I can't forget Novak's ashen skin, his lifeless eyes. I can't get it out of my head that I *killed* the man I loved." Layala's throat tightened, and she closed her eyes, drowning in the memory.

They kissed and made love, tangled in each other's arms in a meadow outside Briar Hollow. The evening sun warmed their skin; butterflies swirled around them as if blessing their union. But after the high ended and she lay on his bare chest, he went utterly still. The steady beat of his heart she listened to stopped. Confused, she lifted her head. "Novak?" she whispered. His wide-open eyes stared at the sky... never blinking.

With a gasp, she jumped back. Panic swirled in her, her skin too hot. She grabbed his face, gently shaking him. It was just a bad dream; he must be sleeping. He had to be sleeping. "Wake up." Tears slipped down her cheeks. "Wake up!" His lips were such a dark purple they almost looked black... the color of her lilies. He did not wake.

Blinking several times Thane set his jaw. He continued rubbing her back and moved a piece of hair off her cheek. "Laya, it can't be true. It doesn't make sense. You didn't use your magic against him. It doesn't just lash out on its own accord."

"It doesn't matter what you believe or what makes sense. It doesn't make sense that I was born with a black lily's mark on my arm either. What happened to

Novak is my fault." She kissed the soft skin of his cheek. "And that's why I said I wish. Because I may have wanted to kill you once," she looked up at the stars and let out a short laugh, "but I don't anymore." She fisted his tunic tightly in her hands. "There are other things I'd much rather do."

Thane closed his eyes for a moment and took a deep breath, letting it out slowly. "I am sorry that happened, and to blame yourself for this is such a horrible burden you've had to bear. But you must let it go. This will slowly kill you, and rob you of happiness you deserve. I *know* the pain you feel, but I am not him. I am not a fragile human."

She slowly shook her head. "I won't risk it. It's why I asked Atarah for a way to break our bond. We can't ever be together. Not really. I can stay and fight and be your friend but that is all."

"Friends don't feel this way about each other."

"It's this cursed bond, Thane. Once it's broken the feelings will go away. We must seek the All Seeing Stone."

He slowly shook his head. "What I feel for you couldn't simply go away. It's more than the bond."

"How do you know?"

"We certainly are more attuned to each other than most now, but you didn't feel a pull for me when I came to you or before. I think your attempt on my life proves that."

He smirked and she sighed, wishing she could scrub that day from her mind.

Thane added, "I cared about you before because I was aware of our connection and I hoped you would want to know me, if you felt it too. But that isn't the reason I—want you now. I thoroughly love your mind, and even your stubbornness." He smiled. "You're determined and witty, and fierce. As fierce as any Raven. But you're also kind and gentle. I've seen the way you care for those in need, like the children and your gnome." He brushed his fingers across her collar bone. "You are more beautiful than I ever imagined. I have never wanted anything more than I want you. I am drawn to *all* of you, Laya."

She kissed him then, softly. "*Maker*," she breathed, and a tear rolled down her cheek. "Why did you have to be perfect?"

Layala rested her head against his shoulder, half curled around his body and stayed like that until the music stopped and the celebration ended.

Chapter 34

If Layala wasn't having a nightmare about pale ones, she dreamt of Thane. Thane touching her and caressing her, kissing her, calling her lover, and—Layala shot her eyes open, breathing heavily. *Ugh not again.* The ghost of his dream lips pressed between her breasts had her cheeks burning.

Tifapine stared above her. Those chocolate curls of hers dangled on Layala's forehead. "Whatcha dreaming about there missy? Not another nightmare, I hope. I keep having this dream that a pale one comes into the tent and eats me whole. Doesn't even have to chew, and I'm stuck alive in his belly punching and screaming and yet no one can hear me."

"That's disturbing." Layala groaned and sat up. "And I've told you not to hover over me while I'm sleeping. It's creepy."

"Every time I do you wake up. Like you can sense it."

"So, tap my arm or something like a normal person."

"I tried that, and you swatted my hand away. Like I was a bug. Were you dreaming about bugs?"

The last thing she was going to do was discuss her dream with Tif. A dream she had no business having. After sitting up, the previous night came flooding back to her. She straddled Thane on his throne and kissed him as if no one watched—everyone had been watching. She even confessed about Novak's death and Thane didn't believe it. But he wasn't there to see the obvious signs of poison. It wasn't a coincidence. "No, I wasn't dreaming about bugs." Layala tossed her blanket aside and picked up a clean pair of pants. "Have you heard any mention of anything that happened last night?"

"Oh, about you and Thane getting handsy? I wish I hadn't missed it. It's been the talk all morning."

Layala tugged the maroon dress she still wore over her head and pulled on a clean top. "Great," she murmured.

Tifapine fidgeted with the hem of her dress and rocked back and forth from heel to toe. "I also heard something last night that I think you should know."

A tap against the tent and a, "Layala, I need to speak to you," from Thane had her dressing faster.

She heard enough to know that whatever Tif needed to tell her would be embarrassing. "Tell me later. I need to go."

"But," Tif called as Layala pulled the tent flap aside. "I think it's important. Like really important."

"Is it life or death?" What Tif thought was important usually wasn't and it could be a long conversation about nothing. After running her fingers through her hair, she tied it back into a high ponytail.

Tif tapped a finger against her lips. "Um, I guess you wouldn't die but—"

"Then it can wait. I'll see you later." Layala stepped out into the morning sun. It was warm but the air was cool. Staring at Thane's back as he talked to a couple soldiers compelled her heart to thud louder and harder than usual.

As if he sensed her standing there, he turned and smiled. "Good morning." His voice was warm honey oozing through her.

"Hello." She returned a smile and they stood in awkward silence. The soldiers looked at her differently. Each wore a mischievous smile like they had a joke they wanted to tell.

"You're excused," Thane said to the soldiers. They dipped their heads and wandered off.

She dreaded that he might bring up anything she'd said or done. It wasn't as if she hadn't wanted to do those things, but the wine certainly gave her the carelessness she wouldn't have otherwise had. "So um," she couldn't find anything to say.

"So, you want to attempt to retrieve the All Seeing Stone?"

"I think we should, given the circumstances." She

couldn't make herself meet his eyes. "I think it's dangerous to stay bonded." It was dangerous because she craved his touch, when she knew he wanted her more. How long could they resist?

"Because you think your magic would kill me if we have sex."

In surprise, she finally looked at him. He came right out and said it, no hesitation. "Yes."

A slow smile tugged at his mouth. "And you want to?"

Out of habit, she rolled her eyes and walked by him. "It doesn't matter what I want. It's not going to happen. It can't ever happen."

He fell into step at her side, brushing his hand against hers. "We'll find the All Seeing Stone and you can ask it what you want and I'll ask it what I want."

Making a course correction, she headed for the horses. "And what is it that you want to know so badly?"

"If I ask the stone if your magic would kill me and it says no, then will you change your mind about breaking our bond?"

"Is that what you're going to ask?"

"I'm asking you that."

Tapping a finger against her lips, she pretended to contemplate it for a long time. "Hmmm, I'll think about it." But what she wouldn't give to surrender, to have his warm lips all over her bare skin. She wanted him to whisper naughty things in her ear.

He chuckled. "Ever the vixen." With a wave of his

hand, he caught Aldrich and Fennan's attention. They made their way over quickly.

"Mornin' sire," Fennan grasped Thane's forearm in greeting. "What's on the agenda today?"

Aldrich bit into his crunchy apple. "Something other than digging holes and whittling spikes I hope."

"We're going to get the All Seeing Stone. Pack a bag."

Fennan and Aldrich looked at each other. Aldrich stopped chewing. "You do realize that it's never been done before."

"That's because I've never tried."

"Arrogant bastard today I see," Aldrich said with a grin.

"Funny, you took the words right out of my mouth," Layala said.

Thane gave Aldrich a light shove. "Just because she calls me that doesn't mean you can. Get Piper, too. The tomb might be surrounded by pale ones."

SITTING on top of a hill that overlooked the Void a few short miles away, Layala's insides squirmed. The land was hills of ashes and rotting flora that smelled like eggs long past due. Black pools of tar bubbled, and dark mist rose off the ground, creating low visibility beyond where the Void touched Palenor. She thought there was movement somewhere in the darkness, but it was difficult to distinguish a shadow from mist.

Holding her hand over her eyebrows to shield the sun, Piper stood higher in her saddle. "I don't see anyone near the tomb."

"I thought it would be bigger." Aldrich pushed his hand through his wavy hair.

"Said every girl you've ever slept with," Piper said.

Layala's hand flew to her mouth to stifle a laugh.

Aldrich shot her a glare. "Piper, darling, you can just say you want to see it. No need for the rude lies."

Piper giggled. "Got you good with that one."

"Shh, we need to be serious right now," Fennan said.

The tomb was on the grassland of Palenor but fifty yards from it, the inky Void lurked. Everything in Layala told her to go back, that this was a mistake. It was much too close to the Void where if she was taken, she could be used to bring back the Black Mage... but she also needed that stone.

Fennan visibly shuddered and tilted his head side to side, cracking his neck. "This place gives me the creeps."

"What makes this tomb hard to get into?" Layala asked, stroking Midnight's smooth neck. The horse whinnied and tossed his head.

"It's riddled with traps of course," Piper said. "I heard getting the door open is the easy part. It's inside that's challenging."

"Who created it?"

"No one knows," Thane said. "The Black Mage was immune to magic attacks through one of his spells. Rhegar found the All Seeing Stone. It's how he had the knowledge to kill the Black Mage when no one else could—I never thought about it before, but you know the old stories about how he went mad after he killed the Black Mage?"

"Yeah," Piper said slowly. "We know the stories. It was the Black Mage's last curse."

"What if it was the stone that drove him mad and not the Black Mage? Maybe that is why it's been guarded so well."

Everyone turned to stare at Thane. Layala gulped, twisting toward the tomb. It was a square building at least twenty feet high with a silver spire at its center. Nothing else was around it for miles save for a boulder here or there.

Fennan huffed. "So, we should turn around right now then. Good talk."

"We could ask it how to destroy the Void," Thane said. "The sole reason our people believe Layala can do it, is because they think she's the only mage born in the last four hundred years. We have no real idea how."

"And who is going to ask if we can even get it? I'm certainly not losing my mind," Aldrich said and spit off to the side.

"I will," Thane answered.

Layala was suddenly sick to her stomach. She

couldn't see Thane go mad because of her. Maybe part of the reason he wanted it was to find a way to destroy the Void, but it wasn't the only reason. He never tried to get the stone before. "We should go back."

"We're already here," Thane kicked his horse forward and trotted down the grassy slope. Fennan cursed and followed after him.

Layala, Piper and Aldrich met them at the bottom. The rotten stink of the Void drifted on the wind; Layala tried to stifle her growing nausea with slow breaths. "Ugh, it's horrible."

"We need to decide who's going in and who is standing guard," Piper said, jumping off her horse. Everyone followed her lead.

Sunshine made his way to the tomb and ran his hand over the stone. "I'll go in."

"No, Fennan and I will go in. Aldrich and Piper, you stay with Laya." Thane pressed his palm flat against the door that read: "He who enters here will die a horrible death."

"It's too dangerous for you to go, *King*." Piper folded her arms. "I'll go with Fennan."

"Why am I automatically out?" Sunshine balked.

A nervous sweat warmed under Layala's arms. "You all can read what is inscribed on the door, can't you? No one is going in there."

After his hand dropped from the door, Thane turned. "You want your answer?"

"Not if it's a death sentence for any of us. Or

madness." Layala nervously looked toward the Void. "Look, we can go back to Palenor and I'll marry you."

"But you'll never be intimate with me."

Their three companions suddenly found everything but them more interesting. Layala's cheeks burned with shame and sorrow. She didn't want to talk about this in front of their friends. Had he already told them?

Piper looked troubled as she nibbled on her lip. Her eyes almost pleaded with Layala, silently begging her for... something.

"Why are you looking at me like that?" Layala snapped.

She shook her head but turned to Thane and raised an eyebrow. Something about the exchange unnerved Layala.

"She's just scared to go inside but wants to look brave," Sunshine drawled. "Aren't you, Pipe."

"Shut up, ass."

Ignoring everyone, Thane placed his hand on the engraved circle then whispered something inaudible. The stone popped slightly ajar with a groan and dust billowed out. With her heart thundering Layala stepped forward and grabbed Thane's arm. "Please don't go in there."

"I have to."

Have to? Why did it sound like there was more to that statement than him wanting an answer? Gripping the edge of the door, Thane pulled. The stone scraped and groaned. Thane gritted his teeth; the veins in his arms bulged with his effort to pull it open. Layala rocked from one foot to the other, holding onto her dagger's handle. Anything could be inside waiting to devour them. When the opening was wide enough, Thane slipped inside the darkness without even glancing back. Fennan followed right after.

I can't let them go alone. What if they need me? The mist of the Void shifted and thickened in the distance, swirling as if someone controlled its movements. *But what if pale ones come?* She was torn; if she went inside pale ones could attack Sunshine and Piper, and if the enemy was able to close the door Thane, Fennan, and her could be trapped in the tomb. But what was inside could be much more dangerous than even a horde of pale ones. Her mate line to Thane almost thrummed, tugging her to follow. "I'm going." Before Piper could protest, she dashed into the tomb's opening.

It was pitch black inside save for the light coming in behind her from the outside. She couldn't see Thane or Fennan or anything but the faint outline of walls. The air was stale and smelled like a thousand years of dust and mold, nearly suffocatingly strong. She had the urge to cover her mouth and nose, but it wouldn't do any good. "Thane? Fennan?" she breathed. It felt too intrusive to speak more than a whisper. A torch sparked to life ahead revealing the males standing at the far end of the tomb and at the top of a stairwell. The room they currently stood in was entirely empty.

"Go back outside," Fennan ordered.

"You can't give me orders, Fen. I outrank you."

"Laya," Thane started but she marched toward them, cutting him off with a scowl.

"I'm coming." She'd done nearly everything Thane asked her to in the name of safety and this time she wouldn't let him win. She pulled her sword and dagger and waited beside them. "Are we going to stand here all day?"

Thane's worried eyes searched her face. "Stay close to me."

Fennan took a deep breath then descended the stairs first, weapons in hand. Thane nudged Layala next, and he took up the rear. Their light footsteps barely made a sound, their shallow breaths were almost inaudible, but in this endlessly silent place it felt as if they were a pack of bumbling trolls screaming. Torches lit on their own the further they descended.

"At least we can see," Fennan said over his shoulder.

On the last step of what could have been a hundred, Fennan stopped. Fire lit along the walls of the tunnel ahead, which also appeared empty. Each of Layala's senses was heightened with her anxiousness. She heard Thane's heart thumping behind her. She picked up on the smell of sweat from Fennan, and even the air tasted mustier down here. But there was also a quiet *tick tick tick*, coming from somewhere in that long tunnel. They knew there were traps, but they couldn't be seen.

Fennan went to take a step and Layala grabbed his shoulder. "Wait." She tossed the knife in her boot ahead. When it clanked on the stone ground, a massive double-edged ax swung out of the wall, slicing back and forth at a fast rhythmic pace.

Wide-eyed Fennan looked back. "That would have killed me."

"There are bound to be more," Thane said. He grabbed a torch from the wall and tossed it further than the knife; when it clattered, the floor dropped, crumbling into a crevice at least three feet across. "Alright, we get past the swinging ax, jump the pit and then it looks like the tunnel turns." He pushed by them and stood before the ax, waiting and then leaped. Layala's heart lurched when the ax swung behind him moments after. "I hate spiders."

"Spiders?" Layala whispered.

Fennan darted past the ax, leaving her alone on the other side. *You can do this, you can do this. Swing, swing, swing*, the ax gave her only a second to get by. It moved so fast it was a flash of silver. *One...* she breathed, *two,* she breathed out... *three*! She sprang forward and felt the wind of the ax *whoosh* behind her.

Peering over the edge of the crevice, her skin crawled. Thousands, if not millions, of spiders covered the walls below with draping silver webs as puffy as clouds. "Oh my—they're climbing out!" Layala exclaimed and kicked a fat brown one off her boot. She wanted to take a step back but if she did, she'd be sliced in half.

"Can you jump that far?" Thane asked, stamping a spider as big as his hand. It crunched under his boot and Layala shuddered.

Without a running start she didn't know, but she didn't have a choice. Fennan launched himself across, clearing it with at least several inches length behind him, but Fennan was almost an entire foot taller than her. Could she make it? The alternative was falling into the bottomless pit of spiders. A crawling sensation tickled her arm. She looked down to see a red spider inching up her skin. She squealed and batted it off. Then she slapped at the rest of her body, certain there were more.

"I'm going to throw you across."

"What? No," she protested even as Thane grabbed hold of her. "No, no, I can jump. I can do it. Or I could use my magic and create a bridge."

"Oh great idea, we're like five feet from the Void, and your magic calls to the pale ones," Fennan bellowed. Fennan aggressively stomped his foot several times. "She won't make it. Toss her."

"How do you kn—" she screamed as she went flying through the air, arms waving in wild circles. When she landed on the other side, she crashed into Fennan's solid form. Thane leapt right after her, landing at the edge but started teetering backward. Another scream caught in her throat as she and

Fennan snatched him by his tunic and jerked him forward.

"Whew, that was close," he said with a stupid grin.

Layala's heart crashed so hard against her chest she thought it might beat right out of her skin. "I'm going to kick your ass when we get out of here."

"I hope so."

Fennan crept around the corner and halted. Solid wall. A dead-end... but at the top carved in the stone it read: Give me drink and I will die. Feed me and I will live.

"It's a riddle." Layala touched the engraving. The rough stone under her fingers was like dried sand; bits of it crumbled. "Do we just say the answer aloud?"

"We need the answer first," Fennan said.

She dropped her hand to her side. "What needs to be fed but can't drink?" Thane looked deep in thought when she glanced over at him.

Fennan shrugged. "Insects? They hate water."

"They still drink," Layala replied and turned to check the spiders. A clump of them moved her way. She slammed her hand against the wall. "They're coming!"

Thane ran his hand around the edges. "It can't be anything living."

Layala grabbed a torch off the wall and jabbed the flames at the spiders. Some raised their spindly legs up in defense, others backed up. Then it hit her. "Fire. Fire!" She whirled around and yelled, "The answer is fire!" Nothing happened. It was the answer, wasn't it? Or had she guessed wrong?

Thane snatched the torch out of her hand and held it against a small pocket in the wall. It began to move upward, scraping and popping as it did. Thane put his arm around her shoulder and squeezed her to his side. "I love you! You're a genius." He turned and tossed the torch at the spiders then with a wave of his hand a line of fire zipped from one wall to the other, keeping the spiders at bay.

Fennan slapped her palm then fist pumped.

While they celebrated all she could think about was what came out of Thane's mouth. *He just said, I love you.* Somehow that made her heart ramp up even faster than it already beat.

When the wall lifted fully, the three of them stepped inside to a small room that held a rectangular sarcophagus at its center. The lid was a male elf carved in thick pale stone. Thane carefully touched it and waited. With bated breath Layala waited too, wondering if the ceiling would come down or if any more weapons would shoot out at them, but the room stayed utterly still. Seemingly satisfied nothing would happen, Thane started to push. Layala and Fennan joined him until the lid moved enough to peer in. A corpse of bones laid inside, with a ceramic vase resting under his hands.

"It must be in the jar." Fennan reached for it then paused. "What if something happens if we pull it out?"

"Something will definitely happen," Layala said.

"We don't really have another choice," Thane grabbed the vase, tearing it out of the dead elf's grasp. He peered inside, cursed and drove his hand in the opening. When he pulled out a piece of paper, he dropped the vase, letting it shatter. "To whoever finds this. I found the stone first."

Layala's stomach plummeted as the words sunk in. She snatched the note out of his hand and read it herself. The writing wasn't faded, the paper not worn. It wasn't very old, months at most. "So, we went through all that shit for nothing," Layala said, crumpling the note.

"We need to go!" Thane shoved her toward the wall that was now lowering. She held in a scream, running for the opening getting smaller by the moment. She dove, and slid under it on her belly. Fennan came rolling out right after but Thane—there was only a foot left. "Thane!" she shrieked. Fennan and she both grabbed the bottom, fighting to keep it open longer.

His beautiful dark head of hair showed then he skidded underneath and cleared the door inches before it was too late. Holding out her hand to him, Thane looked up and smiled. She jerked him up and then pulled him into her. Wrapping her arms around his waist, she pressed her face into his chest. "Don't ever scare me like that again."

The floor began to quake, breaking and cracking

the stone walls. Layala jerked back. "This place is going to come down!"

Fennan jumped over the flames, and landed with the sickening crunch of spiders. "Disgusting!"

In globs, the spiders scurried up the walls and into the cracks trying to escape. Holding her hand, Thane pulled Layala across the flames. The swinging ax fell as the stone above it crumbled. Without a word, Thane threw Layala across the crevice again. She hit the other side, slamming on her hands and knees. Fennan landed beside her and pulled her to her feet. The ground shook harder, pieces of stone crashed down on them. A chunk slammed into her shoulder. She cried out, clutching the injury.

"Come on! Move, Layala!" Fennan waved frantically ahead of her.

Thane swept an arm across her back, and they sprinted up the steps. As soon as they reached the top, the stairs caved in, and they ran for the open door to the outside. When they burst out into the fresh clean air, Layala coughed and fell to her knees, still clutching her shoulder. It throbbed and burned. The fabric of her sleeve was torn, leaving a scrape that oozed.

"Please tell me you got the stone," Piper said, crossing her arms.

Thane scowled at her. "Someone got to it already."

"Who?"

"They didn't sign the note if that's what you're asking. I have no idea."

Aldrich stepped around the corner of the tomb

which on the outside looked perfectly untouched. "There's movement in the Void. I can hear voices. The quaking of the ground must have given us away." He glanced back over to the swirling mist. "We should go. There will certainly be too many for us to fight alone." He jumped onto his horse with such ease it made Layala jealous. Meanwhile she struggled to get to her feet, but moved much faster when she heard the horrid shriek of a pale one.

Chapter 35

When they crested the top of the hill, a lone pale one in full black armor emerged from the mist and stood unmoving as he stared. He didn't give chase or screech or shout threats. He watched. It was more unnerving than if he charged. Layala kicked Midnight into a gallop, catching up to her companions.

"They're not chasing us," Layala said.

"Nevertheless, we'll keep up this pace until we're certain," Thane responded.

It wasn't until Doonafell came into view that they slowed to a pace they could talk without difficulty. "Who would have the ability to get the stone?" Layala asked.

Fennan shrugged. "It wasn't actually that difficult. It could be anyone."

Layala balked, holding her aching shoulder. "Not that difficult? We almost died back there."

Thane chuckled. "I've been in much closer calls."

"Well, I haven't. And neither of you even got hurt. My shoulder feels like it's going to make my arm fall off."

Turning toward her Thane pulled back on his reins. "Why didn't you tell us you were hurt?" When he stopped everyone did.

"It wasn't bad enough to keep me from riding."

Aldrich shifted in his saddle. "I gotta hand it to you, Lightbringer. You're tough for a female."

Both Layala and Piper grunted. Layala tugged the fabric of her short sleeve up to see the real damage. It was scrapped and bruised but not life threatening. "I remember kicking your ass not that long ago. Perhaps you should stop underestimating *females*."

"I still won that bout in case you've forgotten. Besides, I was afraid to hurt your pretty face, so I took it easy on you."

"Liar," Layala retorted. "I'm up for a rematch if you are."

"Perhaps when your shoulder isn't injured," Thane cut in. "I need to speak with Atarah about the stone."

That's when she noticed the dried blood down the side of Thane's face. "Thane, your head. You *did* get hurt."

He lifted his shoulder and rubbed his face on his sleeve. "It's nothing. You four get back to camp."

The urge to ask to join him bubbled up in her throat but before she could get the words out, Thane took off in the opposite direction they would be heading. "Is he really fine or is he just saying that?"

Fennan answered, "Thane heals quickly."

"He's mentioned that before but what does that mean exactly?"

"Whatever injury he had on his head will have already healed on its own. Probably within minutes if it wasn't that deep."

She had never heard of such a thing before, especially not without the aid of magical plants. "But elves don't heal that fast. Maybe faster than humans but not minutes or even hours." She gestured to her shoulder. "Obviously."

"Thane isn't your average elf, just like you aren't. But it's not because he's a mage."

"Then what?"

"You should ask him that," Aldrich said.

LAYALA WAITED outside Thane's tent until it was long past dark for him to get back. Not only did she need answers about the All Seeing Stone, which was their best lead to break the spell between them but she wanted to know what made him different. Why hadn't he told her? What could it possibly be? Did he have a rune mark for healing? If he did, that meant it would have come from the Black Mage's spell book because according to Atarah all rune magic was from the Black Mage. Maybe that was why he hadn't told her. But then again, she'd seen most of his flesh aside from his thighs and private areas and the only rune mark was the mate rune on his wrist.

She glanced at her tent where Tif and Piper were already asleep, then looked about to see if anyone was around. A few guards walked by on patrol, but mostly everyone had gone to bed for the night. Peeling aside Thane's tent entrance, she slipped inside. The light from the moon penetrated the fabric enough that she saw everything once her eyes adjusted. Was she being too bold coming in here without him? She knew what he might think when he came back, but she sat on his bed anyway. The sheepskin was soft under her fingers. She tugged her boots off and then kicked her feet up. She'd jump up when she heard him coming. But after a while the softness of the bed and the heaviness of her eyelids pulled her to sleep.

A light clinking stirred her awake. After remembering whose bed she lay in, she shot up. Thane was unlatching his weapons with his back to her. Her cheeks suddenly burned—did he know she was here? She didn't want to scare him by speaking or getting up, so she waited silently. He tugged his tunic over his head and kicked off his boots. When he pulled at the belt to his pants, she was certain he hadn't seen her. Part of her wanted to keep watching; he had a body to be admired and she was admiring. She imagined running her hands over the muscles on his back and shoulders.

He dropped his pants to the floor and stepped out of them, standing in his black braise shorts.

Say something. Say something. Then she remembered he watched her undress once upon a time. Instead of speaking, she cleared her throat.

Thane turned his head slightly but wasn't startled. "I wondered if you were going to say anything but clearly you were enjoying the show too much."

So, he knew she was there and undressed to his undergarments anyway. "Clearly."

He smiled and pulled another pair of soft sleeping pants out of his trunk and stepped into them. "Why are you in my bed, dearest? Not that you are unwelcome."

Her heart started beating faster. She suddenly thought of all the things they could do in this bed if she wasn't cursed. "I wanted to ask you something and fell asleep waiting."

"Is that all? What a shame."

She smiled and couldn't remember why she waited here in the first place. What did she want to ask again?

"How is your shoulder?"

"It's a little sore but fine."

He sauntered over without putting a shirt on. She fought to keep her eyes off all that delicious bare skin. When he sat beside her, he looked at her expectantly.

"Um, what did Atarah say?"

"Unfortunately, she has no idea who it might have been, and we're back to where we started."

"Not entirely," Layala said. "We know it exists, and there is the dragon shifter." She fidgeted with the sheepskin, pushing her fingers through its softness, trying to get her mind off how close Thane was. She could feel him through their mate bond like a caress against her skin although he wasn't touching her. Her mate rune tingled, and she stood.

Thane's fingers deftly wrapped around her wrist. His thumb stroked skin. "You know how I feel about seeking out the sorceress. She's not the answer. I have a feeling it would end badly."

"Then what?" Layala sighed. "Then we just marry to stop from turning into pale ones and fight the pull of desire forever? Unless we find the All Seeing Stone and have an answer for certain, we can never truly be together."

"And that is what you want? Do you want to be with me?"

For how much she hated him all her life she couldn't believe her answer. "Yes."

A small smile tugged at the corners of his beautiful mouth. "Then we'll find it."

Every fiber of her being desired to be with him. Something in her demanded she reach up and drag her thumb over his lips and kiss him again and slowly strip him of his clothes. She couldn't. Maker above, she couldn't even though everything about him drew her in. But Novak's death was there, haunting her. His funeral flashed in her mind. Images of his mother sobbing on her knees, hugging his headstone. While

Layala watched from a distance like a coward. She wanted so badly to apologize, to tell his mother the truth of how he died but she never could say it, and the guilt ate away at her to this very moment. They deserved to know the truth; that she poisoned him, that her *body* poisoned him. Her chin trembled and tears seeped from her eyes. "Can I stay? Can you hold me? I just want to lay next to you."

His brows raised slightly, and he nodded. "I'd love nothing more."

As they laid together clothed, bodies tangled, they talked. About their lives before, about places they wanted to see in the future, and adventures he went on as a kid with Fennan and his friend Osric. They laughed about how the boys set traps for pixies to get their dust, and tried to wrangle gnomes and force the poor creatures to make them treats. The time made Layala fall for him all the more. She forgot about the war and pale ones and curses. Her heart ached with a pleasant sort of pain, loving their conversation and his arms snuggly around her middle until she drifted off to sleep laying on his chest.

When morning came, Thane woke Layala to a platter of fruit and scrambled eggs for breakfast. She smiled as he set the tray on her lap while she was still in bed. "Thank you."

He nodded and took a sip of his juice then said, "You're welcome. My sister wishes to spend some time with you. She wants to make up for how she's treated you."

Layala picked up the fork. "She does?" Layala was skeptical at best.

He grabbed the single chair, flipped it around and straddled the back, resting his forearm across the top. "I know she hasn't been nice, but Talon has a lot to learn. She's young, and I think being here the last few weeks has opened her eyes. Will you please allow her to apologize?"

Lifting a shoulder, Layala nodded. "Sure. Maker knows I've needed to apologize for things." Thane smiled and the sight of his happiness made flutters erupt in her chest.

When she'd barely had a chance to finish her breakfast, Talon burst into the tent. "Are you ready to go, dear sister?"

Thane smirked at Layala. She set the tray aside and straightened her top. "Where are we going?"

Talon wrapped her arm around Layala's like they were two children skipping off into the forest on an adventure. "Somewhere special."

Layala glanced back at Thane as she was dragged out of the tent. He winked and said, "Have fun."

Talon walked them toward the woods. "So, I know tensions have been high between us. And even though you are a low-born elf, you are my brother's mate and destined to be queen."

It was a backhanded apology, but Layala didn't expect much else. "I apologize for not being very nice myself."

Talon tugged her toward the encroaching woods.

Everything in Layala told her to stop, that this was far enough. The closest elf was at least fifty yards away but what did she have to fear from Talon? She couldn't wield a sword, and she didn't have magic. She wasn't a threat. "Where is this special place?"

"There is a really pretty waterfall. Have you not seen it?"

She had but was it this way? "I have. Piper, Fennan, Thane and I went there a few days ago."

"Uh, my brother is falling for you so hard. I can see it all over his face." She grinned. "I thought you two might kill each other before you could ever get married." She cackled at Layala's stare. "I'm exaggerating of course."

Thane had mixed feelings for her. She knew it because she felt it through their connection. Just as she had mixed feelings when it came to him. He wanted to love her, but it was like they stood on opposite sides of a canyon with a gap wide enough that they could reach and be inches from grasping but never touch.

"I think we should stay close to camp," Layala said even as she crossed into the woods. The thick canopy of trees let down small rays of sunlight, but it was markedly darker in this part. "There could be pale ones near."

"Don't worry, Aldrich is waiting for us there. He checked the whole area. I told him to grab a bottle of wine for us." The mention of wine had memories of kissing Thane and telling him she wished she could have her way with him come to mind.

"I guess if Aldrich is here, it should be fine."

"So shouldn't we be planning a wedding? Thane did set a day and it's not far away." Layala hadn't given thought to what she would want a wedding to be like since Novak died. Before, she dreamed of a lavender gown with lace and long, draping sleeves with a crown of white flowers. He would have worn his finest tunic with a traditional black groom's cape. The entire village of Briar Hollow would have been in attendance and even a few families from neighboring towns. They'd drink the finest wine and dance and sing until midnight.

Picturing a wedding with the High King of the Elves of Palenor was much different. More extravagant than she could even imagine. There would be thousands in attendance, most strangers. But it would be glorious and beautiful.

The seven-foot or so waterfall came into view, crashing loudly into the pool below. A cool misty breeze drifted toward them bringing the smell of moss and wetness. A bottle of wine with two glasses set on a cut tree stump waited. Frogs croaked in sync with one another, and a pair of silver butterflies fluttered by them. But she didn't see Aldrich anywhere.

"I had to sneak us out here because Thane got upset with me yesterday when I drank a whole bottle of wine and," she smacked her own forehead, "and started dancing for a huge group of the Ravens. He says I should be embarrassed."

"Dancing isn't anything to be embarrassed about," Layala said, confused that Thane would reprimand her for it.

"With your top off it is. I had on my bralette of course but he jerked me away so hard it left a bruise on my arm." She huffed. "*The Ravens* weren't even upset with me. They threw flowers at my feet. Fennan was even there."

Fennan should have stopped her. "Well, you are the Princess of Palenor. You must know certain behavior is expected. You've given me the lecture, remember. Thane wants to protect you."

Talon poured them both a glass and handed the first to Layala. "Here you are taking his side again. I know I never told you but what you did to save that mother and her children, it was very brave of you, even if you have remarkable magic. I wouldn't have fought those horrible things... I was terrified and I ran." She filled her own crystal goblet and raised it. "So, here's to letting go of old grudges and building new friendships."

Layala arched an eyebrow but clinked her glass against Talon's and took a long drink. It was more bitter than the others she'd had lately. "Is this from here?"

"Yes, not as good as the drink from the woodland elves I'm afraid."

"Speaking of woodland elves," Layala cleared her

throat nervously. "Would you ever consider marriage to—" a shadow moved among the yew trees on the other side of the river.

"Marriage to?" she prodded.

Movement directly to her left drew her attention and her magic tingled. "I think there's someone—" a quiet whistle cut through the air. She jerked Talon aside and an arrow sliced into Layala's ribs inches under her left breast. She gasped as the pain registered seconds later, and wrapped her hand at the arrow's shaft protruding from her. Her magic waffled, wanting to break free but Layala couldn't see a target. Talon screamed, dropping her glass; it shattered with a spray of red wine.

She came to Palenor to kill the Athayel family and instead, she took an arrow for one. She choked in pain, staggering on her feet. On instinct she pulled Talon aside instead of reaching for her magic. She kept it hidden for so long it didn't come naturally. Something she was regretting. "Run," Layala said, in a hoarse voice. She choked trying to drag in a breath.

When the world began spinning, Layala pawed at a nearby tree for balance but missed and fell, rolling onto her side. Her heart crashed until it ached. Sweat beaded on her brow. Gasping with pain, each breath she pulled in was like fire filling her lungs.

Crawling over to her, Talon tentatively touched the arrow. "What do I do?" Looking around frantically she started to cry.

"I said, run!" Layala said angrily. "This arrow was for *you*."

Her eyes widened and she shoved up, panting. "I'll get help." Then she was gone and Layala was alone with the sounds of the waterfall to lull her into a daze. Truthfully, she didn't know if the arrow was for Talon or not. It could have hit either of them but if she hadn't pulled Talon to the side, it would have nailed her right in the back. She didn't see the face of who fired the arrow, only a hooded figure among the trees, but she didn't think it was a pale one.

Footfalls drew her out of her stupor. She struggled to open her eyes, wishing she had the strength to reach for her dagger to defend herself. Was this it? Her last moments? Maker, Thane was in danger too.

A soft voice called to her. Was it her mother? Did she wait on the other side?

"I'm here." A light feminine voice said, and small hands pried open Layala's mouth and shoved something soft and velvety in. "Come on, chew it. It will help stop the bleeding. You have to live. I can't stay here with the jumbos by myself. I can't. This world is too scary without you."

"Get Thane,"' she murmured and closed her mouth but couldn't work up the strength to chew and she succumbed to the darkness.

A sharp sting hit Thane through the bond. He whirled around to see Talon bursting through the tree line. "Thane!" she yelled. Blood splattered across her light blue dress, and cheek.

"What happened?!" He ran to her as did the group of soldiers he'd been talking to. She fell into his arms out of breath, sobbing and speaking inaudibly. His eyes zipped from side to side scanning the forest. Layala had been with her. "Where is she?"

"I left her by the waterfall," she choked, "I'm sorry. I didn't know what to do."

He didn't have time to ask more questions of Talon. He grabbed two soldiers by the front of their uniforms. "Come with me." They raced past trees, weaving around them until they were but a blur. When the crashing of the waterfall pressed upon his ears he went even faster until there she was, curled up on her side, unmoving. The gnome knelt beside her, crying into her hands. Thane's heart seized when he saw the tip of an arrow protruding from her back. He dropped to her side, gathering her into his arms. "Layala?" His chest ached at the bluish color of her lips, the marked paleness to her usually warm skin, but she still drew a shallow breath.

"Secure the area!" The little gnome held onto Layala as he lifted her off the ground. "Find who did this and bring them to me. *Alive.*"

Orion nodded grimly. "We'll find them, sire."

Thane tore through the woods with one destination in mind. He couldn't risk removing the arrow without a skilled healer present or she could bleed out in under a minute given the location of it. "You have to hold on," he whispered. "I know you're strong. You're one of the stubbornest elves I've ever met."

As fast as his legs could carry them, he sprinted. Somehow it was as if they shifted through time and space, everything blurred, and they arrived at the Mage's Tower. He could manipulate matter with his magic but what was this? He crashed through the door unable to take the time to consider what happened. "Atarah!" he roared.

She turned from her position at the table and jumped up. "Dear maker, get her to a room. This way, hurry!"

Thane dabbed a damp cloth on her forehead as he watched her life slipping away. He didn't even care for himself. He didn't care that he was growing weak. Atarah helped him remove the arrow, and the stream of blood that it released made him grateful he didn't try to remove it himself. Atarah gave her a tonic and helped him bind the wound dangerously close to her heart, but things hadn't changed much in the last hour.

"I don't know if the healing herbs are enough."

Atarah rested a hand on Thane's shoulder. "And if she lasts the night there may be permanent damage."

Tifapine sat on the edge of the small bedside table looking on with a tear-stained face. This was the first time Thane had ever seen her out in the open. She held onto Layala the entire sprint there. Thanks to her quick action with the healing leaf, it bought them more time.

"Is there anything more we can do?" Thane asked, unable to keep the unsteady emotion from his voice.

"I've done all I can but," Atarah paused. "I'll be back shortly." She turned and left the room, closing the door quietly.

Thane climbed into the bed beside Layala and rested his head against her shoulder. Her skin was too cold; he needed to warm her up. Pressing his hand to her chest a warmness emanated from his palm. If he knew more about how the body healed, he thought his magic might be able to close and heal a wound, but he'd never tried and didn't dare risk harming her further. Slowly, he stroked her hair. "Please wake up," he whispered and pressed his lips to her cheek. "You can go back to your aunt and to Briar Hollow after our wedding. You can find plants and drink ale to your heart's content if that's what you want." He smiled at the memory of their first meeting. "But if you want to stay, I promise I'll love you so fiercely that they will write sonnets about our love. I will tear this world apart for you, I will fight until I have nothing left to give and destroy anyone who hurts you, and I will guard your heart most of all. Just, please, wake up."

"I don't think she can hear you," Tifapine said, wiping a tear from her ruddy cheek.

Thane sighed. "I know."

"What if your sister set this up?" Tifapine stared at him unblinking. "I've thought about it for a while. She brought Layala out there, alone."

Thane closed his eyes. The thought made him sick. "I don't think she would do that. That would mean she was trying to kill me too."

"Maybe she didn't know." Tifapine nibbled on her lower lip and looked away muttering, "It was just a thought anyway."

The door slowly creaked. Thane turned and sat up when Atarah carried an open leather-bound book in her hands. It was thick, at least five hundred pages. Atarah's heavy expression made Thane nervous.

"I fear the only thing that will save her now is a healing rune. She lost too much blood and the paleness of her skin worries me. Her breaths are too shallow. Her heart has slowed."

Thane stood and scanned the page. "This is one of the Black Mage's books."

Tentatively nodding, she placed the tome on the table. "It is."

Chapter 36

The loud pop from a fire stirred Layala from a heavy sleep. She fought to peel her eyes open. The dim evening light created long shadows. *Where am I?* The carved stonework above marked with runes was both unfamiliar and jarring now that she knew where all runes came from. As she moved a sharp pain sliced her side and she hissed. With a quick look down she touched the bandages that wrapped around her breasts and torso. She briefly wondered who bandaged her. Pushing her hair off her forehead, she thought back to what had happened. Her memory was a little foggy, but she knew she was impaled with an arrow.

Pushing through the pain she sat up. The single bed she rested in had silk lavender coverlets. A white armoire with carvings of roses was against the wall. The round fireplace had remarkable blush-colored stonework. Directly at the bedside there sat a hip height table with a bouquet of spring flowers and dried herbs in bunches, more bandages, uncovered tins with brown salve, a bowl of rust-colored water, and a pair of tiny boots with holes in the toes. "Tifapine?" Layala called, carefully swinging her legs over the sheets, and setting her feet on the soft rug.

"Laya." Thane's deep voice washed over her. He rose from a corner chair she hadn't seen and crouched before her.

Her head pounded and her mouth was as dry as a summer desert, but she placed her palm against the side of his face. "You're here. I didn't know if I'd ever see you again."

"How do you feel?"

"My head hurts but," she touched where she'd been shot through, "this doesn't much. What did you do?"

The dark-stained wooden door creaked open and Tif peeked her head in. "You're awake!" She scurried across the matte floor, climbed up the corner bedpost and crashed into Layala's side, wrapping her arms as far around as they would reach.

Thankfully it was her uninjured side, but the jarring motion still stung. "Be careful, Tifapine," Thane chided.

Tif pulled away, and gently patted her arm. "Sorry, I was just so excited. They weren't sure if you'd wake up." She took in a huge breath. "But I knew you'd wake up. She's a fighter, I said. I hope you aren't mad, but I followed you into the woods. Something didn't feel right. And I keep some of those healing leaves in my belt like you do."

"Of course, I'm not mad." Layala pushed to her feet. Her head swirled and she teetered. Thane held her arms to steady her. "Can one of you get me a drink of water? My throat hurts."

Guiding her to sit back on the bed, Thane then kissed her forehead. "I'll get a glass for you. Sit and rest for a moment."

"Thank you."

Thane slipped out the door and Tif started her report, "I helped bandage you. Thane turned away when the mage lady and I had to cut your top off. He's such a great male. So sweet and mindful of propriety since you aren't wedded yet."

"That's great, Tif," Layala had wondered if he'd seen her breasts or not.

"Piper, Fennan, and Aldrich are all giving their opinions on what needs to be done. Piper thinks Talon—"

"Talon is here? Is she alright?" Normally she wouldn't be so concerned about the princess, but she still wasn't convinced that the arrow wasn't for her. "And where are we?"

"The Mage's Tower. Atarah had King Thane mark you with a healing rune about half an hour ago because the plants weren't working fast enough. They thought you'd die otherwise."

Layala gripped the blanket so hard her hand

ached. "And what will that cost me? It will come with a price." She tapped her wrist with the mate rune.

Tif twisted her hands together. "Um, you should ask Thane."

Anger fueled her with enough energy to stand and she marched toward the armoire. She was grateful to be alive but the last thing she wanted was to be further indebted to the Black Mage's power. Pulling it open, she found a thick blue robe with a collar of gray fur, among other attire, but it would be the easiest to dress in. Sliding it from the hanger, she carefully put it on and headed for the door. The wound at her side hurt even less than it did only minutes ago. The healing rune worked quickly.

"You need to be resting," Tif said, following right behind.

"I'm fine."

The stone was cold on her bare feet as she quietly whisked down the hall. She passed paintings of elves both male and female, stands with blue flowering plants, and statues of chilling gargoyles built into corners. Open windows let in a cool breeze and torches were placed every ten feet or so all alight to chase away the night. When she reached the staircase voices traveled up and she paused.

Tif bumped into the back of her leg. "Sorry," she whispered.

"This is treason, Thane," Piper spat. "She should be imprisoned or you'll be showing everyone they can make an attempt on you and your mate's life without consequence."

"I didn't lure her out there to have her killed!" Talon sobbed. "I swear it. Aldrich said he checked the area, and it was safe. All I wanted was some wine, that you forbade me to drink."

"Lies," Piper snarled.

"If you weren't such a lush this wouldn't have happened. You shoulder some responsibility for this, even if you didn't set this up, Talon." Thane's resonant voice cut in. "Have they found the shooter yet?"

"They're scouring the woods as we speak," Fennan said. "But no sign of him yet."

"I'm sorry. I wish I could take it back," Talon sobbed. "Layala saved me. She pulled me aside and took the arrow."

Piper let out a humorless laugh. "So, you say. Why would she take an arrow for *you?*"

Since Layala was the only one who could put an end to the argument, she tucked the robe tighter around her and swept down the stairs. When she stepped into the great room the group fell silent. Each one of the elves gaped as if she was a ghost. Even Talon stopped her blubbering. In three strides, Thane was at her side, grasping her arm. "You shouldn't be out of bed."

"I'm alright now. But what Talon said is true. The arrow would have hit her in the back. I don't know who the target was but whoever did it, didn't stick around to finish me off when I was alone in the woods."

Talon nodded fiercely. "See."

"They also didn't chase you down either. Maybe the assailant was a bad shot," Piper argued.

Why was Piper so intent on making Talon the bad one here? Layala would expect this sort of fierceness from Thane but not her, even if they had become friends.

"We'll discuss this later." Thane tugged on Layala's arm and assisted her up the stairs although she felt almost no pain anymore. When they got to the top, she was a little winded but her strength was returning. Tifapine carried a glass of water ahead of them and spilled half its contents on the way up the stairs, but it would be enough to quench her parched body for the moment. After she sat on the bed and downed the glass, she watched Thane pace. "Tif said you used a healing rune." She tried to keep the disdain from her tone. "What is the price associated with it for me?"

He didn't stop pacing. "Nothing for you so don't worry about it."

Layala stared. "Then you?"

"I said don't worry about it."

"I'm going to worry about it because if it affects you, it affects me." And she meant that more than physically, more than their lives being tied. It would hurt her to watch him suffer in any way.

"I had to use my blood to mark the rune on your

flesh. The price was my pain, and it was a small one to pay. I'm used to pain." He held up his left hand where a fresh bandage was wrapped.

"Oh..." she paused thinking it seemed a little too simple. Didn't Atarah say the price of the Black Mage's rune spells was the soul? She supposed that meant only if their end of the bargain wasn't paid. But the spells were meant to be tricky, like their wedding and mate ceremony had to be under the full moon before twenty-five years. "Thank you."

"You're welcome." He stopped his pacing and really looked at her as if he could see into her soul. "Are you alright?"

Absently she touched where the wound was. She felt no pain at all. "I think I'm completely healed now."

"I know you're fine physically. I made sure of that." He stepped closer clenching his bandaged hand into a fist. "But you... you almost died. Do you know that?"

Maybe the shock of it hadn't hit her or the whole ordeal ended so fast it didn't seem real, but she wasn't afraid or traumatized, at least more than she already was. It wasn't as if this was her first brush with danger. She was more concerned with finding who made the attempt than worrying about what *almost* happened. "It's strange to think I almost died when I feel fine. You don't need to worry over me."

He clenched his jaw. "You can tell me if you're scared."

"I'm fine."

"So, you keep saying." He paused. "We need to go back to the valley. We've done enough for Doonafell and," his eyes trailed over her, "we have other pressing matters. We'll leave tomorrow if you can ride."

"I can."

"Pressing matters?" Tifapine chimed in. Layala jumped, forgetting the gnome was in the room. "Like what?" They both stared at her. "Oh, I should leave. I think I know what you're talking about." She wiggled her eyebrows and scampered to the door not without winking at Layala before she left.

The quiet crackling of the fire was the only sound in the suddenly intense silence. He raked his fingers through his dark hair. "I need to know before we leave. Is it enough?" He gulped. "I need to know now because we are running out of time."

"Is what enough?"

"Am I and your people enough to stay? After everything... do you *want* to stay, Laya? Not because you must but because you want to. You were safe in Briar Hollow. All I've done is put your life at risk. I will help you find a way to set you free, if that's what you want."

She didn't hesitate to say, didn't even have to think before she said, "You are more than enough. I told you before I will stay. What do you want?" She didn't realize she was moving toward him until she was a breath away from touching him. She couldn't imagine going back to Briar Hollow now. She knew too much. The elves needed her in this war—Thane needed her.

And if she was being honest, her feelings for him couldn't be denied any longer.

He chuckled as if what she asked was a foolish question, then that beautiful face grew deadly serious. "You. I want you."

The emotions building between them soared and she would burst if she didn't kiss him. If she didn't hold him and touch him.

Grabbing him by the front of his shirt, she dragged his mouth to hers. He reacted by cupping the back of her thighs and lifting her up. Then he pulled back. "Sorry, you're hurt. We should—"

She grabbed his face, "I already said, I'm fine."

He carried her to the bed and set her gently down. She laid back and smiled as he moved over her, kissing her harder on the mouth. His lips trailed along her jaw then down her throat. She moaned and clutched at his shirt pulling him against her. Their kisses grew in passion and need. His hand slid over her breast. She arched and pulled him flat against her, loving his weight against her body. His hands slid along her thighs, and she stilled. Groaning in frustration she pressed her hands against his chest. This was dangerous territory. "You know we can't."

Poised above her, his muscles taut, he said, "I know. I've waited for you this long. I can wait longer... But there is something I need to tell you."

He still hoped that they could be together as mates should be. That they'd find the stone and it would tell them they could be one, but she didn't share his beliefs. Novak died and so would Thane—so would she. She tilted her head, staring into his otherworldly green eyes. "When you say you've waited for me, do you mean..."

He grew a sheepish smile. "I've never," he licked his lips, "I've never made love before. I've waited for you. It didn't seem right to share that experience with someone who wasn't my mate."

She smiled and her heart ached at once. It was sweet and romantic that he waited, but he waited for an experience he could never have with her. "Is that what you needed to tell me?"

There was a knock on the door, and Thane let out a groan. "They have the worst timing."

"Sire, we have a lead on the shooter." It was Fennan on the other side.

Grateful for the distraction she pushed herself into a sitting position. "We should go—"

He cut her off with a kiss. "I'll go. You wait here."

She smiled until he walked out the door and closed it gently behind him. After, she threw herself back on the pillows and groaned.

The door creaked open, and she sat up both nervous and excited. Her smile faded when Tifapine came in. "Are you feeling better? Thane dug the knife into his hand for so long." She shuddered. "I can't imagine how much it hurt."

Layala set her feet on the ground and folded her arms. "What are you talking about?"

"Well, to heal you, the spell required his pain like

he said. It wasn't from simply a small cut for the blood. He had to keep causing himself pain to heal you. It seemed like the more pain he was in the faster you healed. The Black Mage was truly sadistic."

Layala rubbed her temples feeling slightly ill. He tortured himself to save her and then acted like it was nothing. "Why do I have to be cursed?"

"Cursed?"

Breaking down to her knees, Layala held back tears as she confessed everything about what happened with Novak to Tif, leaving out the more intimate details but the gnome got it, and she looked more worried with each word. When Layala had finished Tifapine rocked back and forth from heel to toe. "Well, that complicates things."

"Tell me about it."

"Remember when I said I needed to tell you that thing? You aren't the only one with a secret."

Layala's brow furrowed. "Secret?"

Tif cleared her throat. "Um, I heard Piper talking with Fennan about you and Thane."

"What about?"

"It's about finishing the mate spell. See I only listened because Piper specifically said, 'Layala needs to know the truth.' The full moon story is a lie." Tif glanced toward the door nervously. Layala's stomach dropped. A lie? Why would he lie? Was he lying about the deadline? About becoming pale ones?

"She said that to finish the spell you must be wed

and," Tif gulped, "and consummate the marriage in love. I presume that means…"

NO. Her throat constricted, and bile rose up. "I'm going to be sick," Layala breathed. Maker, why? Why was she cursed? Why hadn't he told her their marriage had to be consummated when she told him the truth?! She struggled to drag in air when she rolled onto her side and curled up. Novak's pale body under her filled her mind, his lifeless brown eyes in an endless stare but no… the face was Thane's. If she didn't end this bond before the deadline, they'd turn or die.

Chapter 37

When Layala picked herself up off the floor, she tugged at the bandages around her torso until they peeled off. The wound was gone, healed completely as if it was never there. She changed into clean clothes from the armoire, all the while trying to stop herself from having a panic attack. *Breathe, just breathe.* She took in deep breaths, pacing the floor.

She wanted to scream at Thane for lying. Damn him! She could have had so much more time to find a way out of this if she hadn't gotten distracted. The war, the pale ones, none of it mattered now. Her love would leave them dead and Palenor without its High King.

Layala started desperately grabbing her belongings, searching for her boots. "We're leaving. Tonight. I must find the dragon sorceress. It's our last hope."

Tif handed her her dagger. "By ourselves? I mean, she's a dra-gon."

"Yes," Layala tossed the bag down. "You know what, no. He's not going to get off that easy."

Storming down the hall, Layala seethed, her magic tingled with her rage. When she burst into the main room at the bottom of the stairs, Thane was alone with Fennan and his back was to her. Everyone had cleared out, thank the Maker. When Fennan saw her approaching, his smile dropped, and he took a step back. Thane turned and Layala smacked him in the chest, hitting him again and again. "How could you lie to me!" She shoved him so hard he stumbled back into the table, knocking over the half-full glasses of wine.

His shocked expression quickly turned bitter when she went to shove him again. This time he grabbed her forearms and held her back. "What is wrong with you? Five minutes ago, you were kissing me in your bed and now you're attacking me."

"Was it all just a ruse? Was any of it real?"

Slowly, he shook his head. "I have no idea what you're talking about."

"Does *consummated in love* ring any bells? How could you lie? After I told you how Novak died!"

He released her and held up his palms to her. "I lied because I knew it would only push you further away from me. That you would have hated me all the more. But I planned to tell you the truth."

"When?"

"Tonight." He said it with such conviction she believed it. "And what ruse would there be, Layala?"

"I don't know," she snapped. "You playing nice to get me to marry you instead of breaking our bond."

"I tried to find the All Seeing Stone to get answers. I know you think you're cursed but you won't kill me. I can withstand more than you think. I've been stabbed, *poisoned*, and broken bones many times and I'm still here."

"You don't know what you're talking about!" When he reached for her, she stepped back. Angry tears streamed down Layala's face as she shoved her finger into his chest. "I found the man I loved a corpse minutes after we made love the first time. It's not some story I made up in my head. He was killed by my magic. Even you can't withstand that."

Both Thane and Fennan stared at her in tense silence. "I never said you made it up."

"Our bond is a death sentence for the both of us. I'm going to the mountains to find the sorceress."

She whirled around to march for the exit. There was no time to be wasted. She mentally counted down the weeks she'd been with Thane. The time passed so quickly—she had *five* days to find this sorceress in the middle of a vast mountain hundreds of miles from where she currently was.

A glass shattered as Thane shoved away from the table and darted in front of her. "Wait. Let's talk about this."

"Do I need to spell it out for you? We consummate this bond, and we will both die. I said I'd never love a man again, and I won't."

Thane pursed his lips. "I am not *him*." He stroked the side of her face. She didn't pull away as he wiped a tear from her cheek with his thumb. "I am not a *man*; I'm an elven male. He was human, and I hate to say it, but they die easily. He could have been sick or—"

Grabbing his wrist, she gently pushed his hand away. "I'm going and this time you're not going to stop me. You *lied* about the one thing that would break us."

He reached for her with pleading eyes. "Laya, please. I *love* you. I know you promised you wouldn't love again, and I'm far from perfect and you deserve better than me but if you could give me a piece of your heart, I promise I will never break it."

Tears streamed down her face. She choked on a sob and furiously wiped her tears. She could give him her heart and that's why saying goodbye was impossible.

"We'll find a way—The katagas serum suppresses magic. We could—"

"It's too late." Even if everything in her wanted to stay, she must say something, anything to stop him from following her. He'd done enough. Sacrificed enough on her account. She needed to do this on her own, and she couldn't stay here and risk killing him. "I don't love you." Those words hung in the air, a shock wave that clearly struck him. "So, either way we'd still be pale ones."

His wounded stare broke something in her. She backed away, heart cracking wide open as his chin trembled. She turned and a sob caught in her throat, and with her hand on the door, he said, "I love you,

Laya and I will for eternity, no matter if I see you again in this life or the next."

He didn't try to stop her when she left.

Layala quietly snuck through the camp, crying again, with her bag slung across her back and Tif hanging on.

"Are you sure this is a good idea? Us two going alone?" Tif asked.

Tears still burned her eyes. "He lied to my face, even after he knew," Layala snapped, angrily swiping at her cheeks. "He lied to me and if he'd told me the truth, we could have done this together but no, he wanted to sell me some fantasy about being married on a full moon." She gritted her teeth. "I knew something wasn't right when Mage Vesstan was so worried. He kept saying it might be too late because I hated Thane. The marriage had to be 'consummated in love'. I feel so—betrayed."

Tif swatted at a bug on her dress. "I still think we shouldn't go alone. Someone tried to kill you and the pale ones are after you."

"We'll attract a lot less attention on our own. They'll never suspect me to leave Thane or the Ravens," Layala said over her shoulder. "This is the only way to save him now."

"So, you do love him. You *lied* to him when we left the Mage's Tower."

Why did the gnome have to call her out like that? "I didn't say that."

"You're willing to risk a lot to make sure *he* doesn't die. You didn't even mention yourself."

"Enough, Tifapine, or I'll leave you here, too." Layala ducked around the side of a tent when voices drifted closer. She didn't want anyone questioning her or reporting on her leaving. Once they passed, she darted out and ran through the shadows until she found Midnight. She patted his shoulder. "I'm going to need you to go fast, boy. You can do that for me, can't you?"

He nickered as if to answer. The saddle rested against the trunk of a tree. With a quick look around, she tossed it on his back and squatted to buckle the belt. "Keep an eye out. Let me know if anyone is coming."

"Got it," Tif said, patting the top of her head.

When she tugged on the saddle horn to test and found it secure, she used the tree for a step up and mounted Midnight. She glanced back toward the glowing light from the Mage's Tower to where she knew Thane was. Her chest ached and her throat tightened. "Goodbye," she whispered and rode off into the night.

Chapter 38

Thane sat with Fennan next to the fireplace at the Mage's Tower. The heat of the flames seeped into him as he stared into the orange glow. He had been so light. So happy when he left that bedroom. When she kissed him and he thought it meant she'd stay, she chose him. He didn't remember ever feeling that way in his life, like he could float up into the sky. Even with everything, all the mess of the war and rebuilding this city, she was all he could think about. The longing to be near her was like the pull of a long night wishing for sunrise.

It hit him hard when she confessed what happened to the man she loved, but the air sucked from his lungs when she said, *"I don't love you."* She wasn't even willing to try to find another way. He held a small bit of hope that maybe, just maybe, in the time they spent together that she could grow to love him even if it was in the smallest amount.

"Thane..." Fennan's voice broke in sorrow, shattering the long silence. "We have to go after her. I'm not letting you turn."

"She doesn't want me," he muttered, dejected. "Even if her magic wouldn't kill me, the marriage and the bond must be consummated in love. I can't force her to love me."

Fennan grabbed him by the front of the tunic and jerked him closer. "Stop it! For weeks I've watched you two gaze longingly, tease, and laugh together. I've seen her stare at your tent at night after you walk in. She does love you, Thane. That's why she left. You will go after her. At least help her find this sorceress. At least try!"

"No," he barked, shoving his hands away. "It is over. I have accepted that this would likely be my fate. I will not turn into a pale one. I will end my life." Anger and frustration and sorrow simmered on the verge of boiling.

Fennan's eyes widened. "You can't give up so easily."

"Easily?" Thane ground his teeth. "I've been fighting for her all my life. I am done now. I have to let her go. This was always going to be my fate. She was always meant to kill me. I just prolonged the inevitable." He pushed up from the chair, picked it up and threw it. The pieces of it splintered and crashed loudly onto the stone floor. The fury slowly turned toward sadness and resignation.

"What about fighting for you? For all of us?" He

didn't respond so Fennan went on, "Then I'll go after her for you. I will help her break this bond."

"You can't."

Fennan slammed his fist on the tabletop. "I'm not going to lose my best friend and king. It is my duty to protect you when you can't protect yourself." Fennan turned on his heel and ran for the tower's exit.

The tower door slammed behind Fennan, and crushing reality dropped Thane to his knees. He would suffer the world for her, and she wouldn't even give him a chance to love her. She couldn't even give him a drop of herself when he'd sacrifice every last bit for her. He would rather die loving her than die alone with a broken heart by his own hand. He couldn't stop the tears from sliding down his face as he pictured her walking out that door over and over. Hearing her say, "I don't love you", again and again.

After a while a numbness overtook him. He had so much hope. He was so sure that they were meant to be... but this was the end. When she left, she didn't just take their lives; she took the last two mages with enough magic to have any chance at defeating the enemy with her.

For well into the night Layala rode hard, feeding Midnight endurance leaves to keep up their pace. She hoped if she followed the road and the stars, she wouldn't get lost. Castle Dredwich was due north as was the portal that she needed to get to in the next couple days. The steady ache in her chest wouldn't shake. She didn't know if it was her pain or Thane's seeping into her. It hurt like losing someone to death, but worse, because this was a willing choice. She chose to walk away. Death didn't force them apart. If only she could make him see—*feel* how much she cared and she was doing this for him.

When Midnight started to slow the next morning despite the magic flora, she looked for water. Sweat dampened around his saddle and his breaths were loud and heavy. He needed a break, or he wouldn't make it to the mountains, and neither would she. She patted his neck, "Good boy. You're such a good boy. We're going to find some water." The looming gray mountain to the right and the city below on the left sparked her memory. She knew this place, it was where she and Thane sparred and the pale ones had dragged her into the crevice. That meant there was a stream nearby. She slid to the ground and tugged Midnight behind her, bringing them closer to the mountainside.

The temperature cooled as the pine trees grew thicker providing shade from the morning sunshine. The sound of rushing water led her to the creek and Midnight stepped halfway in as he drank deeply. She scooped water into her canteen, ever watchful. She couldn't afford to be caught off guard again. Tifapine stirred from her slumber and stretched, standing on the back of Midnight. "It's morning already? That went by fast."

"That tends to happen when you sleep."

"And no pale ones or assassins that I missed, I assume."

A flock of birds took flight from the branches above making Layala's skin crawl. "None so far."

Looking up, Tif visibly shuddered. "Alright, that was creepy. The timing, I mean, uh I hate birds." She pointed excitedly behind Layala. "Look, berries! Get me down."

When Layala grabbed her under the arms and set her on the ground, Tif ran to the bush, plucking plump red berries and shoving way too many in her mouth at once. "Stho gooood," she mumbled.

They stayed there to rest for an hour before she set off again at a slower pace this time. Given that Midnight grazed most of the break she didn't want him sick. She kept her bow on her lap for quick access. Under no circumstances could she use her magic. Doing so would tell the pale ones she was alone, away from Thane and the Ravens. Vulnerable and ripe for the taking.

Another day and night passed without Layala sleeping. Her eyes were heavy, her body growing weak. She'd stopped for hours to let Midnight sleep during the night, but she was buzzing with anxiety, hyper-alert. Every sound was louder. Every break of a branch, creak of a tree, movement of an animal had her tense. She didn't trust Tif to stay awake to keep watch. She brewed herself some tea to keep her awake but eventually it would stop working.

When she passed the Valley of the Sun, excitement kept her going. The bright golden light shone off the roofs of the homes, like a beacon of hope. She was close to the portal now, only a couple hours away. When she came upon the dead tree split in half that Thane and she raced to the day he brought her here, she turned and entered the dark, twisting woods. This was where she worried about getting lost. Nothing here was familiar and the portal was somewhere deep within. After riding for an hour, she stopped, looking for any indication that they passed through here previously. There was no trail, no broken branches or disturbed grass. Weeks had passed and all signs had grown over. "Shit," she mumbled dismounting. The forest groaned and creaked. Creatures with big eyes watched from the shadows. The wind here wisped around her, seeming to carry light voices. Was she hallucinating or were they real? She rubbed her stinging, dry eyes trying to clear the blurriness.

Layala grabbed hold of her mother's willow necklace, slumped against the trunk of a tree and waited. "I'm just going to rest for a minute."

Sliding down Midnight's reins, Tif landed and then patted Layala's knee. "You need to rest. You have some serious bags under your eyes."

"Thanks," Layala murmured.

"I know we are in a hurry but if you're half dead you can't get to the dragon shifter and you certainly won't have the strength to fight her or any other enemies if you have to. I will keep watch. Sleep."

She fought to stay awake but in the end her body's need for rest won.

⟡

"Psst, wake up," Tif hissed, shaking Layala's shoulder.

Her eyes shot open, and she sat upright jerking her dagger loose from its sheath. "What? What is it?"

"The sun is setting, and this forest is scary."

Layala blinked rapidly looking up at the sky. It was indeed stained orange and pink. "That means I've been sleeping for like seven hours. I don't have that kind of time to waste."

"I didn't have the heart to wake you while there was no danger," Tif said with a wide smile. "But I think there might be when it gets dark. I've heard stories about this forest. Mama said that wicked things live here. Giants with one eye and serpents and scorpions as big as you."

Layala's pulse raced as panic seeped into her gut. "Giants? Scorpions as big as...?! It will be dark in minutes. I have no idea how to get to the portal. You should have woken me sooner!"

Midnight neighed loudly and took several steps closer.

"You mean we're lost?" Tif tugged at her dress

nervously.

"I should have never fallen asleep," Layala berated herself, peering around the gnarled and twisting tree she rested under. She slammed her fist against the trunk and then hissed when the bark scraped her flesh. "Damn it, I don't know where to go. Does your mother know these woods? Could she take us?"

"No, and I don't know how to get back even if she did," Tif whined and scurried under Midnight.

"I think I could follow our trail out," Layala said mostly to herself, slipping the reins over Midnight's head. "And then I could find someone to lead us to the portal." The ground rumbled once, then again and again like—giant footfalls. "Don't move," Layala whispered, catching movement ahead.

"What is it?" Tif whimpered.

"Shh." She held her trembling finger to her lips. Midnight shifted, pinning his ears back. Dipping under Midnight's neck Layala saw the creature and it was the last one Tif listed. A massive tail with a stinger loomed above the reddish-black body with pincers that could easily take off Layala's head with one snap. And it was much much bigger than Layala. Its tail reached the tops of the trees.

Layala sighed with relief when it appeared to be moving away.

"Maybe if we don't move it won't see us," Tif whispered.

The creature stopped and its eight legs turned in time. Its huge black eyes glistened in the dying light.

When it moved toward them it didn't make stomping noises, which meant there was something heavier and possibly bigger nearby. Scooping Tifapine up, she tossed her on Midnight's back and struggled to grab hold of a low enough branch to be able to reach the saddle. She jumped, grabbed hold of the saddle horn and pulled. Midnight spooked and reared up, tossing her back down.

The giant scorpion charged, taking down full trees in its wake. "Go!" Layala cried, slapping Midnight's rear. He took off with Tif screaming.

Layala knocked an arrow back and launched it. It hit the scorpion in the shoulder and bounced off. *Shit shit shit.* She reloaded and fired a second time. It whistled and impaled one of the scorpion's many eyes. It let out a shriek but kept coming, cutting its pincer through the air right for her. She dove under it and stuck her dagger on the top of its neck, but it was like hitting solid stone and she was thrown back. Its stinger slammed into the ground spraying dirt into her eyes. Backpedaling, Layala tumbled and fell. The stinger came down again. She rolled with a scream. It barely missed.

Shoving to her feet, she pulled her sword and ran, arms pumping as her legs carried her as fast as they could manage. The crashing trees and roar of the monster gained on her. *Magic! Use your magic!* Her magic screamed in her to be let loose, but it could make things worse, bring more enemies. What if it wasn't only pale ones that it drew but all manner of evil things? One of the pincers crashed into her, sweeping her through the air until she slammed into the trunk of a tree and hit the ground. *Get up! Get up!* Her arms shook as she pushed her aching body. She looked up in time to see the stinger careening down. A scream tore from her throat, and she hacked her sword, cutting deep into the stinger. The creature wailed and jerked its tail. Layala tried to wrench it free but was dragged through the air and forced to let go. Before she could get up one of the pincers encircled around her torso. It squeezed so hard she thought her ribs would crack and concave at any moment. Then she let her magic tear free. Black vines tore from the ground wrapping around the pincer forcing it to drop her. She landed on her feet in a crouch, calling forth more and more vines.

The giant scorpion chopped and hacked at the magical stalks even as they closed around it. "Holy troll piss, it's going to break free," she murmured to herself as she turned to run. She threw up more magic behind her, more barriers to block the beast's path. Ahead, two figures moved in the shadow and made an abrupt turn left. Her pounding heart stilted: pale ones. They had to be. What if they'd been following her the entire time from Doonafell? Where was Tif? Where was Midnight? She frantically looked among the knotted ever-hulking trees. The scorpion screeched in the close distance. *Where are they? Where are they?* She had to escape this forest. Darting into a hollow in a trunk she hid in the dark, praying to the Maker she wouldn't be seen.

Please don't find me, please please please. She gripped her dagger and knife tightly, having lost her sword and bow somewhere.

Those loud pounding footfalls she heard earlier drew closer. Layala pressed further back into her hiding spot. A huge pair of hairy legs and feet stomped by. She held her every breath. It stopped outside the hole and then one huge eye peered in at her.

Chapter 39

She stood frozen, staring back at the cyclops. It grumbled something she didn't understand and then its massive face disappeared. Seconds later its fingers poked inside. This forest was a nightmare, a terrifying nightmare. Layala drove her dagger into its flesh. It howled and jerked its hand back. The entire tree shook over and over as the beast slammed into it. The roots snapped and tore as it began to lift free of the ground. Dirt and debris and insects landed on her head. She squealed, batting the crawling things away and darted between the cyclops's legs. In a full sprint she ran, no destination in mind just to get away. *I have to get out of here!* She risked a glance back. The eleven-foot cyclops was still fighting against the tree. The breath stole from Layala's lungs when she slammed into something hard.

Hands wrapped around her arms and held her steady. "It's me. Fennan!"

Wild-eyed she stared at him, hardly believing it.

"Fennan?" she touched his face and then pulled away. "Oh, thank the Maker. I got lost then there was this huge scorpion and then a cyclops and I had to use my magic."

He nodded. "I've seen them. We need to get out of this forest."

Piper came into view holding the reins to Midnight; Tif sat on his back. "We thought you could use some help," Piper said. Layala ran to her and wrapped her arms so tightly around her, Piper wheezed, "Can't breathe."

With a smile she looked around expecting to see Thane. She missed him. The constant ache had yet to yield. She needed to apologize to him, beg for his forgiveness. It was wrong of her to leave him like she did. After days alone to think, she understood why he lied. A sinking feeling intensified the longer she searched and found no one else.

"He's not here," Fennan said gently.

"Oh," she breathed. A dull ache began throbbing in her chest.

The forest floor shook when the tree the cyclops fought with hit the ground. It sniffed and bent down.

"It's realized you're not in there. We need to go," Piper said. "Get on your horse. We'll come back when it's light."

Fennan put his hands out for her to step and mount Midnight. "What about you two? I'm not leaving you."

The cyclops turned and narrowed its one eye on them, speaking inaudible jargon.

"We have horses," Piper shouted as she ran. Fennan smacked Midnight's hindquarter and started running beside them. A pair of horses grazed next to a tree ahead. Both Fennan and Piper leapt and kicked their horses into a gallop in one easy fluid motion. Holding tight to the reins, she followed them, trusting Midnight to see any protruding roots or rocks. When they burst through the edge of the forest and into the open, Fennan and Piper pulled their horses to a stop. "Why are we stopping?" Layala asked, tugging back on Midnight. "They could follow us."

Fennan stood in his stirrups and looked back. "They can't leave the forest's edge. It's enchanted. We're safe here."

"I didn't see anything like that when Thane and I went last time." It struck a chord in her to even say his name so casually. To think of the time they spent together and she threw it in his face as if it meant nothing. "Also, in case you've forgotten…" Layala looked around worried. "I used my magic. We're not safe."

Piper pushed wild red hair out of her face. "The creatures of this place were cursed to die by sunlight, so it is only the dark we fear when going inside. But we could go back to the castle to avoid pale ones. It's not far."

Fennan groaned, running his hand down his face.

"Then we'd have to deal with Orlandia and explain why we left Thane."

"We make camp here then," Piper said, dropping to the ground.

"Is she not better than facing pale ones?" Layala stayed firmly in her seat, eyes searching the dark around them.

"No," they said in unison.

Even Tifapine joined in on that statement. "She's mean, most especially when it comes to King Thane and his safety."

Layala couldn't help but laugh and she slid off Midnight. "You three are more afraid of Thane's mother than pale ones? That's saying something."

"Not afraid of dying but you haven't seen her angry." Piper sat in the grass and laid back. "I'd rather fight pale ones. Besides, we only killed two on the road. I doubt there are any nearby here. They don't come this far north."

Still on his horse, Fennan trotted over to the old tree and hacked at some branches.

"I'm exhausted." Piper crossed her ankles and kept her arms flat against the grass at her sides. "Layala, you are relentless. We followed your trail. Did you even sleep in the last two days?"

Sitting cross-legged in the grass, Layala glanced back at the forest, not trusting that something might not come out. She'd been scared many times in her life but fighting a giant scorpion was at the top of that list. Just the look of its beady black eyes and those pincers, she shuddered. Nightmarish. "I don't have time to sleep. We have three days."

Piper closed her eyes and inhaled deeply. "We have less than three days. Thane will take his own life on the morning of the third day. He won't risk turning into a pale one."

Her insides churned and nausea rose in her throat. Layala looked at the forest once again, this time with different eyes. Perhaps it was worth risking to gain more time. The sun wouldn't rise for six more hours.

"Don't even think about it." Fennan approached with an arm full of branches. "We could spend all night fighting our way to the portal. We wait until first light. You should sleep. I'll stay awake."

"He would do that? He would really—kill himself?" she whispered.

"Wouldn't you?" Fennan asked. "It won't matter. I have faith that the Maker will lead us to our salvation. We will find a way to save both of you. Thane is the closest friend I have left. Osric is gone. I won't lose my other brother."

They were both quiet as Fennan hit two stones together creating sparks. One caught and flames slowly grew among the dry grass and branches.

"Is he upset?"

Fennan gave her a long hard stare. "What do you think? You told him you didn't love him and left on what he believes is a fool's errand. He thinks you left him to die alone."

Her chin trembled. "That's not what I did. I want

to *save* him. I—I didn't want him to follow me. He's done enough, sacrificed enough for me. I don't deserve it."

"So, you wounded him more deeply than anyone ever could have, instead."

A tear trickled down her cheek. Tif put her tiny hand on Layala's knee and patted gently.

Fennan walked over and put an arm around her shoulders. "Don't cry. I know why you did it. He's too close to the situation to be able to see it clearly."

"When we break this bond," Piper sat up and pulled dry grass from her already unruly hair, "will you come back with us?"

Layala shrugged. "I don't know." She wanted to but it would be impossibly hard to face Thane and never get to be with him.

"Because it isn't only Thane you'd be leaving. You'd leave the Ravens and us. You'd be leaving our people." Piper's eyes were filled with emotion. "And the pale ones will never stop hunting you."

Sometimes she wondered if it would be better if she died, as long as she didn't take Thane with her. The groups who wanted her dead weren't entirely wrong. She was the weapon that could be used to bring back the Black Mage. "What did you find out about the person who shot me?"

As he dug through the pack on his horse's backside Fennan answered, "At first, I thought the assassin was one of ours. It was one of our own arrows. But Aldrich found a tree broach, a type of tree that only grows in

Calladira. I think it was a woodland elf. And I believe Thane was the end target. With Tenebris dead and Thane having no heir, they know if he died, we'd be vulnerable. They would try to take Palenor."

She thought back to when they'd come up against the group of them after meeting with Mage Vesstan. One had been scared enough to piss his pants. It made sense they'd want him dead. "Even with the war against pale ones?"

"Even then."

"But why did they leave me there alone? Why did it look like they wanted to kill Talon?"

"Aldrich was scouting the woods around you two and said he chased the shooter but lost him," Piper answered. "And the assassin probably wanted to kill both of you, given that Talon is an heir too. I was a little too harsh to blame her so quickly."

"So, we are at war with Mathekis and the pale ones, and Calladira," Layala sighed as anxiety crept up in.

"It's no longer small squabbles over land," Fennan said darkly. "They tried to assassinate our High King and you. They will pay dearly."

The conversation ended on that note and Layala allowed herself to doze off again. Her dreams were filled with the many ways Thane could kill himself and each time, she was there as the knife plunged or as he drank the poison but never in time to stop him. But she was there to watch him die in her arms where she'd soon follow him to the afterlife.

Even as she rode behind Piper and Fennan into the terrifying woods, all she could think about was the horrid dreams she had. She was so caught up in her thoughts it wasn't until they reached the portal that she realized how far they'd gone. Piper and Fennan dismounted and waited on her. "You'll have to activate it. Only a mage can," Piper said.

Tif whimpered as she poked her head out of the bag. "Be careful."

Remembering what it was like the time before, Layala tentatively touched the rounded stone archway. It stirred with a soft voice and a quiet wind picked up. "Hello again, Layala Lightbringer."

"Can you take us to the Sederac Mountains?"

"Perhaps," it cooed. "What for?"

"To find the dragon shifter Varlett. Please, it's to save Thane."

"She will not willingly give you what you seek," the soothing voice said, as if it could read her mind.

"She doesn't need to be willing. I will get it."

There was a long pause and then the pull of the portal draining her magic activated with a swirling pool that looked similar to water in the center of the stone ring. "Good luck."

The four of them stepped through into a wind so cold it burned Layala's lungs.

Chapter 40

Thane barely spoke a word to anyone after he gave the order to return home. Although many of the Ravens tried to make him laugh or get him to converse, he was a drone. Talon begged him to go find a way to save himself, but he stared up at the winking stars unable to muster up the strength to argue with her. Aldrich stayed beside him at all times, watching him carefully. Thane knew his friend worried that at any moment he would try to take his own life. Aldrich knew that was his plan even if he hadn't spoken it aloud to anyone but Fennan.

Through the bond he felt Layala's terror the night before. It was the only feeling he had in days. It jolted him from a dreamless sleep. Even after everything he still worried for her, regretted not going if only to spend a few more days with her, to see that she was safe until then. And he knew he was pathetic for wanting that. For wanting her when she clearly and painfully did not want him.

When Castle Dredwich came into view, he turned to Aldrich with a folded piece of paper. "Here are my orders. Upon my death, everything goes to my mother. You are to be the defensive general. Fennan is your second should he return home. You and he will need to lead all military movements, and defend Palenor with everything you have. You are the commander of the Ravens."

With emotion-filled eyes, Aldrich stared at the paper. "Thane, you can't do this."

"Don't make this harder than it already is." He shoved his will into Aldrich's hand.

He gripped Thane's shoulder. "But you still have a few days. Don't leave yet. At least say goodbye to your mother."

"She'll never let me go. You know that. She'd sooner watch me turn and keep me in a cell hoping to find a cure. There isn't one."

Aldrich shed a tear as he jerked Thane into a hug. "Let me come with you."

"No. I need you here for Palenor. You, Fennan, and Piper are the only ones I trust, and they aren't here. You must stay."

Chin quivering, Aldrich nodded. "At the very least give Layala a chance. Wait until the very last moment." The wetness from his tears seeped into Thane's shoulder.

"I will." Before he could change his mind, he pulled away from Aldrich and swung into his saddle. Not meeting the gaze of any of his soldiers, he rode toward

Calladira. For days he traveled, only stopping to sleep and eat when he grew weak and shaky. The hunger pains were welcome. It was the only thing keeping the numbness at bay. He thought of taking the portal which would be faster, but he took the long way to the woodland elves' land. There was no reason to rush into his doom. He promised Piper and Aldrich he'd wait until sunset on the eve before.

The change from Palenor to Calladira was evident by the trees. From sparse pines and ash, an occasional luminor, to thick woods of colorful leaves with trunks three males wide. After a couple days of travel, he was half a mile from reaching their border. The sentries likely already spotted him, but they wouldn't make a move unless he crossed into their land. There he made camp, waiting to freely walk into the hands of his enemy.

Resting under the heavy foliage of an oak tree, he stared at the horizon, taken by the beauty of the evening golden hour. The yellow orb hanging low in the sky pleasantly warmed the skin of his face. He watched the bees buzzing from flower to flower. He took a deep breath, filling his senses with honeysuckle. He wanted to remember this moment. The calm before the storm. A time he could picture for serenity when he'd need it in his darkest moment. When he closed his eyes, he dozed off to the lullaby of wind bustling among the leaves of the treetops.

It wasn't long before he heard footsteps, and on instinct drew the dagger from his belt. Three woodland elves in their garb of browns and gold held arrows pointed at his chest. "Well, if it isn't the scum High King," the redhead on the left said. "Stepping where he doesn't belong again."

"You're technically on *my* land," Thane didn't move from his sitting position.

"That's debatable," said the shorter dark-haired elf in the center. "What are you doing here?"

"I wish to meet with Brunard."

"It's Lord Brunard, and weren't you already informed? He doesn't want to meet with you. You spit in his face when you entered Calladira unannounced with your female and attacked our soldiers."

Thane rolled his eyes and slowly rose to his full height. The three elves moved several paces back, to which he smiled at. "I have a feeling your soldiers and I have vastly different accounts of what happened that day. And I know Brunard would be angry with you if you denied him the chance to get back at me."

The three of them looked amongst each other. "What does that mean?" the red-haired male asked.

"You can either take me to him or I'll go myself. The choice is yours." Thane slowly set all his weapons on the ground and stood with his palms up in surrender.

"Is this a trick?"

"Take me to your lord." He was exasperated at this point. "I won't harm you. I need to speak to him leader to leader. Things aren't going well with the pale ones. I came alone for a reason."

The dark-haired one lowered his bow looking him up and down. "We'll need to bind your hands."

"Now that's not fair, is it? I never required Brunard or any of your emissaries to be bound." Thane glanced down rubbing his thumb over the calluses on his hand. "Besides we all know I don't need my hands to cause a ruckus. If I wanted to harm you I'd have done it already."

"This could be a trap," the third with a scar across one eye finally spoke. "He did threaten our lord not weeks ago. He might simply want to get close to him."

"I don't want to kill Brunard." Thane walked over to Phantom and patted his shoulder. "This is goodbye, boy. Go home." He slid the reins over his head leaving him bare. All three of the woodland elves watched him curiously but none spoke. Phantom nickered and pushed his nose into Thane's hand. "Go home." He stroked his forehead one last time. Phantom dug his hoof into the dirt and stubbornly waited. Emotion built up in him as Phantom stared with those big brown eyes. It was the first time he felt emotional in days. Why was it so hard to say goodbye to a horse? Harder than it was to leave Aldrich. But Phantom wouldn't understand why he'd never see Thane again. He looked to the guards. "Bind my hands if it makes you feel better."

Taking a leather strap from his waist, Scarface tentatively approached Thane. He held out his hands. "Behind your back." Letting out a sigh, Thane turned and allowed the woodland elf to tie his hands. One took the lead, one stood at his side and the other walked behind him toward Calladira.

They passed through a forest of some of the tallest and widest trees in Adalon. Critters chittered above and birds nested. The leaves were hues of amber, gold, and red with some spots of the brightest green. It smelled of fresh baked bread and cookies. The aroma was from the many gnome holes they passed. Calladira had the largest butterflies he'd ever seen. As large as birds and a rainbow of colors floating about bringing a euphoric feeling as if he wasn't at the mercy of his enemy.

More guards gathered around them as they passed until there were twenty-two elves in front and behind. "I get my very own procession. How generous of you all." Thane closely watched the male next to him with a twitchy left hand. He was familiar but Thane couldn't place him. "Do I know you?"

The blond male cut him a glare. His keen brown eyes held such hatred it had to be personal. "Keep your mouth shut."

When he spoke it hit Thane. "You were there a few weeks ago when I killed your friends." That twitchy left hand slammed into Thane's side, stealing the breath from his lungs. "For a coward, you hit pretty hard," he wheezed.

"I'm no coward. You are. You had to be saved by that wicked female. That arrow would have pierced your heart."

"Calling me what I called you, how original." He

wanted to break free of his bonds and punch this elf so hard he wouldn't remember his own name for calling Layala wicked, for even speaking about her, but he stayed his hand.

The doors and windows in the wide tree trunks, the vegetable and flower gardens told him they'd entered the city. Goats and sheep wandered about grazing on the lush undergrowth of the forest as they went. A group of three female fiddlers played near a large spraying stone fountain. Gathered around them were children laughing and dancing, she-elves twirling in their dresses. Some males clapped and tapped their feet.

"Whose horse is this?" someone from the back called. "He's beautiful."

Thane whipped his head around and gritted his teeth when the elf stroked Phantom's neck, not a guard by the looks of his attire; a farmer. "Do. Not. Touch. My. Horse." The elf snapped his hand back to his side. Phantom trudged along, pushing through the elves to catch up to his side. "You were supposed to go home." The horse tossed his head as if he understood but chose to stay faithfully at his side.

Although most of the woodland elves built their homes within the trunks of trees, Lord Brunard had a manor completely covered in deep green foliage. Even the white pillars at the front entrance were wrapped in grapevines with plump purple fruit. The steps to the front doors were cushioned with hundreds of years of moss. It wasn't even half the size of Castle Dredwich, but somehow it was more magnificent. As if it was made by the hands of nature rather than elf or man. It was an escape, this whole place was, from the evils of Adalon. Especially an escape from the pale ones that the woodland elves had left the high elves to deal with on their own for hundreds of years.

When the front doors were opened to him, Scarface nudged him inside. The walls were painted a simple beige. The chandelier hanging above was made of gold with white blossoms that glowed bright as any candle. The gold crown molding and trim around the doors were ornately carved. This was the first time he'd ever been in these walls decorated in paintings of those in Brunard's family, both alive and dead. Ahead a long red carpet stretched leading to an open set of stairs. To the left of the stairs was a wide-open archway. Music came from within, a haunting melody that only brought one word to mind: seduction.

"Wait here." The red-haired elf took a pair of guards with him through that archway. It wasn't long before they appeared at the entrance. "Brunard will see you."

Hands still strapped behind his back, he trudged over the red carpet and through that entrance. He paused in surprise. Females wore clothing barely covering their private parts. Strips of fabric that could hardly be called a dress. Several males in red velvet high-backed chairs with one, sometimes two females on their laps. Brunard, the auburn-haired Lord of Calladira had none of the she-elves on his person but his eyes greedily took in their bare flesh. One poured wine into the waiting goblet he held. He took her free hand and kissed it gently. "Thank you, my shining star."

When his gaze connected with Thane's, he rose. "Ah, the noble High King Thane comes to me in his last hours. Although I must say you aren't looking very noble or kingly. Is that blood on your neck? Dirt on your cheek?"

So Brunard knew about Thane's deadline. He wasn't surprised that his rival knew. He'd likely been keeping track for years. "We need to talk."

Brunard arched his dark brow. "The only reason I allowed this visit is because I'm intrigued." He looked around the room. "Leave us."

Only one guard stayed behind near the exit with his back to them. Brunard gestured toward a chair. Thane took it and Brunard waited with a sneer on his face. "As you know my contract is up soon."

"I thought you found your mate?"

"I did." Thane had no desire to elaborate on that. "I need you to join the fight against the pale ones. If Palenor falls they will be here soon after."

Taking a sip from his wine, Brunard never took his eyes off Thane. "I heard you almost lost Doonafell. Your father was able to hold your kingdom easily. The great Thane Athayel doesn't seem so great after all."

Gritting his teeth, Thane took a steading breath. He couldn't believe he was about to offer his sister to this arrogant prick, but he knew she could handle her own. "We drove them back. But it is high time you join us instead of fighting against us. This is a problem for all of Adalon. I am sorry I killed your father. I truly am. If I'd had another choice, I wouldn't have but he would have killed me. It was battle."

"Why are you truly here, Thane? To beg?"

"I want to offer you marriage to my sister Talon. To secure an alliance. It's a peace offering."

Brunard narrowed his eyes. "Your sister... I'm sure she would be quite delicious to bed but as you saw I have plenty of she-elves."

"This isn't about who is in your bed. She is the Princess of Palenor. It's about an alliance between the elves. We are the same. Fight with us."

"There is no reason for me to believe anything needs to change."

"I will be dead in two days. What do you think will happen after that? You think my mother can hold the kingdom?" Thane shook his head. "No. She is soft and has no desire to fight. It wouldn't surprise me if in her grief of losing my father and me so close, she went into hiding and let the kingdom fall within weeks. Right now, I don't care if you sent an assassin that almost killed... Layala." It pained him to speak her name aloud.

"I didn't send an assassin for anyone, let alone one of the only mages in Adalon."

Trying to gauge him, Thane looked him over. Was he lying? If he hadn't then who? Where was the broach from?

"Maybe you have a traitor in your midst. Too bad you won't live long enough to find out." He paused, setting his mouth into a firm line. "Although, the Black Mage's spells don't kill—they turn an elf into a pale one." The corner of his mouth tugged up. He stood, pulling a knife from his belt. Thane tensed ready to fight. He couldn't let Brunard kill him yet. "Let me cut those ties. You need a drink."

Skeptically he stood, trying to judge his rival's expression. He looked sincere but that meant nothing. Thane rarely trusted anyone outside his close circle but right now he needed to show Brunard that he was genuine. He turned his back to the elf lord and he cut the leather, freeing Thane's hands.

"You didn't think I was going to stab you in the back, did you?"

Thane lifted a shoulder, absently rubbing his wrists, and sat once again. As Brunard walked over to a table with several bottles of wine in crystal vases he said, "You remember when we were younger, and our fathers brought us to meet each other. The elven princes of Adalon. You showed me where you trained, and we ate chocolate cake until we were sick."

"And that time you stole one of my father's horses in the night. And I, of course, followed you." Thane smiled at the memory. They'd gotten into quite a bit of trouble as adolescents for only being together on a few occasions.

"Yes. You said it was all your idea, and you took that beating for me." Brunard chuckled. "Ah the simple days of children. We were friendly once. There's no reason we can't be once again, if only for a moment."

This was what he was hoping for when he came here. That they could put their differences and past sins aside for the greater good. "I need to ask you a favor," Thane began, with a nervous twist in his gut.

"I thought you already did. Asking me to become allies with your kingdom to keep it from falling into the hands of the pale ones. You know that would mean I would basically rule over Palenor."

"I do know that." Thane could hardly stomach the idea, but the woodland elves were happy. The people had always been well taken care of. Brunard wouldn't let Palenor be destroyed if he ruled over it.

"I'll need to have your sister agree and sign a binding contract. I won't have some murderous Athayel in my bed waiting to kill me the first chance she gets."

"She'll agree. But this other thing I ask of you. This... this is for me. For an old friend."

Looking up from the wine he'd poured, Brunard waited.

"I need you to kill me." He gulped down the sickening feeling rising in his throat. "In two days, before I turn into a pale one. The amount of horror I could cause as one of those creatures is unspeakable. You know I have magic. You've seen what I can do, even without it."

A long time of silence, of Brunard staring at Thane passed. "You're actually serious," he finally relented.

"I could do it myself but I fear that my drive for self-preservation could win out in the end." Thane stood. The nervous energy running through him drove him to stand, to move. "I've known elves who've committed suicide. They were not mentally stable. They had such deep sorrow that it drove them to death, but I am of sound mind. What if my fear of being a pale one isn't strong enough?" He paced the room. "I don't *want* to die."

"And what of your mate? Surely, she is the answer to your problem."

Tears threatened but he blinked them back. "She left me."

"You would have me believe that this female hated you so much that she would rather die? I don't believe that for one second."

"It's complicated."

Brunard waved a hand aggressively toward Thane. "This High King begging me to kill him is not the Thane Athayel I've always known. The High King of Palenor *begging* me, his enemy, to take over the rule of his land... You're pathetic. The Thane I knew would never let his mate go. He would have fought for her until the end, not give up like a coward. This is how you want to be remembered? Because this is the only thing people will remember. That you gave up."

Those words hit him harder than anything ever had. Thane froze, letting it all sink in. Brunard was right. He should have never come here. He should have gone after Layala, but no, he couldn't even do that. He let his friends go in his stead. He left her to fight for their lives on her own, while he, like a coward, came here to get his enemy to end his life? Nausea hit him like a hot blast of wind, enough that his legs grew weak, and he had to grab onto the back of the chair. He was so blinded by her rejection that he'd lost himself. Lost who he was entirely. How could he have ever left the person he loved so deeply?

There wasn't much time now. He had to leave. He had to fight until his last breath for her, for himself. He could make it to the portal in a few hours, maybe faster if he could use his magic to shift through space again, and beg it to take him to Layala.

"Thank you," Thane said. "For making me see when no one else could." He marched with a sense of urgency that propelled him into a run.

Until Brunard called, "Wait!"

Thane stopped and looked back. "I have to go. We'll discuss alliances when I get back."

Brunard smiled. "Share a quick drink with me. Then go and save your Layala." Brunard quickly closed the distance between them and held out the crystal glass.

It was the least he could do when Brunard all but saved him. In a rush, Thane grabbed it but froze with the glass touching his lips. He hadn't seen Brunard pour it. The eagerness in Brunard's eyes said everything. He pretended to take a sip. "Thank you again, Brunard."

"Oh, you're very welcome."

Thane handed the glass back. When Brunard took it, Thane felt a sharp jab in his side. He sucked in a breath, and stared down at the knife sticking in his flesh. His vision blurred and his limbs became weak after a couple heart beats. Thane staggered back, falling to his hands. Brunard must have poisoned him with that stab.

"You think after you killed my father, I'd let you walk out of here? Unlike you, I loved my father. I've had to watch my mother cry every day for years because of what you did. And when I take your sister and your kingdom, this will make it all the more sweet. You deserve everything that's coming to you." His boot slammed down on Thane's face, and he blacked out.

When Thane woke with a pounding head and blurry vision, something cold and hard bit into his wrists. Blinking rapidly until he saw clearly, he looked up to find manacles and chains. He jerked as hard as he could, but it only made the metal cut into his flesh. He had no shirt on; his boots had been taken, leaving him only in his trousers. Metals bars surrounded him in a circular cage, like one might keep birds in. It hung from a tree swinging in the air three or four feet high. Woodland elves stood all around, staring at him. Some pointed and laughed. A huge tomato flew through the bars and splat across his forehead; the liquid slime seeped down his face burning his eyes. The hundreds of gathered elves laughed. "Throw another one!" someone shouted. And another they did, hitting him in the chest. An apple slammed into his temple, then a rock popped his chin, splitting it open.

"Murderer!"

"Killer!"

"Not so high now, are you?!"

"I hope you burn in the afterlife!"

Shame rippled deeply through him. Shame for letting himself get into this situation in the first place. For letting Layala leave. It took his enemy to tell him he made a mistake, for him to listen and it had gotten him into a horrific situation. He reached within himself for his magic, finding it odd that it wasn't immediately there. With it, he could break these chains and pry open the bars.

"You didn't think I'd be that stupid, did you?" Brunard came through the crowd with a pair of friends on either side. "The Maker wouldn't have given us magic if there wasn't also a way to fight it." He held up a black barb.

Thane's stomach sunk like a rock. They'd poisoned him with katagas. It took Layala's magic at least six hours to come back. "Let me out or so help me—"

"You'll what?" Brunard lifted an eyebrow. "A steady drip of poison will make you like the rest of us. You'll be a pale one soon and I'm going to let you turn. Death would be too easy for you."

Gritting his teeth, rage pulsed through him. "No. You must let me go."

"You're not in any position to make commands."

"You don't know what you're doing!" Thane roared. "If you miss a dose by even a second, I will get my power back and if I've turned into a pale one, you'll all be dead!"

The crowd murmured in low tones.

"Well, I guess we won't miss until I decide I've had enough of you." Brunard turned to the male beside him. "Dose him every four hours." Then he grabbed a spear that had been lodged into the ground beside the cage. He slashed the sharp tip of it across Thane's rib cage sending a sting of pain. Blood oozed down his obliques. "Or perhaps we'll do death by a thousand cuts or however many it takes. Two thousand, four." He turned to the crowd. "Feel free to cut his flesh like he and his *high* elves cut our hearts, but don't kill him until I say. Make him suffer."

Thane wildly jerked and tugged on the chains shaking the entire cage, making the blood pour out even faster. It spilled onto the metal floor. Fear and fury boiled in him like the angered mountains as they shook. There was no sorrow, no self-pity in him. He was the killer, the Warrior King now. "I will kill you! I will flay the flesh from your bones and laugh as you writhe in pain! Let me out or you'll suffer much more than your father ever did!"

Brunard handed the spear to a female and glared. "Ah there he is. The Thane we all know too well."

The she-elf holding the weapon scowled as she pushed the spear through the bars and cut into his thigh. Not deep but enough to burn, to draw blood, and there were enough elves lined up for this torture to last more than the two days he had left.

Chapter 41

Standing in a cavern of deep brown rock, Layala and her companions shivered in the bitter temperatures of the far north. Despite the cold outside the cave, water trickled down the walls and from the top of the stalagmite hanging in large cone shapes above them. Either the cave was enchanted or the walls were naturally warmer, but it did nothing to keep the chill from Layala's body. Her nose ached from exposure, and they hadn't been there long. All of them wore coats and gloves but there had been no respite, no escape from the winter. By fortune alone the portal that brought them there was within this cavern. The storm outside the wide opening was so powerful, when she attempted to venture out, the snow and whipping winds ripped at her clothes and nearly drove her to her knees.

"This storm has to let up soon," Piper said with chattering teeth.

There was nothing close by and they all feared

losing their way in the storm. The snow was but a wall of white, making it impossible to see a distance barely even feet ahead. "Ask the portal to take us back," Tif groaned. "I'm too cold. My toes will fall off, if they haven't already."

"We can't, not without answers," Layala said.

Fennan rubbed his hands together. "It might always be like this. We've heard the stories of the tearing winds of the Sederac Mountains. We have to push through it."

Layala stood and stared out at the blinding white as it cascaded sideways across the opening with a howl that chilled her to the bone. She scooped up her bag and threw it on her back. Then she stepped out into the storm at the cliff's edge. She tucked her hair into the hood of her coat. "I'm going. And I'm not coming back without finding that dragon." She summoned the vines that wrapped around her waist to carry her down the cliff. Pale ones were the least of her worries in this place.

Piper started forward. "Take us with you. If you don't make it back, we'll die in this cave. The portal will not open for us."

Layala nodded. And her vines wrapped around her companions, and carried them to the hard-packed snow fifty feet below. Tifapine huddled in the backpack, poking her head out occasionally. They walked until Layala couldn't feel her feet, pushing through the cold that burned her exposed skin. She trailed vines behind them so they could find their way back and hoped their lifeline wouldn't be buried in snow entirely.

The powdery snow crunched under her boots for what felt like hours. Her legs weakened when the sun dipped behind heavy clouds and the temperature dropped. Her whole body shook. Her hands ached so she tucked them under her armpits. Her lungs and throat burned, as great plumes of mist appeared as she exhaled. "We have to stop," she said and clenched her teeth to keep them from chattering.

"Keep going!" Fennan grabbed her arm and tugged her onward. "If we stop, we'll die."

Piper wrapped her arm around Layala's. "Maybe if we huddle together it will help." Side by side they trudged. Layala kept her eyes down. Every time she looked up, bits of snow and ice stung her eyes.

"I think I see something." Tifapine pointed over Layala's shoulder. "There's something dark ahead."

"It might be a house," Piper said excitedly. "It's a square outline."

It did look like a house. Shelter at the very least. That gave her motivation to move faster, fighting against the driving wind. When they were close enough, they came upon a square stone cottage. The door was half buried in snow, but smoke rose out of the chimney. "Even if it's not her, it will be warm," Layala yelled. She was the first to get there and pounded her fist on the door. "Please let us in!" Even though she should be nervous if this was the home of the dragon shifter who worked with the Black Mage, all she could think about was a fire that had to be waiting inside.

The door slowly pulled inward, but no one stood in the opening. Looking back at the others, Piper nodded, and they stepped inside. They trailed in snow covering the round purple rug. The room had a warm orange glow from the roaring fireplace set in large cream-colored stone. A wide brown armchair sat before it with a small table beside it. A steaming cup of tea waited on it and beside it a saucer of cookies. The tea would be welcome right about now.

Layala looked to the far wall where a bed with straw poking out from under heavy sheepskin blankets was set. She swung her gaze to the other side that hosted a shelf full of books with pages hanging out of the deeply used leather. But most peculiar was a station with cauldrons and vials of various sizes on a table. Animal skulls hung with string from the ceiling, along with bunches of dried herbs and flowers. There was a vase of dark red liquid that the twist of Layala's gut told her was blood. Unlit candles and feathers from various birds scattered over the table.

"Hello?" Layala finally called. "Is anyone here?"

Fennan had his dagger in hand stepping in front of Layala. "Stay behind me. I don't like this place."

"You came here and now you insult me by saying you don't like my home? Perhaps you'd prefer the storm," said a light melodic voice.

Layala set her jaw and stepped around Fennan, despite Tif's quiet protests. The shifter had to be sitting in the chair. There was nowhere else to hide. Keeping her distance, she moved to the side putting the shifter into view. Tapping her long black talons against the armrests, she smiled. She was young and beautiful. With wavy golden hair and matching eyes of amber. Her deep bronze skin had a shimmer to it much like dragon scales would. "Hello, Layala. I've been waiting for you."

Gulping, Layala resisted the urge to pull out a weapon. "Then you know why I'm here."

"Yes," she mused, looking Layala over from head to toe. "I expected your High King to be with you. Where is he?"

"Not here."

The sorceress chuckled. "You thought you'd break a mate spell with him not present? How very naive of you."

"Just tell me how and I'll go to him. I'll give you whatever you want."

"It isn't wise to go around making promises like that. I could ask for your soul or your life, or the life of your little friend in your bag."

"No. Not lives and not souls."

The cackle that echoed through the room made Layala's warming skin tingle. "I should tell you that you already have the key to what you seek."

Gritting her teeth, Layala's cheeks flared hot. She didn't come here for riddles. "I don't know what that means. I need a way to break a mate bond created by the Black Mage."

"He was my lover, you know." Her three-inch talons at the end of her fingers tapped steadily. "I did love him once, but you know what they say, about a woman who's been scorned."

"He cheated on you? Left you?" Layala asked. Not that she cared in the slightest but if she was going to get an answer it seemed conversation might be what the woman wanted.

"Oh dear, he would never have dared bed another. But you know what he did care about more than me?" she paused. "His power. And you know what I cared about more than him? *Mine*."

Layala took an involuntary step back. This dragon craved power as much as the Black Mage. "What do you want for the answer? I know you were able to get free of him. They said you used to have a rune on your forehead. You don't now." She glanced at Piper and Fennan who stood starkly still a few feet away.

"You're so young, mage. You haven't even tapped into your power, but I can feel it." She slowly bobbed her head. "It's like a thick heavy cloud, wanting to snuff me out. It knows a threat when it encounters one. But even you can't break that mate bond on your own."

"Then what?" Layala demanded. Her pulse picked up; the talking in circles made her anxious. "Another spell?"

"You'll owe me a favor in the future. And you can't deny me when I come to collect. If you attempt to deny me, you'll be cursed."

"What kind of favor?" And what kind of curse?

"The nature of the favor will be disclosed at the time. It won't cost you a life or a soul."

Fennan and Piper both shook their heads. Layala clenched her fists. She didn't have a choice. "I agree."

"The mate bond can be broken by an object infused with dying-sacrifice. That kind of object can undo any magic." Layala reached up and touched her willow necklace. Varlett nodded. "I was there the day your mother forfeited her life to see you free. I watched from the shadows as she tore it from her neck. That necklace represents her love. With the right incantation it could break your mate bond."

"What is the incantation?"

Varlett stood and held out her hand. Tentatively, Layala took it, and the sorceress's talon pierced the inside of Layala's wrist, drawing a bead of blood. The sorceress ran her fingertip over the blood then pressed her bloody finger against her tongue. She closed her eyes as if reveling in the taste of it. Layala cringed and took a step back.

"You fear that Thane will die during the consummation of the mate spell." She kept her eyes closed.

Wondering how she could know that, Layala said, "Yes because of—"

"Your previous lover," Varlett cut in, opening her big golden eyes. "There is a clause in the mate spell—loyalty. I know this because I helped him create the spell. When loyalty is broken there is a consequence. Your lover Novak died because he was *not* your mate. It wasn't your magic that killed him. So now you have a choice. Do you wish to break the mate bond, or will you go to your mate and become one?"

Layala felt both relieved and nauseous. The whole time it wasn't even her? She spent years hating herself, and it was the Black Mage's fault? It was that horrible evil mage who wasn't even alive anymore that killed Novak, and the reason she feared being with Thane. Layala's hand was still wrapped around the cold metal of the willow tree. Maker, she bargained for an answer and owed this woman an unknown favor, and consummating the bond wouldn't even hurt Thane, let alone kill him.

She thought of Thane's smiling face. No matter how she treated him, he still chose her. He laughed when she called him names. He never gave up on her. He loved her despite everything. "I choose Thane."

Varlett smiled. "Go to your mate. I think he might be in trouble. I do look forward to seeing you again, Layala."

"In trouble?" A pain so sharp it took her breath away, hit Layala in the chest. And with it a fiery rage. She whipped around to face Piper and Fennan. "Something is wrong." She knew exactly where it had come from.

"What?" Piper asked.

"Something is wrong with Thane. He's—hurt and, very," his wrath was like a burning sun, screaming at her through their bond. "Very angry." She clutched her chest and then voices flew around what sounded like within the cottage, but she knew it was in her mind. People laughing and screaming insults.

"What is happening?" Fennan moved closer, eyes wide.

She pushed her hands against the sides of her head. "It's too chaotic. I don't know." Flashes of a cage and elves standing on the other side of the bars zipped through her mind's eye. She wanted to scream herself. His rage was so palpable. Layala took deep, slow breaths trying to calm herself, focusing on Thane. There had been absolutely nothing from him since she left but a quiet sadness that she couldn't distinguish from her own feelings. Maybe she could send him tranquility as he'd done to her. *It's alright, it's alright, it's alright. I'm coming,* she chanted taking soothing breaths, picturing Thane feeling their connection like a tunnel that only needed opening. That fire in him died down enough that she heard clearly as if he stood beside her, *"Layala. I am sorry."*

"Don't give up. I haven't given up on you," she whispered, hoping he could hear her.

The dragon lady watched her curiously with a coy smile as if she enjoyed his suffering.

Layala didn't say another word as she threw the door open. The snowstorm had stopped. It was as clear as a summer day with the sun shining in a perfectly blue sky. Layala ran. She knew Piper and Fennan followed her by their footfalls crunching over the packed snow. There was nothing left to do now but go to Thane. To save him from whatever or whoever hurt him, and finally be together before they turned into pale ones.

They reached the portal quickly without the forces of nature against them. Her magical vines lifted them up and she slammed her hand against the stone. "Take me directly to Thane. Take me to him right now! I know you can."

The portal warmed and glowed. "Hurry," is all the voice said and the stone's center swirled to life.

Layala shoved Piper through first, then nodded to Fennan. "GO!" He briefly hesitated then disappeared into the swirls. Layala stepped right after him into a forest of colorful autumn trees that could only be Calladira.

Chapter 42

Piper and Fennan pressed their backs against a thick trunk, waving Layala over to them. Music drifted in the air from somewhere nearby. Laughter and chatter too. Tif leaned onto Layala's shoulder. "This is Newarden, the capital city of Calladira."

Sliding beside Fennan, Layala peeked around the tree trunk. In the near distance a pair of elves walking together leading sheep, headed their way. "How do you know that, Tif?"

"Because no other city in Calladira has the Lord's Manor." She pointed to where deep among the trees was the back of a large manor.

"What would Thane be doing here?" Layala pulled the dagger from her belt. If she had to take out the two elves headed their way she would. Flashes of the cage and his fiery anger stirred in her memory. Was he being held captive?

"I have no idea, but it can't be good," Fennan said.

He slipped off his coat and tossed it on the ground along with his gloves. It was a pleasantly warm day and heavy clothes already had sweat building under them.

"We'll need to sneak around and find him," Piper said. "They'll recognize us as outsiders right away with our Palenor attire."

Layala gasped, remembering what she'd been given at the Summer Solstice. "I brought some leaves from the invisibility plant. How long will they last?" Layala rifled through her bag, pulled out a small leather pouch and found the white leaves now dried and crumbling at the edges.

"Fresh, maybe an hour. Dried, a few minutes," Piper said inspecting them. Layala peeked around the tree trunk again to the two elves. "Maybe we can get new clothes in case it fades too quickly." She hooked a thumb toward the two farmers.

Fennan smirked. "What a splendid idea." He pulled his bow off his back and quickly knocked an arrow. "But there are only two."

"We'll draw sticks," Piper added, taking her sword from its holster.

Layala dropped into a crouch beside Tif. "Stay here. Stay hidden."

The trio swept around behind the two unknowing sheep farmers and with weapons ready Fennan let out a whistle. The two stopped chatting and turned.

"Don't make a sound or this arrow will go through your head," Fennan said.

Piper sneered. "And this sword will cut it off."

The two male elves silently put their hands up. "Now strip," Layala ordered. Using the farmer's own lead ropes to tie them up, they left the two elves bound at the base of a tree.

"Where is the High King of Palenor?" Fennan asked, holding a knife to the throat of the older one.

"We'll never talk, scum."

"Would you rather die?" Fennan pressed the blade harder against the elf's throat.

The elf who couldn't have been more than fourteen years old answered, "He's getting everything he deserves." Then the teen spit and the glob of saliva landed on Fennan's shirt. The older male beside him glared at his partner. A father-son duo if Layala had to guess.

"You're lucky you're still a child," Fennan said, rising up and wiping the spit off with a leaf.

Piper kicked the young male in the side of the head and sent him face-first in the grass. "He is a child in need of a lesson."

"Don't hurt my son!" the other called.

"Keep your mouth shut," Piper snarled and then kicked him too. "They won't talk. It doesn't matter. We'll find him." Then she held up two sticks. One was short. "Short stick stays behind and guards these two to make sure they don't get loose and warn anyone. The other goes with Layala." After closing her hand around the sticks, she held them out to Fennan. "You go."

He tugged one loose. It was certainly the short stick. Throwing it down, he cursed under his breath. "You yell as loud as you can for me if something goes wrong."

"We will," Piper said, gathering the green and brown garb of the two elves into her arms. Layala and Piper quickly changed. The older male's clothes were baggy on Piper, but she belted the waist tight to keep them from falling. "We can't openly wear our weapons. The people here don't unless they are soldiers and given that this isn't a soldier's uniform..."

"So, all we can take is a dagger and a knife then," Layala prayed that they wouldn't have to fight anyone and somehow they could sneak Thane away.

Gripping a leaf in hand, and heart thundering Layala and Piper walked around the backside of the Manor. It was covered in moss and foliage. She ran her hand across the plants feeling for any magical properties, but nothing shifted in her. "Should we save the leaves for escape?" Layala asked.

"They're supposed to be steeped in tea, I honestly don't know if it will even work, but we should save them for when we see Thane."

A trio of chatting soldiers headed their way. "Don't speak unless they ask a direct question," Piper murmured.

The soldiers slowed as they neared. "Good afternoon, ladies," one said with a big smile.

Layala dipped her head and quickened her pace. Thankfully the soldiers kept walking. It wasn't long before they came into the bustling center of the city where small crowds gathered. Her eyes swept over the area looking for any sign of Thane... of a cage. She had a terrible feeling that's where they'd find him. A glimmer of light caught her eye, and the top of a gold cage hung from a tree mostly hidden by the crowd around it. "I think he's over there."

Throat constricting the closer she drew, Layala slid around elves, and gently nudged them aside, making her way to the front of the crowd. When she saw all the blood, both dried and fresh, covering Thane's half-naked body she froze. The invisibility leaf dropped from her fingers. Hundreds of small cuts, some oozing, some partially closed and scabbed over. His head was slumped forward, his sticky, bloody hair hanging over his face. His arms held up by chains cutting into his wrists taut above him. She couldn't stop herself. She ran to the bars, wrapping her hands around them. They'd tortured and humiliated him. "Thane! Thane, it's me. It's Layala. I'm going to get you out."

"Layala," Piper snapped. "Think about this for a moment. We're vastly outnumbered. You're going to get us killed."

Thane's head slowly rose. They'd even cut into his beautiful face. Small scabs marred his cheek and forehead and chin. His eyes flashed wide. "What are you doing?" he groaned. "Get out of here."

"I'm going to free you." Tears burned Layala's eyes, momentarily blurring her vision.

"Get away from the cage." One of the guards

gripped her wrist tightly and tugged her hand free of the bar.

Layala tore out of his grasp and shoved him. "Don't touch me! How could you do this to him?" She lost all sight of reason, of worry, of fear, and only saw red.

He came at her again and she leveled him with a punch to the jaw. The crowd began to question. "She's a sympathizer!" someone shouted.

"Damn it, Layala," Piper said at her side, pulling her dagger. "There are thousands of people here. We must go and come back with the cover of night."

"We will do no such thing," she snapped. She'd be damned and dead before she left him again.

"Shit," Piper cursed, readying herself.

A set of guards came at them with cuffs in their hands. Her chest heaved up and down; her fists clenched at her sides. The guard looked confused at first. "Settle down, maiden. We don't wish to hurt you. Come explain your behavior to Lord Brunard and I'm sure he'll be lenient." The guard narrowed his eyes and reached for her.

Drawing her blade Layala plunged it into his gut, shoving through the metal platemail. She felt his breath whoosh out before she wrenched it from his body. "Here's my *explanation*." Another guard rushed her; she whirled and slashed his throat. Blood sprayed as he went down. "You will all pay for what you have done to my mate!" Another side of Layala she'd never known let loose a murderous rampage. She slashed and hacked at guards coming at her, dropping them like insects. Her blade plunged into the soft flesh of necks, sliced across chests. She moved faster than she ever had. Saw only weak points in her opponents. She was a goddess of death, lethal incarnate.

More guards rushed. Piper was taken down. The soldiers swarmed her in great numbers until a wrathful scream that scorched Layala's throat let loose magic that roared like a beast. Vines tore through the ground, louder than a crack of thunder, wrapping and tangling around elves as they screamed and attempted to flee. The vines punched through the guts of the soldiers, killed and maimed with fatal precision.

Elves ran in every direction, trampling over the fallen, screeching and wailing in a panic to get away. Poison leaked from the lilies, dropping many who hadn't been caught in the vines' destructive path. More guards came running. Arrows flew at Layala but her magic stalks sprouting up like a wall, defended and stopped any and all attacks.

She'd never felt more rage than seeing what they'd done to *him*. She moved and waved her hands killing those who sought to attack. Blood pooled at her feet from the fallen around her. As far as she was concerned, they were all guilty of torturing Thane. They all stood by and watched, and cut him. The only elves she consciously spared were children or mothers who held their children.

A howl that couldn't be mistaken for anything but

a pale one soared over the sounds of chaos. Then another and soon, a horde of pale ones invaded.

"Kill the pale ones!" a voice rose above the chaos. "Forget the mage! Kill them or we will all die!" An auburn-haired male stood on the edge of the raised fountain. As much as she despised the pale ones, this bought her time to free Thane.

Fennan dashed in from the scattering crowd, shooting arrows at pale ones. Piper was at the cage door attempting to get it open. Layala turned and ran, skidding to a halt once she reached him. The door needed a key... She laid her hand flat against the lock; vines pushed in and tore it apart allowing her to swing the door open. She climbed inside, and grabbed his bloody face in between her palms. "I'm here. They can't hurt you anymore." He met her stare as the corner of his mouth crooked upward. Then she quickly broke the chains with her power.

Piper caught Thane's upper body before he fell. "Fennan!" she shouted. "Some help!"

When a pale one slammed into the side of the cage, he stuck his head through the bars and screeched. The sound hurt her ears, ringing after he shut his mouth. Layala shoved her dagger under his chin, sinking it to the hilt. Black blood gurgled out of his mouth and down her hand until she jerked her dagger back.

She whirled around to Fennan sliding his arm under Thane. "Come on, let's get you out of this cage," he said in a tender voice one might use speaking to a sibling in danger.

When they jumped to the ground, Thane groaned, clutching his side where blood still oozed. The deep red covering most of his body made Layala sick. She looked for a way through the mobs of pale ones and woodland elf soldiers when Phantom came from out of nowhere, rearing and neighing loudly. "Just in time, boy." Layala wanted to cheer at the steed's arrival.

Fennan struggled to push Thane onto his back until Layala and Piper helped. It was much harder to lift someone who couldn't help much themselves.

When he was finally on Phantom's back, Thane slumped heavily forward, and to one side as if he might slip off at any moment. He wouldn't be able to hold on for long once Phantom started moving, especially bareback. Using her magic as a step, she leapt up behind Thane, and wrapped her arms around him hoping she could hold him upright. His pain radiated into her stronger than before. "I'm getting you out of here."

"Go, Go!" Fennan shouted. "We're right behind you!"

Layala reached around Thane, grabbing Phantom's mane and kicked him into a run.

"Get the mage! Get the female!" one of the pale creatures bellowed.

Phantom slowed for not a soul, running pale ones down and darting around elves. Layala kept glancing back to make sure that Fennan and Piper were still close behind and they were. When they made it out of the city and deep enough into the woods where no one followed, Layala pulled Phantom to stop.

With a groan, Thane started slipping to the side, "Thane," she cried, trying to keep him upright but he was too heavy. They slid off and hit the ground hard. Layala scrambled to her knees, and leaned over him, tears spilling down her cheeks. "I'm so sorry," she sobbed, "I'm sorry I left you. I shouldn't have. I lied. I do love you." She wrapped her arms around his neck. "I love you, Thane Athayel."

Chapter 43

Love was a powerful force. It could not be bought. It could not be taken or stolen. Although sometimes it must be fought for, it must be given freely.

"And I love you. You were magnificent back there." Thane's voice was hoarse, but he still managed to smile.

Crying harder, Layala pressed her lips gently to his. "Tell me how to do the healing rune spell."

He shook his head. "No. No, I would never let you do that for me."

"Thane," Layala chided. She knew the spell required her pain, but she could handle it. It was the least she could do after leaving him.

"These wounds will be closed in an hour at most," Fennan said. "He will be fine."

She'd seen him heal before, but it was still hard to believe, difficult to watch him suffer in the meantime. Looking over his body Layala found that many of the cuts were already healing. All the wounds had stopped bleeding and were scabbed. Some looked almost completely closed. She sighed and let tears flow in a steady stream down her face. "I'm sorry I left you. And you were right."

"I hear a stream," Piper said. "I'll get some water for you, Thane." She took off at a sprint.

Tif climbed down from Layala's bag that had been slung over Fennan's shoulder and stood at the crown of Thane's head. "The sorceress said it was the mate bond that killed Novak, not Layala's magic! Yay! Now you can get it on!"

Layala laughed. Of course Tif would break it to him right then in such a blunt way. "Tifapine," she drawled.

Tif looked down and rubbed her face. "Sorry. I should have let you tell him, huh?"

Thane chuckled and searched Layala's eyes. "Is that true?"

Grinning with so much happiness Layala nodded. "Yes. We can be together as mates should be. We won't turn into pale ones. We don't have to die."

"I guess going to the sorceress wasn't all bad." He reached up, wiping tears off Layala's cheek with his thumb.

"She owes the sorceress an undisclosed favor," Fennan said, folding his arms. "Which was worth the information, but we don't know what she'll ask for."

Thane slowly pushed himself upright, guided by Layala's hand. "I'm sorry I didn't come for you. I could have helped. I could have made that bargain for you. I shouldn't have let you leave on your own, and then you had to come to *my* rescue." He pushed his messy hair out of his face.

"Stop it." Layala took his hands and kissed the tops of both. "I don't want to hear any of that. I pushed you away. This was my mistake."

Piper came with a canteen of water and both of her ripped-off sleeves soaked in water. Thane took them with a thank you and started by wiping his face. Tif offered a stale lemon cookie that she'd made over a week ago. He ate it in two bites.

Fennan still had his bow in hand. He stood doing a quick scan of the area. "We should get moving. The woodland elves might find us. Or the pale ones could be tracking us."

Piper snorted. "Brunard's soldiers will kill the pale ones, even if it's a bloodbath, and after what Layala did to them, I don't think they'll send anyone any time soon."

Still on her knees beside Thane, Layala glanced back. She thought she should feel some guilt for what she'd done. That it would hit her suddenly and she'd be a mess, but when she thought of the screams and her blade plunging and slashing and her magic tearing them apart, all she felt was... satisfaction. She knew she shouldn't, but she did. Thane promised to destroy anyone who hurt her... she did the same for him.

"Thank you," Thane said and shakily rose to his

feet. "You are remarkable. You did what it would have taken an army to do."

Layala slid her arm around his lower back and her hand rested against his chest to balance him. "Let's get you onto Phantom until we find shelter."

Fennan held out his clasped palms and helped lift Thane onto the horse. "There is an old-abandoned ruin halfway to the portal from here. It would at least provide some cover so you can rest. Fennan is right. We can't stay here in the open no matter how much they may fear Layala."

On the walk Thane told them how he came to be in Calladira and the story twisted Layala's insides. He'd come here to ask his enemy to kill him. It made her sick to think if she hadn't made it in time, he'd be dead as would she, over her false belief.

When they came upon the stone structure Thane had spoken of, Piper and Fennan went inside to scout it out. With a half-caved-in roof that maybe once had been made of straw and mud, and crumbling stone walls nestled against a small hillside, the only thing that might be in there were wild animals.

Thane slid down from Phantom and stretched his arms over his head. His wounds all healed and hadn't left a single scar. Every inch of him was as perfect as it had ever been. She couldn't help but touch the bare skin of his back that once had so many slashes. "How is this possible without magic? I know they say you can heal but why?"

He lifted a shoulder. "It runs on my mother's side

of the family. The natural ability to heal quickly is in my blood. It has long been said that her bloodline—Voness was descended from a god of the old world. The ones time forgot."

Her eyebrows furrowed. "But I thought they weren't real? Just old stories."

"You asked why I can heal quickly. I gave you the only answer I know."

Piper emerged through the broken doorway first. "It's clear."

Fennan stepped out right after her. "There's an old bed made of straw in there. A little dusty and certainly not for a king but you can get rest there. We'll make for the portal in an hour."

"We're going to search for something to eat so you can regain your strength."

Layala made her way to the entrance and stood in the doorway. The weeds had taken over most of the inside and the roof opened up into the sky and trees above. She glanced over her shoulder to see Piper scoop up Tif and put her on her shoulder then handed Thane her pack.

"We're coming back, right?" Tif asked.

"Yes, but they need time to talk, alone."

Thane gave Fennan a hug. Turning away, Layala stepped inside.

Sitting on the makeshift bed that at least had an old cotton blanket, Layala laid back and stared up at the sky. Thane's footsteps made her heart beat faster. She sat up with a smile. His very presence made her happy. It took leaving him for her to realize how much she loved him.

He paused just inside the doorway. The light cascaded around him, making the edges of his form glow. "They said they'll be back soon. I'm going to wash off in the stream."

Layala nodded. Heart suddenly racing, she stood and with each step closer to him her breath shook. "I'll come with you." Blood still covered her hands from her warpath.

The stream ran merely a few yards from the ruins. It was only knee-deep and a leg's length wide, but it was fresh water. Layala removed her boots and then dipped her hands in and scrubbed at her hands and arms. The water ran a light pink color until it washed clear downstream.

Thane waded into the water and sunk down until his body was submerged. Through the bond, his inner turmoil seeped into her. Anguish and fury from what he endured. He floated on his back, scratching his scalp. When he rose up water rolled over the hard muscles of his body. He was so beautiful and good and a pulse low in her gut throbbed. She stared without pause, without embarrassment.

She wanted to ask him to make love to her right then. To give them what they both craved but how could she ask that when they'd just saved him from being tortured? He wrung out his dark hair and came out of the stream with his pants clinging to his powerful thighs.

Silently, she stood and placed her hand on his chest. She couldn't find the words for what she wanted, couldn't make them form but they only had tonight. "I know I said I was sorry but, I need you to know I truly am," she began. "You were tortured because I left you." Tears blurred her eyes. "And I feel horrible."

"Please don't blame yourself. I chose to come here. Brunard will get what is coming to him."

"What can I do to make you feel better? I can sense your unease."

His mouth twisted into a smile. He dropped to his knees and kissed the tops of her knuckles on both hands. "Marry me, Laya. Marry me and be my true mate. I will worship you in every imaginable way."

She swallowed hard. Maker above, he actually got down on his knees after teasing her about it. She knelt before him, taking his face into her hands and softly kissed his lips. "I would love to marry you."

"I have something." He got up and dug in Piper's bag and pulled out a small wooden box. After he removed the lid, he reached in and pulled out a ring. "I gave it to Piper to keep safe. I figured since she was a female, she would be the only one who wouldn't lose it."

With her hand against her mouth Layala laughed. It was so true. He took her left hand and slid it onto her finger. Layala inspected it for a moment. It shined and sparkled in the sunlight. It had a silver band in swirls and leaves leading up to a light purple stone surrounded by tiny diamonds in the shape of a lily. He must have had it made specifically for her. It would have to have been after he saw her magic to get this kind of detail. "It's beautiful. I love it."

Her gaze lifted to his face. He stared down at her face, unreadable. Overwhelming need and want consumed them. Layala pushed her trembling hands up his chest and slid them around his neck. His heart beat louder than ever before. With aggravating slowness, he leaned down and finally pressed his lips against hers, gentle at first, growing in urgency. He lifted her, and she wrapped her thighs around his waist. The desire burning for him soared when his fingers pressed into her back. They kissed and tugged at each other making their way to the shelter ruin. Thane stumbled through the doorway, almost dropping them both to the ground. He caught himself with one hand on the wall and held her with the other. They both laughed against each other's mouths when the fragile wall caved, and a new hole opened up.

He set her on the straw bed, and she dragged him down on top of her, kissing him with fervor and a need that pulsed low within her. She caressed the hard muscles of soft skin, worshiped the taut planes of his shoulders and chest with her lips. Her tongue slid along the line between his abdominal muscles, and he shivered.

"Laya," he groaned with need, grabbing the bottom of her tunic. Thane tugged it over her head. He pressed his lips between her breasts like she'd once dreamed he would. She gasped at the sensual touch; his feline smile grew wider. They kissed and caressed and explored. It seemed to surprise and delight him with every sound she made when his lips touched a different part of her: the back of her neck, below her navel. When his lips touched the inside of her thigh, she gripped the shabby blanket to keep herself from trembling.

"You know I've never done this," he murmured. "But Fennan gave me a book with some—details. It was interesting."

Layala giggled. "You're doing very well." Then she sat up and shoved him down. "It's my turn." Her lips trailed down his chest. He moaned and flinched and trembled the further down she drew. She tugged on his pants, laughing as they stuck, until she finally jerked them off and he lay there bare. She bit her lower lip at the sight of male parts she'd threatened to cut off more than once. There was no doubt he desired her.

Thane took hold of her wrist and kissed her mate rune. "You are my queen."

Layala stood on the bed and slowly pushed her underwear off. Then she slid out of her bralette, standing fully nude in front of him. "And you are my king, whom I will protect and love until the end of time."

Thane visibly swallowed hard, taking her in. He never looked more enticing than he did in this vulnerable state. "You're the most beautiful thing I've ever seen. It is an honor to be your mate."

She dropped to her knees and climbed on top of him, and they became one. He moaned deeply as they rocked together. Thane was both gentle and vigorous, and their bodies melded and moved until she pulsed with euphoria.

When they finished, sweaty and with heavy breath, they laid in each other's arms, faces inches apart, waiting in heart-pounding silence. Thane's mouth curled into a grin, and they started all over again.

Chapter 44

"Are you two still alive?" Tifapine stood just below them off to the side of the old bed.

Startled from slumber, Layala's head snapped up and then feeling Thane's naked body under her, she pressed her ear to Thane's chest. His soft beating heart was the most joyous, wonderful sound she'd ever heard.

"He's alive," she breathed. She sat up and held a hand to her own chest. "I'm alive. We're alive!" She sang and threw her hands above her head. "The sorceress told the truth."

Tif jumped up and down, clapping her hands. "Yay! You're alive." She stopped and then cocked her head to the side. "Wahoo!"

Thane's eyes fluttered open, and he glanced over at Tif. With a groan, he reached for the closest piece of clothing, which happened to be Layala's underwear, to cover his male parts. "Good lord, gnome. What are you doing?"

"I drew the short stick." She shrugged. "Someone had to see if you two were alive or not. I thought maybe the dragon lady lied so you would both die, and I would find you both lifeless. Then we'd have to bury you here in Calladira in this ruin and it would be a tragic story for the ages but unfortunate nonetheless."

"Get out. I'm not dressed," Thane said.

Tif waved a hand. "I've already seen you both naked before. It's fine."

"What?" Thane balked.

"Oh, by accident, I saw you. When I was roaming around your room once looking for a snack. You know how you keep chocolate by your bed sometimes, then you came out of the bath as I stuffed my mouth full. I'd never seen a naked male elf before. It's both oddly satisfying and strange."

Layala laughed and Thane did too.

Fennan and Piper both appeared in the doorway and immediately turned around but stayed in place. "You're alive," they both said in unison.

Layala slapped her arm over her breasts. Thane reached down and picked up the tunic and covered her with it. "Yes, we've established we're alive. I don't know why you were so worried about it!"

"Now we can go back home, and you can have an official wedding with the kingdom. We have a day before your deadline ends. I know you fulfilled the —*latter* half of the deal, but you haven't promised your wedding vows, so we better hurry to the portal," Piper said with her back to them. "And then we can kick some pale one ass."

"Layala is rubbing off on you," Fennan said. Piper shoved him and they both disappeared from view.

"You leave too, Tif." Layala pointed at the exit. "We're fine, as you can see."

She winked at them both then scampered out. Thane and Layala locked eyes and a slow smile pulled at his lips. "That was the most—magnificent thing I've ever experienced. I need to have you again. Just once more before we go."

Grinning, she wrapped her arms around his neck. "You're going to wear me out."

"Most certainly," he said.

After, Layala lay on his chest, twirling a piece of his hair around her finger. Her eyes flicked to his ear and she tugged on it. "So." She gently slid her fingertips down to his earlobe. He shivered at the touch. "I was wrong. I'll admit it."

His eyebrows furrowed. "Wrong about what?"

She smiled and licked her lips. "Remember when I commented about pointed male ears with small tips and therefore small lower bits?"

A slow smirk grew. "I do."

"So, that was a definite myth."

He chuckled and pulled her down for a rough kiss. "I told you, you'd find out. And you said you weren't interested in my male parts. Actually, I think your exact words were 'not remotely interested'. But have you come to crave me, Laya?" His rough fingers slid along her ribcage, bringing goosebumps to her flesh.

"Yes."

He cupped her bottom and squeezed. "And will you show me just how much later tonight?"

She smiled and kissed him again. "As soon as I can get you alone again. It will be a long walk back to Castle Dredwich."

He grabbed his pants off the floor and shook the dirt off them. "And we'll have to wait until we have the ceremony to finish the spell, but absence does make the heart grow fonder."

"I need to wash off in the stream." Layala peeked out in the massive hole in the side of the ruin. "Make sure they're not close enough to see, please." She hoped outside and dipped into the water.

"I'll keep watch, my love."

When they dressed and stepped out to meet Piper and Fennan and Tif, they sat a ways off near the stream, with Tif in between them and Phantom grazing nearby. "You think they heard us?" Layala asked, feeling a blush creep up her neck.

"I think the whole of Calladira heard you." She smacked his chest and stamped ahead. He wrapped his arms around her middle and his lips grazed her ear. "I loved it. Don't be embarrassed." He scooped her up into his arms and she giggled, pulling herself up to kiss him. "Let's go home."

When the Valley of the Sun came into view, lit up by golden light, Layala grinned. It was so beautiful, and it was... home. She once thought it never could be, but Thane was home, and this was where he resided.

Thane cleared his throat. "We'll need to have a small ceremony, completing the mate spell by voicing our vows, and—we'll be forced to hit the sheets, I'm sure."

"What a terrible thing," Layala said smiling, and took hold of his hand. She brought his knuckles to her lips and kissed them. "I only wish my friends and my aunt could be here for it." Even if she knew she would never go back to Briar Hollow to live again, she missed them. As much as she liked the luxury of the castle, she'd miss the cottage and her simple life. But Thane was worth staying.

"They will," Thane assured her. "We'll bring them when we have our celebration and for your coronation, of course. Anyone you want."

"Am I going to have to find another room?" Tif whined. "I can hardly be present with you two—naked and doing the nasty."

Everyone laughed. Layala couldn't help the blush from taking over her face. "We'll find you somewhere, Tif," she said. "A room of your own."

They started up the slope, leading to Castle Dredwich on the other side when a figure appeared at the top of the hill. Dark blond hair waved in the gentle breeze, black armor glinted, but the sun behind him made it impossible to tell who it was. A soldier by the look of his attire. "Who is that?"

"I think it's Aldrich," Piper said and waved. "He'll be so happy we got this mess sorted out."

Another soldier joined him and another until the hill was lined with them. A welcome home party, perhaps? Unless something happened while they were gone, and they were guarding the hillside into the city.

An arrow zipped by and slammed into Thane's thigh. He groaned and stumbled. Layala gasped, keeping hold of his hand and was dragged back with him. He cursed and snapped the arrow's shaft off, but the metal head was still lodged.

"It's us!" Piper screamed, jumping in front of Thane, sword drawn.

Fennan waved his arms wildly. "You just shot your High King!" he roared. "Stop!"

"That arrow is laced with katagas," Thane said. "My magic is fading again."

Another whistled through the air. Layala dropped just before it flew past her head.

"Something is wrong," Piper said, backing up into Thane. Driving into him. "They're not listening. We can make a run for the portal."

"No," Thane barked. "I'm not running from my own soldiers. I am king."

"Thane," Layala pleaded as the soldiers began marching down the hill. Something was very wrong. They knew who they shot at if the arrow was laced with katagas.

Thane stepped out in front of Piper and Fennan. "Stop! By order of your High King!"

They didn't falter in their advance.

"Holy Maker above," Fennan said in disbelief. "That is not Aldrich—it's—"

"Tenebris," Thane breathed. "That's impossible. He's dead."

"He looks very much alive," Piper said, hysteria growing in her voice. "Run!" she turned and shoved Thane hard in the chest. "Run!"

"I refuse to run from him. This is *my* kingdom."

Piper pushed him again and this time Thane stumbled back. "He will take Layala! Run!"

Layala stared at the elf who murdered her parents. Her magic itched at her fingers; her blood roared in her ears. "I can kill him," she said quietly, stepping forward. Another arrow flew by her, barely missing her torso.

Large hands gripped her shoulders and dragged her backward. "No. You can't," Thane said in her ear. "He's immune to magic—your vines would wrap around him and all he would have to do is touch them and they'd dissolve. It's a rune he has—and I can't let you kill our people to get to him."

Thane practically tossed Layala onto Midnight's back and leapt up behind her.

"We'll hold them off," Fennan said with a dip of his chin. "Get her away from here."

"Layala!" Tif screamed.

Layala twisted around, reaching a hand toward Tif. "We have to get her."

Thane shook his head. "We can't."

"Run, Tifapine!"

Thane didn't slow Midnight as they tore down the dirt road. The steed's heavy breaths shot out loudly with his speed. Layala's stomach churned as she gripped his mane; it was wrong to leave their friends. Would Tenebris kill them?

"We can't abandon them."

"If my father gets you and the Black Mage rises, too many will die."

They turned at the rotten old tree and tore across the long grass leading into the scary woods. Thankfully it was daylight. A whooshing sound above and a huge shadow cast over them, Layala's lifted her eyes. Her breath caught in a scream—a huge black dragon flew overhead. "Dragon!" she shrieked.

It dropped like a hawk, hitting the ground in front of them with an earthquaking force. Midnight reared up, screeching. Then the form shifted in the blink of an eye to a woman—Varlett. Oh Maker, was she here to call in her favor already?

She trudged at them with determination. "Get off the horse," she commanded.

Layala pressed into Thane's chest behind her and shook her head. Her magic was ready to raise hell.

"Stay with me," Thane whispered.

"Or don't," Varlett said. "It doesn't matter to me." She raised her palm up, the necklace around Layala's neck tore free and flew to the sorceress's hand.

Layala clutched at her neck. *The mate bond can be broken with that necklace...* "No!"

The dragon shifter began chanting quietly. Layala jumped down and rushed her, dagger drawn. Varlett held up her other hand and Layala slammed into something invisible and suddenly every fiber of her being was being held hostage. She couldn't move, could barely breathe. Thane charged past her, but he was stopped just as abruptly.

Layala's magic broke free, tearing through the ground, gathering around Varlett like a cage but it couldn't touch her. There seemed to be a barrier around her. Layala pushed more and more, rage fueling the barbed vines until they completely encased the dragon shifter. Layala regained control of herself and crept closer.

If the dragon's power no longer held them... "Maybe she's dead."

A searing, burning pain like fire, dug at her mate-marked wrist. Layala hissed, grabbed her arm, and watched as the mark began to fade, first going a light gray, then pale as flesh. "No!" Layala cried. "No!"

Thane grabbed Layala and pulled her against him.

"It's alright. Whether we are bonded as mates or not, I love you... We must go while she's trapped."

The familiar essence of him slowly faded away with the mark. The feeling of love and passion that flowed in her from him, and then her chest started to ache. It was sadness and pain felt like when Novak died, all over again. Her knees buckled and she cried out falling against him. Why did it hurt so much?!

Thane dropped to the ground, clutching at his chest. He pulled in ragged breaths. It was like a limb they shared was severed and bleeding. "Get up," he said, his voice breaking. "We have to get up." He grabbed her arms and dragged her to her wobbly legs.

With her arm across his shoulders, and his around her middle, he carried Layala toward the woods. They crossed into the heavy shade of the thick gnarled trees. Loud snapping and popping pushed Thane faster. Layala glanced back; Varlett broke free and was following them. A mass of soldiers crested the hill and ran down. They'd be upon them swiftly.

"You're making this harder than it needs to be," Varlett shouted. "King Tenebris got his favor from me and now I'm calling in mine from you, Layala."

Layala's foot caught on a root, and she stumbled. Thane held her tighter and kept pulling her along. "Don't look back," he warned. "Keep looking forward. We're going to make it."

They rushed past the downed tree from when Layala fought the giant, and the mass of her broken and tangled vines from the scorpion. But she heard Varlett's footsteps gaining on them. Layala pushed through the pain and pulled free of Thane, breaking into a full run. He kept in step beside her but the blood spilling down his leg from the arrow still embedded, and the pain of a severed mate bond slowed him.

The portal came into view. Tears flowed down her cheeks faster. *We're going to make it. We're going to make it.* She chanted silently. The portal was so close now, only a handful of yards away.

With a strangled cry, Thane was wrenched backward. Varlett's dragon paw protruded from his middle. Her hand now covered in black scales and with talons at least three inches long. Blood and pieces of his flesh covered her hand. Layala screamed.

"Go Layala!" Thane bellowed. "Go!"

She ran at Varlett and slashed her dagger across the woman's arm, nearly severing it. With a hiss, Varlett wrenched her hand free of Thane and he dropped to the ground. Layala hacked at her again, driving the blade deep into the right side of Varlett's chest, missing her heart. She jerked it free and was thrown back with an invisible force and crashed into a tree trunk knocking the back of her skull hard. Her breath whooshed from her lungs and her head throbbed. Black spread across her vision. Thane lay unmoving on the ground. She wanted to call out to him, but nothing came out of her open mouth. Layala tried to lift her arms, begged her body to rise, but she succumbed to darkness.

When Layala woke, she lay on a straw cot. The domed ceiling above had wood rafters across where birds nested. The one window in the dark gray brick room let in a fresh breeze and warm sunlight. Placing her hand on the back of her head, she sat up. On instinct she reached out to feel for Thane but there was nothing. She turned over her wrist and no trace of the mate mark ever being there existed. A single tear slid down her cheek. The last time she saw him he was unconscious and gravely wounded in the woods. Where was he? Did they—she couldn't let her thoughts drift to that dark place. But Maker, why had the dragon sorceress broken their bond if not to be able to kill Thane without Layala dying too? She said she did Tenebris a favor. Would he want Thane dead?

Shoving herself up she hurried to the door and tugged on the handle. It was locked from the outside. She dashed to the window of the tiny room. She stood in a tall tower of Castle Dredwich. Perhaps its highest peak. Soldiers patrolling below looked like small creatures from this height. The next level down, a peaked stone roof was at least seventy feet, a fall she wouldn't survive without the aid of her magic—her power was absent.

She ran to the door again, jerking harder, slamming her fist against the thick, hard wood. "Let me out! Where is Thane?!"

The sun moved significantly across the sky before the door creaked open. Layala jumped to her feet. The blond elf king stepped out from the shadows. His harsh face looked nothing like Thane's. With his hands behind his back, he stepped into the room. In the dark hallway behind him, Layala spotted Aldrich.

"Aldrich!" she called stepping toward him. He closed the door. Her jaw dropped. Was he on Tenebris's side? Was he just following orders until he could help?

"Layala Lightbringer," Tenebris said, in a clipped tone. "I've waited a long time for this moment."

"Piss off," she snarled.

"That isn't any way for a lady to speak."

Clenching her jaw tight, she stared at him. Waiting for him to make a move. She might be able to take him in a hand-to-hand fight.

"Thane is dead. Even though he was my first-born son, he was a traitor."

Panic clawed at her chest. Her hands trembled at his words. It couldn't be true. She slowly shook her head. No no no no. She wouldn't accept that, *couldn't* accept it. The rush of her blood filled her ears. Tenebris's mouth moved but she heard nothing. The room began to spin.

"You will stay in this tower with no food or drink until you decide to cooperate." His voice finally broke through. "It's time for the Black Mage to rise."

"I will never do it," she said, swallowing the lump in her throat. "I'll die first."

"We'll see about that."

He turned away; she took the opening and charged. She leapt onto his back and hooked her elbow around his throat. His nails dug into her arms as he scratched to break free of her hold. "You fool," she spit. "Never turn your back on an enemy." She squeezed harder, willing this prick to die. The satisfaction of hearing his ragged breaths brought a crazed smile to her mouth. The king who killed her parents. The king who hurt and abused her Thane, would be gone forever.

The door burst open, and Sunshine pulled his sword. Layala lifted her head, now was his chance. He cracked her on the temple with the pommel of his weapon. She fell to the ground, clutching her searing wound. Aldrich kicked her in the ribs, and she wheezed in pain. She scurried back until her shoulders hit the cot. It hurt even more than the physical blow to know that Sunshine turned on her. What was happening? Why would he do this?

He held Tenebris's arm and led him to the exit. The

High King gave her one last look, "You were born to raise the Black Mage. It is inevitable. It is your destiny." Then he was gone.

A minute or so after the door closed behind Tenebris, Aldrich appeared. Layala still held her bleeding temple, trying to make sense of everything. She flinched when he stepped into the room, the sound of his boots heavy in the silence.

He stood near the window and looked out. "If Thane was smart, he would have surrendered and lived to negotiate with our father. But he had to get himself killed."

"Our father", echoed in her mind. *Our father?!* "He's alive." She said as much to herself as to him. She wouldn't believe anything else.

Aldrich sighed. "When I shot you in the woods, it was to get him to bring you home. I didn't foresee—everything else. It should have been simple, but then you went to the dragon and Thane to Brunard and screwed everything up. He didn't need to die."

"*You* shot me? *You?*" Her voice was barely a whisper. Maker above, it didn't make sense. "You almost killed me. And you nearly shot Talon."

"My aim was—off. I meant to injure you less severely."

"Were you working for Tenebris this whole time?"

"I was promised things if I remained loyal to my father. He contacted me shortly after Thane tried to kill him. And yes, Thane was my half-brother, but no, he never knew."

She was going to be sick. Aldrich was the traitor; the reason Thane might be—gone. "Where are Piper and Fennan?" And Tifapine?

"In prison."

"I won't help you or him. I won't raise the Black Mage. It won't matter what you do to me."

"You say that now, but you will change your mind when he starts to kill people you care about. I already told him about Briar Hollow and your aunt."

She felt the blood drain from her face. "Aldrich," she wheezed. A sharp pain throbbed in her chest. "Why are you doing this?"

"Because one day I will be High King of Palenor."

"Bastard," she gritted out. "That's all you are and all you'll ever be. Bastards *never* rule."

Aldrich finally pulled his gaze from the window. "You should give Tenebris what he wants. He's already taken a lot from you, and he will take more."

"Get out."

Aldrich slipped silently from the room. Layala lost all composure and sobbed into her hands. Her chest still ached from the severed bond. Pain throbbed all over her head making it difficult to think, and she was trapped here with her worst enemy, not knowing if Thane was dead or alive. They could just be saying it to leave her hopeless. But she had to prepare for the possibility that it was true. If he was truly gone, what would she do? If all there was left was watching her friends be tortured to death or raising the Black Mage and watch the world burn... She glanced toward the window. The fall would kill her...

Night came and went, and the morning sun shone brightly. She hadn't slept. The anxious energy coursing through her body like fire wouldn't allow it. She'd searched every inch of the tower room for a way out, but it was only the door or the window. The stone on the outside was too flat and smooth to climb down. If only she had her magic, she could use her vines to escape and find Thane, but they wouldn't be foolish enough to allow her to regain her power. She saw a steady dose of katagas serum in her future.

Caw! Caw! A raven flapped onto the ledge. Its head cocked to the side and it ruffled its feathers. Caw! Layala grabbed the pillow and tossed it. "Go away!" The pillow fell short and hit the wall.

The bird lifted into the air, flapping its wings loudly and then settled back down. Caw! She jumped up to shoo it off when she caught sight of the small piece of rolled paper tied to its ankle. She smacked herself in the forehead; it was a *raven*. Her heart thudded loudly when she reverently tip-toed toward this raven. "I'm sorry I threw the pillow—don't leave," she whispered.

The bird cocked its head again and chittered its black beak when she reached for the paper. She pulled the string free and unrolled the note.

I'm coming for you, Laya.
~ Thane

~ **To be continued** ~

Want to know the details of how Thane and Fennan took King Tenebris to the Void to have him killed? Read this bonus scene for free at jmkearl.com/freebies

ACKNOWLEDGMENTS

Acknowledgments to my beta reader team: Jess Boaden, Rachel Theus Cass, Tiffany Boland, Brittany O'Barr, Melody Kiernan, Debra Spencer, and Diana Tracy. You ladies made me laugh so hard with your comments! That was entertainment in itself. You all also provided invaluable feedback that took this story from good to great. There was much editing involved!

Thank you for your honesty and time and fun! I've loved working with all of you, and thank you and appreciate you all so much.

Charity Chimni aka Hawkeyes, my proofreader who catches everything, thank you! She's my behind the scenes lady who helps make things happen.

My husband Travis encourages me to keep writing and living my dreams. He's amazingly supportive and is a wonderful dad.

David Farland, who sadly passed away in 2022, was a wonderful writing instructor. His tips and advice helped me become a much stronger writer and through his classes and books, Bow Before the Elf Queen became a reality.

And my dad, who made me a lover of the fantasy genre!

About the Author

J.M. Kearl is a fantasy romance author keeping it PG-13. She writes feisty heroines to love and hunky heroes to fall in love with. She's also a mother of two and happily married to the love of her life. She lives in Idaho but is usually dreaming of somewhere tropical.

Sign up for J.M. Kearl's Newsletter: http://jmkearl.com/newsletter

Also by J.M. Kearl

For more titles by J.M. Kearl, please visit:

http://jmkearl.com

Printed in Great Britain
by Amazon